## THE ROLE-PLAY

And at Renaissance Faires throughout the land, you can see countless players in all their regalia, fighting in jousts, singing to fair maidens, hawking their wares. But what if all of it isn't playacting? What if sometimes the play is real, sometimes the magic is true?

Now you can enjoy Renaissance Faires in a whole new way with these fifteen original tales that take you from annual faires to magical realms where an elf-lord may lure a human child to his timeless realm . . . a young couple may find that the Renaissance wasn't nearly as idyllic as they might have assumed . . . a man may be called on to face a knight's challenge to pay back a childhood debt . . . and both those who participate in the Renaissance Faire and those who merely come to be entertained by it may be caught up in far more adventures than they could possibly have imagined. . . .

# RENAISSANCE FAIRE

### EDITED BY
### ANDRE NORTON
### AND JEAN RABE

## DAW BOOKS, INC.
### DONALD A. WOLLHEIM, FOUNDER
375 Hudson Street, New York, NY 10014

### ELIZABETH R. WOLLHEIM
### SHEILA E. GILBERT
### PUBLISHERS
http://www.dawbooks.com

First Printing, February 2005
1  2  3  4  5  6  7  8  9

DAW TRADEMARK REGISTERED
U.S. PAT. OFF. AND FOREIGN COUNTRIES
—MARCA REGISTRADA
HECHO EN U.S.A.

PRINTED IN THE U.S.A.

# ACKNOWLEDGMENTS

*Introduction: Faire Game* © 2005 by Jean Rabe and Andre Norton

*Jewels Beyond Price* © 2005 by Elizabeth Ann Scarborough

*Diminished Chord* © 2005 by Joe Haldeman

*Splinter* © 2005 by Wordfire, Inc.

*Girolamo and Mistress Willendorf* © 2005 by John Maddox Roberts

*A Time For Steel* © 2005 by Robert E. Vardeman

*One Hot Day* © 2005 by Stephen Gabriel

*Wimpin' Wady* © 2005 by Jayge Carr

*Brewed Fortune* © 2005 by Michael Stackpole

*Marriage á la Modred* © 2005 by Esther M. Friesner

*A Dance of Seven Vales* © 2005 by Rose Wolf

*Moses' Miracles* © 2005 by Roberta Gellis

*Grok* © 2005 by Donald Bingle

*Renaissance Fear* © 2005 by Stephen D. Sullivan

*The Land of the Awful Shadow* © 2005 by Brian A. Hopkins

*Faire Likeness* © 2005 by Andre Norton

# CONTENTS

# FAIRE GAME

## by
## Jean Rabe and Andre Norton

LORDS AND LADIES flock to Renaissance Faires for many different reasons:

To watch knightly jousts and birds-of-prey exhibitions.

To see belly dancers sway in the summer heat.

To hear minstrels perform charming centuries-past pieces.

To chomp down on smoked turkey legs and throw back a pint of ale.

To dress in elaborate costumes and buy fanciful medieval-looking knickknacks . . .

To be swept away to a romanticized era.

Picture it! Parades of nobles and jesters work their way through the grounds. Swordsmen call out for an audience. Women braid flowers in revelers' hair, while artists paint butterflies on upturned faces. Archery competitions are waiting to be joined. Jewelry and cloaks and tall mugs of lemonade are waiting to be bought. There are kissing bandits, mud wrestlers, crafters, and courtly dancers—all vying for attention. And don't forget the flowery headdresses to try on, the outdoor taverns to sing at, and all the new exhibits to discover.

And everywhere there are imaginations daring to be stirred.

Historically, the faires in Elizabethan times were held to celebrate the beginning of spring. There were artisans, musicians, and acrobats. Farmers brought their first crops to hawk. Not so different from what can be found now, eh?

When was the first "modern" Renaissance Faire? No one is really certain, though in the United States many faire enthusiasts point to May of 1963 in Hollywood, California, when Phillis and Ron Paterson ran what was called the "Renaissance Pleasure Faire." It drew about 8,000 folks, and the following year it was said to grow to 12,000.

Now the faires are found across the globe: the Bristol Renaissance Faire in Wisconsin; the Grand Valley Renaissance Faire in Colorado; the Kansas City Renaissance Festival; King Richard's Faire in Massachusetts; the Minnesota Renaissance Festival; Oregon Days of Olde Renaissance Festival; Silver City Renaissance Faire in New Mexico; Tennessee Renaissance Festival; Brisbane Medieval Fayre in Australia; Festival Medieval in France; and on and on and on.

Often they are the haunts or the productions of members of the Society for Creative Anachronism— an international organization dedicated to re-creating and studying the Middle Ages. Always they are the passion of the visitors who return season after season. For example, one of us has made a few trips to the Bristol Renaissance Faire in Wisconsin. Always, there would be a stop by the gaudy wooden stage to watch Dirk and Guido duel with their swords and spar with their verbal barbs. And, always, there would be time set aside to wander by the musicians, the dealer selling those oh-so-delicious almonds, and the mudmen wrestling in the pit.

Many faire-goers have poofy-sleeved shirts in their closet. We do, too.

And some of us try to employ the language of the faire performers and visitors—one must get in the spirit, after all.

Nay: no
Aye: yes
Ne'r: never
Wherefore: why
Belike: maybe
Verily: truly
Prithee: please
My Lord, My Lady, Is it even so, Forsooth, and Alakaday.

So good morrow to you kind readers! Within these pages are exquisite tales by fantasy's finest, all involving Renaissance Faires—ones the authors have visitied and ones they have created from whole cloth. Verily, thou shall find genies and gentlemen, thieves and faeries, and magic enow to entertain and delight thee from cover to cover. Prithee sit back in thine favorite armchair and immerse thyself in this literary feast.

Anon,
Jean Rabe and Andre Norton

# JEWELS BEYOND PRICE

## by Elizabeth Ann Scarborough

Elizabeth Ann Scarborough lives in an antique cabin on the Olympic Peninsula with four-going-on-five cats and a lot of paints, paperwork, and beads. She is currently working on the sequel to *Channeling Cleopatra* and is coauthoring the Acorna series with Anne McCaffrey.

AMID THE FLYING PENNANTS and heraldic banners topping lances, pavilions, and hot dog stands, nothing flew higher in all the realm than the voices of Master Daniel the Jeweler and Baron Bruno the Brazen raised in dispute.

"Look, Bruno," Master Daniel began.

"That's *Baron* Bruno to you, dear, but a simple 'milord' will do if accompanied by the proper obeisance."

Master Daniel proceeded in an even more strident tone, "I don't know how many times I've told you now, *no more freebies*."

"You offend me, sir. Were I not a gentleman of honor and aware that you are a simple tradesman unskilled in the noble arts or weaponry, I would challenge you to a duel."

"Try it, scumbag, and I'll break your arm off and

beat you to death with the bloody stump," vowed Master Daniel, who was something of a poet as well as an artisan.

"Aren't we just the macho old crosspatch today? That time of the month, my dear?"

"Knock it off, Bruno. You know I've been waiting three years for you to pay me for your signet ring and the coronet I made you."

Bruno sniffed. "Most artisans would be honored by my custom."

"Well, please don't let me deprive them of it, then. Give them my share with my blessing," Master Daniel started to turn his back and leave. However, he recalled in time that Baron Bruno couldn't be trusted alone with the goodies in the display case.

"But no one else does stuff as good as yours!" the baron half-wailed, half-wheedled, not an easy thing to pull off, even for the nobility. During the nonfair part of his life, Bruno was a highly trained professional telemarketer, so that probably explained his verbal dexterity.

Master Daniel folded his arms and glared at Bruno, which made no more impression than it ever did. "Like I told you before, dude, I can't make jewelry out of dirt. Silver is expensive, stones are expensive . . ."

"I've brought you stones."

"Some cracked CZs not worth the metal it would take to surround them? Give me a break!"

Bruno's expression turned sly. It didn't have far to go. His expression always bordered on sly, but now it went all the way and he really ran with it. He held up a huge clanking bag. "I have metal. Silver. Stamped, even. Hallmarked some of it. You can melt it down and make me a paper crown for when I'm king."

"Like that's gonna happen!"

"It's good stuff." Bruno plopped it on the fragile glass of the display case.

Daniel snatched it up. "Fine. Then I'll take it on account for what you owe me on the ring and the coronet. I'll let you know what you still owe for the other pieces I made you when I figure out what this is worth."

"You'll see! It's worth a lot. So I'll use my credit on that pectoral there, the one with the dragon in the Celtic knot. Please put it aside for me. There's the queen! Gotta go schmooze."

Master Daniel sighed. You just couldn't get through to some people with anything more diplomatic than a baseball bat between the eyes. He picked up the bag and bounced it. It clanked.

Disgusted, he dumped it out on the workbench inside his pavilion. Some stainless steel silverware, silver colored pot metal pins and earrings. Worthless. The biggest piece that caught his attention, the only thing he thought he might be able to use, was a silver-plated cigarette lighter in the shape of Aladdin's lamp. Master Daniel smoked. A lot. Of course, he couldn't carry the damn thing around in his pocket but it might be cute to have around for a while.

He examined it more closely. It seemed a little tarnished. Maybe there was more silver there than he'd thought at first. There was a mark on the bottom. Probably the manufacturer. He took a rouge cloth and rubbed away the tarnish to see if he could read it.

"You're shittin' me," he said aloud.

"Whosoever owneth this lamp commands the djinn thereof." Damnedest manufacturer's label he ever saw.

But it was not the last surprise.

"Some cigarette lighter," he muttered. "It doesn't even wait for *me* to smoke." For indeed, smoke billowed forth from the teapot-looking end of the lamp. The top of the cloud, instead of wisping on its merry way to pollute the environment as smoke was supposed to do, solidified. Master Daniel, like most vendors and attendees at Renaissance Faires, had steeped himself in fantasy, myth, legend, and fairy tales most of his life. He did not need the label on the bottom of the lighter to tell him that what he was seeing was a djinn, or genie. The guy looked exactly like one, only better.

Also, he had more hair. Genies were usually shown as bald, but this guy had wavy black hair pulled back in a ponytail, a goatee, and a killer mustache. His chest between the wings of his wine-colored, standard-issue genie bolero was also hirsute. But his muscles were as advertised, large and powerful-looking enough to perform any wishes that might involve some hard manual labor.

"I am the genie of the lamp," he began in a pleasant baritone with a faint Middle Eastern accent.

"I gathered," Master Daniel said. "How are you at selling jewelry?"

"This is your command, that I sell jewelry?"

"Well, no, not really. But that's what I'm going to be doing here and if you want to hang with me instead of going back inside your lamp, that's what you'll need to know how to do."

"As a matter of fact," he said, "I come from a long line of jewel merchants."

"Got feet?" Master Daniel asked.

"What?" the genie looked down. "Oh, yes. Certainly. Excuse me." He drew his legs out of the re-

maining smoke. They were clad in the requisite
baggy pants—deep teal—and held up with a sap-
phire colored silk sash that had a scimitar stuck in it.

"You'll have to have your weapon peace-bonded,
man," Master Daniel told him, nodding at the scimitar. "I'm head of security for this faire. Can't be having my help break the rules."

"Peace bonded?"

"Duct taped to your—uh—scabbard. You don't
have a scabbard, man."

"Of course I do. It's in the lamp. I'm going to get
a shirt, too. It's chilly here."

"It's eighty-six degrees, man." He kept calling the
genie "man" not because his vocabulary was defi-
cient but because he was at a loss for what to call
him. Somehow it didn't seem polite to call him
"genie" or "djinn" and he really wanted to be polite
to a dude so well endowed in the musculature
department.

"It is much balmier in my native land. Perhaps I
will fetch a surcoat, too."

Master Daniel had just been getting used to the
guy and thinking the smoke part had been a halluci-
nation when the genie turned back into smoke and
dove into the lamp again. He emerged a short time
later without the scimitar but with a floppy-sleeved
Ali Baba kind of shirt and a long embroidered vest
that reached the top of the tall boots for which he
had traded his sandals. He drew forth a length of
scarlet silk and said, "Pardon me while I wind my
turban."

One thing about it. With the knights in armor,
wenches with their boobs hanging out, jesters, minstrels, wizards, princesses, and a kid or two with
fairy wings, the genie blended really well at the faire.

"What do I call you?" Daniel asked.

"I am your humble servant, Master," the genie said, making a flourishing bow worthy of a stage magician.

"Yeah, I got that. But even though it wouldn't seem really out of place here for me to call you servant or you to call me master, I'd rather call you by your name. And if you call me master, call me Master Daniel. Or just Dan is fine."

"Very well, Master Daniel. I was known as Habib before I became the servant of the lamp."

"Hi, Habib." Daniel stuck out his hand. The genie bent and kissed the ring on his middle finger.

"Honored, Master. Daniel. My, what a lovely ring. Your work?"

"Yeah. I sell a lot of those. When things sell. This has been a slow year. Economy is down. Now, look, Habib, here are the prices. You can read them, can't you?"

"One has much time for study while imprisoned in the lamp," Habib told him.

"Hmm," Daniel said. "I'd think it would be kind of tough to get a library in there."

"It is. That's why I got the laptop."

"You have a computer?"

"Oh, yes, we djinn even had our own server for a time, but it was plagued with malicious ifrits. Handy for keeping in touch with one's colleagues. I also keep a spreadsheet of wishes made and granted, best places to pick up a premanufactured castle, how to make someone instantly the wealthiest man in the world without upsetting the world economy, where to get a quickie divorce for the most beautiful lady in all the land so that my master can marry her himself if he so wishes, that sort of thing."

"Cool. Now, look, everything here is marked. I guess if you can run a computer you can make change. This is the cash box. No taking it back into the lamp with you and disappearing, right?"

"Master Daniel, I could protest that I am a man of honor but I am no longer, strictly speaking, a man. So instead let me assure you that I am forbidden to harm you or your goods while you hold the lamp."

"Good. So, sell stuff, make change, and hold down the fort—uh, tend the shop—while I get on the walkie-talkies with the security crew and make sure everyone knows where they're supposed to be and that they're not supposed to act like super cop. Okay?"

"Your wish—"

"It's strictly voluntary, Habib. This is not my wish. If we make any money, I'll even pay you."

"I have no need of money, Master Daniel. Perhaps an attractive ring such as the one you wear, however?"

"Done. And look, under no circumstances does anybody—and I mean anybody—get any credit. And watch out for thieves."

"Your wish—yes, I will do that."

Daniel repaired to the back of his pavilion and engaged in lengthy discourse with the several members of the security team. He had difficulty keeping track of the conversation however, because there was so much noise going on out front. The faire was in full swing now, he thought. He had a smoke, using his usual lighter, not the genie's lamp, and returned to the front of the tent and the canopy.

The djinn stood about where Daniel had left him.

"Anyone come by?"

"Oh, yes, Master Daniel. Great multitudes of folk."

"But everything went okay?"

"Yes, except that you neglected to tell me where

you keep your stock of other jewels. The case is looking a bit bare."

Daniel gave a low whistle. All of the low-end merchandise he had carefully arranged in the case that morning was gone. "It sure is. You sold all that?"

"I did."

He lifted the lid of the cash box. What he saw made him smile deeply. He pulled out a twenty, one of several, and handed it to the genie. "See there down the hill where those little pavilions are? Those are the food vendors. Why don't you go get us something to eat? I'll have a Coke and a hot dog. You get whatever you want."

Habib looked at the money as if he'd never seen money before. "Truly, Master—Daniel? You would give me money to buy food for myself when you know I could provide you with enough to make you a rich man forever?"

"Listen, Habib, all I really do well and like to do is to make jewelry. If a wish can keep me in whatever it takes for me to do that for the rest of my life, that's great. I've known guys who were filthy rich and they were very messed up by it. You earned this money. I'm not real hungry, so if you want to look around the faire on the way to the food booths, that's cool."

Habib nodded, assessing him with raised eyebrows. "As it has been said, so let it be done. A very wise wish if I may say so. Many people try to expand one wish to include many, but greed betrays them. You have done so in all sincerity. *And* I must say this is the first time I have ever been paid for services rendered to one who commands the lamp. You are as beneficent with your bounty as you are beauteous, Master. Hearing and obeying."

Beauteous? Daniel prided himself on having nice

hair—blond, worn long in the back, cut shorter at the top and sides—but such an offhand compliment took him by surprise. He mused about it so long that it took him a moment to notice that the display case was one of those very beautiful ones he had admired in a catalog. It had fine carving all around the edges and looked like an antique. However, it folded into the size of a suitcase for travel and locked securely.

Then he noticed that the pavilion had been upgraded. His patched and worn old tent was now made of that new waterproof velvet, scarlet, with gold piping and tassels. At the corners! The pavilion was of a brand he recognized as being superior for its easy transportability and assembly as well as dramatic good looks. The interior was now shrouded with a shining curtain of glass beads that twinkled when he pulled them back. Inside, his bed was no longer covered with his sleeping bag, but with down comforters and embroidered pillows with little mirrors sewn on them. His workbench contained a vast array of high quality tools and, when he checked the locked box where he kept the silver and stones, he saw that it had a companion. The first box was filled with silver in sheets, wire, and lengths of beaded and roped, filigreed and straight trim. The other case was filled with gems of all types, but each was finer than the next and all were ones he would have picked out himself.

He gave a low whistle of appreciation. Habib was very good at the genie thing.

Master Daniel was in a good mood indeed when Bruno returned.

"Uh—Dan? About the silver? You know, you're right. I owe you cash and I should pay you cash. Give me back the sack and I'll write you a check right now."

Daniel picked up the empty sack and handed it to him. "Write away. Fifteen hundred dollars and fifty cents is your total."

"Where's the silver?"

"What silver? You gave me stainless steel, pot metal, and silver plating."

"I know. And I'm very ashamed of it. So just give it all back to me, I'll give you this check, and we'll be even. No hard feelings."

Daniel went inside the pavilion, piled everything but the lighter back into the sack and handed it to Bruno, who peered in and pawed through it. "Where's that crappy old lighter?"

"I'm keeping it. Call it interest on your debt."

"You want interest, I'll write this for a little over. Another fifty bucks, say?"

"Fifty bucks? The lighter isn't worth fifty cents. But I like it, so I'm keeping it."

"Look, man, it got in there by mistake. It belonged to my grandfather. My mother will be really upset if she finds it missing."

"Just like I'll be really upset when I find out this check is no better than the last one you gave me?"

"No, it's good. Honest. You can call the bank if you want to." Bruno pulled his authentic period cell phone from his medieval purse and handed it to Daniel, who handed it back. It was sure to have Bruno cooties all over the mouthpiece.

"Forget it, Bruno. I'm keeping it."

"But I didn't get *my* turn with the genie."

"Genie?" Daniel asked.

"The one who gave you this pavilion. The good-looking one I saw from across the field. He was selling jewelry right and left."

"Bruno, it's a hot day. You'd better go find a shady spot and a cool drink. I've got a good new assistant and a new cover for the pavilion he helped me put on just now."

"Right. Then why are you so attached to the cigarette lighter? It's obviously just a tacky old thing from a second-rate flea market. I laughed at the guy who tried to tell me there was a genie attached when he wanted to pay a gambling debt he owed me. I told him he shouldn't take me for an idiot—that I'd take the lamp, since he had added the charming story that would make it a conversation piece, but I also wanted his torc. He gave both up rather grudgingly, I must say. And I stuffed them in a drawer and never thought about his story when I was gathering up bits and pieces to repay you. Then when I saw your so-called assistant and the new pavilion—*well*, I connected the dots you might say and realized I've been cheated out of my wishes."

"You haven't been cheated out of anything. You gave me a worthless old lighter and now you even want that back and it's the one thing out of that sack of junk you gave me that I can use. To light my smokes."

"Sweetie, I'll *give* you a book of matches if that's all you need. If there's nothing special about it, why are you so determined to hang onto it?"

"Because you're trying to take it back after giving it to me. That's why. Are you writing the check or not?"

"I am not."

"And *I* am not surprised about that."

"I am taking this up with higher authorities."

He stalked away, no doubt straight to the royal pavilion to bend the queen's ear.

Habib materialized, hot dogs and cold drinks in hands.

"A fan of yours just left," Daniel told him.

"A fan? I brought no fan. I could install one if that is your wish, of course."

"No, no. Don't you talk about this stuff on the Internet? I mean Baron Bruno, the guy who had our lamp before me."

"I recall no such master."

"That's because he never let you out."

"Most inconsiderate. And now, I presume, he feels cheated because I did nothing for him?"

"That's Bruno, okay. Oh, well, screw him. He can't have the lighter back and that's it. I need to get back to the workbench. I've got a few things to finish and the inventory is down, thanks to those sales of yours."

"How may I assist you, Master?"

Daniel started to say he didn't need any help. If he went in back, leaving Habib to sell the few things left in the case, however, Bruno might try something. Kidnap the genie. Have him arrested. Daniel knew the baron well enough to realize he wasn't about to give up on getting what he thought was due him.

"I could, of course, magically produce an inventory that would be the envy of real kings and queens if that is your wish," Habib suggested doubtfully.

"No. Absolutely not. I want to sell the stuff I create, not somebody else's crown jewels."

"You continually astound me with your wisdom. The truth is, in order to provide jewels by magic, the jewels must be obtained from other sources and that can get very complicated. I could tell you of many instances in the annals of geniedom . . ." Habib's voice trailed off and then suddenly brightened as he said, "However, dear Master, if you will but show me the designs you have created and indicate the sort of materials you would use, I can greatly speed the production of your wares."

"Great," Daniel said. "But I want to see the first thing you make so I can tell if you know your way around a torch or not."

"Quality assurance—oh, yes. I understand such matters.

Daniel showed Habib the sketches he'd made for new designs, described some other things he had in mind, and also brought out the unfinished projects he'd had laying around for a long time.

"Now this," he said, showing Habib a circlet of silver with a design drawn on the top edge and empty bezels already soldered onto it, the largest in the middle, three smaller ones on each side decreasing in size, "is supposed to be a tiara for the queen."

He held up the drawing for it with the gems colored in. "She wanted a big amethyst in the middle, then blue topaz, smaller amethyst, another blue topaz."

Habib shook his head. "Very plain for a queen, Master Daniel, if it does not offend you that I say so. Would not this be more suitable?"

An image of the tiara finished spun in the air like a holographic computer simulation. It was Daniel's design, but done in gold, with tanzanites and very large aqua sapphires. Daniel didn't quite gasp, but he did feel like it.

"You forget, Master, that with me at your command you are no longer a poor man. You need not confine yourself to lowly materials when working for royalty."

"You're right, Habib. I don't know how I forgot about all that new stuff you came up with. But we'll stick with the original for this one. However much Regina Wallewski pretends to be real royalty, she's actually a shyster ambulance-chasing lawyer who thinks everybody owes her anything she wants.

She'd decree sumptuary laws if she could so that anyone who has anything nicer than what she has would have to give it to her or go to the stocks. I'm darned if I'll give this to her for free."

"Calm yourself, Master. It could be worse. Much worse."

"No way."

"Way indeed, Master. She could pay you handsomely—by giving you the gift of an elephant. He whom rulers would ruin are paid thusly. The appetites of royal elephants quickly ruin modest artisans who can neither work the beasts nor sell them and must somehow feed them or risk insulting the sultan. Or queen."

For the first time in quite a while Daniel flashed a sincerely amused grin. "Fortunate for us there are no elephants here."

"You must leave this matter in my hands, Master. I will see that events weave themselves into a cloth of your liking."

Just then a bugle blew outside and Daniel groaned.

"What is it, Master?"

"Not what, who. Speak of the devil! That was the royal herald. The queen is coming."

Outside a shrill tenor announced, "Her Majesty the Queen of the Faire commands the presence of Daniel Firethorn, master jeweler."

Daniel poked his head outside, "What do you want, Regina?" he asked disrespectfully.

"Is that any way to speak to your queen?" Her Majesty demanded, fanning herself rapidly with a fluffy feathered fan. Her Tudor collar almost drooped around her neck and he imagined she must be smothering in the glass-pearl encrusted brocade gown complete with six layers of undergarments. No wonder she was usually in a nasty mood. But every other "noble" at the faire dressed almost as heavily and nobody else threw their weight around like Regina and Bruno. "We've come for our tiara." Just in case he had any doubt who she was, she employed the royal we to make him feel outnumbered.

"The terms were payment on delivery, if you'll recall. I'm assuming you have something in your purse other than your lipstick and hanky?"

"Don't be common. We will settle with you later. We need the tiara for the feast this evening."

He rubbed the first two fingers of his right hand against the ball of his thumb. "And I need it paid for before . . ."

Behind Her Majesty's back, Lady Morgana rolled her eyes and gave Lady Raven, the other lady-in-waiting, a knowing look. They had seen Regina operate before.

"Ah, Master Daniel, I could not help overhearing," Habib said, emerging from the pavilion with a velvet box in his hands. "I am sorry it took me so long to finish the polishing." He kept bowing and scraping and averting his face from Regina as if blinded by her radiance. "Here is the royal commission and I only pray that the polish is not too badly outshone by Her Majesty's beauty."

"We *like* him!" Regina said. "Where'd you get him, Daniel?" but she wasn't really listening. Habib had gone down on one knee to offer the velvet box to Daniel to make the presentation, but Regina snatched the box from the genie's hands and tore it open. "Ooooh," she said. "You outdid yourself, Danny boy. This is so terrific that if we had one, we would reward you with an elephant to show you how tickled we are with your work." Lady Raven was helping her remove the white froufrou headband she wore on her red curly wig and replace it with the tiara. She patted her hair and patted the tiara.

Habib produced a full-length mirror from the pavilion. It hadn't been there before. Regina admired herself, posing and primping as a crowd gathered. The tiara fit perfectly and looked like white gold and precious stones to Daniel, something a real queen would envy.

She caught his look as she replaced the tiara in the box. "Don't look so sour, Master Daniel. You have pleased your queen mightily. That ought to make you happy." Before he could reply, she turned to Habib. "And you, cutie. We were told that you are actually a magical genie who came out of a cigarette lighter that rightly belonged to our loyal servant Baron Bruno."

"The baron obviously mistook me for an old flame, Your Majesty," he said with a wink.

She tapped him lightly with the feathery fan. "Oh, you. He'd never have let *you* get away."

"And yet, here I am, happily serving my good Master Daniel. Now then, Majesty, you'll be wanting to know, since you know I am a magic genie, if there is an enchantment that comes with your new tiara."

"Oh, a tiara and an enchantment, too! That's great. Do tell us, magic man."

"The magic is very simple. Like all good jewels, it merely enhances the inner qualities of the wearer and makes them more visible."

The queen, Daniel could see, did not really believe Habib was a genie. She did believe he was a babe, however, and continued to flirt: "So you are one of those people who believe beauty is only skin-deep. And this tiara is going to show off our inner beauty?" She handed the box with the tiara to one of her flunkies.

"Even so, Your Majesty. Your generosity of spirit will shine through you once you adorn yourself with this bauble."

But before he had finished speaking, several of the courtiers approached the queen, lavishing compliments upon her and telling her what they planned for the evening feast. They surrounded her, and before Daniel had a chance to ask when he'd be paid for the tiara, the whole gang swept down the path between booths like a flock of migrating macaws.

"You see what I mean, Habib. Precious metal only flows in one direction where Her Majesty is concerned, and that's toward her."

Habib put a comforting hand on Daniel's shoulder. "Be not so cynical, O Master. These things have a way of working out."

They didn't work out quite how Habib had planned, however.

The part where everyone at the faire felt they just had to buy one of the new "enchanted" jewels worked fine. Once the queen told her courtiers that she was going to wear an enchanted tiara Master Daniel and his hunky new assistant made for her that evening, everyone had to check it out. All afternoon Daniel and Habib filled orders for jewelry the buyers hoped would improve their love lives or their prosperity or their luck. Anyone wishing for guarantees or more extravagant enchantments was quoted such an exorbitant cash-up-front-for-a-commissioned-piece-later price that they changed their minds.

"Will these things really do what you're claiming?" Daniel asked Habib.

"As much as any of the other things people seem to believe these days—astrology, geomancy, charms and spells from mortals claiming special knowledge, even that which is referred to as modern medicine.

The seeker brings belief that carries its own power to grant the wish—or not."

"So it's just BS, then?"

"That depends on who is buying and how strong their power of belief may be," the genie replied. Daniel thought he was a wizard at rationalization if nothing else. "We promise them very little. At the moment, they seek to be fashionable—to acquire some part of what they believe the queen has acquired. Perhaps later this will not seem so desirable."

"Meaning what?"

"Meaning is it not time that we close your tent and attend this court, this feast, where the queen will display our work?"

"Vendors aren't exactly invited."

"We will not be refused," the genie promised.

Of course, just about anyone could stand around and watch.

The courtiers assembled on the green around the throne, a large chair with a plywood back covered in quilted silk. The heralds blew their trumpets. Then came the ladies-in-waiting, who kept glancing nervously at something within their midst. It was the tiara, floating above a rather nice crystal-encrusted cloth of gold court gown, also a commission paid for by command-extended credit, from what Daniel had heard.

"Where's the queen?" someone whispered.

"I see her new clothes, but where's Her Majesty?"

"I'm right here," Regina's irritated voice came from somewhere between the tiara and the ropes of pearls suspended beneath it. "What's wrong with you people anyway?"

Baron Bruno rushed forward and offered his hand to a dainty crystal-encrusted white gauntlet. "Never mind them, Your Majesty," he piped in his shrill voice with its phony English accent. "They simply don't recognize you, you've lost so much weight!"

"I'll say! She's so thin we can see right through her!" a teenaged wench cried.

"What kind of trick is this anyway?" bellowed her champion, tugging at his peace-bonded sword.

"She's like—under a spell or something," someone else said in nonperiod parlance.

In the hush that followed while the populace digested this observation, Lady Morgana's whisper to Lady Raven, the other lady-in-waiting who had been with the queen when she bought the tiara, was heard all over the green. "I bet I know what it was. Remember that new guy at Danny the Jeweler's? He told Her Maj the tiara would reflect her inner qualities—like her inner generosity."

"Shee-it," Raven replied. "If I'd have been her, I'd never have touched the thing, no matter how pretty it was. If Her Maj has any generosity, it's so totally inner that it will be the last part to decompose when she dies. You know she never pays her bills."

"You're busted, both of you!" shrieked the voice between the tiara and the necklace. "I'll show you how not generous I really can be! Oh, if I could only have people really executed!" The tiara lifted in the air and sailed to the ground, first ricocheting off the armor-plated leg of the champion. "Okay, now, you can see me now, right?"

"Uh—not really, no," Baron Bruno said.

"Well, the damn thing can't work after I've taken it off, can it?" Regina's voice demanded.

Lady Morgana got a funny little smile on her face. Apparently her royal mistress' lack of apparent substance and also her own recent demotion emboldened her. What else did she have to lose? And of course she and Lord Balthazar had just had their own

very cool Renaissance Wedding two events earlier.
Lord B was a Microsoft millionaire when he wasn't
being a lord. "Maybe, ma'am, now that it's—uh—
displayed your inner qualities, you're going to stay
invisible as long as you wear anything else that dem-
onstrates the same—uh—frugality on your part."

The costumer stepped forward and knelt before
her own creation, "Perhaps Lady Morgan is right,
Your Majesty. I'm sure if Your Majesty would be so
kind as to cough up the six hundred bucks you
promised me for making this gown, including materials, you'd reappear."

"And—ahem—the pearls?" squeaked a voice from
the sidelines. This, Daniel recognized as belonging to
Lady Berengaria of Berengaria's Baubles.

The pearls exploded in midair and flew to the
ground, but as the gown began popping open, bits
of Regina sprang into view. It wasn't a pretty sight
by thirty years and seventy tightly laced pounds or
so. Lady Raven, who was not recently married to a
millionaire, quickly flung her own cloak around her
mistress as the dress crumpled to the green.

Regina's pinched and furious face searched the
crowd until she found Daniel and Habib. Habib wag-
gled his fingers at her.

Regina's finger pointed at him so aggressively that
she almost lost the cloak. "You two I'll see in court,
and I don't mean this one! Court dismissed!" she
bellowed.

Daniel and Habib gave each other a high five and
headed back for the pavilion. Behind them, they
heard Bruno: "But, Majesty, my claim!"

While Habib carefully began packing up the display cases, Daniel wasn't even thinking about the
queen. He was thinking that sometime soon he
would have to make the third wish and see the last

of the genie. Sure he'd have his jewelry-making business, but Habib wouldn't be there anymore and Daniel knew he was going to miss him.

Regina, clad in a rather humble long skirt and shift she probably made herself early in her Renaissance career, stalked up to the pavilion. Her courtiers, including the simpering Bruno, trailed behind her.

She flung the tiara at Habib, who caught it without looking up.

"That was a filthy trick, disrespectful of the crown. Master Daniel, I will see to it that you are barred from ever selling at any Renaissance Faire in this state or any other for the rest of your miserable life." Before Daniel could digest this, she turned to Habib. "As for you, you really are some kind of a miserable Middle Eastern demon, aren't you? Well, let me tell you, you are no match for a queen. If Daniel doesn't want me to strip HIM of everything he owns including his shorts when I take him to court, he had better surrender that lamp of yours to Baron Bruno now. It's for your own good. Daniel is a bad influence. Bruno has better plans for you, don't you, Baron?"

Had Bruno a mustache, he would have been twirling it. "Ah, yes, Your Majesty."

"Well, that's not going to happen," Daniel said. "I still have one wish and I'm using it to set Habib free of the lamp."

"You can't do that!"

"Watch me."

"Search the tent!" Regina commanded her flunkies. "Bring the lamp to Bruno."

To his dismay, Daniel saw the lamp teetering on top of the pile of goods Habib had been packing. He reached for it, but the queen's champion knocked his arm away and grabbed the lamp.

He started to kneel before the queen, then gave the

lamp an appraising look as if he was having second thoughts. After all, a magic lamp could be useful.

Bruno snatched the lamp from him. "It's mine! And I command you, genie, to make this nasty jeweler boy and all his goods except the ones he owes me disappear!"

Habib salaamed before Bruno, and Daniel's heart sank. "As you have said, it will be done . . ."

Bruno smirked.

"As soon as Master Daniel has declared himself ready to quit this unworthy place."

"I commanded you."

"And you should not have done so, for I am now, thanks to the goodness of my former master, a free being. To attempt to coerce me is a violation of my civil rights and therefore punishable by my final piece of magic."

The lamp dropped to the ground as Bruno turned into smoke and was sucked up into the spout. Habib picked it up and stuck it in his sash. To Daniel he said, "It really is silver, friend. Have we need of fresh metal, it will melt down nicely."

Regina continued sputtering with rage. "You'll have no more need of silver or anything else! You've just murdered Bruno—or kidnapped him at least! I'll see to it that you never work this faire again, I'll see to it that . . ."

A small crowd had been gathering behind the raging queen and her friends. Lady Morgana pointedly abandoned her liege's side to step back and clasp hands with a fifteenth century Italian lord whose watery eyes blinked rapidly behind contact lenses he'd been wearing too long.

Lord Balthazar nodded toward a man in mundane garb—naked, by Ren Faire standards—who said, "Excuse me, Miss Wallewski."

"That's 'Your Majesty'!" she tried to thunder, but she'd been shouting for so long her voice was starting to crack.

"I'm afraid not. The board of directors for the faire had an emergency meeting called by the chairman—that would be my client, Mr. Ballou here. The board feels that in extorting favors and goods from vendors at the faire, as has been demonstrated publicly this evening, you have sullied the position entrusted to you.

"Therefore, you might stay a—er—junta has occurred and you have been deposed in favor of a new Queen of the Faire—Mrs. Ballou."

Morgana sashayed forward to smile up at Daniel and Habib. She dropped gracefully into what appeared to be a low curtsy and picked up the tiara, polishing it on her skirt, then looked over at her shoulder questioningly at Lord Balthazar, who nodded, grinning idiotically. She then extended both the tiara and a large check toward Daniel. "Kevin says I can have this tiara and he thinks it will be really becoming on me, except I'm more of an emeralds and sapphires sort of girl. Would it be too much trouble to replace the stones for me and maybe do a little filigree here and here?"

Habib and Daniel almost bumped heads bowing low before her, "It would be our pleasure, mistress."

"Good. See you at the tourney in October, I hope?"

Dan nodded and Lady Morgana slipped back into her lord's embrace.

Balthazar's attorney pointedly offered his arm to Regina, who pointedly ignored it, clinging instead to her champion who grinned wolfishly down at her.

"Aw, forget it, Reg. Come on, you can polish my armor for me before you pack it."

And then it was strangely quiet, the voices receding into the distance. Most of the other vendors had packed their goods and pavilions into their cars and vans by then. Daniel and Habib looked at each other awkwardly.

"Daniel?" Habib said at last.

"What?"

"I was wondering. You were so kind as to set me free. Perhaps since I granted you three wishes, you would see your way clear to granting me one."

"Name it," Daniel said, staring into the genie's eyes, which no longer seemed mysterious and impenetrable, but instead frank, honest, and openly admiring.

"That even though I no longer possess any magic, you would permit me to continue to serve as your assistant, salesperson, and apprentice . . ."

Daniel grinned. He had wished for creative prosperity and for comeuppance from those who abused their positions to take advantage of him. What he had not dared to wish for was an ·end to his loneliness. Instead, he had spent his final wish granting Habib his freedom, thereby keeping him out of Bruno's clutches. Now he could see in Habib's eyes that the genie himself was making that last unspoken wish.

Daniel salaamed. "Hearing and obeying, O wise and clever assistant, salesperson, apprentice, and companion of my bench and booth. My pavilion henceforth shall be your pavilion as well."

And they quietly folded their tent and stole off to their state-of-the-art van.

# DIMINISHED CHORD

## by

### *Joe Haldeman*

Joe Haldeman is best known for *The Forever War*, a novel that won the Hugo, Nebula, and Ditmar Awards, and is now considered a classic of science fiction. He's won five Nebula awards and four Hugos for his fiction, as well as three Rhysling Awards for his poetry. He's published one book of poetry, *Saul's Death*. His latest novel, *Guardian*, follows the adventures and misadventures of a Victorian woman who takes her son away from his wealthy but brutal father, going from genteel Philadelphia to rough Dodge City and Skagway and finally, in desperation, into mysterious worlds that have no name. His twenty novels, three story collections, six anthologies and one poetry collection have appeared in eighteen languages. His mainstream novels *War Year* and *1968* are based on his experience as a combat engineer in the Central Highlands of Vietnam. He teaches writing at Massachusetts Institute of Technology in the fall semester each year, is an avid amateur astronomer, paints watercolors, and plays the .guitar. His website is: home.earthlink.net/~haldeman.

WHEN I WAS MARRIED, I played in a pretty good band and made pretty good money. But when the marriage went south, so did I. Wound up being a sideman in a college town in Florida. Jazz and swing and rock, whatever—need a banjo, I can frail along; pluck a mandolin.

Or a lute. How I got the lute, and the lute got me, is a story.

A sideman's a musical hired gun, and a chameleon. You learn to pick up the lead's style really fast and get under it. You make them happy and you get more work; word gets around.

I was a noodler as a kid, with a no-name classical guitar my father left sitting around. Always had a good ear. When a song came up on the radio, I'd pick up that soft-string and just start playing along somewhere in the middle of the fingerboard. I learned how to read music with piano lessons, but the main thing was always ear to fingers without too much brain in between. That turned out to serve me well.

I also did a little teaching at a local music store, classical on Wednesdays and rock on Thursdays. That eked out my sideman income, which was irregular all the time and shrank to almost nothing in the summer—bands that book college towns when the students are away don't make enough money to hire someone like me. (Someone who's the best damned guitar player in town, and modest besides.)

The teaching gig is how I met Laura, got the lute, fell in love, and turned my life into something mad and magical. And I do mean madness and magic, not metaphor.

I later found out that Laura had seen me perform at a gig that turned out to be a kind of one-man band freak show. It was a pretty good folk-rock quintet that changed its name about once a week. When I worked for them, they were Jerry & the Winos, though if you've ever heard of them it was probably as Baked Alaska, with their hit single and album *Straighten Up and Die Right*. Cheerful bunch.

Anyhow, one of Jerry's winos was poleaxed with something like Montezuma's Revenge—they'd just come from New Mexico and figured the spices might have gotten him, not to mention the thirty-two-hour drive. So they hired me to pick up for the guy, who doubled on twelve-string and electric bass, no problem.

(I have an apartment so full of musical instruments that you have to move one to sit down. That's relevant.)

It turned out that it wasn't the food, though, but a bug, and the quintet that had become a quartet wound up being just Jerry and me, with the rest of his band in the hospital. Jerry may have beaten the thing because he was such a total drug addict that he couldn't tell the difference between being sick and being well. Or maybe the heroin killed off all those microorganisms before it finally killed Jerry, six or seven years later.

But that was one hell of a gig. He had the lungs and the energy of his namesake Garcia, and a kind of stoned concentration that was a marvel to watch. The afternoon that three of his guys took a fast cab to join their buddy in the GI ward, Jerry and his sound man laid out all their arrangements on the floor of the stage. We walked down the line, the two of them basically arguing about what instrument I was going to play when. Jerry knew I could play anything from a Roland to a rattle, and he decided to make a virtue out of a necessity—not to mention saving a few hundred bucks by not hiring another sideman or three.

I was in seventh heaven. I also got a lot of ego gratification and local publicity out of it, because Jerry was generous in explaining what had happened and how I'd saved his sorry butt. So I just danced from keyboard to fingerboard; frets to fretless—if there'd been a saxophone on stage, I would've tried to learn it. We had it set up so Jerry went between electric and acoustic while I went from one music stand to the next, reading like a son of a bitch on five instruments. Jerry vetoed the sound man when he wanted to use the Roland's computer-generated percussion, which was good. Jerry did rhythm while I did lead, and vice versa. By the end of the second night, we were playing like we'd been together forever, and Jerry said if the other guys weren't pals, he'd leave 'em in the hospital and we could hit the road together.

But he and the Winos moved on, and I went back to doing what I did, with one huge difference: Laura had been there both nights. Friday with a date, and then Saturday alone.

I hadn't seen her—with the lights you don't see a lot past the stage—and if I had, I probably wouldn't have taken special notice. She was one of those women who could be beautiful when she wanted to be, but preferred the anonymity of being plain. A kind of protective coloration: whatever she was, it wasn't ordinary.

She showed up the next Wednesday at the store and asked about classical lessons. No, she didn't have a guitar, which was good; my secondary function at the place, maybe my primary one, was to sell guitars to my defenseless students.

I'm a reasonable guy and usually start them out with something good but not too expensive. An expert can get a pretty good sound out of anything, but a beginner can't. On the other hand, you don't want to talk somebody into a thousand-dollar guitar that she'll be stuck with if she quits in a month.

Nobody'd ever done what she did. She asked me what my favorite chord was—an open A major seventh in the fourth position—and listened to me play it on every classical guitar in the store. She didn't buy the most expensive one, but she was close, a custom-made ¾-size that a luthier up in Yellow Springs had made for a guy who died before it could be delivered.

I said it had a haunting tone. She said maybe that was because it was haunted.

She was clumsy the first day, but after that she learned faster than anyone I've ever taught. Once a week wasn't enough; she wanted lessons on the weekends, too. Sometimes at the store on Saturday; sometimes elsewhere on Sunday, when the store was closed. We practiced down at the lake on campus when the weather was fine; otherwise her place.

Her apartment was as plain and neat as mine was cluttered and, well, not neat. Mine looked like a bachelor had lived there alone for five years. Hers looked like no one lived there at all. It had the understated rightness of a Japanese Sumi-e painting—a few pieces of furniture, a few pieces of art, all in harmony. I wondered what was hidden behind the closed bedroom door. Maybe I hoped the room was heaped high with junk.

When I did see it, I found it was as simple as the rest of the place. A low bed, a table and chair, and a place to hang our clothes.

She was no groupie. I'd had plenty of experience with them, both before and (unfortunately) during my marriage. Sidemen don't get groupies, though, and groupies don't approach you with quiet seriousness and explain that it was time to move your relationship to a higher spiritual plane.

I hesitated because of age—I'd just turned forty and she seemed half that—and I did respect her and not want to hurt her. She smiled and said that if I didn't hurt her, she would try to return the favor.

Later I would remember "try to." She must have known.

Our first night was more than a night, in both time and consequence. She revealed her actual beauty for the first time, and gave me more physical pleasure than any woman ever had, and took the same in return. I didn't question where she could have learned all that she knew. Sometime around noon, she left me exhausted in her bed, and it was getting dark again when she gently shook me awake. She said she had a present for me.

There were two candles on her table, with wine and cheese, bread and fruit. She lit a few other candles around the room while I opened the bottle, and then brought over her gift, a large angular thing in a cotton sack. When I took it from her, it knocked against the table with a soft discordant jangle.

It was a big ornate lutelike thing, which she called a chitarrone. At least that's what the antique dealer had called it when she bought it at the big flea market in Waldo.

It didn't sound very musical, missing some strings and not in tune with the rusty ones it did have, but even in its beat-up state it was an impressive piece of work, a cross between a lute and a kind of string bass. The wood was inlaid in a neat pattern, and there were three ornately carved sound holes. It came with a diagram showing how the strings should be tuned, drawn with brown ink on paper that felt like soft animal skin, a kind of hokey attempt at antiquity,

I thought. The notes were square, but the staffs were recognizable. I knew I could string it with modern mandolin, guitar, and cello strings.

It couldn't possibly be as old as it looked, and not be in a museum. And she said no, the dealer only claimed it was a twentieth-century copy. It hadn't cost enough to be that old.

I looked forward to trying it out; I could get strings at the store the next day and tune it up between students—maybe I'd have it sounding like something when she came in for her 4:00 lesson.

She said she'd look forward to it, and we got to work on the wine and food. We talked of this and that, and then I played her some old ballads on her small guitar. The food of love, the poet said, and we moved back into her rumpled bed.

I woke to the smell of coffee, but she was already gone; a note by the pot said she had an 8:00 class. I made a breakfast of leftover cheese and bread and cleaned up a bit, feeling unnaturally domestic. Went back to my place sort of drifting in a state of *I-don't-deserve-this-but-who-does?* Shaved and showered and found a clean shirt, and got to the store an hour and a half before my first pupil.

The chitarrone looked authentically old in the cold fluorescent light of the store's workroom. I cleaned it carefully with some Gibson guitar spray, but resisted waxing it. That would make it prettier, but would have a muting effect on the sound, and I was intensely curious about that.

Over the course of the day, during two dead hours and my lunch break, I replaced the strings one at a time and kept tuning them up as they relaxed. I tuned the thing two whole tones low, since it obviously hadn't been played in some time, and I didn't want to stress it.

It had a good sound, though, tuning: plangent, archaic. It was a real time trip. They don't make them like that any more—or they do, but not for working musicians like yours truly. A twenty-one-string nightmare, I don't think so.

The other guys at the store were fascinated by it, though, and so were two of my students. But not the one I wanted to see and hear it. She didn't make her 4:00.

I called and her phone had been disconnected. After work, I rushed over, and found her apartment door open, the living room and bedroom bare. The super, miffed because I'd interrupted her dinner preparations, said the place had been empty since June, two months. When I tried to explain, she looked wary and then scared, and eased the door shut with two loud clicks.

The chitarrone, lying diagonally across the car's back seat, was solid and eerily real. As I drove home, it played itself at every bump in the road, a D diminished, slightly out of tune.

Amazon.com didn't have *The Chitarrone for Idiots*, or for madmen, but there were plenty of lute books with medieval and Renaissance music, and it was easy to incorporate the instrument's bass drone strings into the melodies. There wasn't much call for it in jazz and rock gigs, but I brought it along when folk groups were amenable. I'd worked out some slightly anachronistic pieces like "Scarborough Fair" and "Greensleeves" that were easy to play along with, and singable. And they led to the unlikely gig that demonstrated the thing's true power.

I got a call from a music professor who asked whether I really had a chitarrone, and he got all excited when I demonstrated it over the phone. Could I clear up two weekends in February and play with his consort at the upcoming Medieval Faire?

In fact, I was free those weekends. We set up a couple of practice dates and he faxed me some sheets. They were lute and the robo parts, and it was easy to cobble them together into something that used the instrument's resonant bass strings.

We met at the professor's crumbling-but-genteel Victorian mansion. He'd gathered eleven students who played an assortment of modern replicas of period string, wind, and percussion instruments, and they were all enthralled by my medieval Rube Goldberg machine. The professor, Harold Innes, was especially impressed, not only at the workmanship but the careful aging of the instrument. Could it possibly be a "misplaced" museum piece? I told him it came from the Waldo flea market, and God knows where it might originally have been stolen from.

Innes' wife Gladys was a piece of work, setting out tea and cookies with a kind of smoldering resentment. If she had ever been charmed by her husband's fascination with old music (and perhaps with young students), it had not withstood the test of time. Maybe it was the unfortunate choice of a husband whose last name made a jingling rhyme with her first—thirty or forty years of being "Gladys Innes" might push you toward being "Gladys Anything Else."

Halfway though the rehearsal, they had a quiet but intense argument in the kitchen. One of the students wondered aloud where they would rehearse if Gladys got the house, and the others just nodded sourly.

Gladys did know music, though. She asked me intelligent questions about various tunings and techniques for playing the thing, and when Harold asked me to do a couple of solo numbers, she came out and listened with rapt attention.

I got the job, and looked forward to it even though the six days would pay less than a normal weekend, and I would have to rent and wear a ridiculous houppelande thing, tied around the waist with a rope, that made me look and feel like Falstaff.

A curious thing happened at the second rehearsal, which was a dress rehearsal. Gladys was all smiles and flirting, with me and the students, but especially with Harold. He himself wore a kind of stunned honeymooner look. Their marriage was obviously off the rocks, and the consort responded to that with more than relief; their playing was superbly controlled and had a new emotional depth.

There was another emotional aspect. After the tea break, I played a couple of pieces, a solo of "Twa Corbies" and a duet of "Lord Randell" with a young man who harmonized with a doom-laden tenor recorder. Neither is exactly romantic, plucking eyes and poisoning your lover with eel-broth, but the students paired up while they listened, mostly boy-girl but also a pair of men who leaned together, touching each other shoulder to knee, and two women who held hands and whispered quietly.

It wasn't my singing, which a critic once neatly pinned as "accurate," but some quality of the chitarrone's sound. The damned thing was aphrodisiac, at least in that setting, the old musty Victorian parlor with everyone dressed up for a passion play. The passion was so thick you could bottle it and sell it online.

The Medieval Faire was the killer, though. I was

prepared to endure it—thee-ing and thou-ing everyone, wearing a quarter inch of beard and the woolen
houppelande, not exactly made for Florida spring.
But I did wind up enjoying the phony ambience, and
not just because the concert tent was next to the
mead tent. I've never played to a more appreciative
audience.

The pattern of the gig settled down to this: we
would rotate among three sets of period music, during which I would play lute parts with my regular
classical guitar. That would be about forty minutes'
worth. Then I would pick up the chitarrone, holding
it like a mandolin on steroids, and play a couple of
tunes with light accompaniment.

Crowds would form in those last ten minutes;
crowds that filled the tent and spilled out into the
muddy mess outside. The crowd was composed completely of pairs, doing body language as if it were
an Olympic sport.

Two successful CDs later, I shouldn't complain,
but I will. Laura left me with a magical gift, and a
hole in my heart that grows deeper every time I use
it. Not just because I miss her, though I miss her like
a wounded soldier must miss his lost limb.

I watch people while I play; I watch them go all
soft and fall in love. But never with the player. Never
with me.

# SPLINTER

*by*

## *Kevin J. Anderson & Rebecca Moesta*

Kevin J. Anderson has over sixteen million books in print in twenty-seven languages. His original work has appeared on numerous "Best of the Year" and awards lists. In 1998, he set the Guinness World Record for "Largest Single-Author Book Signing." He has written many popular *Star Wars* and *X-Files* novels, as well as prequels to *Dune* written with Frank Herbert's son Brian. Recent novels include *Horizon Storms, A Forest of Stars, Hopscotch,* and *Captain Nemo.* He is married to Rebecca Moesta, his frequent collaborator. An avid hiker, Anderson dictates his fiction into a miscrocassette recorder while out exploring the wilderness. Research for his novels has taken him to the deserts of Morocco, the cloud forests of Ecuador, Inca ruins in the Andes, Maya temples in the Yucatan, the Cheyenne Mountain NORAD complex, NASA's Vehicle Assembly Building at Cape Canaveral, a Minuteman III missile silo, the deck of the aircraft carrier Nimitz, the floor of the Pacific Stock Exchange, a plutonium plant at Los Alamos, and FBI Headquarters in Washington, DC. He also, occasionally, stays home and works on his manuscripts. . . .

Rebecca Moesta is the author of more than twenty-five books, including the award-winning *Star Wars: Young Jedi Knights* series and two original *Titan A. E.* novels, which she coauthored with husband Kevin J. Anderson, along with the hardcover *Star Trek: The Next Generation* graphic novel *The Gorn Crisis* from DC Comics/Wildstorm. Her novel based on *Buffy the Vampire Slayer, Little Things,* was recently published. She is the daughter of an English teacher/author/Bible scholar, and a nurse—from whom she learned, respectively, her love of words and her love of books. Moesta, who holds an MBA from Boston University, has taught every grade level from kindergarten through junior college and worked for seven years as a publications specialist and technical editor at Lawrence Livermore National Laboratory.

SOMETHING ABOUT THE RENAISSANCE FAIRE beckoned to him like the sound of a hundred sirens luring a lonely sailor from the sea. In spite of the nearly hundred-degree heat of a California summer, he never tired of the beauty of it all—the jostling crowds in brightly colored clothing, the noisy parades of "royalty" and minstrels, the jugglers, the candlemakers, the serenity of a young mother with ample breasts exposed suckling a newborn child as if it were the most natural thing in the world. He loved the spectacle of a hundred different kinds of entertainers and artisans and food vendors, all putting on Elizabethan microperformances minute by minute, doing their utmost to lure money from the cash-fat pockets of the faire-goers.

And it was those cash-fat pockets that brought Wil to these open-air festivals year after year. He never could resist the magic of thousands of bodies jostling together, muttering loudly, kicking up dust . . . never noticing the slender young man with the wispy beard and peasant clothing who expertly and discreetly relieved them of their excess valuables. Pickpocket, thief, rogue, highwayman—after all, that was a legitimate part of the time period, too. Certainly more authentic than either the churro or cappuccino seller.

It wasn't long before the first opportunity presented itself. Wil had learned to recognize those opportunities while he was still in high school, furtively watching for an unguarded purse or backpack; by now his instincts were so well-tuned, he hardly had to think about it. He had just passed the booth from which he'd shoplifted his own costume two years earlier, when he came upon a couple in casually elegant street clothes. They were having a heated discussion just outside a palm reader's tent.

"Why not?" the young woman said. "Are you afraid she'll tell us we should get married, after all?"

The young man scoffed. "Come on, they only say what they think you want to hear, anyway."

Quickly assessing the situation—it was quite important to be a good judge of character—Wil deduced from shoes, hair, makeup, and demeanor that the young woman would be carrying the money. *I'm even doing them a favor*, Wil thought. *A few arguments about money will give them a more accurate sense of their marriage compatibility than any palm reader could.*

He conveniently joined a cluster of people passing by, allowing himself to be crowded into the arguing couple. It took only one brief bump and a mumbled "Excuse me" to liberate an expensive Tumi wallet from the young woman's equally expensive Dooney & Bourke leather purse.

A little farther on, Wil ducked between two booths to determine the value of his acquisition. He was immediately impressed with himself: $281 in cash, and the wallet itself would fetch a good price at the local flea market. Wil tucked his prize into an interior pocket of his billowy brown knee breeches and moved on with a spring in his step. He would dispose of the credit cards, of course. Too easy to get caught using stolen cards.

And he didn't plan to get caught. Ever.

The next two hours proved considerably less satisfying. Discouraged, Wil bought a roasted turkey leg, then removed the pewter tankard he wore at his belt and had it filled with chilled ale. He sat down to eat on a bench in a small amphitheater where two jugglers were throwing knives at each other while making witty banter.

After polishing off his lunch, Wil tossed the turkey leg bone to the ground, not even bothering to look for a trashcan. If someone scolded him about it, he could argue that his gesture was certainly truer to the Renaissance spirit than using a trashcan was. If it really bothered some do-gooder, let *him* dispose of it. Wil had never believed in much except himself . . . and he'd gotten over himself long ago.

Wil headed up a rocky, hay-strewn path, his eyes beginning their automatic sweep. His vigilance was quickly rewarded when he spied a middle-aged man with a chest-length salt-and-pepper beard counting out bills from a leather pouch at his waist. One of the bills fell to the ground and was caught by a hot breeze and blown a few feet behind him onto the path. Noting that the foot traffic was light and no one else was watching, Wil bent smoothly for the merest second, plucked the bill from the ground and continued up the path before the bearded man even had a chance to turn and look for the fallen money.

Wil passed a tarot card reader and a cluster of

college students singing madrigals beside a fake wishing well. At the glass blower's tent, he spotted a man in his mid-thirties making a purchase. He wore safari shorts, a golf shirt, designer sunglasses, and sockless leather loafers. A grade-school-aged boy and girl pranced impatiently beside him. A quick glimpse told the pickpocket that the man's wallet contained enough cash to pay Wil's expenses for weeks.

"Come on, Dad! You promised we could see the storyteller."

"And that's just what we're going to do." The man slid his wallet into the front pocket of his shorts and accepted a wrapped package from the glass blower. Wil hung back and decided this man might be worth following.

The man began herding his children up the path. "Why'd we have to buy Mom another glass unicorn?" the boy said.

"We get her one every year, Evan, whether she can come or not. It's not her fault Grandma broke her hip," the girl answered. "What a stupid question."

"Now, Orli, don't call your brother stupid."

Wil gritted his teeth as he watched Perfect Family Guy, more determined than ever to interject a little bit of gritty reality into the pampered PFG's perfect life. Wil was an old hand at rationalizing to himself. He had been making up excuses and explanations for so long that he had almost come to believe them. Almost.

They came to a small pavilion, where half the floor was littered with hassocks and colorful overstuffed cushions on which children sat or reclined. A man with a leathery face and white shoulder-length hair walked among them, telling stories. Wooden tables running along one side of the breezy tent held books bound in hand-tooled leather. The sign over the pavilion said, "Tales of Glorye."

Wil watched as Orli, Evan, and Perfect Family Guy seated themselves on cushions. Pretending a casual interest, Wil entered the pavilion and began browsing the books. The storyteller spoke in a rich, expressive voice. Wil let the words wash over him, but his concentration was focused on PFG.

When the tale ended about ten minutes later, many of the listeners came up to drop money into a hat beside the old storyteller. Most of the audience left, but Wil's three marks lingered to ask questions. He suppressed an impatient sigh, picked up another leather-bound book and leafed through it, pretending to admire the meticulous hand lettering.

The storyteller plopped the hat full of money onto a table not far from Wil.

"So what happened next?" Orli asked the old man. "I mean, after the knight went back and told the king."

"Ah, now that's a much longer story."

"Do you have a book that has the story in it?" PFG asked.

"Over here on the table." The storyteller moved closer to Wil and selected a thick tome with a burgundy leather binding.

Perfect Family Guy showed it to his daughter. "Say, aren't you worried about leaving all that money just lying on the table?"

Finding the comment particularly ironic, Wil glanced over to see the old man smile. "I find that when you take care of the really valuable things, everything else takes care of itself. That's why I keep everything that's truly valuable to me right here in this pocket," he said, patting the left side of his leather breeches.

"I can admire that philosophy," PFG said.

"Look," Evan said, pointing at the pages of the book. "There's the story he told today."

"And two stories that come before, and three that come after it," Orli said. "Daddy, can we get this?"

PFG stroked his daughter's hair. "It would be the perfect souvenir."

Wil gritted his teeth again. *Perfect.* The very perfection of this family was driving him insane.

"Let me wrap that for you." The storyteller moved to Wil's right, reached under the table, and came up with two sheets of heavy paper that looked handmade.

The children began looking at the books on another table. PFG got out his wallet and began counting out the money. When the storyteller laid the sheets of paper on the table and began wrapping the book, Wil saw his chance. The pocket that held the old man's "true valuables" was within a foot of Wil's hand, so he clumsily dropped the book he had been looking at. Pretending to reach for it, Wil awkwardly bumped the old man with his hip, at the same time slipping his right hand into the pocket and apologetically steadying the storyteller with his left hand.

The whole maneuver took less than a second. Wil felt an uneven lump in the pocket, something strange—but just as his hand closed around it, a searing pain shot up his arm. It was like nothing he had felt since the age of ten when he'd lost control of his bicycle going down the driveway, veered into the neighbor's yard, fallen, and ripped his leg open on a sprinkler head.

With another jostle, Wil snatched his hand back

and bent to retrieve the fallen book. He fumbled around, momentarily blinded by the pain and sucked in a sharp breath.

The old man put a hand on Wil's back. "You all right, lad?"

For a panicked second, Wil wondered if the old man knew he'd been pickpocketed, but when his eyes focused on the kindly face, he saw no suspicion.

"No, I, uh . . . sudden migraine." He put a hand to his head. "Probably the heat."

He handed the book back to the storyteller. As quickly as it had come, the scorching pain subsided, but Wil's hand still throbbed as if he had slammed it in a door.

Perfect Family Guy was beside him. "My wife gets migraines. They can get pretty nasty. Maybe you should lie down somewhere in the shade."

"There's plenty of room on the cushions," the old man offered.

"No," Wil said a little too quickly. "Thank you. I, uh, probably should take some medication for this. It's out in my car." Damn. Now that both men were so solicitous of him, Wil stood little chance of slipping in under their radar.

The storyteller regarded him with solemn eyes. "I hope you feel better really soon. Sometimes there's a trick to it."

"Do you need help out to your car?" PFG asked.

"Thanks. I'll manage." He left the pavilion, cursing himself for attracting so much attention from two potential marks. Surely he could have toughed out just a little bit of pain when he stood to profit so much. Already the searing stab had receded to a mere pinprick in his mind. It had been foolish weakness, but he would not call attention to himself again.

Once he was out of sight of the pavilion, Wil hur-

ried to put as much distance between him and the
two annoyingly helpful men as possible. Safely on
the other side of the faire, he scanned the crowds
once more for opportunities. *This is easy.* He struggled to focus. *You're a natural.* But nothing felt natural
right now.

He was filled with a sensation that was simultaneously pleasant and unpleasant, a fizzy alertness of
the mind not unlike the way he felt when, after an
all-nighter, his body replaced sleep with pure adrenaline. Wil forced himself to move into the flow of
shoppers and sightseers.

There. Wil saw his opportunity. A young woman
with hot pink polish on the nails of her manicured
fingers and pedicured toes was pushing a baby car-
riage. The mother stopped and bent to comfort the
child as it continued to wail. Her attention was fully
focused on the brat and not on the purse dangling
from the stroller's handle.

He moved in. This was almost too easy. A simple
swoop would do it. His hand dipped into her purse,
but the moment he touched the wallet, a lightning
bolt struck the index finger of his right hand, shot
through his wrist, traveled up his arm, and spiked
into his brain. He simultaneously jerked his hand
away and fell to his knees. The young mother looked
up in alarm, her concentration startled away from
her child who, also startled, stopped crying for a
moment.

"Sorry," Wil gasped. "I tripped."

"You okay?" She moved around to the back of the
stroller, darting a cautious glance down at her purse.

"Yeah, I'll be fine." Wil forced himself back to his
feet and dusted off his breeches. "Good as new."

He backed away and lost himself in the crowd.
That had been close. Damndest thing about his hand,

too. In a patch of bright sunlight, he examined his finger. It still stung, as if something small and sharp was embedded in it, but he could see no burn or blister, no cut, no sliver, *nothing.* Yet the pain—the pain in his hand, his arm, his head—had been real. He frowned. Maybe it was a pinched nerve, or maybe he really was having a migraine.

Wil always kept a bottle of ibuprofen stashed in his glove compartment, so he headed out the front entrance, remembering to get his hand stamped for reentry. The parking lot offered no shade at all, and Wil considered waiting for the "shuttle," a wide, canvas-covered horse-drawn wagon that ferried attendees to and from their cars for tips. But the wagon was at the far end of the lot, and Wil didn't want to wait.

By the time he got to his battered '83 Dodge, he had worked up a substantial sweat. He got the bottle of extra-strength pain reliever, took twice the suggested number, and washed them down with a grimace and a swallow of the flat, and by now hot, soda he'd left open in his car.

He rolled down the windows and took a short nap in the front seat to give the analgesic time to work. By the time he woke up, it was late afternoon. The faire would be closing in a couple of hours, and parts of the parking lot had already begun to empty out. Wil felt greatly refreshed, in spite of the heat, and decided to get back to work.

He got out of his car and strode through the lot in the general direction of the entrance. As he walked, he glanced through car windows, looking for wallets, merchandise, or purses left behind by faire-goers in the "safety" of their locked cars. For the most part, he ignored the older cars, like his, which usually weren't worth the trouble. He also avoided anything too new and too likely to have an alarm. Within ten minutes, he had found one with a purse on the floor of the passenger side, "hidden" underneath the morning paper.

He grinned. "Haven't lost your touch, Wil."

All the doors were locked, of course, but he easily found a substantial rock that would remedy the situation. After a quick glance to make sure no one was around, he hefted the rock and swung it toward the window.

Several seconds later, Wil opened his eyes to escape the blinding white explosion in his head. He found himself flat on his back in the dirt, still grasping the rock. The slicing, stabbing, burning pain that grated up his arm was less intense now, but still impossible to endure.

When he dropped the rock, the pain finally began to subside. He hauled himself back to his feet, looked at the car window, and blinked in surprise. The window was not broken. Not even a crack. But he couldn't have missed—not with the force he'd used, not at such short range, and yet . . .

Carefully, afraid of triggering the terrible pain again, he picked up the rock, this time with his left hand. He swung with all his might at the window— *Bam!* Flat in the dirt again. Wil's head pounded as if a grenade had gone off in his right ear, and his right arm felt as if an elephant had walked across it. He whimpered—something no one had ever heard him do. He wondered if he might be having a heart attack. Wouldn't that be the left arm? It was hard to think.

His fingers let loose of the rock, and he lay on the tire-flattened grass until the pain had subsided to a mere prickling in his right index finger. He brought it up to his face and studied it again, but still found nothing.

Something was very wrong with him. Wil didn't have medical insurance, but there was a first-aid tent inside the faire. He could describe his symptoms, maybe have them examine him. At least it would be free.

He got up slowly, not even bothering to brush the dirt off. It might add an air of authenticity when he explained his symptoms, make the first-aid workers take him more seriously. On his way to the entrance, much to his chagrin, Wil passed the Perfect Family waiting to take the wagon shuttle back to the parking lot. The wagon was coming, the horses clomping forward, the people pushing closer to get a seat aboard.

Wil hoped to walk past the annoying family unnoticed, but Perfect Family Guy saw him right away and managed to look genuinely concerned. "Hey, how's that migraine doing?"

Wil's first instinct was to lie, but what was the point? "I thought it was gone, but it seems to keep coming back."

The little girl, Orli, trotted out in front of the wagon, grinning. "Look—what pretty horses! Where's the video camera, Daddy? Can you take a picture of me with them?"

Two rowdy young boys began to clatter against each other with wooden swords they had purchased as souvenirs.

PFG nodded his sympathy toward Wil. "Could be one of those cluster headaches, I suppose. They come and go, and they can be as bad as migraines." Wil made a noncommittal response and stepped around the crowd, wanting to be away.

A younger boy, frustrated at being left out of his

brothers' sword fight, pulled out his "Renaissance souvenir" pop gun and pointed it at them. "I'll get you both!" He fired the pop gun, augmenting the sound with his own yell, "BLAM!"

The hot and tired horses responded to the noise. Startled, they flinched in their harness, snorted, and lurched forward. Orli was standing right in their path, still waiting for PFG to film her with the video camera. The wagon driver wrenched at his reins, the horses lifted their hooves, and the girl shrieked.

Because he had been trying to get around the crowd, Wil was closest to where the girl stood. He jumped forward, knocked Orli out of the way, smashed into the nearest horse, and fell to the ground. Before he could roll away, he felt a hammer strike his chest. The girl had fallen backward to sprawl in the dirt and had already begun to sob, but the weeping came more from startlement and confusion than from severe pain. Wil, on the other hand, thought he might have cracked a rib or two.

The wagon driver backed the wagon up several feet and jumped down from the buckboard, and other people hurried forward to Wil and the girl. The horses snorted, as if embarrassed by the incident. Orli continued to cry softly, and her father quickly checked to make sure she was uninjured before moving to take a look at Wil.

"Wow, that could've been bad! I don't know how to thank you. Are you all right?"

*Surprised* was the first thing that came to Wil's mind. He had acted completely without thinking, with no regard for his own safety. Stranger yet, he felt very little pain. "Fine." And he found it was true. His entire body was suffused with a pleasant tingling sensation. "Better than fine. I'm great."

Perfect Family Guy still looked concerned. "Could

just be endorphins and adrenaline talking. You'd better have a doctor check you out."

A distant part of Wil's mind seemed aware that his body was hurt. He pulled open the loose neck of his muslin peasant shirt and looked inside. A red flush of bruising was already beginning to appear beneath the skin. How odd. After the inexplicable agony he had experienced several times today—each time while trying to ply his trade—now he felt euphoria when he should *really* be hurt. And he'd only been trying to help someone, after all. There was definite irony in that: invisible pain after trying to steal, and a feeling of well-being when trying to help, despite a visible injury.

Wil's eyes narrowed as the thoughts flashed through his mind. *Was* it irony, or was this something more sinister? It had all begun after he'd tried to pick the storyteller's pocket. Had the old man done something to him, administered some sort of drug or hypnotized him?

He smiled up at the PFG. "You're probably right. I'll head back inside to the first-aid tent."

Perfect Family Guy still looked concerned. "They won't be able to do much in there. You might need an X-ray. Do you have insurance?"

Wil shook his head. PFG pulled out his wallet and removed a business card. "Here's my card. If you end up needing to see a real doctor, I'll make sure that your expenses get covered."

"Thanks." Wil glanced down at the little rectangle of paper, then put it in his pocket. *Bentley Watson-Taylor III, Attorney at Law.* "I hope I won't need it. I'm just glad Orli's okay." A tingling rush of good feeling started in Wil's hand and swept up his arm and through his body.

"Thank you, Mister," Orli said, and gave him a hug. "I hope you're going to be okay, too."

Wil knew the hug against his sore ribs should have hurt, but he didn't even wince. "I'll be fine. You just stay out of trouble."

Back at the entrance he showed his hand stamp, went through, and headed toward the storyteller's pavilion.

On the way, he tested his theory. He tried to pick a pocket and received a fresh jolt of pain. Then, after helping an older woman push her husband's wheelchair up an uneven slope and position the man where he could watch a troupe of players perform humorously abbreviated Shakespeare plays, Wil felt the rush of euphoria again.

The old storyteller had definitely done something to him.

When Wil reached the pavilion, the old man had just finished spinning a tale and the few late-afternoon audience members left quickly. Wil walked straight toward the storyteller, stepping over the scattered cushions. The leathery face registered recognition and concern, but no surprise.

"What did you do to me?" Wil demanded. His voice was rough with mixed emotion.

The old man considered the question. "I shared something with you, as I do with all who listen to me. How is your headache? Are you feeling better now?"

Wil felt an acid spurt of frustration burn in his stomach. "You know it wasn't a headache, and, no, I'm not feeling better. You tricked me."

The old man's expressive eyebrows climbed a millimeter up his forehead. "How so?"

Wil cast about for an answer. He wasn't sure how

he'd been tricked or what had been done to him, but he traced the strangeness back to *here,* in this tent with gauzy walls and cooling breezes, and this enigmatic man from whom he had tried to steal something of "true value."

"You . . . you tricked me by saying you had something valuable in your pocket."

The old man nodded soberly. "You heard that, did you? That is true. I carry what I value most in my pocket. But how is that a trick?"

Wil seethed inside. Wasn't the answer obvious? "Because you knew I'd hear you, and that I'd try to find out what was in your pocket."

"Ah." The storyteller's voice was barely a whisper. "And . . . ?"

"*And?* When I touched whatever was in your pocket, it gave me a jolt of some sort. It hurt so much I let go and fell to the ground. That's how you tricked me. What was it? Some kind of trap?"

"I admit, I did speak the truth in your hearing, yet no one can choose what another person will do with the truth once they hear it. I did not make that choice for you."

Wil couldn't believe his ears. Was the storyteller actually implying that this was all his own fault? "Oh, no you don't, old man. You still did something to my hand, and I'm betting you know how to undo it. Every time I try to practice my . . . business, my hand, my arm, my body, my brain, *everything* hurts like hell. Well, fine. You made your point. Picking pockets is bad. Stealing is bad. I get it." He raised a fist. "Now make it stop or I'll—"

An excruciating pain sizzled up Wil's arm and blinded him for a moment. As soon as he lowered his arm and forced his fist to relax, the agony began to fade. "For God's sake, just make it stop."

"Make it stop? For God's sake . . ." The storyteller looked troubled. "Let me tell you a story—it's what I do. Please, sit down."

Wil wasn't sure why, but he sat. And listened.

"In the time of the Third Crusade, the Year of Our Lord 1190, many brave knights, greedy lordlings, and hapless soldiers traveled across Europe by boat or by foot, in order to secure the Holy Land from the evil Turks. Some crusaders truly felt a calling from God, but the real reason for most of the lords and commanders—third and fourth sons without lands to inherit—was to capture new domains to rule. Other knights simply came for the chance to fight, to kill the infidel, to find glory on the battlefield.

"One such knight—let us call him Roderick the Brash—led his soldiers into battle, cutting his way through Turkish lines to establish a foothold in Jerusalem. There, while attempting to occupy the ancient holy city, Roderick came upon a kindly old leatherworker, who went by the name of Julius. The leatherworker did good deeds for his neighbors in Jerusalem, without giving thought to whether they were Christians, Moslems, or Jews. He claimed to have been a centurion in the Roman army in the time of Jesus Christ."

Wil scoffed. "That would have made him over a thousand years old."

The storyteller simply looked at him. "It's a story. Would you like to hear more?"

"As long as there's a point."

"Julius himself was present at the crucifixion and had come into possession of a fragment of the True Cross, and a Splinter from this remarkable artifact had kept him alive for so long. Though he wasn't wealthy, the leatherworker had sufficient means to meet his needs and was content. No doubt, he experienced the same euphoria you can feel if you perform a selfless deed."

"That's a stretch. Are you telling me—"

The old man calmly went on. "When he learned that Julius the leatherworker had such a treasure, this holy relic, Roderick the Brash came at night into his shop and demanded to see the fragment. Julius told him the story I just told you. And then Roderick struck him down with his sword and took the fragment for himself."

The old man's gaze was distant, and his voice hitched. After a brief pause, he reached into the pocket where he kept his treasure, where Wil had felt the first sharp sting. He withdrew an oddly shaped and unimpressive lump of very old wood, less than two inches long. "When the fragment encounters someone who needs its . . . assistance, it shares a part of itself. A Splinter.

"Roderick the Brash had great need of it. After touching the fragment, Roderick attempted to ignore the message of the Splinter. He continued to fight and kill until the pain became so overwhelming it rendered him unconscious, and his men left him for dead on the battlefield. After that, Roderick had no choice but to change his ways. He performed his penance for many centuries, made his way through the world, and found his own contentment. And, over the years, the fragment grew smaller, bit by bit, as it found others who needed it."

Wil's impatience mixed with wonder, annoyance, and indignation. "So, I'm supposed to believe that you're a knight named Roderick the Brash, who lived during the Third Crusade? And that I've got a Splinter of the True Cross stuck in my hand?"

"I simply told the story." The old man gave him a noncommittal look. "Believe what you wish."

Wil blew out an angry breath, looking at the lump of wood. It wasn't the least bit impressive. "If I believe that's a real holy relic with magical powers, and an invisibly small Splinter is embedded in my finger, then I'd also have to believe that I no longer have free will. I'm just a rat in a maze, and God is some sort of cosmic experimental researcher dispensing either treats or electric shocks, depending on whether or not I do what He wants."

The storyteller did not answer the accusation directly. His pensive gaze seemed to look through Wil. His eyes seemed very, very old. "There are many possible interpretations—some harsher than others. Some say that the Splinter is a sort of . . . conscience for those who have discarded the conscience that God gave them. But I don't believe that.

"Others believe that because the cross is a symbol of sacrifice, a Splinter of the True Cross might bestow peace and happiness for every deed that is selfless or sacrificial, while selfish acts are rewarded only with pain."

The storyteller paused. "But I don't believe that either. All of my experience and knowledge have led me to conclude one thing, that a Splinter is distilled truth. No more, no less."

Wil wanted to object, to interrupt and call the man's words bullshit. He didn't believe in Biblical morality or in miracles and had never felt a need to go to church. He had certainly never let himself be bound by superstition. But something kept him silent.

"Each Splinter senses the good or bad potential of a person's actions, then gathers those effects, concentrates them into the *now*, and transmits the truth back to its owner. If a thief takes a wallet, he causes financial injury to the person he steals from. He also steals some of that person's time, and robs him of his feeling of safety. Like a pebble dropped into a pond, there are ripple effects."

Wil rubbed his forefinger but felt no twinge of pain. "Now you're getting pretty esoteric."

"It is concrete enough. Perhaps the thief's victims would not have enough money to buy necessities for themselves or their families. Imagine that a person needed to fix the brakes on his car. If there wasn't enough money to fix the brakes, and the brakes failed, then a terrible accident could result. All these things factor together and are condensed by the Splinter into a single manifestation of pain, great or small. In the same way, a kind or unselfish deed helps both the giver and the receiver. The Splinter concentrates consequences, intensifies truth."

"But . . . but, if I believe you, then you've just taken away my livelihood!" Wil squawked. "That's how I survive. You don't have any right."

The storyteller smiled. "Imagine what the ruthless warrior Roderick the Brash must have experienced. How difficult it was to give up hatred, pillaging, and violence, stranded in a hostile foreign land, suddenly prevented from looting and killing. . . . Still, he learned to get by. So can you."

Wil squirmed. Something about the old man's interpretation rang uncomfortably true. "So is there anything I could do to get rid of it? Short of amputation? I mean, if I did a lot of good deeds would it go away . . . and leave me in peace?"

"I have met a few people who tried amputation. Strange, no matter how much they cut off—finger, hand, arm—the Splinter stayed inside them, as if it were in their blood. Perhaps you stand a better chance of finding peace if the Splinter remains in your finger."

The old man began to stack up his fine tooled-leather books. With a callused finger, he rubbed the intricate designs and workings, smiling at the craftsmanship. "It's not so hard to learn a new trade, given a little incentive, although you might find it comforting to revisit . . . familiar surroundings from time to time."

Outside the tent, criers were announcing the closing of the Renaissance Faire for another day.

Wil just stood, unsettled, staring at the storyteller, not knowing what to do. "This is impossible. You don't really expect me to change who I am and what I do for a living just overnight, do you?"

"No, my friend. But you will have plenty of time. After all these centuries, who would know better than I?" He paused for a moment, holding up one of his ornate books. "You might discover talents you never knew you possessed. You already have quick hands, sharp eyes. Think about what you could become."

The old man's words were too much to absorb all at once. Wil had to let the implications sink in, and questions piled up in his mind. "I have plenty of time . . . ?" Then, as he began to consider the possibilities, a familiar pleasurable sensation tingled in his hand. "You mean I could be a fine artist, a poet, a rock guitarist, even a surgeon? How would I choose?"

A small smile flickered at the corner of the storyteller's mouth. "Why choose? You could do them all. But use your abilities to help people, and you will find contentment."

The pleasant warmth seemed to be growing stronger. "Well, I guess I've always wanted to see other countries. Maybe I could join a service organization and travel while I learn some job skills—new ones, I mean—and some foreign languages."

Now the tingle seeped from Wil's hand into his entire body and, for the first time in memory, he felt a true sense of wonder.

# GIROLAMO AND MISTRESS WILLENDORF

## by

## *John Maddox Roberts*

John Maddox Roberts is the author of some fifty books and numerous short stories in the SF, fantasy, mystery, and historical fields. Among his works is the Edgar Award-nominated *SPQR*, first in the best-selling Roman mystery series. Born in Ohio, he was raised there and in Michigan, Texas, and California. After service in the US Army, including a stint in Special Forces and a tour in Vietnam, he attended college in Albuquerque where he met his wife, folklorist and musician Beth Van Over. While John and Beth were living in Scotland, he wrote his first book and sold it to Doubleday. He hasn't had honest work since. John and Beth have traveled over large parts of the world and now reside in the tiny town of Estancia, New Mexico, with an ever-varying number of cats. His most recent book is *Hannibal's Children*, an alternate history about ancient Rome and Carthage.

*Gladius Domini Supra Terram Cito et Velocitor*

SOMETHING HAD AWAKENED HIM that morning. Troubled as he had not been in a long time, he had risen from the hard plank that served him for a bed, knelt on the concrete floor, and purified himself with flagellation and prayer. Then he had dressed himself and walked out into the city.

Now he wandered, seemingly without aim but knowing that his steps were guided. He had a mission. He knew not what it was, but he would carry it out with obedience, diligence, and humility, as he had with every other mission sent to him.

As always, he shut out the distracting vanities of the city: the immodest dress of the women, the depraved entertainments, the heathen music, the sheer, overwhelming abundance of material things. He kept his mind focused on the only thing of importance: salvation. Salvation was a precious but slippery thing. It could be won only through a lifetime of prayer and austerity, but it could be lost through a moment's inattention, through the smallest vanity or indulgence of the flesh.

By late morning he was out of the center of town, climbing through hills cloaked with scrub oak and cedar, studded with gray boulders. Here and there, set well back from the road behind gates and tall hedges were the homes of the rich, well-watered and overgrown with alien verdure, flowers of every color in riotous profusion, fruit trees in bloom spreading an intoxicating perfume through the air. This was wrong. This place was supposed to be desert, a harsh, clean, and purifying place where the questing soul could find peace. Instead, the worldly rich brought in water and fertilizers and alien growth to infest the land with crawling, disgusting life.

He climbed higher until, looking back, he could see a broad sweep of ocean. Ahead of him, somewhere just around a bend, he heard music and voices. It was not the driving, thundering music of the town that so offended him, but light melodies of flute and string and voices in harmony. No matter, it was abominable, the work of the devil.

The bend was shaded with tall, fragrant eucalyptus and then the road widened to a broad, open lot, jammed with automobiles. On its far side a huge sign arched above a pair of half-timbered booths. In ornate lettering it read: "Renaissance Pleasure Faire."

*Renaissance!* How he hated the word. It was the darkest of times, when men turned from the grace of the life to come and began to celebrate the world and its temptations, its fleshly traps and snares. From the true religion they reverted to paganism in all but name.

And for some reason he was called to this unholy place. He crossed the lot to one of the booths and paid for admission. A costumed attendant gave him a ticket and a guide packet. Girolamo took a deep breath, said a brief prayer for strength, and passed inside. Immediately, he nearly collided with a juggler who avoided him adroitly, never interrupting the rhythm with which he kept what seemed to be innumerable balls in the air. A few steps farther on, a team of tumblers in particolored clothing assembled themselves into improbable, towering arrangements. Morris dancers armed with sticks, their limbs girded with ribbons and tinkling bells, danced out an absurd story of death and resurrection.

The frivolity of it all repelled him. He glanced at the map in his guide kit, then folded it away. He did not need it. His steps would guide him where he was commanded to go. Fearlessly, he strode into the celebration of iniquity.

The place seemed laid out according to no special plan. It was a series of shaded alleys lined with booths, stages, small clearings for entertainers, all winding about and running into each other, so that it was easy to get lost or find oneself going over the same path repeatedly.

He passed a stage where long-haired men with billowy sleeves dueled with rapiers, setting the air ringing with clashing steel and shouts. In a clearing a bevy of bodiced women sang bawdy songs. In another, people sat at long tables while barmaids, also in bodices, served tankards of ale and platters of heavily carnivore-oriented foods.

In fact, the bodice seemed to be a minor theme of the place. Everywhere he looked, there were women whose garb of long-sleeved blouses and ground-length, layered skirts seemed modest enough except for one thing: bodices that supported bulging breasts and displayed veritable acres of cleavage. Every time he saw one, he looked away, but they seemed to come at him from all directions.

In a bazaar merchants sold attire of all sorts from court gowns to armor. There were woodworkers and tinsmiths and calligraphers and tapestry weavers and artificers of all sorts. The place celebrated the work of hands, a thing not utterly repellent to him were it not for the abounding vanity of it all. But what he sought was not to be found here.

Eventually, he found himself away from the centers of activity. It was a narrow path that led from one of the clearings, and for some reason he could not remember which. Where it began, small yellow flowers that looked native dusted the ground beneath the trees. As he progressed, the flowers grew in greater profusion, larger and of multitudinous colors. Shrubs began to grow high on both sides, and then vines began to appear, draping the tree limbs. Broad-leafed plants intruded, as if the desert place had turned tropical. He stopped dead, heart pounding, as a large snake slithered across his path, its scales gleaming like jewels in the dappled light of the sun falling through the leaves. He did not fear the fangs or venom of serpents, only what they portended. He knew who their father was.

At last he came to a tiny clearing within growth that had become impenetrable. There was a hut in its middle, if the term applied to a house that seemed to be made of living withies, intertwined into circular walls, parting to form graceful windows, joining at the top to form a leafy, conical roof. As he approached, he heard laughing voices. People emerged from the high-arched door of the hut: a young couple. The man was slender, with long, dark hair. The woman wore a wreath of flowers around her fair hair, and her long, diaphanous gown bulged at the belly with new life. They said something to someone inside, then walked arm in arm to the path. They nodded to him as they passed, but their faces clouded, as if, despite their outlandish, period clothing, he were the anachronistic intruder.

When they were gone, he noticed the sign beside the door of the hut:

> Mistress Willendorf
> Fertility Specialist
> Conceptions and Safe Deliveries Assured
> For Humans and Beasts
> Reasonable Rates

All of it was in the ornate calligraphy that prevailed in this place, an almost blasphemous imitation of the illuminated manuscripts of old.

He began to tremble, fearing what he would find inside that hut. He was ready to face anything, but this had the reek of the most ancient of enemies, the terrible adversary from the very beginning of time. Why was he called to this battle? This was a task for the heavenly hosts, not a humble servant of God.

Nervously, he looked around the little clearing. If the estates of the wealthy were repulsive with their imported water and plantings, this was positively unnatural. There was no visible source of water, but it crawled with life. He could almost hear things growing. The verdure buzzed with insects and rustled with animal life. Things slithered along the ground and birds squawked above in what should have been an arid, barren hillside.

Why was he called to this unholy place? He shuddered, reminding himself that his was not the right to question his mission. He steeled his soul and passed within.

At first he could see nothing in the dimness. The smell of the place was strange. It was that of growing things: the perfume of flowers, the scent of damp earth, but of other things as well: sea bottom, and blood, and, very faintly, putrefaction. As his eyes adjusted to the dimness, he saw that there was another person in the hut's single, small room. Despite his iron self-control, he gasped.

The woman was mountainous. Seated on the ground, her eyes were almost on a level with his own. A billowing skirt covered massive thighs. She wore the inevitable bodice, and it half-exposed breasts the size of prize pumpkins that rested atop a bulging belly. Her features were oddly small and fine in the midst of the broad platter of her face. Her black hair reached the ground, dressed in innumerable serpentine locks, adorned along their length with flowers and with ornaments of wood, bone, amber, coral, pearl. It occurred to him that nothing about her was of mineral origin. All was living or had lived.

Even as this thought occurred to him, a tiny snake emerged from her hair, its slim, elegant body green-scaled. It regarded him with unblinking, yellow eyes. Another showed itself, this one blue with red eyes.

"And what business might you have with Mistress Willendorf?" the woman asked. Her voice was surprisingly light and full of mockery. "You don't look like the type to seek my favors. Quite the opposite, in fact."

"What are you?" he half-whispered. "Are you a minion of Satan?"

Her laughter sounded like falling water. A few more snakes emerged from her hair, as if to see what might be the source of her mirth. "Satan? That pipsqueak upstart? That two-bit Middle Eastern tribal bogeyman? Why would I ever serve such a creature? You serve a small god if you fear the likes of him!"

He was stunned. Could there be an evil even more ancient and powerful than Satan? Yet surely one of his followers would never speak thus of her master.

"Who are you?" he asked again, this time more firmly. "I don't know why, but I have been called to face you. To do battle, if need be."

She placed strangely small and delicate hands upon her knees and leaned forward, as if to see his face more clearly. "Oh, yes. I remember you. It's been a while, hasn't it, Girolamo?"

"You know me?"

"I know you and all your kind. You are the people fond of fire. You burn anything and anyone you don't like. Personally, I dislike fire. It destroys living things without returning their richness to the earth."

Now he began to understand. "You're one of those

earth-worshipers, the people who bow down to dirt. Are idols of stone and wood not low enough for your sort?"

"Has it never occurred to you that every bite you or anyone else eats comes from the soil? And what you eat becomes your flesh, blood, and bone and from your flesh comes your progeny and in time you and all your progeny return to the soil to nourish future generations without end. What's not to worship?"

"Distractions! Life is to be endured, to be suffered. The life of this world is contemptible. It is only the life to come that has meaning. All this—" he gestured to the forest and the festival beyond, "—all this is frivolity. It is the vanity of this world. It distracts men from the only important thing."

"And what might that be?" she asked, idly stroking one of her snakes.

"Salvation, of course!"

"My followers don't need salvation. They were never damned in the first place."

"*Your* followers? Are you a priestess? A cult leader?" He had shaken off the shock that had unsettled him. What was there to fear in this monster of flesh? Nothing, to one who wielded the power of God's own sword.

"I am She who Always Was," proclaimed the woman. "I am she who quickens the earth and brings forth life. I am she who devours the dead and creates it all anew, every day." Now a multitude of little snakes emerged from her hair. She held out her hands and a pair of larger serpents wound around her arms, their spade-shaped heads coming to rest in her palms.

"Blasphemy! God and God alone brought forth all living things. God breathed into clay and created man!"

She chuckled and the snakes withdrew. "You'd like to believe that, wouldn't you? Isn't that the whole point of the Sistine ceiling? A male creating another male without having to deal with anything female first? It doesn't work that way, Girolamo. It never has."

"You know my name," he said. "How?" But things seemed to be coming back to him.

"From the last time you and I contended. That was, oh, about five hundred years ago. Pretty recently on my scale of things, but it may seem like a long time to you. That was in Florence. I was on the ascendant again, in the Renaissance, and you were trying to turn back the calendar. You wanted the Middle Ages back. People were beginning to rediscover the glories of Greece and Rome."

"A pack of pagans!" he spat.

"The Greeks and Romans had their good points," she said, "though all that pales in comparison to the Neolithic. Ah, well, those were the good old days."

He was beginning to remember. "You should have stayed dead and buried long ago."

"I'm frequently dead and buried, then reborn."

"More blasphemy. There was only one Resurrection!"

"How blind you are. But then, you've always taken pride in your blindness. Resurrection is the law of life. It was never the monopoly of your religion."

"What do you mean, *my* religion? There is only one true religion. All else is error and blasphemy and idolatry!"

"And that's why you're back," she said.

"Back? What do you mean?"

"Think, Girolamo: where were you before you came here?"

This was a bewildering change of subject. "Where?

Why, I was down in the city, when I received the call to come here."

"And how long have you been in the city? Where were you before that?"

"Before that? I've—I've been in the desert, meditating."

"I've been away from here for a while, too," she said, smoothing the cloth over her massive knees. "We've been lying low, you and I, ever since Florence. They've been depressing times, mostly, a lot of wars and witch-burnings and plundering and despoiling of the Earth. But I started waking up about a hundred years ago. Slowly, at first. I was down deep, but I could feel my old aspects being reestablished. I think it was the cinema that got it started."

"That is absurd. The cinema is nothing but moving images flashing on a screen, nothing but light and shadow. It is as silly and vaporous a vanity as the old carnival masks."

"The masks you used to burn. Blind then and blind now. You see, the cinema brought back an ancient concept: *glamour!* Once only the gods had glamour. This age has raised up new gods. It began slowly, but it spread worldwide. Then came rock and roll, which revived the ancient rites of orgiastic ritual: what the Greeks called *extasis* and *enthousiasmos*."

She meant that thunderous music that was nothing but an annoyance to him. "You cannot be serious."

"Someday," she said solemnly, "Elvis will be recognized as the first high priest of the new religion, which is the ancient one. Jerry Lee and Chuck and Buddy will be remembered as his acolytes. Check out a Madonna video if you want to see how far this movement has come in a short time."

"This futile vanity is raised up to challenge God himself? Is this why I have been called back?" They

were all coming back to him now: his sermons that
had terrified the most sophisticated state in the
world, his visions, his burnings.

"No," she said sadly. "You're back because your
kind are rising again, too. They're trying to worm
their way into the halls of power, the way they always have. They want to wield their old weapons
again: fire and sword to destroy the unbelievers.
They aren't all of your own religion either. You
should see your Satan's old playground, the Middle
East.

"There it's imams and mullahs offensive imams
are just priests and would-be mahdis. There's even a
bunch that want to rebuild the Temple of Solomon
and go back to sacrificing bulls. They're all the same.
They're all like you and the ignorant preachers who
want to manipulate presidents and premiers and
prime ministers. They all want to go back to the Middle Ages when their kind had all the power."

"It was a time when faith reigned, woman! People
abased themselves and begged for salvation. The true
believers were saved, and all others were damned. It
was simple and it was true and it will be true again!"

"Not so fast. At the same time the true believers
were working to regain power, something new appeared: the Internet."

"Internet?" He was vaguely aware of the word. It
was yet another of the distractions.

"Exactly. It was nothing ten years ago and now
it's everywhere. Where the fundamentalists want
iron-fisted tyranny controlled by themselves, the Internet is utterly anarchic. Nobody controls it, nobody
planned it, it just grew. Where they want to control
everything anyone sees and hears, it is totally unrestrained in words and imagery. It's completely without boundaries, full of commercialism, a forum for

mystics and visionaries and lunatics of every sort. Where they want to regulate sex, abolish it if they could, it's utterly awash in pornography. Where governments try to censor the news, people can go online and report what they actually see happening."

She leaned back and took a deep breath. "It's a chaos come again, Girolamo, and it's the future." She smiled at him. "Behold my beloved daughter, in whom I am well pleased."

This final blasphemy was too much. "I will fight you, and I will find others to fight you!"

"Go ahead. It should make for an interesting fight. It will mean a great deal of bloodshed, but I've never objected to blood. It nourishes the soil." She smiled. "Do you believe that I am weak? Those earth worshipers you spoke of: most of their love of nature is just the pretty parts. Nature is beautiful, but nature is terrible, too. They love the budding flower, but they turn away from the hyena devouring the newborn wildebeest. They want to look at nature without living in it. They beweep the extinction of species, but microbes are as much animals as elephants and whales. Already, those little creatures of mine are taking their vengeance."

"Liar! Pestilence is not your weapon, but God's! With it, he chastises the wicked and makes men turn back to him!"

"You fool. It's no weapon, just creatures doing what is in their nature to do. The only evil is in men like you who try to turn such plagues to their own advantage. But I don't doubt you'll find plenty of catastrophes to turn to your account. The world is full of it, just now."

"To the death, woman!" He whirled and strode from the hut. On the path he met with another young couple and they stepped away from him in alarm, frightened by his sunken-cheeked, skeletal face, his eyes that burned with utter certainty.

He paid no attention to his course, but in time he found himself in the middle of the festival, surrounded by dancers and jugglers and barmaids. He stopped as if in a daze and gazed toward Heaven.

"Hear me, you sinners!" he bellowed. Such was the force of the voice emanating from his wasted body that the music fell silent and the onlookers gazed at him in awe. "The sword of God hangs above this place! It is swift and sure, and soon it will plunge to Earth, and with it will come war and pestilence and famine and the cleansing fire that burns away all dross! Only the faithful will be saved. All the rest will perish, and spend eternity in fire everlasting! This is the judgment of God!" The silence held, then he felt a touch at his shoulder. He blinked a few times, then turned to see a young man standing beside him, booted and gloved, holding a blunted rapier: one of the dueling performers.

"Hey, man, you do a great Savonarola, but it's kind of a bummer, you know? Why don't you have a couple of ales and lighten up, okay? You're scaring the kids."

Girolamo shook the hand from his shoulder. He glared around him at the silent, staring people in their colorful garb. Did they think he was part of the entertainment?

"I will be back!" he shouted.

He stalked out beneath the arch and away from the place of revelry. Somewhere out there, he knew, he would find followers, as he had before. He would restore men to the true path. He would put an end to all this. He had done it before.

Behind him, the music began once more, then the sound of voices singing.

# A TIME FOR STEEL

*by*

## *Robert E. Vardeman*

Robert E. Vardeman is the author of more than fifty fantasy and science fiction novels, in addition to numerous westerns under various pen names. Titles include the fantasy *Dark Legacy* and SF novel *Ruins of Power*. Short fiction includes "Feedback" in Al Sarrantonio's *Redshift* anthology, the zombie horror story "Middles" in *Book of All Flesh* and the forthcoming "Soul Juggler" for the Circus anthology. He has also had the story "Road of Dreams and Death" in another Andre Norton anthology, *Tales of the Witch World I*. Vardeman is a longtime resident of Albuquerque, New Mexico, graduating from the University of New Mexico with a B.S. in physics and a M.S. in materials engineering. He worked for Sandia National Laboratories in the Solid State Physics Research Department before becoming a full-time writer. For more information, go to http://www.cenotaphroad.com.

"SHE DOESN'T HAVE A STITCH of clothing on!" exclaimed Sheriff's Deputy Ben Rodriguez. He pushed a couple of tourists out of the way to get a better look at the shapely woman riding the prancing white horse down the main concourse of the Arizona Renaissance Faire. The arid desert wind blew her long blonde hair about, but not enough to suit the deputy.

"What?" asked his partner. Jason Hardin almost dropped the huge turkey leg he was gnawing on when he caught the merest flash of slanting afternoon sunlight against creamy white thigh. "She can't do that!" he exclaimed, moving in his partner's wake to get to the front of the crowd gathering to watch the unclothed spectacle.

The woman laughed and waved cheerily, giving them just enough glimpse of skin under her flowing hair to let everyone know she wasn't wearing a body stocking. She was naked. Entirely.

Hardin cursed the day the Pinal County sheriff had assigned him and Rodriquez to police the Renaissance Faire with more than its share of weirdos and freaks. The immense crowd, more than twenty thousand people jammed into the thirty-acre re-creation of a medieval village, proved less of a chore to police than the semipermanent resident vendors and actors. Hardin had never quite gotten into the spirit of the Ren Faire, although he knew that Rodriguez was continually ooh-ing and aah-ing over the displays and performances, the wares and the clever costumes.

None of it made a lot of sense to Hardin, in spite of numerous eager participants explaining to him that the people wanted to relive the Middle Ages, but with running water and CD players for their folk music.

"There she goes!" he cried, breaking through to the front of the crowd in time to see nothing but the golden cascade of hair draped decorously down the woman's back and over the white charger's hindquarters like some silky blanket.

"Wow," Rodriguez said.

"What are you doing just standing there?" demanded Hardin. He towered over his shorter partner, but Rodriquez was ten years younger and in better shape. Hardin started to throw down the turkey leg he had been eating for a late lunch, then decided against it since it was all he'd had since breakfast at six AM. Let his partner chase her down.

"What do you want me to do?"

"That's public lewdness. We've got to arrest her."

Rodriguez laughed. "Can I order a lineup? I wouldn't mind seeing a lot of these babes without clothes. But identifying her's not going to be easy."

"You weren't looking at her face," guessed Hardin, standing on tiptoe to see which way the horse had gone when it reached the main concourse. From there, the naked woman could have gone any of four ways. He thought she would leave behind a wake of curious bystanders, but it was as if she were nothing more than a drop of water in a vast ocean. She had vanished quickly, and no one in the crowd was inclined to keep staring after her. As odd as that seemed, too much else competed for their attention.

"Nope," Rodriguez agreed cheerfully, "but she has a cute little rose tattoo. I *was* looking there." He pointed to a spot on his groin, then moved his finger down a bit more. "Maybe lower. I'll have to—"

"We're supposed to enforce the law," grumbled Hardin. Sometimes he didn't understand Ben. His partner looked at this as a lark, a plum assignment, while he saw it as an inch away from a living hell when there were real crimes being committed throughout the county. The sheriff was investigating a murder twenty miles out in the desert, two other deputies were after a major league drug dealer, and here he was chasing a naked woman for public indecency. It wasn't right, and it made him mad.

"If you cut through and go around, you might get to the concourse faster," Ben suggested, but Hardin was already squeezing between booths selling turkey legs, steak on a stake, and lemonade.

Hardin popped out behind the vendors and coughed as a cloud of dust enveloped him. The last bulldozer rattled away from the artificial lake gouged into the sun-baked ground. The lake was almost full, with foot-high waves breaking against the sloping shoreline as the wind picked up, as it always did around sundown. The dozer had merely added a final touch to the far shore and was being loaded onto a flatbed trailer. Hardin had asked the Ren Faire director, Pita Hewell, about the lake and had been told they intended to have a Viking boat display and some simulated sea attacks on a mock castle tower as program items later in the fair. Possibly some of the crowd might like to go along for the siege.

*Anything for a buck,* he thought in disgust.

Hardin skirted the lake and turned back into the main concourse when he heard a whistling sound, quickly followed by, "Drop the turkey leg!"

His sense of danger was acute enough that he tossed the half-eaten meat in one direction and dived in the other. The whistling sound turned into ferocious flapping. A peregrine falcon caught the meaty leg before it hit the ground. Hardin landed hard, rolled and sat up, fumbling for his holstered service revolver.

"No, wait, don't!" came the same voice that had warned him. Hardin quickly shifted his gaze to a man dressed in medieval jerkin over a blue silk doublet and sporting a well-worn, heavy leather glove on his left hand. "I warned everybody about eating during the show."

"Show?" Hardin asked, still pumped from the

nearness of flashing claws strong enough to rip off his arm.

"The birds of prey show. No raptor's quicker on the attack than the peregrine." The bird handler made certain Hardin wasn't going to draw his pistol, then rushed back to the elevated grass area of Falconer's Heath and thrust his gloved hand into the air. The falcon landed with enough force to stagger the burly man.

Hardin got to his feet and brushed himself off, glad the crowd gathered for the bird show was more intent on the falcon than the damn fool deputy who had almost been the predator's dinner. He hurried to the middle of the concourse and looked around.

The crowd had swelled, pouring in for evening events. A half dozen shows ran simultaneously, including the hunting birds. Ventriloquists, sideshow blockheads, jugglers, more dancing and singing acts than Hardin could tolerate—and all obstructed his view enough so that he couldn't find the Lady Godiva wanna-be.

"Officer? You're a real policeman, aren't you?" asked an older woman.

"Yes, ma'am," he acknowledged. "A sheriff's deputy."

"I want her arrested!" the woman exclaimed. "I've never seen such a thing."

Ben Rodriquez came up in time to hear the complaint.

"We never have either," Hardin said, looking fiercely at his partner, silently warning him not to speak. "Which way'd she go? Lady Godiva?"

"That way," the woman said. "I hope you catch her. Why, there are children in the crowd. This is supposed to be wholesome entertainment."

"Yes, ma'am," Hardin said, glaring at Rodriguez

some more. His partner grinned from ear to ear. "You head that way, Deputy Rodriguez," he said pointedly. "I'll check the jousting arena."

He had been told to stay out of sight as much as possible. The public wanted to know they were safe, but a constantly patrolling uniformed deputy took away the festive air. At least the sheriff hadn't insisted he wear a silly costume. Hardin shuddered at the thought of a Robin Hood cap with a jaunty feather stuck in it.

Angling to the side of the concourse, he moved past some of the audience participation booths. One that intrigued him was simple enough, but the mechanics verged on a scam. A guy stuck his head out of a hole in a wall and insulted the crowd. For a few bucks they could buy tomatoes to throw at him. The part that irked Hardin was the man passing over the tomatoes. If they gave him a large bill, he made certain to lay their change in a puddle of tomato juice. No one took it and shoved a soggy wad of one-dollar bills into his pocket. They bought more tomatoes to throw. Hardin had counted more than $800 an hour going across that counter.

He shook himself and tried to remember this was a modern-day sideshow without all the freaks and geeks of days of yore. At least not all of them. There were glass eaters, people dressed as chickens, and executioners, and others Hardin had not wanted to identify. He took a moment to jump onto a crate and look around. Lady Godiva had vanished from the earth, as if she had never existed. He considered letting the matter drop. Then he knew he couldn't. She had gotten away with her ride once. She'd do it again, thinking the laws of the twenty-first century somehow had been nullified in this bubble of the Middle Ages.

To the east lay the jousting arena and stables for the knights' horses. Just the place to find Lady Godiva. Hardin kept a low profile but hurried to the climbing wall and went through the fake castle portal to the arena, then turned left to the stables. A grin came to his face.

"Gotcha," he said, spotting the white horse Lady Godiva had ridden. His excitement died when he saw the horse standing alone in a stall. The saddle was draped over the stall divider and a long blonde wig hung over it. Hardin picked up the wig and saw the wearer had left a bit of herself behind.

"Red hairs," he said, thinking hard. He had seen this particular, peculiar color before. The grin returned to his lips. The magician's assistant! Merlin the Magnificent was on stage now. It wouldn't take much to match his assistant's hair to this strand. Hardin picked up the wig and turned to leave.

He went cold inside when he saw the armored body, partially covered with straw, in the stall opposite Lady Godiva's horse.

The deputy knew then that this nothing duty had become more. Much more.

He carefully made sure that the man was dead. A single savage slash had cut through the light armor he wore, severing his right arm. Shock had probably set in and the man had bled out on the spot. But the stroke that had sliced through arm and armor had been prodigious.

Hardin backed off, pulled out his walkie-talkie and let Rodriquez know what had happened. Then he used his cell phone to call the sheriff and get an investigative unit dispatched.

It was well past sunset by the time the body had been removed and the sheriff had gone, leaving behind several detectives to carry on the investigation.

But with twenty thousand visitors, the crew seemed overwhelmed. Rodriguez stood close to his partner and spoke in a low tone.

"What aren't you spilling, Jase?" he asked.

"The sword beside him wasn't his," Hardin said. "It doesn't fit into his sheath. I tried. What blood's on the blade got there after the death stroke. I think he was killed with his own sword."

"And the killer took it with him?"

Hardin nodded.

"So why not tell Gizmo and his boys?" Rodriguez spoke with contempt of the detective unit under Deputy Gizzarello. "Afraid they'll grab the glory? Like usual?"

"I don't care about that. I want the murderer, and Gizzarello's not asking the right questions of the right people," Hardin said. "This guy's part of the show with the fake king and his court."

"Yeah, the king's champion. So?"

"He was also a vendor when he wasn't in the show. He was a metalsmith, sold chain mail, swords and daggers at a booth on the main concourse."

"Gizmo'll get there eventually. There's something else," Rodriguez said, urging his partner to tell the rest of what he suspected.

"I think Lady Godiva might have seen something. The time of death is close enough to when she rode into the stable."

"You sure she's Merlin's assistant?" Rodriguez asked eagerly.

"No looking for the tattoo," Hardin cautioned. "Unless it comes to her being a suspect in the murder."

The two made their way through the increasingly chilly Arizona desert night and came to the stage where Merlin had performed. The audience was half gone; those lingering were fumbling out a dollar or two to put in the jester's cap being passed by the redheaded assistant. Hardin looked from the strand of hair taken from the wig to the woman. He was no judge of dyes and what women did to their hair, but it was close enough.

"Officers," greeted the magician, putting away the last of his stage tricks. A tall, thin man with a wispy beard, Merlin was younger than his costume suggested. He took off a pointed cap festooned with mystical symbols and dropped it on the small table to the side of the stage and ran his hands through longish brown hair. He looked tired from his performance, but Hardin thought there was more to the sharp-eyed gaze that fixed on him. He tried not to shiver as Merlin the Magnificent bored into his very soul with those gray eyes of his.

"Your assistant was seen this afternoon," Hardin said, holding up the blonde wig. "She left behind one of her own hairs."

Merlin chuckled and relaxed. "Rachel is quite a handful," he said. "I'll talk to her about her, uh, riding apparel. Like the rest of the Rennies here, she sometimes takes odd jobs during her breaks. This might not have been the best way of making a few extra ducats."

"I didn't mind," Rodriguez piped up. Hardin silenced him with a cold look.

"Most of the crowd wouldn't, I suspect," said Merlin. "The *male* half. She's a bit on the wild side."

"Why don't you and Deputy Rodriguez come to a meeting of the minds on this?" Hardin asked. "I need to attend to some business." He glanced in the direction of the porta-potties.

Merlin laughed and said, "Some things remain constant up and down the corridors of time."

Hardin let Rodriguez lead the magician away so they could talk to Rachel, but he didn't go to relieve himself. Instead, he went behind the stage and found Merlin's gear. Something struck him as wrong about the man. He had been too relieved that the law wanted to discuss Rachel's naked riding—relieved because he didn't have to address some other matter, Hardin guessed. Depending on what he found, Hardin might have a suspect in the knight's murder. The magician could have killed the knight for putting the moves on his assistant. Jealousy was a decent motive for murder.

A quick search of two boxes and a huge trunk unearthed a dozen well-read volumes of Arthurian legends and an expensive leather-bound personal diary. Knowing this was an illegal search didn't stop him from flipping through the pages. A diary, nothing more. As he leafed through the pages, he noted something odd. The first page was dated almost five years in the future. Every subsequent entry came closer to the current date, as if Merlin was Japanese and worked from the back of the book forward. But that couldn't be right, because a quarter of the journal's pages were blank from this morning's entry to the last page and everything was penned in precise English.

He read a few of the entries, then quickly replaced the book when he heard Rodriguez and Merlin returning to the stage.

"I do have to get my equipment stored, Officer."

Merlin looked around, startled, when Hardin stepped onstage.

"Did you know a man named McLeod? A metalsmith?" asked Hardin. Again, he saw the flash of emotion that didn't mesh well with the question.

"He's done work for me. For most of the performers. McLeod's a talented artisan."

Merlin was as tense as a man can get without bolting in fear.

"He was killed this afternoon."

"His sword," Merlin started. "I mean, he was making a sword for me."

"There was one beside the body. It wasn't the murder weapon. Your assistant had just finished her bareback ride when he was killed."

"Rachel doesn't know anything about it. She would have told me."

"About the stolen sword or the murder?" asked Hardin, taking a shot in the dark and hoping to get additional information from the man. He read the answer on Merlin's face. He was upset that McLeod was dead but more upset about his sword. Hardin could come to only one conclusion. Merlin knew the murder weapon was his sword.

"Tonight is a full moon," Merlin said unexpectedly.

"I suppose. So?" asked Rodriguez.

"Let's take a ride, you and Rachel," said Hardin. "We can go to the district HQ and get a full statement. I'm especially interested in this sword McLeod was making for you. Was it sharp enough to slice through armor and bone?"

"It's a special titanium alloy," Merlin said distantly. He looked east where the moon poked a thin sliver above the Superstitious Mountains. "Yes, it's full tonight."

"Come on," Hardin said, reaching to take the man's elbow. "Get his assistant, Ben." Rodriguez hurried off to find Rachel but Harrdin hesitated. Merlin was tall, gaunt, and didn't look as if he had the strength to push open a door, but Hardin found it impossible to move the man along, even with the special come-along grip police used.

Hardin tightened the punishing grip, but Merlin still didn't budge. He stepped back to get out his cuffs, then blinked. The deputy looked around in surprise and saw . . . nothing. Merlin had been there one instant and gone the next.

"Ben, he's skipped!" he shouted to his partner. "Keep an eye on his assistant."

He hardly heard Rodriguez's quick acceptance of looking after the magician's sexy assistant. Hardin thought Merlin might go back to his equipment. He saw the curious journal where he had left it. On impulse, he picked it up and tucked it into his broad leather belt. Then he did a quick mental inventory of the items and decided nothing was missing. Wherever the magician had gone, it wasn't here to pick up anything incriminating.

Even as that thought crossed his mind, Hardin was making his way behind the shops and to the stables where McLeod had been killed. The deputy ducked under the yellow tape marking off the area as a crime scene. The criminalists' work was done, and they wanted everything left intact should they need to go over the area again, but two uniformed deputies who should have been more attentive looked away—*past*—Hardin as he went by.

"Has anyone come in?" Hardin asked the new-hire whose nameplate was hidden by his crossed arms. The deputy ignored Hardin. "I said, have you seen anyone in here recently?"

When he got no reply, Hardin grabbed the deputy's arm and squeezed hard. He might as well have not bothered for all the response he got. Hardin ran his hand in front of the deputy's eyes. The man wasn't asleep. He simply didn't notice. His attention was focused somewhere else.

So was his partner's, and nothing Hardin did roused them.

Hardin shook his head in amazement. It was as if the pair had been bewitched. He went into the stables and stopped dead in his tracks when he saw faintly glowing green footprints leading to the rear. Hardin dropped to one knee, took out a pencil and poked at a print. Whatever fluoresced didn't come off onto his pencil. Somehow, he doubted the footprints had been here while the criminalists were working the scene.

He started to put the pencil back in his pocket, then thought better of it and dropped it. He followed the tracks to the stall where McLeod had been killed. It took several seconds for him to make sense of it.

"I'll be damned," he said. It was as if the killer had dipped both feet in the glowing green ichor, then tracked it around as he killed McLeod and finally left. The trail was so blatant even the two insensate guards outside should have been able to follow it.

The tracks led out back of the stables, then turned toward the artificial lake. Hardin pulled out his walkie-talkie and told Rodriguez what was going on.

"Meet me at the lakeshore," he said.

"Want me to bring Rachel along?"

"This might get dangerous," Hardin said. "Keep her away from trouble."

Hardin heard his partner's laugh and knew what it meant. Rodriguez wanted to see how much trouble Rachel could be, but he joined Hardin in a few minutes.

"All's quiet on the lakefront," Rodriguez said as

he strode up. Then he saw the green footsteps. "That looks like the perp stepped in a bucket of green paint."

"Come on," Hardin said, anxious to follow the trail. He worried that it might fade. "Watch out while I—"

A loud splash in the lake drew both of them in the direction of ripples moving away from the center.

"What was that? A fish jumping?"

"Look," Rodriquez said. A silvery flash in the light of the full moon was all they saw.

"Bare skin," Hardin said, not sure of his identification. "Could your Lady Godiva be skinny-dipping?"

"No way. She's back at the stage. I told her to wait there."

"If she's mixed up in a murder, you think she'd do what you said?" asked Hardin.

"More likely to hightail it than to go skinny-dipping by moonlight. Maybe that was Nessie."

Hardin cut off a retort. His partner might be right. Or partly right. The Renaissance Faire management always looked for new attractions. A mechanical sea monster might fit the bill.

"It looked more like a woman's hand and arm," he said finally.

"The trail's starting to fade, Jase," his partner pointed out. "We'd better get onto it right now. If it's Rachel out there swimming stark naked, I can deal with it later."

Ben was right. The trail was vanishing as Hardin stared at it. He got a sighting on where the tracks cut back toward the main concourse and ran for the spot, rather than following step by step. Hardin pushed his way through patrons clustering in front of the shops and booths. None of the faire-goers took notice of the fiery footprints—they might have thought it was part of the overall show.

The tracks led across the fortune-teller's green to a shop selling chain mail and other metal implements. A CLOSED sign dangled outside.

"McLeod's booth," he said under his breath. "Come on, Ben." He made certain his service revolver was handy, the leather strap holding it firmly in his holster pulled free, then advanced. Two men were arguing inside.

He recognized one voice immediately as the stage magician's.

"You don't know what you're talking about," the other voice sounded.

"You killed him, Birmingham. Don't deny it. You can't lie to me!"

"Because you're *the* Merlin?" came the contemptuous reply.

"Yes."

Hardin sprinted for the booth and tried the door. Locked. He heard scuffling sounds inside.

"Police! Open up!" he shouted. The struggle between Birmingham and Merlin grew more intense. Hardin heard metal clashing against metal. With daggers, maces, and swords on display, it was nothing short of a miracle one of them wasn't already dead. There were too many weapons a desperate man could use.

Hardin kicked hard and the door sagged. A second kick tore it from its hinges with a screech of nails pulling free of wood. He jumped into the shop, pistol leveled. Rodriguez followed, his pistol ready for action, too.

"Drop it or I'll shoot!" Hardin went into a crouch, both hands steadying his revolver, and aimed at Merlin. The magician held a sword like he knew how to use it.

"You've got this wrong, Deputy," Merlin said. "Birmingham's the one who killed McLeod."

"McLeod was making the sword for him," Birmingham said, holding a pair of daggers, the one in his right hand sporting a foot-long blade; the basket-hilted main gauche in his left was even longer. "He wanted to cheat McLeod and they fought. He killed my boss!"

"Drop those toad stickers," Rodriguez said, moving around beside his partner. The muzzle of his semiautomatic was pointed at Birmingham.

"He's lying. He killed McLeod for the sword," Merlin said. "I followed his tracks here."

"The green glowing footprints?" Hardin couldn't figure it out. "What caused them?"

Birmingham's feet suddenly glowed a brilliant emerald, causing him to hop about as if they burned.

"You bewitched me, like you did the sword! I should never have taken it!" Birmingham was a smallish man, and he moved fast. Rodriguez—and the bullet from his 9mm Glock—was faster. The report filled the small shop with a deafening sound that momentarily diverted Hardin's attention.

Swifter than any man should move, Merlin threw down his sword and grabbed a long black display case from behind the counter. Hardin responded to the movement, turned back, and fired instinctively. But he shot at empty air. Merlin had vanished, as he had before.

"Cuff him. I think we've got our murderer," Hardin said to his partner. Birmingham grunted as Rodriguez rolled him over on the floor and grabbed his wounded arm, forcing it back so he could apply handcuffs.

Hardin vaulted the counter, skidded, and stopped at the rear door before peering out with a quick out-in look. He didn't want the magician slicing his head off, because he was certain the case held another sword. Whether it was the one Birmingham claimed was bewitched didn't matter. It was probably the cause of the murder.

Hardin had seen fancy craftsmanship during his few weekends at the Ren Faire, jewelry selling for more than he made in a year, expensive crystal goblets and even wood carvings he wouldn't have minded displaying in his own home. An expertly crafted sword might be worth a young fortune—and worth killing to get.

His quick peek assured him Merlin wasn't lying in ambush. He darted out and looked around, wondering where the man might have run. Something drew Hardin toward the lake. Long legs pumping and lungs straining, he made his way along the alley behind the shops and burst out onto the path leading to the lake. He saw a dark shape ahead, at the lakeshore.

"Merlin!" he cried when he recognized the magician. "Give it up."

"Birmingham is the killer," Merlin called. "My fate is worse. And better."

Hardin ran along the unlighted path and stepped into a pothole. With a grunt of pain, he twisted his ankle. Pain lanced up into his knee, but he wanted Merlin in custody. Not only was he a material witness, Hardin had questions. Other questions.

He felt the magician's journal grating against his belly, where he had tucked the book into his belt.

"You won't be arrested. We need you to testify."

But his words seemed muffled. Crawling a few yards, he clambered to his feet and hobbled along in time to see Merlin open the dark case. The magician began a low chant that ate away at Hardin's nerves.

Merlin held the polished steel blade high above his head so that moonlight ricocheted off its gleaming length.

A splash sounded far out on the lake. Hardin saw ripples expanding outward from . . . a hand. A woman's hand rising from the depths.

Merlin adroitly spun the blade about, caught its hilt, and then sent it cartwheeling high into the air. Every rotation caused a unique, unnameable color to reflect from its steel, as if moonbeams were being torn apart by an eldritch prism.

"Hold Excalibur well, Lady," Merlin said, "until the time is nigh for its return."

The hand surged high and deftly caught the sword before vanishing without a ripple into the lake.

"Merlin, that was evidence." Hardin limped up, not sure what to do. He tried to fix the location of the sword in the lake. Somehow his eyes had tricked him into believing a hand had grabbed it. Merlin had only tossed it into the water to keep it from him.

"The sword will be returned, many years before now," Merlin said cryptically.

Hardin stared at the man and doubted his eyes. There was something unearthly about him, as if distinct edges were blurred and he vanished into the distance across a heat-shimmered desert.

"Stop," Hardin barked. "Your journal!" He pulled it out.

"Thank you," Merlin said softly, taking it from him. Hardin's fingers refused to close tightly enough to prevent the removal.

"Jase! You okay?" called Ben Rodriguez.

Hardin turned to see his partner running along the path.

"Be careful. There're holes in the path that'll trip you up." He turned back to Merlin. He caught his breath. Merlin stood at the stern of a boat silently gliding across the lake.

"Is he in the boat?" asked Rodriguez, coming up, not even breathing hard. "You want me to fetch him? I got the sheriff to send a half dozen more officers."

"What boat?" Hardin asked.

The lake was still, no sign of movement anywhere except occasional insects dipping down to the surface for a nocturnal drink. The boats to be used for the Renaissance Faire mock battles were docked to one side.

"Where'd he go?"

"Back in time," Hardin said. "Our time. For him our past is his future."

"Huh?"

"McLeod must have been one hell of a fine sword-smith," Hardin said, letting his partner help him back along the path.

"We've got a picture of it. Birmingham's spilling his guts, but he's trying to cop an insanity appeal. The sheriff's trying to get him to shut up until he can get a lawyer."

"Insanity? What's he saying?"

"He says that was King Arthur's sword and that the stage magician was the real Merlin."

Hardin thought about this for a moment, and smiled. He had never expected to see such a turning point in history. Or perhaps it was more properly a nexus. A crossroads? Metallurgy was a science now. Coupled with Merlin's spells and the ambience of a Renaissance Faire, the most important sword in history had been created—and passed backward in time to await the man destined to wield it.

# ONE HOT DAY

### *by*

### *Stephen Gabriel*

Stephen Gabriel holds a bachelor's degree in architecture from the University of Wisconsin/Milwaukee and served in the United States Air Force during the Gulf War. Currently, he is the lead application support engineer at a CAD software reseller and also does computer-based modeling and rendering. In his spare time, he writes fiction and pursues other various creative outlets.

COLLEEN AND MORRIGAN SAT in the shade of a large oak, their dresses spread on the ground around them, hems pulled up exposing their legs to mid-thigh. It was a hot and humid day at the faire, and space in the shade was valuable. Their heavy brocade dresses, full sleeved blouses, and the tightly cinched bodices added to the discomfort. They sat and drank their iced teas and fanned their faces.

Every year, the Renaissance Faire had a free day for anyone in costume, and every year since they had first visited the faire in college, Colleen and Morrigan had dressed up and returned to enjoy the ambience and revelry of the times.

Colleen wiped her forehead. "Well, I don't think I'll be wanting to go to the jousts today."

Morrigan nodded. "No way, not with those bleachers out in the sun like that! I vote for hitting the shops next. Most of those are in the shade and some even have—gasp—fans!"

Colleen laughed at Morrigan's mockery of shock over a merchant at the Renaissance Faire having a not-quite-period convenience. "Aye, my dear friend! We must forthwith see this fan abomination of our distinguished faire and determine for ourselves if it be evil or good!"

Morrigan smiled, "Yeah, verily, must we all not judge for ourselves?"

The two rose, their dresses falling back to cover their ankles, shielding their legs from what little cooling effect there had been. Morrigan shifted her skirt. "I swear mine must weigh ten pounds more than when we got here!"

"At least! We should have dressed as Gypsy belly dancers!"

"That would have been great! If we were still nineteen and single! Then we'd have been cool and hot at the same time."

Colleen's eyes sparkled. "College. Those certainly were the days! Eight years since we graduated. It seems like everything has changed since then. Our lives, our bodies, our world—even the faire has changed!"

"Maybe, but maybe not." Morrigan shrugged. "Maybe nothing has changed but us. Maybe the world just repeats itself, goes through the same motions time and time again, and the only thing that changes is how we experience it."

Colleen raised an eyebrow. "Why, oh why, did I ever pick a philosophy major for a best friend?

"Because all the others were too drunk to walk back to the dorms with you!"

They continued on toward the market, laughing and reminiscing. Soon they slipped into the quieter tree-lined neighborhood of the market where improbable ceiling fans out of DaVinci's dreams and the Swiss Family Robinson slowly turned the air of many of the vendors' shops. In the distance they could hear Rodney on the hammer dulcimer. He was very good and a regular at the faire. Both Colleen and Morrigan would likely buy his latest CD; they always did and he always somehow recognized them each year.

The two began wandering through the shops and stalls, looking at jewelry and pottery, period garb and candles, musical instruments and crafts. Their first stop was their favorite, a jewelry shop owned by a woman named Yvonne.

They entered the jeweler's shop, where a maddening contraption slowly beat the air down upon them and provided a hint of relief.

Yvonne approached. "I see you two are back again this year!"

Morrigan replied, "Just as you are! How've you been?"

"Fine, despite this horrid temperature. I've got some stuff that I picked up recently from various sources, if you'd like to look. It's not sorted or graded, but you two are regulars, and I'll trust you to look through it."

Yvonne pulled out a large wooden jewelry chest heaped with an assortment of finery. They dug into the pile, gingerly untangling and pulling out one piece at a time, examining things before laying them out on the counter. There were necklaces of all types and sizes, gold and silver, semiprecious stones and beads, even some that looked like ivory and coral.

Settled beneath the necklaces were bracelets, rings, and earrings in a myriad of varieties, some matching the necklaces above, but most not.

They searched through the jewelry, holding it up and admiring it. One piece caught Morrigan's eye, a simple leather lanyard holding a medallion of the face of a man made of oak leaves with piercing eyes and foliage protruding from the corners of his mouth. The medallion was heavy despite its small size, the metal cool to the touch and hidden behind a dull gray finish that turned to black in the engravings and in spots across its surface. Morrigan looked at it closely for a while, moved to set it down, then changed her mind and looked at it again.

As she held it up a second time, something in the distance caught her attention. There was an old woman dressed in rags; her clothing and face were filthy and a few teeth were missing from her mouth. The crone was calling insults to the passersby in a screeching voice. Suddenly she turned and stared at Morrigan through the open window across the shop. The crone sneered, turned, and left. Morrigan shook her head, telling herself that the biddy was just an actor hired by the faire for color.

"You seem to like that piece. May I?" Yvonne weighed the piece in her hand, her fingers rubbing over the front and back, rolling the leather of the cord between her fingers.

"It's the Green Man, isn't it?"

Yvonne replied, "Yes, or more accurately, Jack in the Green. An interesting piece, Celtic in origin, though not completely unique. Still, it does seem to have a character of its own."

"Then it should suit Morrigan perfectly," Colleen interrupted. "She's Irish and a character!"

Morrigan gave her a mock dirty look, then returned her attention to the proprietor. "It's a bit heavier than you'd think. What kind of metal do you think it is?"

"It's pewter, a bit corroded, but the workmanship is fine. The lanyard is about done in, so terribly dry and cracked. I could replace that if you like."

"Please. What would you charge for it?"

Yvonne looked at the small pile that Colleen had accumulated and then back at the Green Man, "Honestly, it's worth more as a curiosity than anything else, and seeing as you are such good customers, what would you say to ten bucks?"

Morrigan's eyes widened, "Yeah, okay!"

"Let me get that new lanyard." Yvonne went to a bench behind the counter and began changing out the leather cord.

Morrigan looked over at Colleen's small hoard. Colleen was cutting the selection down by a few, adding others in. Yvonne quickly returned with the medallion on the new cord and Morrigan slipped it over her head, pulling her hair out from under the cord and sitting the medallion on her bare skin.

Morrigan's gaze flicked past Colleen to the door, and then back again with a start.

Colleen looked up. "What?"

"Nothing. It's nothing. Well, I just thought I saw this old lady again."

"What old lady?"

Morrigan laughed, "You know the type, the ones they hire to boo and hiss and insult the guests."

Colleen's eyes lit up. "Really! Where?"

"Just outside the door to the shop."

"I don't see her."

"Me neither. Not now anyway."

Colleen went back to her sorting, finally settling on a dozen pieces, none of them matching. They paid up and then headed out, waving good-bye to Yvonne and thanking her for the opportunity. "See you again next year," Colleen called.

Colleen looked over at Morrigan. "How are you holding up?"

"Hot! Really hot! How about yourself?"

"Same here! What do you say we get something to drink after Rodney's?

"Sounds great, but let's hit a few more shops on the way."

Morrigan was ogling handwoven rugs at the weaver's stall when she noticed the old woman again, sitting on the rocks next to the stairs nearby. She'd call this one a festering warthog and that one a warty toad. No one seemed to acknowledge her, but such was the role she played.

Morrigan smiled inwardly; the faire went to some expense to get good actors to portray the wandering characters that added flavor to the grounds. The old woman was earning her keep. It was a hard role to play, Morrigan suspected, and she waved at the old woman.

In return, the old woman glared, pointed, and shouted, "Witch!"

Colleen came up beside Morrigan. "Find anything interesting?"

Morrigan looked down at the pile of rugs and shook her head, "Not quite what I was looking for, maybe someone else will have it. But the old lady is back, right over there. She even called me a witch!"

Colleen looked around. "Where? I don't see anyone."

Morrigan looked puzzled. "She was here just a minute ago."

"Well, let me know if you see her again. It's always interesting to listen to them go on like that!"

"I will, as long as you promise not to get in an argument with her like you did with that hermit last year."

Colleen giggled. "It wasn't an argument, I was just testing his skill."

They headed up the stairs and turned into the first shop, a place full of candles and overly strong incense. They passed quickly through there, the scents overwhelming in the hot humid air, and entered a silversmith's shop where an assortment of goblets, candlestick holders, and other memorabilia were displayed in cases.

Chatting idly as they browsed, they were more interested in the gentle breeze from the contraption on the ceiling than the silver pieces. Morrigan tugged at her laces, trying to get a little more breathing room in her bodice.

As Colleen looked over some unique candlestick holders, Morrigan's attention wandered out the window where she again saw the old woman haranguing guests with her gush of curses. The old lady looked around and began yelling "witch" to no one in particular. No one responded to her.

Morrigan shook her head; it was not a good day for that actress, the heat must have really gotten to the audience.

They continued their tour of the shops, passing the flute carver and the hanging chair shop, the cobbler and another stall of period clothes that they knew to avoid because of the prices. Shortly, they arrived at a small seating area from which Rodney provided entertainment and wares. They listened to him hammer songs on the dulcimer. The clean sounds of the strings and the rhythm of his strikes was relaxing. A crowd formed, as it always did for his performances, and everyone clapped loudly at the conclusion while he bowed and motioned to the recordings he had available. The air was still hot and thick here, and Colleen and Morrigan watched enviously as a group of men passed by, stripped to the waist.

The crowd soon broke and Colleen moved forward to talk with Rodney, while Morrigan remained seated fanning herself. Morrigan watched the ebb and flow of the crowd, and in the distance, she spotted the old woman again. The woman pointed at someone in Morrigan's direction and began her shrill accusations of "witch" in a voice that sounded like rusted hinges swinging. Morrigan rose, keeping her eye on the old woman as she approached Colleen. She reached out her hand to touch Colleen's shoulder, but overbalanced; she stumbled and collided with her friend.

She pulled herself upright. "I'm sorry!" She craned her neck again, searching for the old woman, while Rodney and Colleen exchanged looks and waited for an explanation.

Morrigan finally turned, "Damn! The old woman was just over there, going into her witch tirade again. She's rather good at it. I wanted you to see her."

Rodney looked at her blankly, "What old woman?"

"Why, she's been here since we arrived this morning, insulting everyone in sight and proclaiming people as witches." Not seeing any recognition on his face, she continued, "You know . . . old woman, gray hair, missing teeth, tattered and dirty clothes, insults people?"

Rodney shook his head, then raised a finger, "But I am the first to admit that I don't notice much that goes on outside my performance area."

All three of them laughed, Colleen perhaps a bit more than the rest. A crowd began to form again as Rodney returned to his music. The women bought their music and moved on.

Next, they browsed through the wares of the first of several pottery shops. As they walked, Morrigan noticed that the faire had put in for more child performers this year. It seemed there were dirty-faced youngsters begging at every corner and alley, adding to the atmosphere of the place.

Morrigan was looking at mugs near the front window when the visage of the old woman again caught her attention. She was standing directly in front of Morrigan, glaring at her, a sneer on her wrinkled face.

"Colleen," Morrigan blurted.

Colleen didn't reply, so she called again.

Colleen looked up and smiled. "Find something good?"

Morrigan shook her head and pointed out the window.

"What?"

Morrigan cursed. The crone woman was gone again, nowhere to be seen.

"Your mysterious old lady?"

"She . . . she was looking at me in a weird way."

Colleen looked out the window, shifting back and forth to get as wide a view as possible. "Sure you're not imagining her? Are you feeling okay? You look a little flushed."

"I'm fine, it's just a little weird is all. And I'm not imagining her. She's starting to give me the creeps."

"All right. Maybe we should stop and get something to drink after this shop."

They finished perusing the goods and headed out without buying anything. They looked around for a vendor with drinks, but could spot nothing within eyesight. Together they shrugged and settled on walking south. Morrigan noted details she'd missed before, like a crippled beggar, the sternness of the guards, how realistic the buildings seemed with their thatched roofs, and how the old woman suddenly appeared again. Once more Morrigan stumbled, catching herself on Colleen.

"Morrigan, you okay? I think we really need to get you some liquids and fast."

"The old woman," she began.

Colleen nodded, "Yes, yes, the old woman. I understand, there's an old woman giving you creepy looks. We can come back to see her later." She took Morrigan by the arm and approached two of the security guards dressed in faux mail and colors, sweat beaded on their foreheads. "Forgive me sirs, which way to the closest drink vendor?"

One of them pointed in first one direction, and then another. "Either end of the market place m'lady! One way 'tis no faster than another, as ye'r in the middle!"

Colleen dragged her along again. But after a dozen steps or so Morrigan fell to the ground. Another hand grasped her by her free wrist and pulled her up. It was the old woman.

"You dirty thievin' witch. We'll hang ya, we will!"

Morrigan stepped back, but the old woman held her fast, and her eyes burned with malice. Morrigan was suddenly flocked by people in traditional garb, dirty children dressed in rags, beggars and cripples stinking of sweat, and stern-looking guards in mail with unsheathed weapons. She squeezed her eyes tight, and in the distance she heard Colleen call her name. When Morrigan opened her eyes again, Colleen was standing in front of her, and the press of the crowd was gone.

"You really don't look good." Colleen slipped her arm around Morrigan's waist this time and began to pull her down the lane toward the now-visible refreshment stands.

Morrigan stumbled along, her eyes searching for the old lady as they passed groups of people. Her head was beginning to buzz and she swayed with vertigo. The people looked at her strangely, as though there were something wrong with her.

They passed another pair of guards in chain mail. Morrigan watched them look at her, saw how their eyes followed her, watched them lean closer together and whisper. She could almost hear them say it, hear them call her a witch.

With each step things seemed to grow wilder and wilder. Now she saw the old woman again, now she didn't. Now she heard the creaky voice calling her a witch, and then it was just a grandmother speaking with her grandson. The images and sounds faded in and out. One moment she was walking up a lane crowded with people in contemporary clothes, and the next it was a narrow street crowded with peasants and soldiers, people covered in filth and smelling of unwashed clothes and bodies. And always now, somewhere, she heard the old woman's accusations, "Thievin' witch!"

Morrigan fell again, and a hand firmly grasped her. She rose up to stare the old woman in the face, her fierce eyes boring into Morrigan's as she cried out, "Let's hang the witch!"

Morrigan pulled back and spotted two guards closing on her. Like a panicked rabbit, she turned and ran as fast as she could. She dodged in and out of the throngs of people, filthy bodies wearing clothes no better than rags. She tripped over something, and callused hands seized her when she tried to rise, strong hands. She struggled, but strangers were pinning her. Morrigan's head spun and darkness claimed her senses. Her world was a nightmare of dirty faces and smelly bodies pressed in tight about her, and through it all she could see the crone glaring.

\* \* \*

Colleen sat in the first-aid tent, still shaking from Morrigan's collapse. Fortunately, two security guards had seen them and noticed that Morrigan looked quite ill and had followed. The guards were there as she collapsed. The paramedic had finished examining Morrigan and had stripped her down to the shift under the heavy dress, removed her skirt, blouse, and bodice. A fan blew cooling air across her.

Colleen dabbed Morrigan's forehead with a damp cloth, then wiped down each of her arms. The paramedic had said it was heat prostration, and that it could be further treated once she awoke. Morrigan apparently wasn't the first case of the day and not likely to be the last, according to him.

Morrigan's eyes fluttered as she drifted back to consciousness. She looked up at Colleen.

"What happened? Where am I?"

"You, my dear, are in the first-aid station. What happened is you passed out from the heat! Apparently, largely due to the garb of the day. Here, have something to drink, but just a little at a time."

Colleen held up a cup of water with a straw, guiding it into Morrigan's mouth.

Morrigan sipped for a moment, then lay back down. "I had the strangest dream. That old woman I mentioned, she was calling me a witch. And they chased me down and hanged me."

Absentmindedly, Morrigan reached for the medallion of the Green Man and found only the broken ends of a badly dried and worn leather lanyard cracked with years and years of wear.

# WIMPIN' WADY

## by

### Jayge Carr

Jayge Carr started her professional career working as a nuclear physicist for NASA, then became a full-time mother. One day she threw a book across the room, and snarled, "I could write a better book than that!" Her engineer husband, little knowing what he was unleashing on an unsuspecting world, said, "Why don't you?" Four published SF/F novels and dozens of short stories later . . .

"B'OOO FAIWE-WE! B'OO!"

Constanza Beatriz Florentin, in mundane—that is real—life Anne Porter, turned her head to look where her two-year-old daughter Lottie, carried in her arms, was pointing.

"Yes, Lottie, that's a blue fairy."

"B'oo," said Lottie, in great satisfaction. "B'oo faiw-we."

Constanza paused in admiration. The "Fairies," people hired by the Renaissance Faire managers to add "mystique and allure" to the faire, varied widely in their talents. But this youngster, whoever she was, was earning her pay. Instead of skipping along, or somersaulting, or pretending some odd step, she was dancing, as sure on her toes as any professional ballerina. Even her shades of blue-winged fairy outfit looked more like a tutu than anything else. As Constanza and Lottie watched, the blue-clad fairy did a pirouette, whirling around, followed by a few graceful gliding steps while dodging scattered patrons. Then, as someone aimed a camera at her, she flowed into an arabesque, a pose straight from *Swan Lake*, arms like wings, one leg back, and held it until the camera clicked twice and the patron said, in a gravelly beer voice, "Thanks, honey."

"B'oo," Lottie said again, in her sweet high baby tones. "Nice faiw-we. Nice b'oo."

"Very nice," Constanza agreed.

But the blue fairy danced off down the cobblestones of the Renaissance Faire's main concourse, and Constanza turned to the path leading to the Society for Creative Anachronism's compound.

" 'Bye, faiw-we." Lottie waved vigorously. " 'Bye! 'Bye! 'Bye!"

"Prithee, wait up, Constanza," came a rich, contralto female voice from behind them.

Constanza turned. Emerging from the ever-changing scatter of patrons and roving vendors, and limping toward her, was a tall woman wearing the standard female faire garb of long skirt and bodice over a white chemise. But the Renaissance-clothed lady coming toward them had touched up her deep blue skirt and bodice with a long tartan wrapped diagonally across her body from one shoulder to the other hip, and topped her buoyant mass of rich brown curls with a matching blue muffin cap, topped with an annular ring pinning a cocky pheasant feather.

For a second Constanza felt a surge of pure jealousy. Not that she wasn't the prettier of the pair, even with most of her dark-blonde hair hidden by her headdress. And her period costume, with the subtle touches such as the chemise enhanced by bands of Spanish blackwork embroidery, that she had done herself, was better, even if it wasn't her best or even second-best garb. (No one practical wore anything but their sturdiest outfits to the muck and mess of faire.) But the approaching SCAdian looked fresh and crisp and clean, and Constanza already felt crumpled and grubby, thanks to Lottie.

Then Constanza had to laugh. "Wait up?" she asked.

The newcomer grinned ruefully. "Well, I got the prithee part accurately, didn't I?"

"Indeed you did. Good morrow, Jennet." A consoling smile. "You just need to keep practicing. We'll keep it more mundane for now." Garb and persona were very carefully chosen by all members of the Society for Creative Anachronism. Though a newcomer, and still amusing herself and her fellow SCAdians with her language attempts, Jennet Stradaquhin—real name Mary-Evelyn Dixon—was doing well with her clothing. And looked good in it. Jennet was what Constanza's grandmother from the old country would have called *zaftig*. Though she was tall and carried her weight gracefully, the current fashion police would condemn her round curves. But her pretty, if full-cheeked and freckled, face, easy smile, and willingness to lend a hand with anything, had quickly made her popular among the SCAdians.

"Do you want me to carry the baby the rest of the way to the compound?" Jennet asked, proving her good nature.

Constanza started to peel the two year old off her

shoulder, then hesitated. "I thought I saw you limping. What's wrong?"

Jennet grimaced. "I hurt my foot when I was helping coach my little brother's soccer team. Mom made a fuss and I went to the doctor. I pulled a ligament. I have to be careful for a bit, that's all."

Constanza settled Lottie on her shoulder. "Then you'd better not put extra weight on it."

Jennet made a pouty face, then smiled. "We'll make up for it later, eh, Lottie pumpkin."

"Not pum-pin," Lottie objected. But she wasn't immune to the contagious good cheer, and smiled back.

"Maybe I can pull your wagon for you. That shouldn't hurt anything," Jennet suggested. Then, "Wow." A blush.

"Ooops. I mean, Gadzooks, how— No," a sigh, "that isn't right either, is it. But you're not pulling a wagon under your tapestry bundle, are you? Whatever, it looks so period. Not like those silly red metal wagons the faire rents, that you have to cover to hide their modernness. Did your husband make it?"

Constanza shook her head, then nodded at the carved wooden horse almost buried under its fat, lumpy, spilling-over-both-sides burden. "No, we got it from a vendor. It doesn't just hold all Lottie's gear—"

"And there's so much of it, isn't there," Jennet said with a laugh.

"Isn't there just! But it's also a riding toy for Lottie, when I haven't overloaded the poor thing."

"And you like that, Lottie pumpkin, right." Jennet didn't wait for an answer, but took the leather strap from Constanza.

The two women fell into step together, heading for the SCA compound, chatting amiably.

"—I missed last week," Jennet was saying a few

minutes later, "and I do want to do my share." A
wink. "I so enjoy giving my lectures on embroidery
and the Bayeux Tapestry."

Both women knew that the lectures and demonstrations of their medieval arts/skills/crafts were
what made the faire managers welcome the SCAdians to the Fairegrounds, assigning them a compound
of their own, big enough to have even small combats
and weapons demonstrations.

"The patrons will adore your lectures," Constanza
replied. "We do, and we're a much rougher audience. You love your subject, and you've clearly done
your research."

"G'een faiw-we!" Lottie suddenly piped up. "G'een!"

Constanza and Jennet both looked around. "I don't
see any fairies, Lottie dear," Constanza said.

"I don't either." Jennet turned in a full circle.

"They're usually all over, but I don't see one now,
green or any other color."

"G'een faiw-we," Lottie said, cherry-pink cupid's
bow mouth in a delightful childish pout.

"Whoever it was probably was in front and turned
somewhere past the compound," Jennet suggested.

"Perhaps," Constanza said slowly. "But this isn't
the first time she's seen a fairy that I haven't. And
it's always green."

"Maybe green is the term she uses for a color that
she doesn't know the name of?"

"No. She knows green." Constanza thought it
over, then shrugged. "Maybe that green one has decided that his or her game should be playing hide
and seek."

Jennet shrugged. "Maybe."

"Wady," Lottie interrupted.

Jennet looked at her. "Yes, honey?"

"Wady foot. Foot bad?"

"Ah. Yes, honey, my foot is bad. So I limp. When it's better, I won't."

"Bad foot. Wimp?"

"Limp, honey. Limp means I don't walk right. My foot hurts, and it's sore. So I'm limping." She took a couple of steps, exaggerating the limp. Smiled broadly. "I can't help it. Limping."

"Wimp. Wimpin' wady."

Constanza grinned at her younger friend. "You may be wimping wady for a while. She still can't come close to pronouncing l's and r's properly."

Jennet shrugged. "From a sweetie like Lottie, who cares."

"Wimpin' wady," Lottie agreed. Then, "Nice wimpin' wady."

"Good heavens," Constanza said. "I think that's her first three-word sentence."

"Happy to be of service," Jennet said with a smile.

"Oooooooooh!" With a squeal, Lottie suddenly ducked her head into her mother's front, hiding her face. Muffled: "Bad faiw-wie. Bad."

Both women turned. Coming toward them, gliding almost, face a mask of cool regality that somehow radiated cold anger, was a woman who could have stepped out of a portrait of a medieval queen. Her black flowing gown was covered with chains of what looked like pearls, plus many other jewels at neck and draped over the bodice. Shining night-sky-black hair was caught inside meshes of more pearls and chains on each side of her head, extending straight outward left and right more than a handspan on each side, larger in size and about the same shape as the pint foam cups in which the vendors served drinks. On her forehead and around the crown of her head was a glittering tiara. Only no human queen ever wore gossamer butterfly wings.

Jennet made a slight whistle. Whispered, "Think she's part of the court?"

"I hadn't heard. Don't take chances," Constanza advised.

Both women sank into deep curtsies, Constanza balancing precariously with Lottie clinging to her.

The Fairy Queen glided by, not ackowledging their obeisances.

"I hope she's not part of the court," Jennet muttered, once the queen was down the pathway a bit. The young SCAdian's nose was still wrinkled. Bending low had brought her face too near to the muddy area by the cobblestones. It had rained recently, and there was more than mud in the mud. Despite all efforts, the horse by-products got onto or into most of the walking surfaces.

"Bad faiw-wie," Lottie agreed. "Mean. Mean."

"Not as mean as my witch of a podiatrist, if she knew I was here," Jennet said to herself, softly enough that neither Lottie nor Constanza could hear. "She blames me because nothing she's done so far has helped. Well, it's my life, and I'm going to enjoy myself. What harm can just a little walking do?"

A few hours later, Constanza was looking unhappily around the private upstairs room of the SCA compound. Usually, there were at least two small children up here, and it had been set up as a children's playroom. But at the moment, it was empty except for her and Lottie, who was happily amusing herself in a corner.

As Constanza watched, the two year old rolled her ball against the wall, and caught it as it bounced back at her. She had been playing with the ball for five minutes at the most, and her pattern was to play with one toy, once it satisfied her, for ten or fifteen minutes before getting bored and going to something else.

If there had been another parent here, Constanza would simply have asked the other one to watch Lottie for a few minutes. But no one else was near, and she didn't have a choice. Her stomach was roiling, she was acutely nauseated. She had to go. Now.

But it shouldn't take that long, and there were bound to be several people downstairs.

"Lottie," Constanza said firmly. "You stay here and play. I'll be right back."

"Pway," Lottie agreed.

"Don't go through this doorway," Constanza added.

"No. No go."

"Stay here. Don't go through the doorway!"

"Pway here."

Constanza bit her lip. But Lottie seemed to understand. Besides, there were adults downstairs, all longtime SCA friends. Constanza headed out, hand pressing against her mouth, all but running.

If she had turned around, she would have seen Lottie throwing her ball awkwardly at the wall, instead of rolling it. And the ball hesitating, as though someone caught it, before coming back.

"Would you like to play with me?" asked the Green Fairy, as Constanza's rapid footsteps on the stairs faded away.

"Pway," Lottie agreed, nodding. The Green Fairy was just her size. His broad, three-cornered smile was infectious, and his short, tight blond-brown curls seemed to bounce, as if he couldn't keep still, even for a second. His green outfit of velvet doublet and silk tights looked more like that of a medieval page than the costumes of the hired fairies. "Pway, G'een Faiw-we." Lottie tossed the ball again.

It wasn't until they'd played ball, then set out some blocks, that the Green Fairy said casually, but with an odd glint in his wide eyes, "Would you like to come to my place to play?"

Lottie tilted her head. "Nice G'een Faiw-we."

"It will be fun," he coaxed. "I have many toys to play with. Magic toys."

"Pway. Toys." Lottie shook her head. "No. Mommy no." She pointed to the door.

"We won't go through the door," he informed her.

"Oooooh?"

"No. We won't go through the door. Your mommy said not to go through the door. So we won't. But you can come play with me, with me and my toys." He smiled, his elfin ears pointing. "All you have to do is say Yes—" He held out a small hand. "—and hold my hand."

"Yesth." Lottie smiled back, putting her hand trustingly in his. "Pway."

\* \* \*

Constanza, who had called "Privy Run" as she dashed through the downstairs, was leaning over the porcelain bowl of the toilet in the nearby facility, still retching miserably.

In the intervals that she wasn't retching, she was muttering, "*Morning* sickness," in disgusted tones.

\* \* \*

"Ma-gick? Oooohhhhh!" Lottie looked around herself, eyes wide.

"Like it?" the Green Fairy asked, tugging her small hand to turn her in a full circle, so she could see all the wonder and the glory.

"Like!" Lottie moved toward a grove of singing flowers.

"P'etty!"

"This is only the beginning," said the Green Fairy.

\* \* \*

When Constanza came back, the upstairs room held no sign of Lottie. Nobody downstairs had seen her either.

\* \* \*

The word spread rapidly through the SCAdians at the faire. Child missing. Constanza and Hrolf's little Lottie had somehow gotten out of the compound.

Soon SCAdians and other faire workers, who had heard the news, were moving out from the SCA compound, asking booth vendors and anyone else if they'd seen a two year old, with straight red hair cut short, dressed in the faire child's garb of long lemon-yellow chemise and crayon-blue apron.

The first pair of trumpeters encountered stopped speaking of the feast, and started asking people to look out for a lost child. Then the second . . .

Vendors passed the word along rows of booths.

But nobody had seen her, alone or with an adult.

An hour passed with no sign of Lottie. Then two. More and more people were looking. Her parents were both frantic, out searching, calling.

Her father, Hrolf, was walking rapidly down a path through a fragrant garden area, his gaze swinging from right to left and back, looking, searching . . . not finding, Constanza was working her way down a row of merchant booths, asking each vendor if he or she had seen a red-haired two year old in yellow and blue. All could only shake their heads. All promised to keep an eye out, and send a message if they saw her.

But no one did.

How could they know that she was no longer on the Mortal Earth?

\* \* \*

The Green Fairy was juggling half a dozen dazzling, glittering objects that changed shape as they moved, from round to pyramid to cube to oblong to conical.

Lottie, out of breath from running and chasing, was laughing while she sat on something softer than grass, sweeter smelling then honeysuckle.

"Watch this!" Suddenly, the Green Fairy was part of what was being juggled. His small figure followed the same path as the objects he had been juggling, now all green to match his clothing.

"Oooooh! Nice!" Lottie applauded.

He landed on his feet in front of her, and held out his hands, and the juggling tools, now all cubical and green, piled in two neat stacks.

"Nice! Nice!" Lottie nodded, smiling as she clapped.

The Green Fairy bowed, still holding three cubes in each hand. "I know many games," he said. And tossed, and the cubes disappeared.

"Yes. Pway. Pway game," Lottie agreed.

"No," said a third voice.

Lottie and the Green Fairy both turned. Where there had been simply a slight hummock, with candy canes growing in profusion, was now a . . . fairy. A very angry fairy, from her expression.

"Uh-oh," said Lottie, flinching away. "B'ack faiw-we. Mean b'ack faiw-we."

But the black-garbed Fairy Queen was not looking at Lottie. 'Tamlittle," she addressed the Green Fairy. "You know better, my lad."

He stood, shoulders hunched, scraping one foot against the soft rainbow-hued ground covering. His lower lip stuck out in a pout. "I followed all the rules, Your Majesty."

"You know very well, Tamlittle, that the rules are not meant to apply to mortal infants."

"The fairies have taken mortal infants before." The slightest of hesitations. "Even you, Your Majesty."

The black-garbed Fairy Queen narrowed her eyes, glaring at him, then stiffened her back and seemed to grow. "Ill-done of you, Tamlittle, to remind me of past mistakes."

"I followed the rules," he repeated stubbornly.

"The mortal babe is too young to have given consent. You have done wrongly, my lad. She must be returned."

"No." He moved so he was between his queen and Lottie.

"No. She walks. She talks. She understands."

"Yes, she walks. Yes, she talks. But understand? No, she hasn't sufficient mortal years for that. So you, my lad, are in dire trouble. She returns, Tamlittle. She returns now."

But the Green Fairy—Tamlittle—didn't move. "No," he repeated stubbornly, defiance clear on his face, a look any human parent would have recognized instantly. "No. She agreed. She stays."

The expression on the Fairy Queen's face grew harsher.

"You are risking much, Tamlittle."

"I'm lonely," he said simply.

"Lonely?" For once, the Fairy Queen was startled, taken aback. "How can you be lonely? There may not be as many of us as there once were, but there are sufficient. You cannot be lonely."

"I am lonely." He hung his head, then looked back up. "I am the youngest. No one else wants to play with me."

"We all play."

"Your games. Older games. I want . . . I want to play my games. I want to play young games."

"Oh." The Fairy Queen did nothing as mundane as chew her lip, but her expression was that of a human doing just that.

"Oh. Dear."

"B'ack faiw-we sad?" asked Lottie in her sweet high little soprano. "Poor b'ack faiw-we. Kiss make well?"

"My, I see why you chose this one. Sweet little mortal babe."

"Yes. She likes me. She likes to play with me. And I like her."

The Fairy Queen sighed and shook her head. "She's still too young. I'm sorry, Tamlittle. What must be, must be."

He smiled. "I can make her older!" A gesture, and suddenly both Tamlittle and Lottie were growing larger, until the black Fairy Queen faced two people, one mortal, one elfin, her own size.

"Oh! Wow!" said Lottie, her voice deeper.

"She grows well, Tamlittle, but it doesn't change anything. She still is a babe in mind."

He turned, was looking at her in a very different way.

"She's beautiful."

"Because of you."

"No. I only made her go along her own path more quickly."

"Interesting." The queen studied the more than pretty young girl. "As lovely inside as out. I see that I underestimated you, Tamlittle."

Tamlittle took Lottie's hand again. "She stays," he said stubbornly.

"Do you want your mother, child?"

"Want Mommy," Lottie agreed.

"Don't you want to stay and play with me, Lottie," Tamlittle coaxed.

"You pway. Me. Mommy."

The queen was right. Inside the willowy young teen body with the magnificent swath of Plantagenet red-gold hair was a two year old's mind, inexperienced, still learning, often misunderstanding.

"I can't. I wish I could." Suddenly, he smiled. He made a gesture, and a life-size moving picture appeared to the side, where he had pointed.

"Mommy!" But Lottie clenched her shoulders. Constanza had been ping-ponging between fear and anger. At the moment, anger was what showed in both expression and body language.

Her lips were thin, her eyes narrow. She looked at each person she passed with suspicion. *You? You? I'll kill you if you're the one!*

"You want to go to your mommy?" Tamlittle asked slyly.

"Nooooo. Mommy an-g'y!"

"Very clever, my lad," the queen said wryly. "Not good enough, but clever."

"Her father's stomping along, too," Tamlittle said.

"They must love her very much," the queen said softly.

'The mother's pregnant. A boy this time. They'll forget her."

The queen shook her head, slowly. "Some mortals might. But somehow, I wonder if these would."

"They left her alone," Tamlittle pointed out.

"But did you walk her away, or did you use magic?" His lip pouted. In fairy terms, he was still a child, perhaps the young teen his form now suggested. "I could have taken her out by mortal means, no one was paying attention."

"You can't be sure."

His lips came out farther. "No," he said simply.

She raised her hand. From it, a stream of light flowed.

He got between her and Lottie, and shut his eyes.

"Wook," said Lottie. "Wimpin' wady!"

All three looked at what had been simply Lottie's mother, striding along.

Now she had stopped, and was talking with Jennet. A gesture, and the three in Fairy Land could hear what the mortals were saying.

"No sign." Constanza was shaking her head. "You sure?"

"I talked not two minutes ago with a SCAdian who had just come from the compound. There are several notes on the bulletin board. But all say nobody's seen her."

"She's here." Constanza straightened her shoulders, firmed her mouth. "Someone will find her. Soon." But the panic in her voice belied the confident words.

"Yes, soon." Jennet's expression softened. "I'm sure."

"I'll keep looking."

"So will I." Jennet turned to go down another side path. But Constanza had already put the other woman out of her mind. She was moving along, her head swinging.

"Oh, Lottie, pumpkin, where are you?" Jennet said, on a sigh.

"Not pum-pin," Lottie said softly.

As the two women separated, the three-dimensional picture started to follow Constanza.

"No," ordered the queen. "The other one."

The picture wavered, then moved slightly. Constanza disappeared, and then Jennet was in the center of the picture.

She was limping along, face grimacing in pain.

"We've got to find her," Jennet muttered. "Got to!" A tear fell, then another. She shuddered, but forced herself onward, continuing to call, "Lottie," every few steps.

"Wady cwy," said Lottie. "Why?"

The queen looked accusingly at Tamlittle. "Her foot hurts."

"She should get off it. Stupid mortal," he muttered.

"She knows that, Tamlittle. She knows she's hurting herself. Not just the pain with every step, but she could be doing permanent damage. Not ever to be able to walk easily again, never to run, never to be normal, ever ever ever. She knows all that, too. Doesn't she?"

He sighed. "Yes. She knows."

"So, tell me, fairy lad, why she is risking permanent damage to the only pair of feet she has. She has no magic to repair herself, does the mortal medicine fail her." She shook a finger at him, deepened her tones. "Now, say out loud why she is risking never being able to walk without pain again. Speak while remembering always that she isn't a fairy, she hasn't magic to fix something that's not working right."

His lower lip came out.

"Tamlittle?" the Fairy Queen said softly.

"Wady cwy," said Lottie sadly. "Kiss make well?"

"Your kiss could make her well, mortal child. Only yours," said the Fairy Queen.

"Kiss make well? Me kiss?"

"Yes, child. Your kiss, Lottie's kiss, will make the Limping Lady well. Only Lottie's kiss."

"Me go. Kiss make well." She moved toward the now openly crying Jennet, who was nonetheless still moving, still looking.

"Tamlittle?" the Fairy Queen asked softly.

"Must I?"

"It is her choice. You are a witness."

"Yes," he said, holding out his hand. "Lottie, you are only seeing your limping friend. She isn't here."

"Not here. 'Ike TV?"

"Yes. Not here." He sighed. "Like . . . ahhh . . . TV."

"Mortals have their own forms of magic now," the queen murmured.

"Wady not cwy?"

"Truth Tamlittle," the queen ordered, sadly.

"Your lady is crying, Lottie. She's jut not here. But yes, she's crying."

"Me kiss? Kiss make well?"

Tamlittle sighed softly. Moved closer to Lottie. "You wish to see your lady face-to-face? Then take my hand."

The queen smiled. "As you were, Tamlittle. As she was. Imagine the commotion if you took her back as she is."

"Oh." He made a gesture, and he and Lottie shrank back to normal two-year-old size.

"Fun!" Lottie giggled. "Do again."

"Maybe later." He looked hopefully at the queen. "Or maybe now. She forgets quickly."

"Go wady now," Lottie said, proving him wrong. "Kiss make well?"

"Soon." He looked at the queen. "I can't take her back where mortals can see."

"A problem indeed." The Queen hesitated. "But wait. Only one person is in the room upstairs, where you took her from.

"And they may be leaving. Yes . . . now. Before someone else comes."

"Take my hand, Lottie," Tamlittle said sadly.

"G'een Faiw-we cwy?" Lottie asked.

Tamlittle forced his contagious smile. "Only that I will miss you later, Lottie."

"Pway 'ater. G'een faiw-we pway."

"No." He shook his head, the short crop of tight curls dancing.

"Uh-oh," said Lottie, her own lower lip trembling.

"Take her back, Tamlittle. Now," the queen ordered. He took Lottie's hand, and then the queen was alone in the magic dell. She bowed her head, swiped a tear from one eye. Even fairies can't have everything they want. Even fairies.

\*     \*     \*

Back in the upstairs room of the compound, Tamlittle looked around, his lips pursed. Then he smiled and nodded.

Lottie was yawning. She'd played hard, and it was past her naptime. Tamlittle moved to some cabinets on one wall. Most were filled with the oddments of the Society. But one was completely empty. If Lottie were to go inside and curl up, she could sleep.

It would explain how she could seem to have been lost. It didn't take him long to encourage her to get inside and curl up. She had picked up the soft cloth doll she called Lovey and was rubbing it against her cheek, slumping into sleep even before he closed the door.

He thought, then made a gesture. Faint glittering particles went inside the cabinet. Now Lottie would have plenty to breathe, no matter how long it took to find her. He hesitated, remembering something he'd almost forgotten, then made another hand movement, and a different magic slipped inside.

Then he bit his lip—and vanished.

"Good-bye, Lottie." His last whisper lingered after he was gone, like the Cheshire cat's grin.

\*     \*     \*

The sound of heavy footsteps echoed up the stairs. Then the door swung open, and hit the wall with a clang.

Lottie, inside her cabinet, heard and was jolted out of sleep. "Maaa-mie," she murmured.

"I heard something," said a voice.

"No, you're imagining it," said another.

"Aaaaaaaawwww." Lottie did not like being rudely awakened, once she'd started her nap. But when nobody responded, she slid back into sleep.

"Toys all over the place," someone grumbled. "Watch your step."

Too late. "HA HA HA, THAT WAS FUN!" screeched the bright red Tickle Me Elmo doll on the floor. Someone had stepped on it just right.

"WAAAAAAAAAAA!" Twice in two minutes was too much. Lottie set up a howl that reverberated inside her little cubbyhole.

"She couldn't be in here," one voice was saying. "We looked and looked."

"You didn't look enough." The owner of the other, deeper, male voice was listening, trying to locate the source of the sounds.

"WAAAAAAAAAA! MAAAAAAAAAA!" Lottie was thoroughly upset, and wanted comfort. Now!

Bang! A cabinet door opened, and was flung back. Bang! Another. Bang! Bang! Ba—

"Oh, you poor darling!" Jennet swooped, gathered up the now hysterically crying baby, and cuddled her. "Bruce. Get the word out. Get her parents here as soon as you can."

"She was here all the time." Bruce was shaking his head.

"Thank goodness that you remembered we had some staffs stored here, and we came back to get one for me to use as a cane." Jennet shuddered, wiping from her memory the argument over coming back to the best-searched area. "Who knows how much ventilation that cabinet has."

Bruce chewed his lip, looking inside. "I'm amazed she managed to get in there."

"Children are like cats. They take up a lot less space than you'd think."

"I don't think there is ventilation. And even cats have to breathe." But he said it softly. No use upsetting anyone. Then he headed out at a near run, to spread the word that the lost was found.

Back upstairs, Jennet rocked in place, the crying child in her arms.

Lottie knew it wasn't mommy holding her. The feel was wrong, the smell was wrong, even the murmuring voice was wrong. But she knew the person holding her. Finally, face streaked with tears, she said, "Wimpin' wady?"

"Yes, pumpkin?"

"Not pum-pin!" Lottie stuck out her lip.

Jennet smiled. "You are my very most special pumpkin, Lottie."

"Wimpin' wady sad?" Lottie asked.

"Not as much, now you're safe."

"Sad? P'ease not sad."

Jennet hugged the small body. "You are such a dear!"

"Kiss make well," Lottie said, and bestowed a good smacking kiss on Jennet's cheek.

"Ohhhh. Thank you, sweetie."

No one else was there to see the small sparkle of magic jump from Lottie's lips, to Jennet's face, and run down her body to surround her injured foot. And sink in to work its wonder.

\* \* \*

Back in Fairy Land, the queen nodded, as the vision of the reunion vanished. "Let this be a lesson to you, Tamlittle. Meddle not with mortals."

"You were right, Your Majesty." Tamlittle knelt, bowed his head. "She was too young."

But after the queen was gone, he continued to stare into nothingness, as though he could still see Lottie, her parents, and the rest of the SCAdians celebrating her return.

He smiled, that broad, infectious three-sided grin that had first attracted Lottie. "But not even you can stop time, Your Majesty. She'll grow. I will wait. Not patiently. She'll grow."

# BREWED FORTUNE

### *by*

### *Michael A. Stackpole*

Michael A. Stackpole is a writer living in Arizona who likely would have headed out on the road and become a performer in Ren Faires had he found them before he found gaming. As it is, gaming gave him the ability to travel and work for low wages, all without needing fancy dress. He's enjoyed the Arizona Renaissance Festival over the past sixteen years, and being able to set a story there was a delight. On his website, www.stormwolf.com, he has another story of Merlin Bloodstone.

IT SHOULD NOT HAVE SURPRISED ME that Merlin Bloodstone, my boss, agreed to attend the Arizona Renaissance Festival. He's an occultist who dabbles with eccentricity the way Stephen King dabbles with writing. Bloodstone acts like a refugee from the nineteenth century, so imagining him feeling at home in the twelfth wasn't very hard.

There were many reasons for him not to go, however. The Ren Faire is an informal outing, with folks wearing everything from medieval garb to the latest fashion trend offered by teen pop idols. In Arizona, you also had the cowboys, who looked ready for a rodeo and pretty much wishing they had six-guns to deal with some of the odder folks. For Bloodstone, however, dressing informally means he might go with a half-Windsor knot in his tie instead of a full, and the closest he ever got to wearing comfortable footware was standing next to someone who was.

Being Arizona, the faire was also out in the sun, which he largely avoided—less because of his being a photophobe than his keeping odd hours—but he did tend to be on the pale side. There would be nothing out at the site Bloodstone would consider even close to tea. On top of that, there would be a crush of people and his dislike of crowds probably should have kept him away completely. In fact, I expected it would.

He decided to come anyway, though, for one reason alone: he was jealous.

Aside from the fact that he is utterly unpredictable and lives in his own little world, he's a good employer—at least I think so when I don't want to kill him. He pays me a good salary. I live in the guesthouse at his Paradise Valley home. I get all my meals there and even have the use of a car. Sure, I'm on call 24/7 to deal with him or his clients—the need for spiritual advising knowing no clock—but there's not too much heavy lifting involved, and when I have time off, I get to use it as I will.

My free time, over the two months leading up to the festival, had been spent helping CROFT, a Celtic living recreation group, get ready for the faire. CROFT has a small Celtic village where members show off traditional skills like spinning, weaving, woodworking, and cookery. Not being particularly skilled at anything, I did what I could. That meant a lot of lifting, toting, and washing up, but it was fun and let me spend time with friends.

Bloodstone had been excluded from the whole process, so he was willing to risk sun, weak tea, and crowds just to see what it was I'd been doing without him.

I'd planned on bringing Bloodstone out in the second weekend of the faire, since I'd worked the first. I'd gotten us tickets, but Friday night Anne called from CROFT and asked if I could come in and work the morning shift. I agreed, then called a car service to drive Bloodstone out the next day. I wrote up careful instructions as to where I could be found, included the faire map, and highlighted a few acts he might want to see until I was free. I paper-clipped the ticket to all that and left it on his desk.

That morning dawned cold and a bit wet, though the weather report said it would be clearing later. This pleased me because it was cool enough that I'd not roast in my garb. I donned knee-high boots, breeches, a homespun shirt, and a brown leather doublet. I added big gauntlets, a belt with a pouch— for hiding my nonperiod camera and cell phone— and topped it all with a brown cavalier hat which sported a jaunty green feather.

It did make me look more nobility than peasantry, but I could lose the doublet and hat while working. To complete things, I did slide a stag-handled dagger into the top of my right boot. As a participant I could wear a weapon as long as it was snapped into the sheath. To draw it for anything more than eating would get me in serious trouble. It was there mostly for show, and I was happy with that.

I left the house pretty early and took the Cougar coupe. The forty-minute drive brought me all the way into Pinal County and the shadow of the Superstition Mountains. I drove past the various sponsor signs, nodding my head in the direction of the Fitz-

Gibbon Industries sign, as we Rennies had taken to doing. Showing all deference to the FitzGibbons was seen as good—much in the same way that kowtowing to Sauron made life easy in some parts of Middle Earth. I checked in, flashing ID three different times, then reached the Thistlewood Cottage.

The earlier rain might have been good for keeping dust down, but it made starting and keeping a fire going with wet wood rather tough. I begged some glowing coals off McLeod the swordsmith, in exchange for working the bellows and the promise of some of the stew Anne would be making, completing my quest for fire. I hauled water as patrons filtered into the faire, chopped veggies, and otherwise did what needed to be done until close in on noon. The whole time I was polite to the patrons, but I kept being more and more distracted as I didn't see Bloodstone among them.

Anne looked up from the bread dough she was kneading. "You're free, Connor. You better go find him."

"I don't even known if he's here." I would have added that I would have called him, but Bloodstone would sooner have an asp in his pocket than a cell phone. I sighed. "I suppose I can do a circuit. If he comes here while I'm gone, you'll recognize him because . . ."

She laughed. "I've met him, remember, that night gaming?"

"Oh, yeah." Anne and other friends had been at the guesthouse gaming when Bloodstone had come in to ask me a question. That night he was quite the sight. He's a small man, with an oversized head and huge violet eyes. His black hair had been combed back and slicked down, emphasizing his widow's peak and his clothes had been something out of the

Count Dracula for Boys line. He looked like a Boy Scout preparing to earn a vampirism merit badge.

I gave her a wink. "I'll be back as soon as I can." I wandered out behind the cottage, pulled on my doublet, my hat, and my gloves, then began to make a circuit of the faire. Most of the people were heading east, toward the tournament ground, to watch knights wheel and pass and bash each other. It was great theater, and I tried to take in at least one of their shows a day. It was closer to professional wrestling than *Braveheart*, but as spectacle it delivered.

Moving against the flow of traffic is not easy, so I sheltered in the shadow of Lord Randall's Chain Maille Fashions shop and watched the parade go by. People who come to the faire tend to drop into three groups—though the professionals call them all patrons, and volunteers tend to call them mundanes. The easiest to spot are the tourists. They look at folks in costume the way they'd look at animals in the zoo, and with a bit more fear since there're no bars between them and us. Then there are the faire-goers, who have been before and get into the spirit of things. Though they're largely dressed for the outside world, if you say, "Good day, M'lady," a woman will usually answer in kind. These folks generally buy bits and pieces of garb over the years and come in some percentage of fancy dress. A booth outside the gate will rent costumes for the day, and another inside lets folks dress up and have their picture taken.

The third group gets just a bit scary. They are called *playtrons* and spend a lot of time at the faire. They fork out tons of money to put together an ensemble. They come to the festival all dressed up, assume their own persona, and watch their favorite performers wherever they are playing. Don Juan and

Miguel—a great sword fighting and comedy act—
will have playtrons who sit in the crowd, mouthing
the lines along with the actors, and will happily jump
in with the correct response or a straight-line heckle
as needed.

I waited for the main crush of folks to sweep past,
then headed toward the front gate. As I went I
passed one of several booths offering palm and tarot
card reading, I got a sinking feeling in the pit of
my stomach. Bloodstone, being an occultist, has an
abiding loathing for fortune-tellers. The folks at the
faire were doing it for fun, whereas the kind he hates
do it for profit. Unfortunately, he's not terribly good
at sorting the two types out, and I could just imagine
him haranguing some faux-gypsy tarot card reader
who didn't know her cups from her wands.

As I came around the corner, cutting between the
birds of prey tower at Falconer's Heath and the
nearby kitchen, one of a pair of women held a hand
up. I slowed, for they weren't Rennies, even though
they did have on nice costumes. I thought they might
need help.

The woman smiled. "A question, if I might, sir?
Do you feel at one with your costume?"

The question surprised me, and made me blush a
little, but I never got to answer.

From behind me, I heard a voice I knew very well.

"Yes, kind lady, I feel most at one with it."

I spun on my heel to face my boss and plopped
straight down on my butt. In point of fact my jaw
hit the ground before my buttocks did. I craned my
neck back, looking up at Bloodstone.

"What on Earth?"

"When in Rome, Connor."

By which he must have meant "when in Camelot—
the Disney version," because he'd rented a purple

velvet wizard's robe, with gold satin lining and a galaxy of embroidered gold stars sprayed all over it. The sleeves had been rolled up several times, and the matching hat sat back on his head a bit, with the tip tilted and crooked. A gold cord belted the robe at his waist and a wand with a star on it had been tucked away at his left hip the way a samurai might hang a sword.

I shook my head. "Pure vanity. You picked it because it matches your eyes."

"Droll frippery, Connor, and unworthy of you." He flicked a hand as if casting a levitation spell. "On your feet, you have to come see something."

I got up, dusted myself off, doing my best to ignore the giggles of the women who I had thought were speaking to me, and drifted off in Bloodstone's wake. He headed north for a dozen yards, then east past the Fairhaven Theater. The crowd parted and he locked onto his target like a Hellfire missile. I knew there was going to be trouble, and I wasn't sure how to avert it.

Bloodstone was headed for a little cottage in the middle of a beautiful greensward. The cottage itself, and the sod surrounding it, had been imported from Ireland by the FitzGibbon family. They were big in the Irish community in the valley, and had donated most of the funding for the import of another Irish cottage in the Margaret Hance Park in downtown Phoenix. They also gave CROFT funding, which is first where I ran into Pierce FitzGibbon.

Him, I wasn't worried about immediately. Among Bloodstone's eccentricities, there is one he clings to with the fervor of convert to a new religion: tea. He knows tea, period. He is precise in how it is picked, prepared, brewed, and drunk. He knows the properties, real and imagined, of every variety available. I got the feeling sometimes that he might not have been there when the very first cup was brewed, but the pot wasn't cold by the time he did arrive.

And that cottage had in it a tea leaf reader, Lady Siany, late of Ireland. I'd only seen her in a hooded green cloak, moving about the faire, with wisps of white hair trailing from within the hood. Being a dyed-in-the-wool skeptic, I had no more use for fortune-tellers than Bloodstone, but for entirely different reasons. For me, they were doing wrong; whereas for him, they were doing *it* wrong.

"Come, come, Connor." He waved me onto the grass and toward the cottage's little door. "She's waiting for you."

I stopped dead beside the little sign that informed me the tea leaf reading would set someone back $35, and it wasn't going to be me. "Oh, no, this is a day off for me. I don't have to do this."

Bloodstone turned, his smile fading somewhat and his eyes half lidding. "Please, Connor. Indulge me in this and I will be at your bidding for the rest of the day."

I smiled. "You'll eat what I tell you to eat?"

"Yes."

"See the shows I want to see?"

"Yes."

"And," I hesitated, my mind racing.

An edge came into his voice. "Indulgence buys indulgence, Connor."

"Okay, I won't push it." I smiled, then doffed my hat and handed it to him. "Won't be but a minute."

The cottage interior measured not more than six feet on a side, and had a cozy feeling to it. I entered through the east, and windows north and south provided a little light. Lady Siany supplemented that by candles placed on a rough-hewn table. Dried herbs and flowers hung from the ceiling and their scent blended with that of the tea being brewed.

A stool was meant for me, whereas she had a high-backed chair. That was nice staging, and my uncomfortable stool would not encourage me to linger. In and out, the faster she could move them, the more money she'd make.

As I entered, she slipped off the hood. Even in the half-light there was no mistaking the platinum paleness of her fine hair. She wore it long and unbound, and the pointed tips of ears poked up through her locks. It used to be, in the early days of Ren Faires, there were a lot more folks playing at the Lord of the Rings, and in the wake of the movies, seeing that again was no surprise. The professional performers usually didn't do that, but she was doing her own sort of act.

She nodded to acknowledge me and guided me to the stool. Her every motion, from that nod, to her turning to the little brazier she used for heating her water, had a fluid and serene quality to it. I did feel at ease which, given my feeling about fortune-tellers, was surprising. She poured the tea into a small earthenware bowl, which might have been Japanese save for the shamrock pattern incised around the rim and painted in the bowl itself. The tea steamed and whole leaves swirled within.

She looked at me and smiled, which added a glow to her delicate features. Her eyes looked gray, but could have been pale blue. I couldn't really tell, and half-wondered if they weren't shifting colors even as I tried to figure out their hue.

"Others, I would have to instruct, but you know what to do."

I did. I'd seen Bloodstone read leaves many times, so I sipped the tea, remaining silent. I did this less to put me into a contemplative mind than to avoid saying anything upon which she would build her little spiel. People going to psychics tend to miss how much their chance comments reveal to the reader. I wasn't going to let that happen here.

Once I'd drunk all but the last, I took the bowl in my left hand, swirled the dregs around three times widdershins, then quickly inverted the bowl onto the table. What little excess tea there was drained out between the boards, but we sat in silence as we waited for the leaves to dry a bit.

Lady Siany reached for the bowl with long, slender fingers unadorned by any jewelry. She turned it over and slowly spun it around. The tea leaves remained plastered against the inside of the bowl. The reader would look at the shapes and interpret them. The images closest to the lip were supposed to happen in the near future.

Her voice, like her presence, soothed. "There is much I see here. You come from a long and storied family, one of nobility and blood, though not always has the way been easy. You have good friends, and you are well loved by them and your family. You are a man of intelligence, discretion, and deep loyalties."

I smiled. I couldn't help but. Now, if you think about it, if you had some beautiful woman you'd paid thirty-five dollars to tell your fortune saying that about you, you'd smile, too. And so would everyone else who heard those same words reading after reading. Who'd not like to think that of themselves? I smiled because I knew what she was doing, and I knew the next step would be to tell me something warm and fuzzy about my future because the cardinal rule is that you always leave the patron—or pigeon—feeling good.

She set down the bowl and pointed to a sharp

leaf right below the rim. "This is an arrow. There is misfortune and urgency close upon you. And here, this leaf, a skull. Violence and danger. I urge upon you caution, and would further urge you to leave immediately save for this."

I stared at the image. Four leaves had combined to look like a heart, torn down the middle, yet with wings. I didn't know what a broken angel's heart might represent, but she clearly attached importance to it. "Tell me."

"There are many ways to interpret the symbol. Suffice it to say, it is hopeful. The velvet lining in a cloud."

Her mangling that cliché snapped me out of whatever sort of lunacy I was slipping into. A cold shiver ran down my spine, then I stood, gave her a little bow, and backed into the doorway. "You're good, I'll give you that." I reached into my belt pouch to give her the money.

Lady Siany shook her head. "No, that is not necessary. Be wary."

She spoke with such sincerity that another shiver ran down my spine. I left the warm confines of her cottage and let the colder air brace me. I snarled at Bloodstone, snatched my hat from him and marched off the greensward toward a drink stand. I was one step away before I heard another voice, one I didn't know as well as Bloodstone's, and one I wish I knew even less well.

It didn't help that the remnant of the sentence I heard ended in the word, "varlet."

I spun on my heel for a second time, but didn't fall. There he stood, all tall and dark in black and silver, including the coronet set in the center with onyx: Prince Pierce FitzGibbon. He wore a rapier and dagger, as befitting royalty, and had a small retinue of musketeer bullyboys around him. They were laughing at me, and while Pierce pointed at me with his right hand, he stroked his goatee with his left.

I bowed my head and dropped to one knee. "You spoke to me, my lord?"

"Yes, peasant, come here."

Every Ren Faire has its royalty. They're all actors chosen to *act* the part of the nobility. They wow the crowd, oversee the jousts, take toy swords from kids and dub them knights. In short, they do everything real royalty used to do, save despoiling the peasantry—though some despoilery has been known to happen after hours. Sometimes, however, the royalty begins to succumb to the crown disease, where they begin to think they are due the homage paid their role.

Prince Pierce FitzGibbon had a terminal case of it. It was no secret that he'd gotten the role because of his family's business underwriting a chunk of the faire. Nominally he was known as Bonnie Prince Pierce, but we all called him Bunny Prince Pierce because during dress rehearsal someone stuck a cottontail on the back of his doublet and he paraded about proudly with it.

I kept my head bowed and my place in the dust as patrons gathered to watch. "There, my lord?"

"Yes, here, peasant." He pointed at his feet. "Now, peasant, I am waiting."

I kept my voice light and clever, when really what I wanted to say was, "Biteth me, you poxed dog." I curbed my ire and instead intoned sweetly, "I could not, sire, for I am so unworthy, the grass would wither beneath my feet. The greensward, my lord, flourishes in your presence alone, and for me to eclipse it would be a crime unto the most high. For me to even consider it is a sin, Highness, and I feel a fair need to be shriven. I beg leave to find a priest and confess."

I bowed more deeply with a flourish and, God love them, the two women who had seen my fall before laughed and clapped. Others joined them, and Prince Pierce was trapped into waving me away. I don't think he would have, save that an old man in a motorized wheelchair—all bundled up against the cold in a cloak, with a plaid blanket across his knees—weakly clapped palsied hands. Pierce glanced at him, then nodded and waved me away.

I melted through the crowd and quickly found Bloodstone beside me. "Well, Connor?"

"Well what?" I jerked my head toward Pierce, his entourage and the man in the wheelchair trailing them. "That was just Pierce showing off for his grandfather. At least, I think it was Gilbert FitzGibbon in the wheelchair."

"I believe it was, but that's not what I meant."

I sighed and dusted my knee off. "The reading? Okay, it came true, she saw danger in the immediate future which, but for the clapping of those angel-hearted women, would have ended in disaster."

He frowned, and his wizard's hat slipped down a little. "You disappoint me."

I shook my head. "No, you're not getting me there. Yes, she alluded to the Moran family legend, but she didn't have to be a seer to know that. After dress rehearsal, Paul Knight, the guitarist with Alannah, sang that old folk song. He did it to needle both Pierce and me. I didn't see Siany there, but she might have been."

Bloodstone said nothing, though being a folklorist, he knew of the story. In theory, back in the days when the festival village would have seemed shockingly modern and a fair-size metropolis, the Morans

and FitzGibbons had dealings. It was Celt versus
Norman stuff, or so the song would suggest. The
Morans had taken in a baby who turned out to be
an elf changeling of incredible beauty. She enflamed
the heart of a FitzGibbon who planned on taking her
as spoils after he wiped out my family. She went to
him and pledged herself to him forever, as long as
no FitzGibbon spilled Moran blood. The deal was
done and everyone lived happily ever after—or as
close as they get in those dirges. In the third verse
everyone slaughtered everyone else though, somehow, FitzGibbons and Morans survived to breed up
families here in the new world.

He blinked his violet eyes. "I'm even more
disappointed."

"Because I didn't believe her or don't believe the
songs or what?"

"I'm disappointed because you missed the point."

"Which was?"

He sighed, which was to the world of sighs what
Placido Domingo is to the world of tenors. "The tea,
Connor, the *tea*."

"Oh." I licked my lips, then thought for a moment.
"Whole leaf, first flush silver needles, very Darjee-
ling, and brewed just right with minimal
equipment."

His face lit up with a huge smile. "Exactly. Very
good. When you come back tomorrow, you will
bring her some of my Phoenix Eyes. She will know
what to do with them."

I sighed. When in doubt, with Bloodstone, it's always the tea.

My stomach rumbled and I was sorely tempted to
burn my indulgence by suggesting Bloodstone eat a
turkey haunch, but the things are bigger than he is.
However, the crowd was coming out of the joust and

heading toward Falconer's Heath for the birds of prey show. If I took him to see that, he'd lament their not having his namesake there. Instead I ducked backstage with him, skirting the place where they were digging a lake for some Viking naval stuff next year, and around to the CROFT area. We took it slowly and, luckily, didn't run into Pita Hewell, the faire director. If I'd been caught with a patron backstage, there would have been hell to pay.

I smelled Anne's stew before we reentered the grounds. She suppressed a laugh at Merlin's getup, but kindly offered to feed us. Bloodstone, whose reputation as a gourmand has struck fear into the hearts of five-star chefs, ate the stew happily and raved about the saffron bread. Okay, so his rave is to ask for another piece, but the smile on his face told me Anne would be getting a gift of tea, too.

After we ate, we wandered the faire. No one recognized Bloodstone per se, but a lot of tourists did ask if they could take his picture with their kids. I expected him to bristle, but he must have really liked the bread because he posed happily with young children, a rowdy group of high school boys in body paint and kilts, and a few Britney Spears wanna-bes.

I quickly escorted him to the Palace Theater where he sat through one of Don Juan and Miguel's shows. They are a favorite at the faire because they live in Arizona and, more importantly, actually write *new* material, unlike some other national acts. Their blend of sword fighting and comedy, Bloodstone commented between laughs, was a distillation of commedia dell'arte. I nodded as if I knew what he meant, and tried not to laugh too hard at the modern media jokes that just zipped past him. He very much enjoyed the show and even paused on the way back out to see when their next show would be.

On we trooped, slowly making our way about the grounds. My shoulders were beginning to ache and my feet hurt. Worse, my mouth was dry, which meant I needed fluid. Living in a desert, one picks up on those signs of dehydration, so we headed for the King's Kitchen. The quickest way there, it turned out, was across the fortune-teller's green, and I must have been really dry-brained because I didn't even see Prince Pierce until he caught me with a shoulder and smashed me to the ground.

"What the hell?" I started to get back up, but Pierce kicked at my right ankle. I dropped to my hands and knees and caught a skirling hiss that I'd heard quite enough of at the Palace Theater. Even before Bloodstone shouted, "Connor, roll!" I'd dipped my right shoulder and moved aside about two seconds quicker than Pierce's rapier stabbed sod.

I came up in a crouch and filled my hand with the dagger from my boot. A million things ran through my brain, first and foremost being that Pierce had gone nuts because he was coming at me with four feet of steel, looking to open a little tunnel from my front to my back.

He lunged and I retreated, parrying the rapier wide right. I'd fenced for fun in college, so watching him, reading him, wasn't that hard, but weird things were beginning to happen. My focus was narrowing. The world of the faire didn't so much go away as it began to seem normal. Right there, on that swath of ground from the old world, Pierce and I had slipped back into the days of the song. It was Moran against FitzGibbon and, somehow, that didn't seem wrong.

This was complete insanity, as complete as his second lunge, which I also parried. I clung to my twenty-first-century self as tightly as I could, recalling things I'd read about sword fighting. The most dangerous thing about a rapier was not the blade having an edge. Usually, they weren't sharpened at all because a rapier didn't need it. It was pure physics: when you put a man's full weight behind a narrow cross section of steel, sharp or not, it's going to puncture a body.

I smiled as I circled after my third parry. One other thing I knew, which I was pretty sure Pierce didn't, was that there were a lot of different tactics for dealing with a rapier. I needed badly to be inside his guard, and there was an easy way to achieve that. Once inside, I'd be able to do some damage of my own and his channeling of a Singer sewing machine would be at an end.

A little knowledge, as they say, can be a dangerous thing. I had a little. Pierce had less. That made him very dangerous.

I continued to circle, barely aware of the people ringing the green. We came full around, with me sideslipping his feints. Finally, when my back was toward the teahouse, I slowed my motion and Pierce lunged.

I leaned right, letting his blade pass between my body and my left arm. I reached out with my left hand and took hold of his blade, swinging it wide. My right foot came up in a hard kick, really hard. It crushed his codpiece and sent many a man in the audience reeling in sympathy. Pierce fell back, dragging his sword with him and I felt a burning sting in my left hand.

Swordsmen of old might not have sharpened their rapiers, but Pierce had been neither a scholar of swordsmanship nor physics. His sword was sharper than he ever would be. As he dropped to the ground, his razored blade sliced through my gauntlet and twisted, cutting my palm.

Reflexively, my hand tightened into a fist as I dropped to my right knee. Bright red blood oozed through the rent leather. One drop hung there, thickly crimson, then fell to splash on the green grass.

A loud gasp sounded, eclipsing Pierce's moaning at first, but ending in an abrupt whisper. Past the writhing prince, the old man in the wheelchair clutched at his chest. His body shook and his head was thrown back. The hood slipped, revealing a liver-spotted pate with a few white hairs in disarray over it. His lips peeled back in fierce rictus, exposing long yellowed teeth, and his eyes rolled back up into their sockets.

Piece somehow heard his grandfather's gasp and rolled over, crawling to him. I watched him go, both surprised he could move, and then feeling sorry as he placed his face on the plaid blanket covering the man's knees. His shoulders shook and there was no hiding his sobs. So intent on him was I that I barely noticed Lady Siany wrapping a silk scarf around my wounded hand.

After a second or two, the yellow-clad first-aid workers cut through the crowd and reached the wheelchair. One of Pierce's entourage helped him to his feet, and they all wheeled his grandfather away toward the backstage area. Some applause scattered through the crowd, but most people turned away, confused and muttering.

Bloodstone appeared before me and handed me a bowl of lukewarm tea. I sipped, then looked up at him. "What the hell just happened here?"

"What you will believe, Connor, is that both of you were dehydrated and a bit touched by the sun. He succumbed to the monomania that fit his role. Both of you, mindful of the song and the enmity between your families, just lost it. You both work here, not much really happened, and those who watched will remember interesting swordplay and the unfortunate collapse of an old man."

I sipped some more tea. "Yeah, and what will you believe?"

He sank into a crouch that puddled the robe around his feet. His voice, likewise, sank to a whisper, though no one else was close enough to hear. "What I will choose to believe is that the song was true."

"If it was true, I'd not be here. The Morans and FitzGibbons would all be dead."

"That third verse was added much later to the song, to mask the truth of it. The Moran changeling did keep her pledge to her lover and husband, Gilbert FitzGibbon. Siany means health, you know. She kept him alive and healthy for seven centuries."

"And this happened because she decided she wanted to go back to the elflands?"

"No, Connor, it happened because, at the beginning of the twentieth century, his health began to fail."

I snorted. "That doesn't make any sense."

Bloodstone mistook my meaning on purpose. "You believe that disease can become resistant to medicines, but not magics? An inexpertly cast spell could promote resistant diseases, and magicks do require precision. Fast-changing diseases can prove difficult to stop, and in 1918 Gilbert got very ill."

I frowned. "The Spanish flu."

"The very same. Siany's magic saved his life, but could not save his health. Through the twentieth century it deteriorated until his quality of life was worthless. But there is where Siany's promise became a curse, for he could not die until a FitzGibbon shed Moran blood on Irish soil."

"That doesn't make any sense. There are lots of FitzGibbons and Morans. Why me?"

"Magics, especially those worked by the Sidhe, have their own peculiarities. It could be purity of bloodlines, it could be names, it could be anything. Perhaps you are just the Moran who most resembles the Moran she originally made the pledge to save."

I sipped more tea and thought for a moment. I remembered how it felt as we were dueling, how it was insane and yet felt right. It was almost as if I had been there before—a sense of *déjà vu* I couldn't shake. "And you think Pierce most resembled Gilbert in his youth?"

"Quite possibly."

I nodded, then looked him square in the eye. "You know I'm going with heatstroke on this, right?"

"Of course, Connor."

"Believing what you believe, you didn't set me up for this, did you?"

"Had I known, I would have warned you, and certainly never brought you to this piece of earth. You have my solemn oath."

I accepted that, which isn't quite the same as believing it. Had the FitzGibbons come to him and explained things, he would have found a way for me to shed blood. Part of my mind begin to wander, wondering what Machiavellian scheme he would have concocted to get me bled, but a shrill voice demanded immediate attention.

"There you are!" A slender, dark-haired woman with a radio on her hip and a clipboard in her right hand, stood over me. "You are in serious trouble."

"Yeah? You want a pound of flesh, you can get it here." I flashed her my left hand, with the white silk—a portion of which was nicely red—wrapping my fist. Pita was the faire director, and Pita wasn't really her first name. I didn't even know what it was, we all just called her that because it was faster than saying "pain in the ass."

My boss rose and smiled at her. "I think you will find, Ms. Hewell, there is less difficulty here than you imagine." Bloodstone used the same calming tone he did when explaining to a skeletal supermodel that getting on the outside of a cheeseburger did not make her look like a python that had swallowed a yak. "Mr. FitzGibbon's family will press no charges, and since both Pierce and Conner are faire employees, no member of the public has been involved.

"Moreover," he said as he reached for my left hand, "I think you will see that very little damage was done." He untied the silk and stripped off my glove. "Unguents and gauze will suffice."

I flexed my hand, then looked at it. There was blood there, but only a few abrasions. My hand didn't quite feel like the ground chuck it had before . . . *Before Siany touched it.*

No, I flatly refused to go there.

Pita's nostril's flared. "That may be, but I have other problems. Where is Lady Siany?"

Bloodstone smiled. "I believe she has gone home." He meant home in a whole otherworldly way than Pita heard it.

"Great. A fight, a death and now I have no fortune-teller."

I smiled slowly as I stood. "Sure you do."

"Who, you?" Pita laughed. "You don't even make a passable peasant."

"Nope, not me." I turned to Bloodstone. "Indulge me."

"Connor, don't be absurd!"

I'd have lost the battle right there, but Pita looked down her nose at him. "Him, tell fortunes, please . . ."

Bloodstone's chin came up. "I am not unacquainted with the prophetic arts, Ms. Hewell. If you are to join me within, I will brew you a cup of fortune."

I smiled as she preceded him into the cottage, not caring to be the recipient of her fortune. I started off for CROFT, but Bloodstone cleared his voice.

"Just a moment, Connor. You have an errand to run. Have Chuck drive you in the limousine."

"I know, I know." I held up my hands. "Phoenix Eyes."

With him, it is always about the tea.

# MARRIAGE Á LA MODRED

## by

### *Esther M. Friesner*

Esther M. Friesner is the Nebula-Award-winning author of thirty novels and over one hundred stories. She is also the editor and creator of the popular *Chicks in Chainmail* anthology series. Her most recent publication is *Death and the Librarian and Other Stories*. She lives in Connecticut with her husband, son, daughter, two cats, and no groundhogs.

EVERYONE AGREED THAT THE GUY dressed up like Friar Tuck was a hoot and a half, especially when he spouted *thee* and *thou* and *forsooth*, *yea*, *verily* like they were going out of style (whither they had already gone, yea, verily, centuries before this). That's what they'd come to the Rowantree Ren Faire for, right? A little of the old M'lord/M'lady/M'chicken/M'whatever. At these prices, you darn well bet that there was going to be a whole lot of enforced picturesqueness, to say nothing of photo ops, or the paying customers would know the reason why. No dragon out of legend was half so ugly as a tourist who suspects he's not getting value for money.

So that was why everyone in the Barre family

party thought it was absolutely, utterly, completely fall-down-and-wet-yourself hilarious when Friar Tuck lurched into their midst, laid hands on sixteen-year-old Bethany Barre, and dragged her forth to stand beside him beneath the shelter of an ancient oak tree. His voice rang out from one end of the faire to the other, declaiming for all the world to hear that it was high time that so likely a wench as this were married.

"Forsooth, I trow it be vile shame that such a love-some chuck remain a maiden in her father's house a moment more!" he bellowed.

A grinning crowd began to gather in the oaks' delectable shade. This was going to be good. For one thing, it was good that one of *them* was not involved. Most red-blooded Americans agreed that living theater was wonderful stuff so long as some other poor *zhlub* was the one having to live through it. (Discounting, of course, such social triumphs as being on *Survivor* or the *Jerry Springer Show*.)

In the midst of spectacle-hungry savages, Bethany cringed and wished she'd never decided to attend Rowantree Ren Faire in costume. She loved the graceful medieval style of dress, but when you were the only one in the immediate vicinity wearing it, it had the same effect on the hired role-players as rubbing yourself all over with raw liver before diving into the shark pool.

"Maiden . . ." Bethany's older brother Vic sniggered, safely removed from the center of attention. "Yeah, sure, *riiiight*." His skepticism as to his sister's purity earned him a slap in the back of the head from his girlfriend Dakota. "Hey! What'd *I* do?" he demanded, rubbing the sore spot.

"Shut up, Vic," she whispered. "You want your dad to hear you say shit like that?"

"Aw, hell, baby, it's not like it's true or anything.

Who'd want to do *her?*" It was the best Vic could come up with by way of gallantry toward his sister.

"Like that'd matter to your dad? He'll give you another one of his lectures even if it means we miss the whole show this guy's putting on with Beth, and *then* he'll give you hell for making him miss the chance to take pictures. You *ever* want to borrow his car again?"

"Oh. Yeah. 'Kay." Vic shrugged and clammed up good. Dakota had a point, and a pretty savvy one at that. He got that, and he hated her for it.

Vic wasn't very bright, but he recognized intelligence in others. It pissed the hell out of him. Girl-smarts were a lot harder to deal with than guy-smarts, because when it was uppity *womenfolk* making him look bad, he couldn't even lure the she-geeks under the bleachers and beat some *real* smarts into them like he did with the male nerds and dweebs at school. And his sister's kind of smarts was the worst because she was a whole two years younger than he and only one class behind him at school (as Mom and Dad never seemed to tire of reminding him). If he screwed up his grades one more time, they'd be graduating together, if he managed to graduate at all. That was why Vic viewed it as a gross betrayal of trust and love that Dakota had been harboring unsuspected brainpower, and he resolved to break up with her as soon as they escaped from this day of family-fun-or-else.

Meanwhile, that Friar Schmuck dude was doing a pretty good job of humiliating little sister Bethany, so at least the day wasn't a total loss. If Vic was Dad's personal prototype of the Total Screwup, Version 9.0, Bethany was the old man's shining star, a true and irreproachable example of earthly perfection in all things. It mattered not at all that Bethany hated the way that Dad praised her and peppered his every lecture to Vic with reminders that *Bethany* wouldn't do anything that stupid, *Bethany* would never act so foolishly, *Bethany* wouldn't even *think* of putting peanut butter on the cat: He still resented his sister with a passion.

It helped a *little* bit that Bethany was deeply embarrassed by any and all unavoidable trips into the spotlight, including Dad's praise fests. When she won the science fair or the declamation contest or the poetry prize (and she did, repeatedly), she looked ready to shrivel up and die. Right now, in the clutches of the *faux* friar, she was probably squirming inside.

Cool. Vic jammed his hands in his jeans pockets and took in the performance.

As for Bethany herself, she had come to the conclusion often reached by women far older than she that there was never a convenient death around when you wanted one.

"Ah, sweet maiden!" Friar Tuck proclaimed loudly enough to knock leaves from the overhanging branches. "How is't that one so beauteous as thy comely self not be yet trothpledged to some likely lad?"

"Um . . ." Bethany shrugged, causing the loose elastic of her neckline to give way, baring her shoulders. She wore a borrowed dress, on loan from one of her school chums who had opted for the Tao of Goth as a way to cope with being outcast. Valerie was what diplomatic souls called a *healthy* girl, but in another triumph of wishful thinking over fact Bethany had imagined the surplus yards of three-sizes-too-big garnet satin would drape, not droop. She was wrong.

"Ahhh." The friar's eyes widened in appreciation as he ogled her bare shoulders brazenly. It was all part of the show. "Methinks the wench showeth herself eager to be wed! Come, lads, who'll step forth to claim so tasty a prize? No need to talk of dowry when delights such as these await a man!"

No one in the crowd stirred. Small wonder: Everyone wanted to be on the shutter-snapping end of their cameras when the mock marriage actually took place.

Bethany took note of this and dared to relax a bit, albeit slowly. Clearly none of the eager mob had figured out that unless someone stepped forth to take her hand in mock marriage, there wouldn't *be* any mock marriage (which would be just fine as far as Bethany was concerned, thank you). She was just about to *ad lib* some twaddle about having decided to go into a convent instead, right before she made her getaway, when Fate raised its ugly head.

"Tchah!" cried the friar. "Fie! *There* you are, my fine young buck, playing the blushing bridegroom whilst thy modesty makes thy winsome wife-to-be grow old and gray, waiting for you." And with that, he plunged into the depths of the crowd beneath the oak tree—dragging a helpless Bethany behind him— and seized a fresh victim.

"Whoa!" Vic crowed when he got a good look at the youth whom the friar had drafted. "*Major* geek alert. *Serious* swirlie candidate here."

To his chagrin, Dakota did not immediately agree with him as to the newcomer's candidacy for a "swirlie"—that quaint and arcane adolescent custom of laying hold of one's social inferior and forcibly dunking his head into a flushing toilet bowl. Rather, she raised an eyebrow and allowed a small, speculative smile to play across her lips as she said, "Oh, I dunno, Vic. He's kinda cute. You know, in a hobbity kinda way."

Vic steamed at the remark. Ever since those dumb-ass movies had come out, all of a sudden it was *cool* to admit you liked all that quests-elves-dragons crap. Strike two for Dakota.

Come to think of it, strike three. Vic reasoned that if you're going to decide that a geekazoid is "cute," you damn well better cough up a justification that makes some freakin' sense. There was nothing at all "hobbity" about Beth's press-ganged groom-to-be. He was too tall, too thin, too pale, and he looked as if he couldn't find *jolly* in a *Nuthin'-But-J* edition of the dictionary. Maybe he was concealing a set of hairy feet inside those pointy-toed shoes of his, but Vic was willing to bet that this guy's toes were as smooth and hairless as his sharp-featured face. Sure, the dweeb had a full-to-overflowing head of hair that went all the way down to his narrow little butt, but it looked as milky and frail as the rest of him, a blond so light it was nearly silver.

"Freakin' albino hippie," Vic muttered.

Dakota smacked him in the arm. "Shut up, Vic. You'll hurt his feelings."

Oh, yeah, *that* was it, *that* did it: Strike three and then some. Vic scowled. His mind was made up: Dakota was about to become the newest resident of Dump City. Now there remained only the question of when to give her the tragic news.

Shutters were clicking, videotape cassettes were whirring, people who'd brought their brand new, as-yet-untried digital cameras to the Rowantree Ren Faire were cursing fluently as Friar Tuck, exuding joviality and sweat from every pore, attempted to pronounce Bethany and her pickup spouse husband and wife.

The key word here being *attempted*.

"Do you, good Sir . . . er . . . what did you say

your name was, lad?" he asked, gazing up into the
unknown youth's blazing green eyes.

"I did not say," came the chill reply. "Nay, nor
will I, lest my foes grow wise therefrom and use that
knowledge to work dark sorceries upon me, to my
detriment and death."

"Oh." Friar Tuck was nonplussed, though he did
his best to recover. "Fie, fie, my proud young sir,
none mean you harm nor hurt in this merry com-
pany! Cans't not see that we are all friends here,
seeking only to celebrate thy nuptials with this
sweet maiden?"

The nameless one glared at him so fiercely that the
good friar stumbled backward, almost as if he'd been
shoved by an invisible hand. "I say thee nay! Fair
words oft hide false heart. 'Tis true, the lass is passing comely, and has about her the look of one brisk
in bed." (Most of the spectators laughed loudly at
this, though those standing closest to Bethany's father took one look at his face and turned their bawdy
guffaws into coughing fits.) "And yet—" he went on,
oblivious to the crowd. "And yet, by my bond and
powers, she is a prize worthy to couple with one of
my highborn house, at least while her beauty lasts.
I've bedded worse."

"Ooooooookaaaaayyy . . ." In the face of a tourist
who had an even better grasp of Fluent Sher-
woodspeak than himself, Friar Tuck let slip his own
"forsoothly" diction and backslid all the way down
to his New Jersey roots. "Yeah, uh, hey, buddy,
maybe you oughta watch what you're saying about
the lady, huh?"

He shot the lad a cautionary look and nodded
toward the crowd. Bethany's father had murder in
his eyes and was attempting to fight his way to the
fore in order to teach this lout a more mannerly way

to speak of his little girl. Bethany's mother was doing her best to drag him back, nervously trying to persuade him that this was all part of the show, let it go, relax, don't worry, take pictures.

Vic was laughing so hard he thought he was going to rupture something. "Oh, wow, that fat-ass jerk in the brown bathrobe is *so* screwed!" he crowed, pointing at Friar Tuck. "Poor bastard snagged a real nutcase out of the crowd. Betcha he'd give a billion bucks if he could go back and pick someone else."

"No, he wouldn't," Dakota said calmly. "The reason he picked Nutcase in the first place was because he's in costume, just like your sister. It's all about the photo ops. The role players like Tuck and the hired wizards and wenches and the whole forsoothverily squadron get trained to home in on visitors who show up wearing garb. Single 'em out, make a big fuss over them, and they'll be back next year, guaranteed. Hey, maybe even next weekend! And it works for the visitors who don't dress up funny, too. They get to take lots of pretty pictures so that when they go home they can pretend they've just been visiting a fairy tale."

"You're not getting me into a fruity outfit like that," Vic snapped at her.

"No way," Dakota agreed. "You don't have the legs for it. Nice costume, though. I wonder how he can wear all that velvet and still look so cool on a day like this?"

"Dumbass looks like a freakin' sofa," Vic muttered, eyeing Sir Nutcase's sky-blue doublet and hose with a hostility born of pure envy.

While Vic seethed, the goodly friar was doing his level best to get the mock marriage all wrapped up. The sooner it was done, the sooner he could escape the uncanny gaze of this weirdo. In desperation he turned to Bethany.

"Do you, m'lady . . . insert name here? *Please?*"

"Bethany Barre." Having concluded that there was no way out of this save seeing it through to the end, Bethany offered no resistance. Her lack of any save the most flimsy of backbones was partly the reason why she did so well in school. Teachers worn down by tussles with Beth's less tractable peers often gave the capital-G Good Girl an A minus rather than a B plus out of sheer, exhausted gratitude.

"*Thank* you." The friar patted Beth's hand and placed it forcibly in that of the groom-to-be. "Do you, m'lady Bethany of Barre, take this, Sir . . ." He cast one last pleading look at the nameless youth.

"Call me Robin-o'-Greenwood, if call me by some name you must," came the rather cranky answer.

"*What*ever." The friar no longer cared whether or not he'd get dinged by his supervisor for letting echoes of Newark pop up in his speech like the animatronic stars of a Whack-a-Mole game. "Thus do I pronounce ye, lady Bethany of Barre and Sir Robin-o'-Greenwood, most rightly trothed, and thereto I bid ye present some token of espousal for all these good folk foregathered to see."

The so-called Sir Robin frowned. "A token? I only meant to bed her." (Bethany's father snarled like a Rottweiler and was shushed again by his wife.) "But by the exchange of mortal goods we would be troth-plight truly!"

"Ummmm . . . Uh-huh." The friar looked like a bobble-head doll. Lowering his voice, he murmured in Sir Robin's ear, "See, this is perfect. You don't have a ring to give her, she doesn't have a ring to give you, I pronounce it a trial marriage until such

time as one of you coughs up the jewelry, and you're
free to hit Ye Olde Foode Courte and buy yourself a
turkey leg or something. Get it?"

"Got it."

"Good." The friar beamed, and to the crowd de-
creed: "Sir Robin begs your kind indulgence, but he
finds himself without any worthy token of his troth.
M'lady Bethany, have *you* any spousal gift to give
this man, thereby to seal your pact?"

Bethany shook her head and managed a small
smile. She was smart enough to see where this was
going. She could almost taste her impending
freedom.

"Your pardon, good friar," she said, curtsying
prettily. (What the hell, she was about to be released
from this uncomfortable little piece of living theater:
she could afford to play it up just a tad.) "I greatly
dread that I have nothing worthy of my new lord."

"Is't so?" The friar folded his hands over his belly
and clucked his tongue, overacting his disappointment mightily. "An it so be, I must declare that this
trothplight be null and void, for a marriage may not
take place if neither of you can provide some proof
of worldly substance."

Bethany smiled and looked very pretty and very
helpless. Her peculiar groom raised one silvery eyebrow and shrugged. The crowd that had gathered
began to disperse, sensing that the comedy was almost over and willing to forgo the last few moments
in order to get a better place in line at the smoked
turkey leg booth. The friar raised his hands to admin-
ister the final blessing before sending everyone on
their way, when without warning:

"Whoa! You mean you're gonna let this dude leave
my little sister at the altar?" Vic swaggered forward
until he stood face-to-face with the friar. "I don't

*think* so. You want at least one of them to lay down something solid, like, you know, a down payment to show they mean business, right?"

"Uh . . . yes." Friar Tuck was starting to get that *Where the* hell *are my security people?* look in his eyes. "A symbolic gift must be made—a ring's the customary choice—to prove that they've the wherewithal to . . ."

"Blah, blah, blah." Vic mimed a rapidly, vapidly quacking duck's head with his right hand, then turned his back on the friar and confronted his sister's peculiar groom. "Don't anybody ever say I never did nothing to take care of my little sister." He punctuated that mare's nest of a sentence by yanking a ring off his own left hand and jamming it onto one of the so-called Sir Robin's preternaturally long, white fingers. The surprised recipient of this abrupt bounty stared at the dark gray circlet, eyes growing wider by the second.

"Vic, you son-of-a-bitch, did you just give him my promise ring?" Dakota hollered. "I got that made especially for you at the blacksmith shop when my parents took me on that stupid trip to Colonial Williamsburg! That's a *real* horseshoe nail, you prick! What's the big idea, giving it away like that?"

"What do *you* think?" an unrepentant Vic hollered back, smirking. If he'd planned it, he couldn't have come up with a better way to tell his former girlfriend that it wasn't her, it was him, he needed more space, maybe they should both try seeing other people, et cetera. "It's *over*."

"Yeah, well, *good!* Because you *suck!*" Dakota stamped her foot and sputtered a few more generic insults at her faithless beau. Vic's mom looked embarrassed and made a few well-meaning attempts at trying to put a comforting arm around the jilted girl before deciding it might not be the best idea. Dakota looked mad enough to start biting people, and given the sort of girl Vic usually dated, that wasn't just a figure of speech.

The crowd that had been in the process of dispersing began to reconvene. A real breakup—especially an ugly one—offered even more viewing pleasure than a mock marriage.

"Talk to the hand, baby! The one *without* your stupid ring!" Vic laughed. His parents, mortified beyond belief, exchanged a long-suffering look and silently agreed to salvage the sane portion of their family.

"Come along, Bethany, there's nothing more for you to do here." Mr. Barre beckoned to his daughter. "I got plenty of pictures; let's go get some lunch."

"Yes, Daddy," Bethany said, and moved to join him.

At least it was her *intention* to move. She didn't. She couldn't. A look of pure panic flooded her face as she realized that she had no power to stir from her place beneath the oak, and when she lifted her skirt to investigate the matter, she screamed to see that her feet had vanished. In their stead, the gnarled and quaintly graceful roots of a young sapling wrapped her shins and ran deep into the earth.

Her scream was not the only one. Those members of the crowd close enough to see her astonishing transformation screamed as well, and those who had no view of it at all screamed out of the lopsided, lemminglike logic that possesses all mobs, viz: It seemed like a good idea at the time.

Though the organizers of Rowantree Ren Faire had enjoined their clerical role players from making any mention of the Christian deity (no sense in alienating cash-paying unbelievers), Friar Tuck took one look at

Bethany's roots and yelled, "Jesus H. Christ!" before taking to his heels.

It was the cue for a general stampede, though Bethany's immediate family stood firm. To be honest, they had little choice: her mother had fainted and her father was pinned to the ground, cradling his wife's slack body. (Mrs. Barre was also a very healthy figure of a woman.)

As for Vic, he stood there gaping slack-jawed at his sister and her ersatz groom. Well might he gape: A crackling nimbus of green-gold light had fallen over Sir Robin like a cloak, waves of arcane energy shifting and crawling across every inch of his body. The fiery light burned away all illusion: Eyes shifted into the shape of birch leaves, grew larger, more luminous; ears took on an outline more proper to fox or wolf than human; pale skin grew paler still, and the bones beneath the face looked keen enough to slice steel like steak. A dagger with a sapphire-topped hilt bloomed at his belt, hidden until now by the same glamour which had made the youth seem human. Pulsations of power rippled out to build a small fortress of concealment and exclusion around the oak and those few people still nearby, though these now numbered only Bethany's blood kin. It was a shielding spell proof against any outward assault, should Friar Tuck return with those pesky security people.

Only when his spell weaving was done did the creature open his long, thin-lipped mouth to speak. Every word resonated with the burden of immortal age.

"Behold, we are plighted by a ring forged of iron, that metal which of all others has power to bind my people to obedience!" He seized Bethany's trembling hands in his own and pressed them to his heart. "Beloved, come! Come away with me now to those sweet, deathless lands beneath the earth where my people dwell in endless song and bliss. Already has my kingdom opened to greet its new-made queen!"

He nodded gracefully toward the oak and the great trunk split itself in two, but instead of the sound of ravaged heartwood, a cry of flutes, drums, and trumpets burst from the sundered tree. Bethany's face was washed in a flood of verdant light that faded only to reveal the wonders that lay beyond the miraculous portal.

"Your . . . queen?" she whispered. Her eyes shone.

"Aye, sweeting." Her transformed bridegroom smiled. "As we are bound to one another irrevocably, it behooves me well to share my woodland throne with you in the true realms, lest my subjects murmur that I've shown little judgment in bringing home a human. Indeed, they've chided me ere this for my ill-reded practice of visiting the mortal realm. I confess, they were right: Had I let you flimsy creatures go your own ways, I had not have been captured by yon false friar, nor had I been brought to such a wretched fate as this."

" 'Such a *wretched* fate'?" she repeated. She had the look of someone awakened from beautiful dreams by being smacked across the face with a mackerel. "Do you mean *me?*"

"None other, my delight." He patted her on the head like a useful dog.

"So you're not taking me with you and making me your queen because you *want* to?"

He laughed. "Why would I *want* to? You are a pretty thing, but you're less than a child to me. I'd have bedded you gladly and gone my ways, yet since this token was forced upon my person—" He made a small, deprecating gesture with the iron ring. "—I make the best of a bad bargain. If I make you my queen, my subjects will presume you are a mortal of great standing and hidden powers, perchance e'en one so great as dread Morgan le Fay. They'll not dare mock me for my misfortune, even in whispers."

Now Bethany's eyes were shining again, but not with joy. Angry tears streamed down her cheeks. "Is that all you care about? That your stupid, pointy-eared subjects are going to gossip about what a moron you were, getting snared into marriage with a mortal?"

Large, beautiful, cold eyes blinked at her in amazement. "What else should matter to me?" he asked, honestly bewildered by her question.

"Well, I can save you a lot of trouble and . . . and *embarrassment*." Bethany's voice broke on a sob. "I free you from your bond! I—I'm taking back the ring! The engagement—the wedding—whatever the hell you want to call this hideous nightmare, is off!"

"I beg your pardon?"

Bethany grabbed the elf by the front of his doublet, yanked him toward her so that they were eye-to-eye, and yelled at the top of her lungs: "*Welcome to Dump City, asshole!*"

Vic applauded, the only conscious witness to Bethany's uncharacteristic attack of assertiveness. (Mom was still sunk in a faint and, when he heard his precious baby girl utter the A-word, Dad swooned as well.)

The elf-lord's pale face darkened. "Girl, you forget yourself. I offer you courtesy and you return ingratitude? Fie! It is not for you to break our bond, even had you the power to do so. I, Eamon Oak-lord, have already set my mark upon you."

He drew his dagger and with one slash of the silvery blade tore away the skirts of Bethany's gown, revealing the progress of the woodsy transformation his magic had wrought. Bark had climbed almost the entire way up her thighs. Mushrooms were springing up from between the roots where her toes had been, and moss bloomed on the north side of her calves.

Bethany stared down at what had become of her legs, then glared at the elf and, without warning, smacked him hard across the face. "You *tool!*" she cried. "I *borrowed* this dress!"

Vic cheered.

The elf-lord was at first too startled by the mortal girl's audacity to do more than cup his stricken cheek and stare. Too soon, though, he recovered, the dagger still in hand. He seized Bethany's chin and brought the dagger's point to her neck with a calmness that was more frightening than any show of rage.

"Perhaps you do not understand, child," he said softly. "This ring makes you as much mine as I am yours. By the laws of my realm, this means that you're my chattel, being a mere female. Your fate's not yours to decide; I may do with you as I will. I trow you'll find it wiser to court my pleasure rather than my discontent. Do you see?"

Shuddering, Bethany managed a tiny nod, dreading the dagger. Her sign of terrified compliance made the elf-lord smile. He replaced the blade at his belt, then traced a pattern on the air with one hand. The bark receded from Bethany's shins; her feet emerged from their prison of roots. The elf-lord bowed and offered his arm, beaming at her as if he were her most devoted suitor rather than the brute who had just browbeaten her to his will.

"Shall we go, m'lady? Your kingdom awaits."

"I don't *think* so."

The glimmering gateway in the oaks' heart was

blocked by the figure of a tall, beefy knight in Tommy Hilfiger armor. Vic Barre folded his arms and gave the elf-lord a hard look. "No means no, dickhead. Now let my sister go."

"You . . . dare?" The elf snarled like a wolf. His hand strayed back toward his dagger.

Vic was paying attention, for once. His own hand shot out, only in this case it was a fist and it was aimed right for his opponent's nose. The elf went flying heels over head out of the oak tree's shadow. Vic was on him almost before he landed, so that by the time he drew his next breath through a bleeding nose his prized dagger was twinkling in the mortal man's hand.

"Nice blade, man," Vic said, flicking it back and forth. "Kinda old-fashioned for my taste, but hey, that's your whole story, isn't it? I mean, where else do you get this retro shit about females being property? Dude, you keep talking like that, people are going to think you're a Republican and then you'll *never* get laid!"

"Mortal cur, do you defy me? Do you want to die?" The elf was on his feet, wiping blood from his nose. "I need not that toy to destroy you. I have the power of my magic!" He raised his hands, the palms sizzling with blue fire. "By the ring she gave me, I will have my bride!"

"Whatever, Eamon," said Vic. And he threw himself upon the elf-lord and planted a huge, wet, no-holds-barred, no-boundaries-respected kiss full on the mouth.

The blue fires of destruction that had been building in the elf's hands exploded into showers of confetti and pink ducklings. Vic broke the liplock, brushed some paper flakes out of his hair, removed a few infant waterfowl from his shoulders, and then said: "And that's just a sample. Wait until the honeymoon."

"Wha— wha— wha— wha—?" Not even the most beautiful elf had the power to stammer gracefully. "*What* did you say?"

"I said that it's *my* ring, not Beth's, asshole, so if that's what says who you gotta marry, it's gotta be me."

"Yes, but— but I— but I didn't mean—" The elf took a deep, centering breath and tried again. "What I *meant* to say was: What did you call me just then?"

"Asshole?"

"No, no, before that. Just before we—we—" The elf-lord wiped his mouth vigorously on the back of his hand. "Just before we *you-know-what*. You called me by—" He dropped his voice to a barely audible whisper. "—*my name!*"

"Yeah?" Vic shrugged. "It's Eamon, right? What's 'a matter, I pronounced it wrong or something?"

"You uttered it again!" the elf wailed, falling to his knees. "Freely and openly, where anyone might hear! Names are powerful, names command! O dread mortal sorcerer, how came you to be vouchsafed the one article of arcane knowledge which gives you sovereignty over me?"

"You told him, moron," Bethany said. "You told everyone within earshot. Right before you ruined Valerie's dress, when you were bullying me, you said it out loud. You were all 'Yadda-yadda-yadda, *I, Eamon Oak-lord*, yadda-yadda-yadda.' Remember?"

"I did?" The elf thought back, then blushed, recalling his momentary indiscretion. "Oh, *shite.*"

"So okay, E, what's it gonna be?" Vic demanded. "Way I see it, you're in a lose-lose situation with my little sister. She's got you by the short hairs, or whatever the hell you elfs got going on in that department. She knows your name; she *owns* you, dog. Way I see it, your best way out is a, whatchacallit, amicable divorce."

"Well would I, fair sir, if only it were possible." Eamon Oak-lord sighed. "But the power of the iron ring binds me beyond my will to sever that bond."

"No biggie, dude." Gracious in victory, Vic patted the elf on the back and gave him a pack of tissues for his nose. "Beth's still free. It's my ring, like I toldja, so if you're married to anyone—"

The elf raised tearful, pleading eyes to Vic. "But m'lord, I— I swingeth not that way," he protested.

"Me neither, but I had to do something, y'know? I mean, you were coming down pretty hard on Beth'. I can't let you do that to my baby sister. That'd totally bite."

"Why, Vic, that was so . . . *noble* of you!" Bethany exclaimed.

Vic blushed. "Aw, forget it."

"No, I mean it," she insisted. "You were wonderful: Heroic; chivalrous; *totally* cool!"

A sheepish grin lit up Vic's face as he forced himself to admit: "Yeah, I guess I was. And y'know . . . it felt good." He shrugged off this epiphany and hastily switched his attention back to Eamon. "So look, even if there's nothing you can do to get us unbound, don't sweat it. I mean, it's all my fault for sticking you with that iron ring, right? So I'll deal. It's just a marriage on paper, or whatever the hell you elf-guys use. I don't care if I'm Mrs. Oak-lord from now till forever, but listen up: It's gotta be an open marriage and I'm staying on *this* side of the freakin' tree, 'kay?"

"Nay." Again the elf sighed fit to break the heart of any who might hear. "There's more to our bond than words alone, alas, for spells that are sealed by cold iron's touch last for the human spouse's life span. It matters not if we dwell apart, nor if you come to wed one of your own kind, for we elves set little store by mortal chastity."

"Swingers, huh? So what's the prob'? It all sounds cool to me," said Vic.

Eamon gave him a mournful look. "Not so, for unless some affection—however small—link us all that while, the bond-spell's barren, and that barrenness will taint my lands and yours. Behold! Already it begins!"

He gestured at the ancient oak. The gateway dimmed and closed, but that was not the sum of the changes in the tree. As Vic and Bethany watched, the leaves began to lose their healthy green, to turn first brown, then black as they shriveled on the branch. Acorns ripened only to rot and fall to the ground, exploding like stinkbombs. A squirrel scampered down the trunk and threw up on Vic's shoes.

"Eeeeuuuuwww!" cried Bethany. "Nasty."

"Tell me about it," Vic agreed. "You can't get squirrel puke off Reeboks."

"There's worse to come," Eamon said morosely. "The blight will spread. All this fair land above is linked to the kingdoms below."

"You mean here? The fairgrounds?" Bethany was aghast. "But this is part of a forest preserve! The long-term ecological effects could be disastrous."

Vic frowned at his sister. "You saying that Smokey the Bear's gonna be pissed unless I french this elf *again?* No way."

"'I' very faith, no way." The elf was on his feet again, cupping his mouth protectively. "Not even though my kingdom fall, ne'er to rise in beauty more."

Bethany rolled her eyes. "You guys are *such* 'phobes. You mean if one teensy little kiss would save his kingdom and this forest, you couldn't just close your eyes and *pretend* you were kissing a girl!"

"Hey! *No means no!*"

Eamon and Vic stared at one another. Had that sentiment truly come from both of them at one and the same time? They blinked at the realization that yes, it had. They high-fived enthusiastically.

Above their heads, the oak tree put out fresh green leaves. At their feet, a still-queasy squirrel scampered off in search of a good mouthwash.

Bethany saw it all and smiled. "Good news, boys: Apparently the bond-spell's willing to recognize more than one kind of affection."

Eamon looked puzzled, but for once it was Bethany's brother who caught on. He threw one arm around the elf-lord's shoulders and said, "Dude, I got it! She means we don't have to get all *Will and Grace* to keep things green; it's cool if we're just good buds."

" 'Buds'?" the elf repeated nervously. He checked his fingertips for any burgeoning sprouts.

Bethany gave him a comforting pat on the back. "He means *friends*."

Eamon still looked doubtful. "Our amity is but newly fledged and brief. How may we cause it to endure? I have small knowledge of what mortal friendship means. Bedding with mortals, yes; budding with mortals, no."

"oh, you know, the usual," Bethany said, ticking off items on her fingers. "Hanging out together, influencing one another, sharing common interests—"

Eamon Oak-lord looked troubled in his mind. "We elves are of an ancient, haughty race. What common interests might we ever have with mere mortals? Indeed, we have been called cruel nigh as many times as we've been named noble, for humans find themselves unable to fathom our motivations in many things."

Bethany laughed. "Eamon, you and Vic were meant to be. You just described what most people say about teens."

Hereat the elf looked totally flummoxed, but Vic reassured him: "Trust me."

"As if I have a choice," said Eamon, resigned.

\* \* \*

"Back off, Loomis," Vic said, confronting the worst bully, bar none, in all Kirkland High.

Robert Loomis, two hundred and thirty pounds of unfocused aggression and ignorance, looked up from the quivering body of yet another hapless victim whom he'd backed into one of the Boys' Room stalls and bared his yellow teeth.

"So it's true," he said. "I heard you was turning into a real nerd rescue hero, but I didn't believe it."

Vic smiled back, unafraid. " 'Cause it's noble. Ah, hell, who'm I kidding? It's really 'cause I got bored. Anyone can give a nerd a swirlie. This is more of a challenge."

"Well, let's see how noble you look after I slam your face into the wall, asshole." Loomis started for Vic, only pausing long enough to glance at the trembling freshman trapped in the stall and say: "You better stay there, unless you want what I'm gonna give him." He turned and leaped for his prey—

—and froze in mid-pounce, spun around twenty times, and executed a perfect dive headfirst into the toilet bowl, which began to flush with abandon. His jeans vanished, revealing a set of tighty-whities whose rear waistband was soon yanked painfully high in the great-granddaddy of all Atomic Wedgies. His intended victim stared, then skedaddled and never looked back, though he did mutter a hasty thank you to Vic as he sped past.

"And there's more where that came from, Looms," Vic announced. "Unless you swear you're gonna lay off the nerds from now on, 'kay?"

Loomis gurgled a reply. The toilet flushed again.

Vic shook his head. "C'mon, E-man, ease up. You *know* it's no good if I can't hear him promise. I can't lay the binding spell on him if I don't get his word of honor."

Eamon Oak-lord, glorious in the full regalia of a rapper-wanna-be, materialized atop the toilet tank. "Thou hast become a noble champion of the helpless, a true defender of the right, and a cherished friend, m'lord Vic; 'tis well. But forsooth, yea, verily, thou never doth let me have any fun."

# A DANCE OF SEVEN VALES

## *by*
## *Rose Wolf*

Rose Wolf holds a Ph.D in fantasy and science fiction. She
has published a collection of poems and several short stories, of which "A Dance of Seven Vales" is her fourth.
She admits that the main character in this tale—teacher
of speculative literature, belly dancer, and former wife of
a Ren Faire wizard—is "authorbiographical." However,
she attributes the Wiccan elements in the story to her
friend Sharon Smith, who maintains that Rose converted
her to the Old[est]-Time Religion. Rose's response is to
dedicate the "Vale Tale" to Sharon and to invite other
readers into its world with the words of George Meredith:
"Enter these enchanted woods/You who dare."

THE JESTER PASSED BY, SINGING, and from
where she sat in her tent Arabis the belly dancer
heard him. Drawn, as she always was, to the sound
of any music, but especially that of the Renaissance,
the woman rose to her feet. Setting aside the finger-
cymbal she'd been adjusting, Arabis pushed open the
back tent flap and blinked. A curious procession was
making its way down the tree-lined aisle that ran
parallel to the main route of the faire. The dancer

shaded her eyes with a henna-reddened hand, wondering whether her sight was playing her false in the bright summer sun. But she knew that the eclectic mix of races now making its way toward the great oak was no more than to be expected. Why, some of the creatures making up the fool's tail of honor were not even human; but Arabis, whose everyday avatar was that of Shirley Webster, professor of fantasy literature, was merely intrigued by this.

Hugh Ambrose the jester, resplendent in satin motley, led the ragtag band, dancing backward and conducting himself with his mock scepter as he caroled Shakespeare's "Under the Greenwood Tree." He was followed by a group of men and women in period costume, representing a cross section of classes from the high to the low; normal-enough visitors to the lawn of Castle Glenn at this time of year.

Next, however, came a plump fairy, who resembled a large soap bubble when the sun struck her iridescent costume, and after her an ogre wearing a sinister garland of shrunken heads about his thick neck. Bringing up the rear was a small personage in a brocade waistcoat and short trousers, carrying a walking staff and making his way barefoot through the grass. Barefoot? Well, perhaps on the soles, but this little wayfarer sported an impressive crop of hair on the tops of his feet. A hobbit, then.

Arabis smiled. For a while, as she knew from having been briefly married to the resident wizard of the Glenn Ren Faire, the admission of beings from fantasy literature to such festivals had been opposed by period purists—sometimes hotly. In the end, though, the ban against nonhumans had been lifted, and now the denizens of every universe from Middle Earth to classical mythology could be seen mingling with the usual crowd of ladies and knights, cutpurses and tarts. *Usual!* thought the dancer/fantasist, suppressing a laugh as she sketched an Arabic salute—hand touching breast, mouth, and forehead—in response to the halfling's shy bow.

But what followed him had no place in any dimension friendly to that of the feudal, agrarian world of the faire. Striding with purposeful tread came seven adults—five men and two women—clad in modern business suits. The men carried posters and charts portraying what appeared to be a housing development; the women bore folders emblazoned with a logo of a double interlocking capital "S" in a font that looked like chiseled stone. The members of the group talked loudly among themselves as they moved, apparently oblivious to either the natural beauty of the Glenn or the human (and other) culture in lively play around them. Indeed, they huddled together and glanced about at the activity of the faire almost as though they feared contamination from this alien environment. And the looks they gave the landscape were not apprehensive but appraising. Arabis saw the man in the lad make a sweeping gesture and heard him call back to one of his cronies, "A lot of these trees'll have to go, except for that big one; that'll be the symbol of the complex. We'll set up our display there." He pointed ahead to a white oak of great size that lay at the end of the tree-flanked aisle through which the procession was making its way.

The dancer was not the only one to catch this chilling statement; the hobbit heard it, too, and he spun about with an expression of horror on his round face. "You can't do that!" he shouted at the businessman who had spoken. "These trees have voices!"

*Treebeard,* the fantasist thought, *condemning the rebel wizard Saruman for his rape of the countryside around his tower.* As she remembered the quote, the entrepreneur at the head of the group laughed sarcastically and called in reply, "Yeah, little dude—and what they say is, *'We're leaving.'*"

Several of his underlings groaned appreciatively at the pun, but Arabis, who ordinarily delighted in such wordplay, felt sick. When the crowd of humans, nonhumans—and *subhumans*, she thought fiercely, and it wasn't the ogre she had in mind—had passed out of earshot down the glade, she realized she was clutching the tent flap with force enough to whiten her knuckles.

Perhaps the hobbit, in repeating the words of the Shepherd of Fangorn, had paved the way for her next thought, but Arabis found herself saying aloud, "They'd better watch out for the Wild Magic."

*Now why did I say that?* the woman wondered as soon as she had spoken. She was no follower of Wicca, though several of her friends—and not a few of her students—walked the Old Way. She had, however, acquired some knowledge of the Craft in order to teach the works of fantasy that made use of it, and she had considerable respect for its adherents. In fact, she had chosen her name as an Eastern dancer from a character in a novel who, witchlike, knew the green gifts of the earth and cherished all its life. When the opportunity came to that plucky Welsh girl to free a race of pixie-folk imprisoned under a mountain, she was able to meet the challenge with this wisdom, the meaning of "arabis" and of "wicca" as well.

*Wisdom*, thought the teacher bitterly. *We've got precious little of that these days, at least about your relationship with the planet—and even less empathy.*

"TESTING! TESTING! ONE, TWO—" The shriek of a loudspeaker shattered the green quiet. Startled, the dancer glanced in the direction of the big oak.

As she suspected, the businesspeople had set up their display and were evidently ready to present their project.

"I don't want to hear it," she muttered. Even as the words left her mouth, though, she knew that employees of the faire would be expected to attend the presentation, if their schedules permitted. With the next dance performance not until three that afternoon, hers—unfortunately—did.

With a sigh that made her red face veil flare out like a dragon's tongue, Arabis stepped back into the tent long enough to snatch up a wide black shawl. Tossing this discreet garment around her shoulders, she covered the metal on her costume, from which the brilliant summer sun would otherwise have woken distracting flashes. She might have been capturing a storm's worth of lightning bolts in a black cloud, an analogy which—her "teacher" persona thought sulkily—was an accurate description of the way she felt. In this ill humor, she barely noticed as two other latecomers seated themselves next to her.

A small platform had been erected at the base of the oak—so close to the tree, in fact, that it resembled a huge shelf fungus protruding from the trunk. *Parasites*, thought Arabis, eyeing the realtor's associates with distaste. The group sat on chairs on the structure, three to the left and three to the right, flanking a small movie screen. The seventh stood at a microphone, and it was not the man who headed the team but one of the two women. She began to speak.

"Good afternoon, lords and ladies, knights, peasants, and—and—" Here either her imagination or vocabulary ran out, for she flapped a manicured hand helplessly toward the rear bench where Arabis sat and finished, "—*creatures*." The belly dancer's jaw dropped; her seatmates, whom she now saw were the jester and the hobbit, both looked equally astonished at this unflattering classification.

"This is the seventh Ren Faire here at Castle Glenn," continued the speaker, "and I do hope you're all enjoying yourselves, because I'm afraid it's going to be the last. Yes, yes, I know—" She made a placatory gesture as gasps of dismay rose from the benches. "But time marches on—"

*"Forward into the Past!"* A stout man in the green tabard of a forester half rose, shaking a gloved fist at the platform as he shouted the motto of the Society for Creative Anachronism.

"Ah," smiled the woman, waggling a coy finger, "there we're ready for you! Why not 'Backward into the Future'? As a matter of fact, that's the slogan of the project we're unveiling today, And now . . ." She turned as a tall, bearded man in a purple robe and pointed cap stepped up onto the stage. "If Wizard Ladoki will honor us with a demonstration of his magic, we'll begin our presentation."

The realtor bowed herself to one side of the screen, and the mage stepped up before it. Dipping a hand into a leather bag that hung at the belt of his robe, he brought forth a palmful of glittering powder and flung it at the blank surface with a dramatic gesture. "Let there be—Greenman's Grove!" he cried, and disappeared behind the display.

Arabis groaned softly and rested her forehead in her hand. Beside her, the hobbit might have been reading her mind as he once more spoke the words of Treebeard: " 'A wizard should know better!' "

A projector whirred, and the legend "Steinheim and Sons" appeared, with both capital letters done in the carved-stone font Arabis had seen on the briefcases of the business folk. Then a rippling arpeggio sounded on an unseen harp, and a picture of a

Tudor-style house complete with plaster-and-lath facade, mullioned windows, and a stone tower at one corner flashed onto the screen. Several admiring "Ooh's" rose from the audience, and the members of the Steinheim team nodded to each other knowingly. Next, a young couple in Renaissance garb wandered into view, stopping before the house in apparent awe; the woman laid an imploring hand on her partner's arm, and they walked to the rustic front door, which opened to admit them.

Now a mellow male voice intoned, "Does your present home lack magic? Do you wish you could escape at the end of your workday to a simpler world, a more gracious age? Come travel in time with us to Greenman's Grove, where the architecture of the future meets the art of the present to re-create the ambience of the past . . ."

The camera dollied forward, sweeping viewers into the model home; there they met up with the man and woman, who were admiring the wood paneling in a cavernous library. The tour proceeded, and shots of the rooms and features of the sample house were interspersed with architect's renderings of variations on the same dwelling. The last such drawing was an overview of the entire development, showing seven subdivisions—one per vale—of graduated size and cost. Each community bore a name from legend or myth, from the cottages of "Puck Place" to the quasi-castles of "Centaur Court."

At last the spiel wound to its close, and the costumed couple emerged onto the doorstep of the tour home. From a purse on the belt of his doublet, the lordling produced an old-fashioned key, which he presented to his lady with a courtly bow. She smiled, and raised her hand to touch his; then both of them looked out toward the viewers. "Come with us to Greenman's Grove," the young noble said cordially, and his paramour finished the invitation by saying, "Where a castle really *can* be your home." With a burst of period music, the couple vanished, to be replaced by a stylized version of the ancient leaf-covered countenance of the Lord of Wild Magic, the Green Man.

A smattering of polite applause (led by the realty people) followed. A few individuals moved toward the small table set up to the left of the platform to hold flyers and photos of the proposed community. However, the majority of the less-captivated-than-captive audience dispersed with unflattering haste back to the faire.

The teacher shivered, despite the heat of the July day and the black shawl she was wearing. Bad enough that these mundanes planned to uproot the fairy ring of the Glenn and replace it with a stone circle; but what a nightmare to think that her ex-husband, who owned a tract of land he maintained as a nature preserve, agreed to this—this—(the fantasist in her groped for a term and had to invent one) "Sarumaneuver!"

As if she had spoken aloud, the hobbit looked up at her with bleak brown eyes. " 'I feel sick,' " he said, echoing Sam Gamgee's reaction to the latter's first sight of the Black Land.

"Indeed, Master Holbytlan," Arabis grimly returned quote for quote, " 'this *is* Mordor, or one of its works.' "

Hugh the jester was evidently thinking along the same lines. He had taken his name from a character in one of the works of Gilbert and Sullivan and made frequent use of their material, and he now began to hum a number from the fairy opera *Iolanthe*. The dancer (who also sang) recognized the air and snickered.

With a conspiratorial wink, the buffoon unfolded gangling limbs and skipped toward the Steinheim stage. Capering up to its edge, he waved a bony hand in a fly-shooing gesture at the woman who had given the introduction and began to bellow: "Go away, Madam!" This is the chorus in which a group of humans vainly attempts to frighten the Queen of the Fairies into withdrawing, and it was both highly insulting and thoroughly appropriate to the case.

"Sic 'em, you merry dog," Arabis urged, grinning as she watched the frozen humor-the-madman smile with which the businesswoman met her tormentor.

"—'So beware, Madam—and *begone!*' " Hugh finished a moment later, with a commanding flourish of his scepter, as though that beribboned stick were truly a king's rod of office with the power to impose banishment—or a fairy's wand.

The dancer knew a cue when she heard one. Stepping up onto the bench, she struck a Wagnerian pose and launched into the Fairy Queen's furious reply. The theme shuddered and rumbled, threatening even in open day:

> *"Bearded by these puny mortals,*
> *We shall launch from fairy portals*
> *All the most terrific thunders*
> *In our armory of wonders!"*

On the last word, Arabis flung wide her arms, then raised them as in invocation to the great tree that rose before her. The noon sun struck full on her bespangled costume, and the effect was dazzling. Several onlookers applauded, but this tribute was lost on its recipient; her attention was all for the mass of leaves overhead, which had begun to toss in a wind that stirred them alone. For an instant—no? *yes!*— they formed themselves into the face of the Green Lord, not an artist's rendering but a living countenance, immemorially old and newly born each instant like the earth itself. Two spots of especially bright light rested where the entity's eyes would be, and the glow of these disks seemed to bore into the teacher's brain, bearing a desperate message: *Dance/ vales!* Then, as quickly as it had taken shape, the image dissolved.

Arabis returned to her surroundings with a jolt. Finding herself still standing on the bench—and the focus of bemused (and amused) attention from the crowd—she hastily snapped into theater mode. "Performance at three in the Turkish Pavilion!" she cried; then, giving the Eastern salute and a smile she hoped was seductive, she stepped down, wrapped her shawl around her, and fled.

*A pretty fool I must have looked up there!* the woman thought furiously as she made her way back to the tent. *Maybe I'd better give up dancing and apprentice myself to Master Hugh. Let's see, what name could I use for that profession?* Arabis, a.k.a. Shirley Webster, stifled a giggle as the obvious answer presented itself: "Shirley: I Jest!"

But even so delicious a pun could not distract the teacher's attention long from the "treepiphany" she had experienced at the oak. Once more in her accommodations, Arabis revolved the apparent vision and its cryptic message while she ate a light lunch, then composed herself for a brief period of meditation. Ha she truly seen the Green Man and, if so, what had been the meaning of his words, "Dance/vales?" Was she intended to use dance to save the vales of Castle

Glenn? Was she to perform using "veils" for this purpose? Or was the phrase she had heard actually "Dance avails," and if the latter, for *what* did it avail?

"Save the vales," she muttered, as nervous laughter threatened again. "Sounds like the Transylvanian branch of Greenpeace." Green peace was what she needed right now: the verdant serenity that still presided over this spot, the color and confusion of the faire notwithstanding. Unfolding herself from her lotus posture, the dancer rose, pushed open the heavy flap of the tent, and stood gazing down the tree-lined corridor to the oak.

What on earth was happening here? She knew that the owners of the castle crowning the hill behind the huge oak were experiencing hard times, but surely the faire, which they had hosted for some years on their land, brought in enough revenue to enable them to meet their expenses. And there was another reason why the idea of a housing complex in Castle Glenn was unthinkable. The septet of small valleys that fanned out from the base of the mountain—really a series of forested aisles lying side by side like seven toes on a polydactyl cat—were famous for their abundant wildlife and lush plant growth.

Wildness . . . plants . . .

A sudden breeze stirred the mass of greenery all along the dim green corridor, filling the air with a gossipy hiss; the trees seemed to be talking among themselves, turning up large leaves like hands behind which they whispered to their fellows in agitation, *"News! News!"*

Then a second gust of wind caught up a pile of leaves that had mounded themselves around the nearest tent peg. Funneling them upward into the air, it spun them in a vortex a yard high. Arabis watched this sprightly dancer with delight, wishing she could capture the grace and speed of its natural ballet in her own performance.

She released the canvas flap and was turning to go back inside when she nearly collided with a small figure that was now standing at her left. The newcomer was a child, perhaps eight years of age, clad in a brief one-shouldered dress of "skeleton leaves and the juices that ooze from trees"—*like Peter Pan*, recalled the teacher—but this youngster was female. Her ears were ribbed with delicate green veining and swept up to leaf-sharp points, while her eyes, of a startling peridot hue, showed vertical pupils like those of a cat. *What a great costume*, thought Arabis. *This kid must really be into role-playing if she'd put up with those novelty contact lenses at her age.*

The dancer inclined her head. "Hail, fair—" She had been about to say "fairy," but remember just in time that such entities did not like that term and emended the salute—"Fair Person. I am Arabis. How are you called, if I may know your name?" The courtly locution seemed natural and right.

"Sylphin," said her visitor. This reply was lisped so softly that the woman could not tell whether the creature was trying to say "sylvan," but she decided that either name was appropriate.

Having introduced herself, the fairy exchanged no further pleasantries. Instead, she shot out a bird-boned hand in the direction of the realtors' platform and stated imperiously, "*They* must go. You will help?"

There was no doubt to whom "they" referred. The teacher certainly agreed that the businesspeople needed to be transformed into slime molds—she had said as much by singing the threatening chorus from *Iolanthe* at them. Most of the listeners would have failed to see the relevance of the song and would probably have put down her wanted-to-be "put down" to a private joke between herself and the jester; still, she was not about to voice this opinion to the wrong person. Suppose the enchanting entity before her had been sent by the organizers of the faire to ferret out opinions on the coming complex? She *had* to be a spy—she couldn't *really* be—

Watching the face of the "fairy," Arabis said carefully, "There can be but one world in this place. . . ."

Sylphin stamped a small brown foot in rage. "Ours!" she hissed. "The one that grows! As *these* will. . . ." She reached toward a leaf that rested on her left hip. This decoration evidently hid a pocket, because the girl's hand disappeared for a moment, to return clenched about something retrieved. In a gesture at once childish and regal, she thrust this fist at the teacher, who offered a palm to receive the contents. Then Sylphin drew her fingers away, and Arabis gasped in wonder.

The gift was another leaf. It shape suggested that it had been plucked from a white oak, such as the tree that stood in the heart of Glen Glenn, but this glorious thing might have graced the living crown of the Green Man himself. Its seven-lobed shape was woven of an emerald stuff whose surface seemed in constant motion, brightened by sunlight, then darkened by shadow; silvered by rain, then whitened by snow. All the times and weathers of the forest year flashed across the leaf in a moment. Yet this wonder was but the humble backcloth to the veins that bisected each of the lobes: every one was a thread of gem-brilliant color, and each hue was different. These, too, pulsed with life.

The human woman stood dumbstruck with wonder, but the elf-child merely shrugged, as though such living jewels routinely carpeted the floor of the woods from which she hailed. Briskly, she lifted Arabis' hand to her lips and breathed upon it, then chanted in a whisper:

> *"Sevenfold strong I bind the charm*
> *To ward my father's land from harm.*
> *Let earth and water and air and fire,*
> *Plant, beast, and man, aid my desire:*
> *Let all who will not join the dance*
> *In stony home abide entranced."*

Folding the dancer's fingers over the treasure, the forest daughter met her eyes with an expression that combined pride, power, and not a little mischief. *Somebody's in for it now!* Arabis had just time to think before the "leaf" gave a frantic thrust to the digits that imprisoned it and a rainbow exploded from her fist.

The teacher cried out in alarm and would have hurled the object away, but Sylphin seized her hand and kept it tightly closed. She felt as though she were clutching a ball of earthworms who were trying to grow up into anacondas as quickly as possible, or a cluster of plant shoots sprouting at time-lapse speed, and she had to grit her teeth to endure the sensation. In seconds the stuff lengthened until it touched the ground; whereupon its movement mercifully ceased. It was then Arabis realized that the substance she held was cloth.

And, oh, *what* cloth! Permitted to open her aching fingers at last, the dancer saw on her palm, in a crumbled green ruin of plant matter, seven scarflike ribbons—the erstwhile veins of the leaf. As before, no two colors were alike, and now each bore a unique pattern wrought into its gossamer substance which was also a texture and—a text? Touching the brown band, the teacher felt moist earth and sensed the rich and varied life hidden by the soil; taking up the blue was cupping a palmful of water. She felt like Iris, the goddess of the rainbow.

A long moment passed before the recipient of the fairy's gift was able to look up from the wonder she held to say, inadequately, inanely, "This is so beautiful—thank you."

"Not for you," the forest girl corrected, "for *them*, the stone-house-makers. At middle-dark this night, they will assemble before the White Tree, and you will dance there. When the moonlight catches my father's eyes, touch each of *them* with one of these." Sylphin indicated the ribbons, and once more her thin lips quirked in an expression Arabis did not quite like.

"And what will happen then?" The dancer strove to keep her tone casual.

"Why," answered the fairy, her smile broadening to show small pointed teeth, "they will be made what they would make."

"Which is—?" the human woman was about to ask, when from the opposite opening of the tent came a call: "Arabis, fifteen minutes!"

"Coming!" She glanced over her shoulder to reply, taking her eyes from her guest for the briefest of instants, but when she looked back, she saw only a whirl of leaves speeding down the green alley in the direction of the oak.

A moment more Arabis watched the leaves; she could have sworn that, as they were about to impact on the trunk of the tree, they suddenly lifted and swept into its crown instead. *Why, of course*, thought the fantasy teacher in her, beyond shock now. *After all, sylphs* do *live in the tops of trees.* She might have stood longer, but the distant burble of a bouzouki signaled the start of the afternoon show at the Turkish Pavilion, and she at last turned back in to the tent.

Relieved to be distracted from the, no, not unnatural but all *too* natural happenings of the morning, the dancer took refuge in her art. Concealing the fairy scarves carefully beneath a pillow, she collected her "floor-work" veil, a pair of sequined foot guards, and a tape of the music she would use: Borodin's *In the Steppes of Central Asia*. Haunting and meditative, this piece suited her mood; it would not overtax her unduly either because she knew she would need all her strength for the night. For *that* routine, she already had a most unique accompaniment in mind—one she was certain no Eastern dancer had used before. *But then,* Arabis reflected somberly as she slipped out the front flap of her tent into the bustle of the ThoroughFaire, *which of us has ever been summoned to a command performance by a god?*

\*    \*    \*

The rest of the afternoon and the entire evening passed in a blur, with time feeling, by turns, weirdly extended and horribly compressed. Scarcely aware of her actions, Arabis ate a nourishing supper from the cookshop booth, did her yoga and warm-up exercises, and assembled her costume and its accessories. She selected a bolero jacket and harem pants, as the interpretive choreography she planned would involve kicking and leaping; she also substituted a tambourine for the traditional finger-cymbals.

For music, she had earlier chosen a little-known orchestral suite by John Philip Sousa entitled *The Dwellers in the Western World*. This composition, an engaging mix of folk themes, hymnlike passages, and, of course, marches, presents a musical portrait of three of the races which have come to America. What Arabis loved about the piece—and what made it a fitting choice for the performance she was about to give—was the contrast in attitudes toward nature that are evident in its themes. The black and the red man live in harmony with their environment, reenacting its cycles and forces in exuberant dance and worship, while the white man, having sealed himself away from the natural world, honors only his own works and makes vainglorious parade of his achievements. *And yet*, the teacher thought as she paced within the tent, her nails digging Islamic crescents into her clammy palms, *aren't we all guilty of offense against the Green Realm—and its Lord—simply by our presence here? It's really a wonder that Earth hasn't risen in wrath like a great beast afflicted with vermin in its pelt, given itself a colossal shake, and flung us all off into space.*

Well, maybe that was about to happen now.

At long, long last, the clock on the dressing table showed a quarter to twelve. Lifting the pillow on her cot, the dancer reverently withdrew the seven ribbon-scarves from their hiding place and tucked them into the top of her harem pants, spacing them at intervals so they formed a colorful fringe. *Looks like I'm planning to do the hula*, she thought, and had a sudden vision of herself as a sacrificial maiden being carried doomward to the heartbeat thump of war drums. Taking up tambourine and tape player, Arabis pushed open the back flap of the tent, half expecting to find an outrigger waiting for her—

—then decided to upgrade to a diving bell or spaceship when she met a wall of solid whiteness. A dense fog had risen sometime in the evening, and the entire faire seemed to have been transported to the bottom of the sea or the surface of the moon.

Sight was dimmed and hearing muffled; all that remained visible of the long and well-populated street of booths were a few diffuse glows here and there, indicating lighted tents.

*Good—maybe this means the show* doesn't *go on,* thought the teacher, and was immediately ashamed of her cowardice. Resolutely, she took a step forward, then another. After a few yards, she discovered that a surrounding bubble of clear air was traveling with her. The farther she moved away from the tent and toward the oak, the larger this open space became, until, by the time she arrived at her destination—or was that *"destiny"?* her nervous brain gibbered—the sphere of clarity had expanded to enclose Arabis, the White Tree, and the audience.

Yes, there was the realty team, seven strong, dressed in casual clothing and—their platform having been dismantled—seated on large cushions arranged in a horseshoe on the ground. Seven *strong*— or were they? As Arabis glanced around the ring of watchers, she saw that each man and woman wore an identical fixed, bland expression. That this was not merely a "PR face" was proved by the fact that none of the businesspeople acknowledged the dancer when she set down her tape player and gave the Eastern salute.

*My God,* thought the woman, really afraid now. *What has already been done to them—and what more am I expected to do?*

Suddenly she wanted out of the whole affair. Turning back the way she had come, Arabis prepared to plunge down the alley until she reached the safe normality of the faire—and once more she met a white wall, one that was truly solid this time. The impact was not painful, but it left her shaken and made her fear escalate to full-bore panic. She had raised her arms to strike at the impossible barrier, opened her mouth to scream, when a voice—a human, familiar voice—called her name in an urgent whisper.

Arabis looked wildly around and caught sight of her ex-husband, standing at the base of one of the smaller oaks in the tree-lined lane. With the wizard were the jester and the hobbit. All three smiled and nodded, each gave her his persona's equivalent of a thumbs-up, and Ladoki mouthed, *It will be all right.*

Reassured by the presence of her own kind in this place of ancient power, and by whatever knowledge they possessed about the night's work that she lacked (what *did* they know?), the dancer lifted her chin, smiled gallantly, and repeated the salutation to her unseen host and his unresponsive guests. And then the same invisible Hand that had reared the wall of mist touched the recorder, the strains of Sousa's "Red Man" poured forth, and Arabis became an Indian brave.

The music began with a stealthy theme; the native was stalking prey, either human or animal. The dancer took small, measured steps to quick lifts of the hip, tapping the tambourine in sharp bursts as she progressed around the circle of watchers. As the hunt motif opened into a victory celebration, her free hand brushed the veils of Earth and Sky, and she bent to thank the soil for its bounty, then leaped up swiftly to acknowledge the spirits of the ancestors, watching from aloft by their campfire-stars.

As the Indian movement drew to a close, her mind was filled with images of a race that could reach for the trees, the sky, and the heavens without ever leaving the earth. Therein, she knew, lay their strength and their secret knowledge of the world's life.

In the few seconds' pause before the next musical

section began, Arabis caught glimpses of gleaming eyes peering from the fog around the perimeter of the performance area; some of the Green Lord's subjects appeared to have joined her audience. A sensation of building power tingled along the human woman's skin, making her want to jump, but no, now such spontaneity would be in (dear, dear!) execrably bad taste—

—for the White Man had arrived to Set Things Straight, and all was as serene as a Sunday stroll in the park. This was Progress, so Arabis progressed, camel-walking to the hymnic strains of the opening and making a slow and stately round of the still-motionless onlookers, the tambourine held before her like an offering plate. When celebration—sedate, of course—was permitted, it arrived in the form of an oompah band, pumping and pompous; the tambourine became a bass drum, carried sideways by the dancer as she majorette-stepped. Suddenly the theme reverted to the first churchlike tune, swelling to a paean of adoration of *Homo civilis;* the tambourine was lifted overhead for the sun that never set on his empire. This White Man, with his assumed (in every sense) Burden, was a creature desirous of, and dedicated to, the imposition of Order upon the chaos he believed characterized the natural world and the other races.

The elements he had harnessed to "spread his conquests farther" were Fire and Water, and those were the ribbons that symbolized him. Arabis was not surprised, as she knelt in the grass at the end of the second phase of the dance, to hear a rumble of thunder and see a brief flash of lightning. The latter lit the leaves of the oak, which began to move in a wind that blew nowhere else. The tension grew, then—

—bursting through its taut-stretched surface like a

clown through a paper hoop came the Black Man! Arms akimbo in a tattered shirt, his feet beat an exuberant rhythm on the packed earth before his cabin; the day's work was done in the fields, and it was time for a dance. A brief dark passage followed, in which the slaves ran for their lives after an escape, but freedom was won, and a triumphant Juneteenth parade followed. Arabis, affirming the unquenchable spirit of a race who filled the Air—the one element that could never be bound—with music for all peoples to hear, skipped, kicked, and played *herself* with her tambourine, bouncing its skin from hip, knee, and foot.

Sousa's irrepressible music flashed with silver; the glockenspiel shimmered, the piccolo hurled darts of the stuff so sharp they stung the ears, and the dancer's instrument seemed about to toss its cymbal-coins to the audience in prodigal glee.

A sudden moon swam into view, lighting the mist-encircled theater with its own full argent round; and two smaller but equally bright disks shone from amid the leaves of the oak. Sylphin's words leaped to Arabis' mind: *When the moonlight catches my father's eyes* . . . Cast the veils—NOW!

As the suite drew its themes together in a rousing finale, the dancer whirled a final circuit round the curve of her stage. Reaping the ribbons in a rainbow sheaf from the waist of her pants, she tossed them one after another to the motionless men and women. Where the cloth touched, it took hold and spread like a colored fire, until each scarf had covered an entire figure with a skin of fairy fabric. The leaf-stuff darkened and drew in on itself, bunching, rounding, curving groundward. When the music ended and silence fell, before the Green Man's oak stood a ring of seven gray stones.

Arabis froze as though she, too, had been stuck by enchantment. Once more she recalled the fairy's words, this time the end of the incantation, which now appeared to have been a curse: *In stony home abide entranced.*

One, two, three, four, five, six, seven, all bad realtors go to—*Steinheim*—

Belatedly, the teacher's numbed mind supplied the translation: "stone home."

Feet whipped the damp grass of the glade, and the three other humans who had witnessed this judgment on all the species hurried to the dancer's side.

The hobbit, earth-dweller that he was, seemed to feel the sentence just; his brown eyes glinted with anger, and he bit out the words of Gandalf to the day-caught trolls: " 'Be stone to you!' "

The jester nodded in rueful agreement, then murmured the words of Jack Point in *Yeomen of the Guard:* " 'Like a stone, my boy, I said!' "

The wizard had opened his mouth to make his contribution, but Arabis chose that moment to finally snap. "So help me, Landon," she shrilled, shaking a finger in her ex's bearded face, "if you quote hat horrid Bob Dylan song, I'll—I'll remarry you just so I can divorce you again!"

"You mean, 'Everybody must get'—"

"DON'T SAY IT!"

Landon/Ladoki slid an arm around the trembling woman's shoulders and drew her in for a hug. "Okay, honey, calm down—I won't say it, but I sure am thinking it. I mean—" The wizard's perpetual grin faded as he scanned the circle of new-made stones. "—I think we all ought to take a turn at getting, um, stiffed like those poor souls, after what we've done to the earth."

He held up a hand as Arabis spluttered a protest.

"Yes, I know, who am I to talk—but I realized how wrong I'd been to help the realty folks when that little—fairy, I guess she was—came up to us" (his gesture took in Hugh and the halfling) "after your performance this afternoon. That's why we're here now."

Ladoki dug into the pocket of his purple robe, saying as he searched, "The Steinheim people paid me to do that little number for their presentation, but I'm going to send back this green." Surprise spread over his face as his fingers closed around the object he sought.

"What—?" Arabis began, then gasped as the wizard showed what lay in his hand. It was a leaf, green in its seven lobes and veined with varicolored fire, identical in every way to the one sylph had presented her—had it been only this afternoon?

All at once, the dancer knew what she had to do. Plucking the leaf from Ladoki's palm, she spun off toward the most distant of the stony homes in the ring, the first she had helped to enchant. Recalling the spell invoked by the Green Man's daughter, she began to recite it, altering its wording. As she spoke, she moved around the circle, brushing the fairy gift on each of the monoliths in turn, until, with the final line of the charm, she touched the last of the stones.

> *"Sevenfold I unbind this charm—*
> *The Green Man's land will take no harm.*
> *Let earth and air and water and fire,*
> *Halfling and men, hear my desire:*
> *From stone homes in deliverance,*
> *Let these repentant, join the dance."*

When she had finished the incantation, Arabis turned until she stood facing the huge oak. Laying the leaf against her heart in token of her willingness to offer herself in place of the enchanted ones, she raised her left hand and addressed the gods of the grove:

"Green Sire, Green Daughter, set them free—"

Once more the vast face shaped itself in the foliage of the tree, and a voice like a forest swept by a mighty wind made answer:

*As you have said, so shall it be.*

In Arabis's hand, the leaf burst into green flame. At the same instant, all around the ring, the stones began to smoke, and in a moment they had melted into the ground like piles of dirty snow subjected to a sudden winter sun.

The woman gave a great cry, but in her mind the green girl was speaking:

*Do not fear. They still live.*

Arabis fainted.

\*     \*     \*

"Shirley, honey, wake up—come on, you've got to *see* this— "

Arabis groaned and pushed feebly at the hand that was shaking her shoulder. Wincing as bright sunlight struck her gritty eyes, she sat up, to find herself on the cot in her tent with the wizard holding the morning edition of the local newspaper under her nose. He brushed a kiss against her sweat-matted hair.

"Glad you're back, sweetie. Check this out—"

The dancer would not usually have been pleased about falling asleep while still wearing her contacts, but she was happy that that had happened last night; this was one read that wouldn't wait for a grope for glasses.

GREENMAN'S GROVE GETS AX, blared the banner headline (*ouch*, thought the teacher); Steinheim and Sons to Scrap Castle Complex, Erect Eco-Friendly Dwellings Instead, the subheading elaborated. Below this announcement appeared a photo of the realty team with placard bearing the project logo, followed by the article:

*In an exclusive interview taken at 2:00 this morning, the prestigious realty firm of Steinheim and Sons announced its decision to abandon plans for the Greenman's Grove Castle Community.*

A description of the nature and location of the complex followed, but Arabis skipped this section, scanning instead down the column until she came to the quotes. How much, she wondered, did the seven men and women who had spent a portion of the night before as pseudo-Stonehenge remember of the experience—and what had it done to them? Ah, here—

*"We visited the grounds of Castle Glenn yesterday morning," firm founder Rockwell Steinheim told reporters. "We gave a presentation about the project and left; but last evening we all felt a need to return." Asked if he and his team had gone back to visit the Renaissance Faire, the senior Steinheim replied in the negative. "We wanted to view the Seven Vales at a quiet time," he explained, "and I'm glad we did; none of us realized how beautiful the area is. It has to be kept unspoiled for future generations." Son Micah declared, "I've been to Japan, and the Vales remind me of a Zen garden." Brother Jasper stated, "You can just sit there for hours and become part of the landscape." Sister Opal offered the final*

*comment: "I don't know why we didn't see it before, but now the veil has fallen from our eyes."*

At this point, the reporter could not resist the obvious pun on veil/Vales and, after a summary of the firm's new plans to purchase undeveloped land and design a completely environment-conscious community, the article concluded.

Not knowing whether to laugh or cry, the belly dancer looked at the wizard in silence for a long moment. Finally she whispered, "Oh, Landon, I'm so glad."

"Well, it's all thanks to you, honey," Ladoki said, drawing her in for another hug. "Those stonehearts or houses, or whatever, got free because you gave them leave."

"No," Arabis corrected, smiling but never more serious, "because the Green Ones gave *us* leaves."

# MOSES' MIRACLES

*by*

*Roberta Gellis*

Roberta Gellis has a varied educational background, a master's degree in biochemistry and another in medieval literature, and an equally varied working history; ten years as a research chemist, many years as a freelance editor of scientific books, and thirty years as a writer. She is married—to the same man for over fifty years (no mean feat in these days) and lives in Lafayette, Indiana, with her husband and a very lively Lakeland terrier called Taffy. She has one child, Mark, who teaches rhetoric (a fancy name for expository writing). She has been a successful writer of historical fiction, having published about twenty-eight meticulously researched historical novels since 1978. Gellis has been the recipient of many awards, including the Romance Writers of America's Lifetime Achievement Award. She has also tried her hand at science fiction (*The Space Guardian* and *Offworld* in the '70s, under the pseudonym Max Daniels) and mythological fantasy, including the novels *Dazzling Brightness, Shimmering Splendor, Enchanted Fire, Bull God, Thrice Bound,*) Currently Gellis is writing historical mystery set in twelfth century London (*A Mortal Bane, A Personal Devil, Bone of Contention*).

"**Y**OU WANT THE CAR to go *where*?" Dov Goldberg asked.

His big brown eyes, usually half lidded to mask any expression, were now wide open, betraying astonishment and, perhaps, amusement.

Rivka Zahara sighed. "To the Misty Mountain Renaissance Festival at Breamville."

Dov blinked twice rapidly as he picked a set of keys out of the top right-hand drawer of his desk. He held them together with a handsome eelskin wallet that contained the registration papers for the sleek Jaguar he knew was Rivka's favorite of the many cars he owned. He bowed his head for a moment, then lifted it and handed her the wallet.

"Right. I'll bite. Why do you, of all people, want to go to a Renaissance Faire? I have a feeling that asking me for the car, which you never do, is an elaborate leg-pull, but I just can't see it."

"It's not a leg-pull," Rivka said, shaking her head and frowning slightly.

The truth was that Rivka did *not* want to go to the Renaissance Faire. She suspected that she would spend all her time at the faire with prickles running over her skin and feeling slightly nauseous, which was why she hated fakes of any kind. Although she no longer told anyone, because very few had ever believed her, any kind of physical fakery produced that reaction in her.

Dov knew; he was a believer, and it was why she was invaluable as his curator/librarian. Dov had, in the parlance of Rivka's youth, more money than God, and his hobby was the collection of ancient artifacts, mostly manuscripts—a hobby notoriously subject to the production and presentation of fakes. Her prickling skin had saved Dov a lot of money—and broken two art-counterfeiting rings while she was at it.

"So?" Dov urged.

"It's Lily that wants to go, not me," Rivka said.

As she said it, Rivka realized that she didn't herself know why she wanted Dov to be aware that she was taking the car and where she was going—only that it gave her comfort to have him know.

Dov looked relieved. "Oh, Lily and her witch-craft." He grinned. "She gets her herbs and stuff and crystals and mirrors at places like that. How anyone who can handle all the appeals for funding that come to me and can see through the smoothest and most plausible con artists and keep them off my back can believe that stuff, I don't know."

"You believe in God," Rivka pointed out. "It's just as sensible. There's even less proof that God works than that magic does."

He smiled at her but then shook his head, a frown pulling his thick black eyebrows into a single line over his eyes. "But Lily can drive herself. Why are *you* going?"

Rivka frowned, too. "She told me that there's a man there who has the most wonderful manuscripts. He promised her some really unusual stuff—hen's teeth, for God's sake—if she would bring me to the faire. He thinks I might buy something for you."

"I don't like the sound of that." Dov's brown eyes no longer looked gentle at all. They had turned into flat brown pebbles. "This person asked for you by name?"

"Yes, and knew I was your librarian. I know it doesn't sound good, but you know that Lily can't be fooled about people the same way I can't be fooled about manuscripts, and she swears that this guy's no fake and he means no harm. These Faire people take odd jobs, like cleaning out cellars and attics. Maybe he found something."

"Hmmm." Dov now looked somewhat less like a bland-faced hit man. "That sounds almost reasonable. All right. Have a good time."

Rivka made a face at him, thinking of the coming discomfort of prickling skin and uneasy stomach; however, when she and Lily arrived at the faire, she was pleasantly surprised to discover that "pretend" and "fake" were not at all the same thing. The clothes and swords many wore weren't fakes; they were acknowledged replicas, sometimes only fanciful costumes, never intended to be regarded as genuine medieval garments, and thus not fakes.

Rivka began to look around with pleasure at the shows in the center of the green and the booths around the edges. After a little time of general exploration, Lily moved toward particular booths. Twice, as Lily examined merchandise, Rivka felt impelled to turn and scan the crowd, feeling watched, but Lily did not react.

Finally, Rivka said, "We'd better go to your man's booth now. I'll look at the manuscripts he has for sale and then we can have lunch. Those turkey legs people are carrying look luscious, and it's been a long time since I got grease on my ears while eating."

Lily laughed and pointed across the field to a small tent almost invisible in the deep shadow of a patch of large trees. "There's Qaletaqua's booth."

It was smaller than most of the others and quite dark inside. From the doorway Rivka could make out a small table with a scroll and two open books atop it and at the back of the tent, shelving holding flat boxes and more books. She stepped in and stopped abruptly, gritting her teeth. A whole hive of ants seemed to be running all over her, nipping her, and she needed to swallow to suppress her rising gorge. She would have backed out, but Lily was behind her and a tall, thin shadow moved out of the darkness behind the shelves.

"Quick," Lily said, her voice angry. "Ask what you want and let her get out. I didn't know all those books and manuscripts were fakes or I never would have brought her."

"Fakes?" Even full of indignation the voice was beautiful, rich and mellow with a hint of music in it. "They are copies, exact copies, yes, and they are almost as expensive as the originals, but not fakes. I never claim . . ."

The open declaration that the books were copies had reduced Rivka's reaction. She was able to raise her eyes to examine the booth keeper and her breath drew in. He was very tall, very slender, with hair so bright a gold that it shone in the dimness of the tent. His eyes shone, too, green, like a cat's in the dark, and like a cat's the pupils were vertical, oval slits. A fine straight nose, a beautiful mouth. He was heart-stoppingly handsome, except for his ears which had long, pointed tips reaching the top of his skull.

"Believe me, the labor and effort involved make the price cheap." He gestured toward the exhibits.

Rivka came forward and examined the display. She sighed and shook her head. "They are exquisite, but it doesn't matter. My employer isn't interested in copies, no matter how careful and exact. He only purchases originals."

"And if no original is available?"

Rivka laughed. "Then he does without."

Qaletaqua sighed. "Then we cannot barter, which I had hoped to do. I have some remarkable works. You should look at them before rejecting out of hand. In any case I asked to see you to buy, not to sell."

Rivka laughed again. "My employer does not sell. Once in a while he will give one of his acquisitions to a cause he feels is worthy, and sometimes he will lend a piece to a museum so that others can see it and enjoy it, but—"

A hand moved swiftly and seized her wrist with such strength that the bones ground together. Rivka cried out. Qaletaqua released her, his lips beginning to form the word "sorry." Simultaneously, the tent opening was filled with a large shadow, Lily was pushed unceremoniously aside, and a flat, very ugly gun was pointed at Qaletaqua's chest.

"Dov!" Rivka breathed.

"Right," Dov said, but his eyes were fixed on the stall keeper. "Now I want to know what you look like, mister. Take off the wig, the fake ears, and the contact lenses."

"If you shoot me," Qaletaqua said, "even if the bullet barely grazes me, I will die. Iron is deadly poison to me. And if you kill me, a whole nation will die with me."

"Lily?" Dov's voice was hard as the gun in his hand.

"He's telling the truth," Lily said faintly. "At least, *he* believes he's telling the truth."

Dov lowered the gun. "Right. I won't shoot you, but I won't swear not to beat you black and blue if you don't get rid of the makeup."

"It isn't makeup," Qaletaqua said. "I am Sidhe." He waited a moment, meeting Dov's hard stare and then, apparently thinking the mortal didn't recognize the word, added, "An Elf, one of the Fair Folk."

Dov took a step forward. Lily laid her hand on his arm. "Whatever he is, Dov, he's not wearing makeup. Maybe it's plastic surgery. Some of these faire people are pretty far around the bend."

Rivka nodded and said, "And look at the stuff he has on the table and on the bookshelves. Just look. Where did he get stuff like that, even if they are fakes? You know, I'm not sure I could prove them fakes even with carbon dating and an electron microscope."

"You couldn't," the Sidhe said. "They are copies, yes, but copies down to the molecular structure."

There was a moment of strained silence, then Dov said, "What's this all about? What did you think you could get by hurting Rivka?"

"No, no." Qaletaqua raised open hands. "I am so sorry for that. I did not mean to hurt her. I forget how frail mortals are. But when she said you would lend something you owned for a good cause, I got so excited I grabbed her hand."

Dov snorted. "A good cause is a large library or a museum so thousands of people could see and enjoy my possession, learn from it, not a guy who thinks he's an Elf."

Qaletaqua swallowed. "What I need is not something beautiful or something that mortals could learn from." He swallowed again. "It is only something that will save my city and my people . . . and eventually yours . . ."

"That's a rather large order for one manuscript— even if it is a grimoire," Rivka remarked.

"Not a maker of spells but an unmaker." Qaletaqua looked at Dov. "Remember finding what they call Moses' tomb?"

"Of course I remember," Dov said. "The dig was my gift to myself for making my first ten million." He shrugged. "Twenty years ago. Finding the tomb was dumb luck."

Qaletaqua nodded. "They called it Moses' tomb because it was just where your Bible said Moses died, and it was all alone. Your prize for financing the dig was the small scroll in the box under the body's hand. It was rolled tight and too fragile to handle, so they let you have it."

"I still have it."

"I know." The Sidhe smiled. "And have you found a way to unroll it?"

Rivka shook her head. "Nothing and no one I would trust has suggested anything reasonable . . . or unreasonable. At this stage I'd probably go for soaking it in babies' blood if anyone could make a good argument for it."

"I can unroll it for you, and without ever touching it."

"Lily?"

She came forward, her face drawn into worried lines. "He believes it," she said. "And if he *is* of the Sidhe, he's probably speaking the truth. But elves— elves don't exist!"

"I thought you believed in magic," Rivka said dryly. "You told me he could get you hen's teeth."

"*He* believed he could. I'm not sure I believed it, but he was only asking me to get you to come here and talk to him. What did it matter if he was a delusional kook? There wasn't much to lose, even if the teeth were fake. And I was sure you would enjoy the Faire. Dov's manuscript scroll is different. That's too much to risk on my intuition."

Dov looked fixedly at Qaletaqua. Rivka, too, looked at the Sidhe's ears, the place where his improbably golden hair met his skin, the oval slits of his pupils. Both of them were practiced in picking out the tiniest imperfections. There were none. Lily's assertion that the person wasn't wearing makeup was true.

"You say you can unroll the scroll . . . without touching it?" Dov asked.

"It will have to be removed from the box, but you can do that. I need never put my hand nor any other instrument on the scroll and it will never be out from under your eyes."

"All right," Dov said quickly as if he were afraid he would change his mind if he hesitated. "Close up here and I'll drive you to my house. If you can—"

But Qaletaqua was shaking his head. "I cannot go to your house nor ride in your automobile. Too much iron. I would be in agony. I might die. Bring the scroll here."

It was Dov's turn to shake his head. "Oh, no. What kind of sucker do you think I am? Bring Moses' Miracles to an open fairground without even normal security? It's worth—"

"It's worth nothing where it is," Qaletaqua snarled. "Nothing! There it sits, protected by walls and bars of steel, growing more brittle and more faded day by day, but you would rather have it turn to dust while you squat on it like a goose on a dead egg. And my people will die, and yours, too, when the curse of Making eats away the walls of Elfhame Machu Picchu . . ."

"Machu Picchu," Dov said, voice flat, "was a city of the Inca."

"It was an elfhame, too," Qaletaqua retorted, the brilliant green eyes full of tears, "When the Inca ruled, the Sidhe of Machu Picchu were welcome to them; they were welcome to the Sidhe of Machu Picchu."

"A brilliant people, but so cruel." Rivka shuddered.

"Brilliant," Qaletaqua echoed. "Then the stupid conquistadors came and their mad priest twisted the minds of the Inca so that they poured through the Gate that had welcomed them and raised weapons—

steel weapons—against the Sidhe. Machu Picchu died, but that was not enough. The priest had heard of Nahele Helaku and wished to destroy that, too."

"Nahele Helaku—Forest Full of Sun," Dov muttered.

Rivka glanced at him; she could read almost any European or Near Eastern ancient language, but Dov was far more expert in Early American culture.

"Beautiful, is it not?" the Sidhe asked. "And it is now dying, inch by inch because the mad priest cursed Machu Picchu with a Making of monsters to creep out of the dead elfhame and poison everything they touched." He sighed. "The magus majors of Nahele Helaku sealed Machu Picchu, but in five hundred years the Making has eaten away the seals and the monsters are finding cracks. All Underhill will die of their poison. Then they will find a way to the mortal world, and you, too, will die."

He stared into nothing, tear streaks on his cheeks. It was a heartrending sight, but Dov had been a very rich man for a long time and had heard every kind of sad tale. He was about to turn and walk away when Lily darted past him and dropped something onto the hand the Sidhe had raised in appeal. Qaletaqua shrieked and jumped back. The object fell to the ground and Lily picked it up and handed it to Dov. It was a very small key, made of steel, and quite cool.

The Sidhe was staring at his hand in horror, and the others saw the key shape on it, blazing red as if the key had been white hot when it touched him. Dov blinked.

"No!" Lily wailed. "Oh, no! I didn't know it would be so bad!"

"Steel *is* poison to him," Rivka murmured. She put her arm around the now sobbing Lily and looked pleadingly at Dov. "We could bring several guards, and you're armed. Dov. . . ? I'd love to see that scroll open, to know what it says. . . ."

Dov was staring at Qaletaqua who was growing noticeably paler by the moment. His hand was swelling rapidly, he wavered on his feet, and he was swallowing convulsively as if to keep from vomiting.

"Would a hospital help?" Dov asked.

"I must go to my own healer," the Sidhe whispered.

"Go!" Lily cried. "Go quickly. Oh, I am so sorry. Don't worry about the stall. I'll find security and tell them you got sick suddenly. They'll shut down for you."

Cradling the injured hand with his other arm, the Sidhe looked at Dov. "Please," he whispered.

"I'll bring the manuscript tomorrow . . . and I'll bring an army with it," Dov said.

The next day, just after noon, four luxury limousines pulled into the faire parking lot. Twenty hard-eyed men got out. Faire security was hastily summoned, but Dov assured them his operatives would cause no trouble. He offered his card. One security man's eyes opened wide and he urged the others to admit Dov's "guests."

Dov paid for twenty-two tickets and they passed through the gates. Once in the field, ten peeled off from the group and spread around. The remaining ten, with Dov and Rivka, made for Qaletaqua's booth. Lily had been ordered to remain at home and, if Dov and Rivka did not return or phone one hour after faire closing time, Lily knew whom to call.

The interior of Qaletaqua's tent looked exactly the same as the previous day. Rivka's breath hissed in softly as she braced herself to resist the sensations his merchandise produced. Her breath hissed in again when she raised her eyes to Qaletaqua. He was not the same. His hair was still golden, his eyes still green, but both were somehow dimmer, and his face was . . . old, lined and bony, the skin pallid instead of fair.

Dov frowned. "You don't look so good, friend. Do you want to put this off for another time."

Qaletaqua's gaze had fastened on the long, flat box strapped across Rivka's chest. Straps went over each shoulder and joined a belt that went around her waist. Another strap seemed welded to the box and went around her body just under her breasts. There didn't seem to be any closures.

"Is that it?" Qaletaqua asked softly.

"Yes," Dov said.

He was wearing a loose safari jacket over a black turtleneck shirt and black cargo pants. Every pocket on the jacket and pants bulged, and Dov's right hand was suggestively in the outside jacket pocket.

Qaletaqua ignored the implied threat, gestured toward the end of the bookcase. "If you will come back here, I think the lady will be less distressed." He led the way, turning sharply at the end of the bookcase. As Rivka turned also, he suddenly seized her and cried, "Watch the step!"

For just a moment Rivka thought the warning had come too late. Her foot lost contact with the ground and a wave of violent vertigo swept over her. Worse, there was no light. She would have cried out with fear, but she felt Dov's hand reassuringly on her shoulder.

In the next instant, she was standing firmly on a wide platform covered with exquisite, glowing sand paintings—paintings that reshaped themselves under her feet as she moved. Ahead . . . ahead was impossible. A forest such as had not been seen in America for thousands of years—a forest with beams of light streaming down between the enormous trees. But beams of light were impossible, too; the sky was black.

That was impossible. They had entered Qaleta-qua's tent just after noon; now above, a lacework of brilliant stars shone in a dark sky. Yet ahead was "a forest full of sun" . . . well, moonlight to her, but she remembered how Qaletaqua squinted outside the tent. It might be sunlight to him. She put her hand over Dov's.

"I don't think we're in Kansas anymore," she said.

"No, nor in Tennessee either," Dov replied.

Qaletagua released Rivka's wrist and spun around, saw Dov, and uttered a word Rivka had no need for translation to understand.

"Thought you'd leave me behind, didn't you?" Dov smiled.

"It would have made for less argument, that's all. And you never would have missed the lady. I would have brought her back at the very instant she left."

"With or without the manuscript?"

"With! I promised not to touch it and I would not have done so."

"You thought Rivka would hand it to you?" Again a smile.

"Over my dead body!" she exclaimed, eyes hard as Dov's.

Qaletaqua put his good hand to his head. "Please," he whispered. "This is what I wanted to avoid. I thought the lady . . . She wanted to see the scroll open. I wouldn't have touched it. I only need to read it slowly to make a copy."

"You haven't exactly imbued us with confidence," Rivka said. "If you want to see this manuscript out of its box, you'd better take us back. Right now!"

"But I need to be *here* to open the scroll. I cannot gather enough power in the mortal world."

"No go-back, no scroll." Rivka's voice was flat.

Tears leaked from under the lids closed over the Sidhe's green eyes. "I swear a fellow magus will see you safe back to your own time and place when I have read the scroll." He opened his eyes, took in Rivka's expression, and sighed. "How I have blundered! Our mortals are compliant."

Rivka stiffened, an angry comment on her lips, but Dov's hand tightened on her shoulder. She looked up and saw he was staring out into the forest, his eyes alight with interest.

"Let's go along with Qaletaqua and let him see the scroll. I want to have a look at this place." His hand patted the bulge in his jacket pocket. "One wrong move and he's dead. The gun is an automatic and I've got enough ammunition to shoot up a fair-sized city. *Someone* will be glad to take us back to be rid of us if this one doesn't keep his word."

It was a strange walk. From the platform the forest seemed a fair distance, but they were under the trees within a few steps. Also, from the platform the forest seemed to be empty, yet within moments of entering it, they were approaching an enormous longhouse, such a longhouse as no tribe, no matter how strong and prosperous, had ever built. And behind the longhouse, lodges, again like none ever seen on earth.

Here their progress slowed and Qaletaqua led them on a weaving path of soft white sand marked with symbols that their steps did not disturb. Narrower paths led from that they walked, and Qaletaqua led them down one. At last the Sidhe stopped by the door of one of the lodges. The place was eerily silent; they had seen no one since they arrived.

The door flap was beaded into scenes of tribal celebration. The outer walls were of a silver-furred hide Rivka—though admitting her real ignorance—would have said it was deer or antelope . . . if a deer or antelope could have grown large enough for one skin to cover a whole house. Qaletaqua lifted his hand and the door flap lifted. He stepped in. Rivka followed. Dov with his gun drawn in one hand and his other hand still firmly gripping Rivka's shoulder stepped in after her.

Rivka stared around. The "branches" that supported the lodge were not only of silver but they seemed to be growing. Her lips parted to ask a question just as a scream of abject terror and terrible pain rang out.

Qaletaqua darted past, snatching up a club. Dov, flicking off the safety of the gun, followed with Rivka hard on his heels. Back to the main path, along it to the longhouse. The door was open and just past the doorway someone was down, convulsing, screaming. A little black *thing* clung to the screamer's ankle until a violent convulsion shook it loose. Qaletaqua shouted a warning, but Dov had already squeezed off a shot, another. The thing . . . or bits of it . . . lay still.

Two more slithered out of the longhouse heading for them. Dov shot them. More screaming from the other end of the longhouse, but this was only fear, not agony. Dov jumped over the wailing, convulsing body, leaped at the seemingly open doorway . . . and bounced off.

Qaletaqua shouted a word and Dov went through, almost falling. Three more shots. The screaming inside stopped.

Two more Sidhe were approaching at a run. Both had the same blond hair and green eyes as Qaletaqua, but both were wearing Amerind dress, fringed deerskin elaborately beaded. Even without touching it, Rivka knew the clothing was soft and supple as velvet. One saw the remains of the black thing, gasped, and went wide around it; the other leaped over. Both flung themselves down beside the screaming man.

One put a hand on the injured man's head and the screaming and writhing stopped; instead the healer began to tremble and whimper. The other put a hand on the ankle. He grew pale and bit his lip but did not remove his hand.

Dov came out of the longhouse. "I think I got them all."

He looked at Qaletaqua, who had not made a sound after releasing the barrier that kept Dov out of the longhouse. The Sidhe was staring at the remains of the three black creatures Dov had killed, then at the straining healers. He looked even older and grayer.

"Merciful Mother," he breathed, "we are lost. Before, at the worst, they came one at a time. Now I fear . . ."

"Now I guess you'd better look at that manuscript." Dov's voice was unshaken.

Sheltered by Dov's big body, Rivka removed the box and its harness as soon as they returned to Qaletaqua's lodge. She was careful not to shake the ancient wooden box in which the scroll had lain for thousands of years. Then she opened the box. She made no attempt to remove the scroll. The lightest touch resulted in fragmentation.

Qaletaqua signed for her to lay the box on a table to the side. Then he looked at the rolled scroll and began to whisper softly, the rhythmically repeated words taking on the nasal singsong of an Amerind chant. The scroll swelled. Rivka drew in her breath, chanced a glance at Qaletaqua. The Sidhe's face now looked like a skull framed with that improbably brilliant gold hair.

When the scroll exactly fit the box within which it had lain loose for so long, Qaletaqua's voice drifted into silence. Rivka, breath held, watched the scroll. Over her shoulder she could hear Dov breathing hard.

"Take it out and unroll it so I can see," Qaletaqua urged impatiently. "It may take hours to generate a copy."

"Do we have hours?" Dov asked.

No one answered the question, but Rivka's hands shook as she lifted the papyrus from the box. She had feared it would feel wet and flaccid and perhaps fall apart, but the feel was that of freshly prepared fine paper and it unrolled readily, opening to reveal closely painted rows of hieroglyphs. Qaletaqua, leaning close, uttered another word Rivka did not need translated.

"What are those symbols?" he cried. "I cannot read it."

"The symbols are hieroglyphs," Dov said. "But why?"

"Well, Moses *was* Egyptian," Rivka pointed out, fixing her eyes on the scroll. "What language did you expect?"

Dov began to laugh. "Silly as it sounds, Hebrew."

Qaletaqua turned his head away. "I cannot read that," he sighed. "I cannot use the spells. Underhill is dead." He shuddered, drew himself together. "Well, we will fight as long as we can. I will go to Machu Picchu with those sworn to the task of stemming the tide. A fellow mage will take you back to the tent in the faire. You can do no more for us."

While he spoke, Rivka had been reading the scroll. The first half gave the ten symbols for the ten plagues. To the side in red was a single row. The other half mentioned the escape to the Red Sea. Beyond were two more rows of red glyphs. Something stirred in Rivka as her eyes followed the symbols and she hastily looked away.

"Do you have to read the scroll yourself?" she asked.

Qaletaqua stared. "You can read it? Can you teach me?"

"If you've got ten years or so to spend—"

Her answer was cut off by shrieks and curses. Dov and the Sidhe charged out of Qaletaqua's house; Rivka paused to reroll the scroll and replace it in its box before she followed. She heard gunfire—not sharp single shots but the stuttering thunder of full automatic. Then she was in an open area near the longhouse.

Dov was standing, legs apart, braced against the jerking recoil of his gun. A number of Sidhe with flat-ended clubs in hand were swatting at a few scattered creatures while Dov blew away the large central group. Rivka shivered. The heads looked like those of vampire bats, the bodies were froglike, the skin black and glistening with mucus. Like frogs, the things could jump, but fortunately they could not fly and were not particularly quick or agile. It was possible to kill them—but not thousands of them forever.

In another few minutes the attack was over. Everyone stared around suspiciously, but no more of the black monstrosities appeared . . . at least in that area. Dov replaced the magazine in his gun, dropped it into his pocket, and reached a hand toward Rivka.

"Got the scroll?" He nodded in answer to his question without waiting for her to reply. "Okay, Qaletaqua, you convinced me. Let's go to Machu Picchu and see if Moses' Miracles will work."

Most of those who had been wielding clubs joined them, faces grim. The edge of the forest was achieved in one step, the Gate—the sand-painted platform—in a second. A moment of darkness and vertigo and the whole party stood on another platform formed of cyclopean stones.

Rivka did not notice any pattern in the stones. She was looking ahead, across a sandy waste to . . . Machu Picchu. She had never been there. Her field trips had been to Europe, the Middle East, Egypt, and even China, but Dov had brought back many photographs from Peru. As they approached—the journey was less swift and easy; the Sidhe who accompanied them breathing hard with effort—she saw that this Machu Picchu was not exactly like the site in the photographs. It was less decayed. The walls of the temples were higher, there were roofs in many places, and the stones seemed black.

Rivka looked harder. "Ooooh," she quavered, clutching Dov's arm with her free hand.

The darkness on the walls and roofs was . . . moving, flowing. And as it flowed it was renewed so that more could run down the walls, down the broad ledges, down the steps, into the ball court. But the walls of the ball court seemed lower than those on the photographs.

Rivka shivered and held Dov tighter as she perceived the real reason for the shorter walls. The ball court was full, yards deep, with a seething tide of the black monsters.

Some crept up the walls and fell back, but more took their place. And she saw where one got over the wall and then two more before a third touched whatever restraint was there and fell. Nervously she opened the box, took out the scroll, and shoved the end of the box into a pocket. The scroll still seemed fresh and new, so she unrolled it to the part concerning the plagues. Dov put a hand over the text.

Rivka looked up. Dov's face was gray and his eyes dull pebbles. She swallowed hard. She had never seen Dov afraid before, even in the face of an attempt at assassination; then he had been angry.

"Qaletaqua," he called, looking around. "When Rivka starts reading that spell of unbinding, are the protections you and your friends made going to come down?"

"I am afraid . . . yes." Qaletaqua's voice was raged. "But they are failing anyhow." He gestured.

Rivka looked. Below the walls of the ball court where the terraces merged into what had been arable land there was a sea of writhing black that stopped abruptly. Although she could see nothing, Rivka could feel a wall of force . . . only it no longer held back the whole sea. Here and there a thin stream forced its way out into the sandy waste.

"We need to be nearer," Qaletaqua said.

Rivka nearly cried a denial, but Dov put his arm around her and she went forward until they came to a little rise. In England or the Scandinavian lands she would have called it a barrow, but she did not know whether the Incas used that form of burial or buried their dead at all.

Now she saw two of the streams from under the wall of force were bending toward each other . . . bending toward them. Bleakly, Dov nodded at her, released her, and lifted his gun. The two streams came together, formed into a black river.

Rivka raised the scroll, called to mind the bright, hot forecourt of her teacher's house, heard his voice, clear, light, correcting her pronunciation from modern to ancient. Whatever had moved in her when she first saw the symbols touched her more strongly as she began the invocation that had ended the plagues four thousand years in the past.

Heat within her, terrible heat, yet it leached out with each symbol she pronounced, symbols she could read and say aloud but not understand. There were echoes inside her head of some kind of meaning, but she could not fix on it; she heard one of the Sidhe cry out, heard Dov begin a litany of obscenity, but she could not stop, could not even lift her eyes from the scroll.

When she had pronounced the last red word, she was chilled, but free. Shaking with cold and fear she looked up and became too frightened even to shake. The barriers were down. Instead of trickles, a whole ocean of writhing black was pouring across the waste toward them.

A Sidhe behind her exclaimed and his voice held . . . joy? Madness! In moments they would drown in the black flood and die in agony. But the Sidhe was pointing up at the ruins and Rivka could see that the walls and towers were no longer black with new growth. The ball court was empty, too, but the blackness crept out toward the waste with no interference.

Beside her Dov's gun began to roar, sweeping from side to side. In a wide arc facing their little hillock the tide ceased to move as the things died. A few escaped. The Sidhe leaped down to meet and destroy the strays.

Rivka began to hope, but then Dov's gun hiccuped, fell silent. Jammed? The ocean of black flowed into the hollow Dov had created and moved toward them again. Rivka remembered the writhing, screaming victim of the monsters' poison.

"Stop!" she cried . . . in Egyptian.

With the word that terrible heat rose in her again so strong she feared she would char inside. Speaking the red symbols had leached the heat away. Salvation was in saying the unbinding spell.

Only it wasn't. Rivka said the first word, but the heat grew more intense. Her eyes blurred; her hand shook. She lost her place, found it again.

Burning, not knowing what else to do, she shrieked the first symbol once more, but it was not the symbol she had spoken before. Yet the heat began to fade. She continued to read. She grew cool . . . cold . . . very cold. She could barely move her lips, but she forced out the last word.

Dov's gun began to roar again . . . and the sand rippled. Rivka wondered why Dov's aim was so bad and then saw that his gun was not pointed toward the ripples. But the ripples spread, away from where she stood, growing deeper, deeper . . . and there was a roaring, not from Dov's gun, a terrible groaning as if the earth itself were in pain.

Between the ripples hollows sank, deepened, widened. The black ocean heaved, swelled on the rising ripples and fell into the ever deeper hollows. There was a grinding, followed by a sharp explosion. One of the terraces of Machu Picchu cracked open and a whole river of black flowed in. Another crack. A higher terrace gave way swallowing up nearly all the monsters near the elfhame.

An even greater explosion followed a violent tossing of the earth that churned what had been the arable land around the lower walls of great buildings into rough clods. Those were swallowed up, taking with them the black curse, and were regurgitated as clean earth. The groaning of the earth was rising to a scream and the land heaved in waves.

Beneath their feet the hillock trembled. The Sidhe shouted. One seized her; another seized Dov, crying out with pain at the nearness to the gun and magazines but holding steady. And they were at the Gate, from which Rivka saw the whole sandy waste rise up into mountains and collapse. The platform trembled, disappeared . . . and they were upon the sand paintings once more.

"What the hell did you do?" Dov breathed.

"I think I read the spell Moses used to part the Red Sea," Rivka said in a small voice.

"Right." He took a deep breath. "Now put the damn thing away and let's not read any more Egyptian spells!"

Mutely, Rivka rerolled the scroll and put it in its box. Most of the Sidhe were gone by then. Only Qaletaqua, still looking gaunt and tired, but smiling broadly, lingered.

"I will take you back to the faire now," the Sidhe said.

But Dov was holding up a hand and looking out at Nahele Helaku—the Forest Full of Sun. His eyes were alight, his expression intense. He grinned at Qaletaqua.

"I wonder if there's any other manuscript in my library that you'd like to borrow? If you tell me how to get here, I will bring it myself."

Rivka's lips tightened. Dov had discovered a new addiction, even more dangerous than archaeological digs. She put a hand on his arm.

"And I'll come along to translate, or at least tell you how to pronounce the symbols."

Qaletaqua laughed aloud. "Come to the faire and I'll find a way."

# GROK

*by*

*Donald J. Bingle*

A frequent attendee of game conventions and Renaissance Faires, Donald J. Bingle is well-versed in role-playing in realms both historical and fantastical. This background has proved invaluable in his written work, which ranges from role-playing adventures and movie reviews to stories and screenplays. He is the author of *Extreme Global Warming*, a darkly comedic screenplay about an environmental organization that is about to save the world, but doesn't want to get caught doing it. He also recently released *Forced Conversion*, a science fiction novel about the all-too-probable future of the government's relationship with malcontents. He has fantasy stories in *The Players of Gilean* and *The Search for Magic*, a science fiction story in *Sol's Children*, and spooky stories in *Carnival, Historical Hauntings*, and *Civil War Fantastic*. He can be reached through www.orphyte.com. And, yes, he owns more than one poofy shirt.

"LET'S BE PRACTICAL for just a minute, okay?" said the young man as his giggling bride pulled him toward yet another of the myriad of gaily festooned booths. He wore jeans and a short-sleeved button-down shirt. A pinkish tinge on the bridge of his nose and the tops of his ears betrayed that he would later regret having refused to don any sunscreen when they had parked in the grass several hours earlier. "I mean, really, how many opportunities am I ever going to have to wear a poofy shirt?"

The pretty maiden stopped giggling long enough to pretend to put on a serious face, her lips briefly forming a pout. "You can wear it the next time we come to the faire!" She smiled broadly and took up her tugging once again. "It's fun. You can get a new piece of the outfit every time we come." She wore a flowered peasant dress in soft pastels, with a circle of daisies in her hair.

He didn't resist her tugging, but the young man's sneaker-clad feet thumped into the soft dirt with a plodding thud as he moved with her toward the colorful booth filled with expensive items of "period" clothing. "So, we pay money to come into a place to shop, so we can pay money to dress differently, so when we pay money to come back the next time and shop, we'll look more like the people we're paying money to?" The young man knitted his brow and shook his head in disbelief. "I thought we were supposed to be saving money for a house."

\* \* \*

Grok watched the couple earnestly. He understood the words, but he didn't really understand some of the people who came to the faire at all. He turned quickly away from the incipient argument, almost colliding with a six-year-old girl skipping along at the side of her mother. The six-year-old screamed. The young ones always screamed.

"Aaaaiiiiieeeeee," she wailed at a pitch so high that Grok could not have matched it ever in his life, no matter how hard he tried or how much pain he might be in. "Mommy, Mommy, Mommy!" The girl swerved left, seeking refuge behind her mother.

Time to go to work.

Grok roared "Yyyyyuuuuuuurrrrrrrraaaaaaaaaggggghhhhh," in a deep, guttural voice that the young girl would never be able to match, no matter how old and cranky she might become one day. He jumped up and landed, with his knees bent, hard on the powdery dirt. The dirt billowed up between Grok's splayed feet and dusted down upon his bare toes. He beat his chest and flung his head wildly back and forth, his greasy, black hair flailing from side to side before coming to rest in a tangle that covered his mud-caked, filthy face. He reared back his head and roared again, spittle flying up into the air and falling back upon his neck, as well as upon the stained and matted furs that were bundled and gathered about his body despite the heat of the midday sun. But he made no move toward the still-screaming child. He never moved toward the screamers. It was a good way to get punched in the groin.

Mommy looked about quickly, her tilted eyebrows and wide pupils demonstrating a panicked fight-or-flee concern. A filthy, disgusting, vile creature crouched at the side of the path. Caked-on mud and dirt covered his swarthy, hairy flesh and an odor of sweat and garlic and rancid grease emanated from every portion of his body and every inch of the foul and torn strips of cloth and fur that were tied with worn leather straps around his torso.

She immediately smiled.

Patting her daughter on the head, she bent down

and twisted to look into her terrified daughter's face. "It's okay, honey. It's just the Dirt Man. He won't hurt you. He's just for show."

They almost always called him the "Dirt Man" or the "Mud Man." Sometimes the patrons who came dressed in wizard's robes or who talked often of lords and rings and such called him "Orc." It didn't really matter.

Grok roared again, but not as loudly. A small crowd of patrons began to gather and point as the mother calmed her child. "See, honey? That's what you'll look like some day if you don't take your bath when you're told."

The little girl looked back at Grok, wrinkling her nose in disgust. "Really?" Grok sniffed the air exaggeratedly in return and looked around, as if to figure out where the stench came from.

"Really," said the mother with a chuckle. "He's just cranky 'cause he needs a bath and some nice, new clothes."

Grok sneered a bit, his lip quivering over his yellow, uneven teeth, then suddenly picked a bit of something disgusting-looking off his tunic and sucked it off his grimy fingers, smacking his lips loudly and letting forth a resounding belch.

The crowd laughed.

"Here, sweetie," said the mother encouragingly, as she handed her young daughter a crisp dollar bill. "Why don't you give him this, so he can buy a fresh, clean outfit and stop scaring pretty little girls?"

Grok stared intently at the money and yipped several times in encouragement, then cast his eyes down at the ground and held forth a shaky hand. The little girl took the dollar from her mother and moved with trepidation toward the foul man-beast, who squatted down lower so as to match the girl's height. With a sudden burst of courage, she darted forward, stuffed the money into his grimy paw, and retreated back to her mother.

Grok took the money, sniffed it thoroughly, bit on a corner of the paper (drawing several guffaws from the small crowd), then used it to wipe his hair and armpits before blowing his nose in the paper and stuffing it beneath his furry garb. Then he scampered off behind the nearest booth to polite applause from the crowd.

\* \* \*

"Dude, I am telling you, we have absolutely got to see the jugglers. Last time they picked some big guy out of the audience as a volunteer, you know, and then they, like, they started throwing things past his head and crawling on top of his shoulders and stuff while they juggled." The lanky teenager wore baggy jeans and a black T-shirt proclaiming the U.S. locations visited by a metal band on their "world" tour.

The teen's spiky-haired compatriot rolled his eyes. This second youth wore baggy jeans and a black T-shirt that declared "I killed Kenny and now I'm going to kill you." "Duh. The guy was obviously a ringer. They can't do that crap with volunteers. Somebody gets hurt and the shysters would be all over those guys."

"Y'think?"

"You are so totally clueless, dude."

\* \* \*

Grok watched the exchange from behind a tree, but stayed clear of the gangly young men. They would sometimes laugh at him and point, but they would never give him money. And sometimes, sometimes they would jostle him around or throw dirt at him. He didn't mind the dirt, but he didn't like the mean-spiritedness of boys of a certain age. And they could run faster than he could.

Besides, there were always more interesting people to watch at the faire.

\* \* \*

"Did you see that?" the middle-aged matron said stridently to her paunchy husband.

The husband looked up from his Royal Frozen Creamery Confection, which was dripping in a sticky mess over one of his hammy hands. He adjusted his baseball cap with his free hand, to block the glare of the sun. "What? Where?"

His wife nudged him with an elbow. "Don't look, you pervert."

The husband looked about quickly with genuine interest. "What?"

"That woman was wearing a chain mail bikini."

The husband craned his neck so quickly in the direction that his wife's eyes had flickered that he almost certainly strained a ligament. "Where?"

"Never you mind where. It's absolutely disgusting."

He turned back to his wife in disappointment, returning his passion to licking at his rapidly melting ice cream. He shrugged as he pushed his face into a mouthful of the cool, mushy sweetness. "It's a faire. People dress up. You know, knights and all that stuff."

His wife snorted in a manner not at all ladylike.

"Nobody dressed like that in the Middle Ages. Besides," she lowered her voice to a whisper, "she didn't have anything on underneath."

The husband's head popped back up and swiveled like a periscope. "So?"

His wife glared at him. "She didn't have the figure for it. A bit on the porky side, like you."

He just shrugged and went back to his treat. "Oh."

"A fine citizen you are. There are small children about, you know." Her foot tapped lightly in the dirt and she crossed her arms in consternation.

"Kids see barely dressed fat people on the beach all the time, not to mention on *Jerry Springer*. What's the difference?"

His wife's voice dropped again to a conspiratorial whisper. "The chain mail, it had big links."

\*     \*     \*

Grok scampered in the direction in which the wife had suggested the chain mail bikini bimbo had gone. Even though no one thought anything about staring at him, he always seemed to get in trouble when he stared droolingly at any of the women for too long. It wasn't fair, but whenever he stared intently at the ample cleavage displayed at the faire by women of all makes and sizes, sooner or later he would get thwacked with a purse or an umbrella or the girl's boyfriend would come at him or security would get called. But the chicks in chain mail, they obviously came to the faire to be stared at; they loved . . . lived . . . to be ogled. And when you were a filthy, dirt-encrusted, flea-ridden piece of flesh encased in rancid animal hide, ogling was pretty much all of the romantic pleasure you could get. And if the chick had a little extra weight, so what? That was just a way to get through a tough winter as far as he was concerned.

Besides, once he had his fill of the view, he could almost be sure that, with all of the head-swiveling going on by passersby, he would be able to steal a pickle from someone. There was nothing like a cold, juicy, garlicky dill pickle on a hot day like today. Oh, sure, the steak on a stake was juicy and garlicky, too, but if you weren't careful, you could skewer yourself pretty badly trying to steal one of those.

\* \* \*

"So, I get initiative, and boom, right away I roll a natural twenty. Crit. Double damage. Then, second attack, another crit. Same thing, both with the plus three sword, plus strength, plus Oil of Sharpening, plus the Bless—thirty-seven points of damage. It was awesome." The young man in the brightly colored, full-sleeved shirt, with leather vest, gesticulated enthusiastically as he strolled along, the feather in his floppy hat and his peace-bound rapier bouncing in time to his long strides.

"Yeah," said his similarly-attired companion, with considerably less enthusiasm, "but I can't believe you didn't have to do an alignment check. You're supposed to be a friggin' paladin. You can't go offing a mayor."

"Detect evil, ten-foot radius, man."

"And did you actually check it before you attacked, or did you just find out after the fact?"

"Same difference. He was evil. I took him out. Solo."

"You didn't know. You didn't check. If you didn't say it, you didn't do it."

\* \* \*

Grok ignored the conversation about violence. He had long ago learned that such conversations were only about make-believe violence, like the make-believe battles in the jousting grounds at the south end of the faire. The crowds would cheer and shout "huzzahs," obviously worked into a frenzy of support for the ersatz knights in their clash of dull weaponry. But he had seen enough of the staging and choreography practiced on the weekdays when the faire was closed, that he was bored by the entire phony spectacle. The horses, though, he liked the horses. Not only could he pick up extra money mucking out the stables twice a day—without even having to worry about getting his outfit dirty—but the horses were big and gentle and never were mean or judged him. He didn't like to watch the jousts, though. The horses were manhandled and spurred and made to work hard in the heat. It's not like they had a choice about it.

\* \* \*

"Why pay four dollars for a hot dog, when we can just go back to the van and make peanut butter sandwiches?" groused Grandpa as a bevy of children scampered around the picnic bench where he had sat to rest as Grandma did her best to corral the grandchildren.

"It's ninety-two degrees out in the shade, dear," stated Grandma as she bustled the last grandchild to the table and rummaged for her change purse in her big macramé handbag.

"I didn't say not to buy cold drinks. I'm not stupid and I'm not mean," grumbled Grandpa.

"The van has been sitting in the sun for four hours," replied Grandma matter-of-factly. "You could *pour* a peanut butter sandwich."

\* \* \*

"Now, I want everyone to sit very still and be very quiet and you'll see something that you'll never get to see in the wild." The presenter waited momentarily for the crowd to settle completely and then briskly raised one hand into the air.

From behind the stands there was a sharp "scree," and the "woof" of heavy wings. A majestic hawk took off from its hidden perch and soared just above the heads of the seated throng, traversing the length of the stands, then dipping one wing briefly and wheeling toward the trainer making the Birds of Prey Salvation Society presentation. The presenter dipped his upraised arm and flung a tidbit of meat high into the air, and the hawk made three powerful strokes as it rose quickly up to snare the morsel at its apogee. Then it glided in a circular path to land on the opposite, heavily-gloved arm of the presenter.

The wide eyes of the children and the simultaneous intake of breath by the mesmerized onlookers as the giant avian winged scant inches above their upturned faces provided a picture of awe and innocence and unity that the world outside the faire scarcely knew.

\* \* \*

It was at the Birds of Prey Salvation Society presentation that Grok first spied them. She was pretty and rosy-cheeked, fully grown, but still retaining the innocence and radiance of youth. Her gown was light and airy, with a shimmer of silver threads that matched the twinkle of her green eyes. Her chestnut hair was braided into a Celtic knot, from the center of which cascaded a fall of silken tresses that moved lightly in the breeze. She watched the massive birds run through their paces with reverence. But between each demonstration, her eyes would wander to the end of the stand kitty-corner from her own position, where sat a handsome young man in a bright white pirate's shirt and black pantaloons, with a leather vest and knee-high soft boots. Though the shadow of the great bird passed directly over him, his strong, gray eyes never left the lady fair. Not staring, certainly not leering, but with respectful admiration and friendly invitation.

At his appointed time, Grok stepped forward into the circle of grass and the best-trained of the birds, a Swainson's Hawk, swooped down and landed on the collar of his leathery garb and began picking tidbits of meat from his hair and clothing to the delight of the audience. The crowd laughed and cheered as Grok reached back to pick lice from the wings of the great bird and eat them. The maiden's laughter was genuine and musical and unrestrained. The young gentleman, who had not seen a thing of Grok's or the hawk's performance, smiled and laughed gently at the joy of the lady he had espied.

Then the presentation was over and a throng of children and parents with camcorders surrounded him. Grok went through his practiced paces, much as had the birds. Only Grok's routine consisted of grunts and howls and groveling and picking his nose and, by the time he was done and had collected yet more of the coin and paper money of the realm, the smitten lad and lass were lost from his sight.

\* \* \*

Grok rushed along the grassy avenues of the Renaissance Faire, anxious to see what had happened to the young gentleman and his lady fair. Children screamed and flummoxed tourists quickly skedaddled out of his way, diving and twisting their suburban bodies in ways they were not accustomed to. All the while they tried desperately to avoid brushing up against the mud and dirt and grease and sweat that covered Grok and spattered in every direction as he swung his arms and shook his mane of hair.

Snippets of conversation were interrupted as he roared along the venue.

"Would you care for mead or diet mead, m'lady?"

"How do I know if it's a good price on a jeweled snood? I don't even know what a snood is . . ."

"Don't you think we should be just a little bit concerned that Johnny knows what the difference is between a mace and a morning star?"

"I'm telling you, all of the arrows were computer graphics . . ."

"More beer, wench! Now there's something you can't get away with saying at home."

"You keep your pet rat where?"

"My feet are tired . . ."

He caught up to his quarry on the outskirts of the Globe Stage, where two men were giving a demonstration of the gentlemanly art of fencing, rapiers flashing and flying in quick bursts of action aimed over one another's heads, as the swordsmen ducked and cavorted. While they clashed, the two supposed gentlemen traded double entendres, barbs slashing and flying in quick bursts of wit aimed over the heads of the younger members of the audience, as their elders chuckled and snorted.

The winsome lady he had seen during the bird show peeked out from behind a massive tree, as the young gentleman who had been watching her stood with one arm leaning against the same tree in a relaxed pose.

"Prithee, miss. Do not hide thy countenance from me behind this sturdy vegetation, lest I be deprived of thy beauty too long and my soul wither from lack of nourishment."

The maiden giggled lightly. "Thou dost have a charming manner about you, kind sir, but I worry that the words flow so brightly and generously only because the spigot is ne'er turned shut."

The suitor clutched at his chest and fell back and to his knees. "Thy words of rebuke strike hard as a dagger into my heart. I fear that I may fall without ever knowing the sweet taste of your lips softly caressing mine own."

"And how know I, sir, that you are not just a cad and a bounder, who feigns injury to prey upon my innocence and virtue?"

"I swear to you, m'lady, upon mine honor as a knight, that I will do nothing that is not done at your own request."

She reached out to her gentleman and he rose gracefully, kissing her hand as he stood. "Then, gallant sir, thy first task is to escort me from this place to my dwelling, where I may take refuge from the hot sun and refresh myself."

"I shall honor each request thou shalt make, fair maiden, and take thy happiness as my life's quest."

The maiden snuggled her face close to the ear of her suitor and whispered gleefully, "You're right. Role-playing can be fun. And we've only just begun . . ."

Grok watched wistfully as the two headed for the entrance to the faire, hand in hand, skipping in merriment and joy. This vicarious moment was as close to love as Grok would ever know, he was sure.

\* \* \*

Grok was sad to see the couple go, sadder still to see the faire ending, for this was the last day of its short, summer run. He made the most of what remained of the day, mock-terrorizing little ones and hanging from the limb of a tree. He ate mud to the delight and disgust of the faire's patrons (who all were quite happy to drop money into his grimy pouch for the privilege of being delighted or disgusted). And he retrieved the leftover ears of sweet corn left at one of the food booths at the end of the long day.

There would be a party tonight 'round the campfires near the tents and the RVs of the faire workers. But in the morning, all would pack up and move on to another faire or back to their real jobs in the city nearby. The faire grounds would be empty till next summer, when the Renaissance would come once again to this world. There would be hugs and back-slaps and handshakes as the Renaissance workers said good-bye to one another, except for Grok.

No one wanted to hug the Mud Man, the Dirt Man, the Orc. Few had ever even reached out to shake his hand. Instead they would wave good-bye from a distance or say that he might give some thought to changing out of his costume now that the faire was done. Once, someone had asked, hesitatingly, what his real name was and where he came from.

"I am Grok!" he yelled, beating his chest. "I live here."

His questioner merely shook his head and walked away, muttering "Get a life, man." Grok stood, watching the questioner depart, confused.

Grok thought hard, but he could remember no place but the faire grounds, no place before this place. He knew no name but Grok, the Mud Man, the Dirt Man, the Orc.

He ran his long, dirty fingernails through the scraggle of his greasy beard and scurried off to bury his wages from the faire season in a secret, safe place. He stashed the money under a loose rock in a Crown Royal sack with his previous earnings. His treasure trove also contained a plastic wrist band with the name "Frank Blevins" on it, a pamphlet from the Center Street Mission declaring that "Jesus Saves," and an old photo of a man about Grok's height, but who somehow stood just a bit taller—a man who looked a bit familiar, but who Grok couldn't place anymore.

All Grok knew was that no one came to this place for most of the year, even though the buildings were sturdy and safe and provided suitable shelter from the cold and the rain and the snow. He made enough coin during the season to last the rest of the year, supplemented with the squirrels and rabbits he would snare from time to time. And in this place, during the faire, people would look at him and talk to him and laugh and give him money willingly.

But whenever he would see people outside the faire, they never laughed. They rarely gave him money, even when he did the same routines he did at the faire. They were mean or, worse yet, they treated him as if he wasn't there. They didn't treat him as a person.

But he was a person. He was Grok, the Mud Man, the Dirt Man, the Orc; the star of the Renaissance Faire.

# RENAISSANCE FEAR

### by

### *Stephen D. Sullivan*

Origins Award-winning novelist Stephen D. Sullivan doesn't believe in anything that he writes about. He doesn't believe in magic—other than the ordinary kind that makes the sun rise every day. He doesn't believe in Dragonlances, dragons of any kind (save on the island of Komodo), elves, Mage Knights, ghosts, or Mutant Ninja Turtles. Or, for that matter, any intelligent, talking animals—except some humans he's encountered. (And even then . . .)

Actually, the first sentence above is not true. Steve does believe in love, heroism, and the power of human redemption. He's written about all those things, and will continue to do so. Sadly, he also believes in fear, greed, and hatred. He'll probably continue to write about those, too. He especially believes in samurai. Winning an award for writing about them in *The Lion* has probably prejudiced him on that front. He also believes in speedy racers running across country at nearly Mach 5. (Though he doubts anyone could run such races without massive casualties.)

Steve barely believes in ghostwriters or immortal teen detectives, whether they've been going for seventy-five years or not. (How long does a fictitious author live, anyway?) Clearly, he also believes in obtuse biographies with mysterious references to his past work. He does believe in

comic books, lost islands, and dinosaurs. He even believes
that he may have seen a dinosaur lurking around the
Kwikee Mart last Halloween—though maybe that was just
Homer on work release from the Treehouse of Horrors.

Despite his belief in dinosaurs, Steve does not believe
in time travel—save the one-directional kind we're all engaged in as we read this paragraph. In this time contin-
uum, more information about Steve can be found at:
www.sdsullivan.com—or—www.alliterates.com.

"**L**IZARD ON A STICK! Get your lizard on a
stick!"
The street vendor loped through the dirt pathways
between the colorful tents and muddy paddocks,
holding aloft his sample of wares—a collection of
brownish, lumpy ribbons of fried meat, each skew-
ered on a thin strip of wood. The young, scraggly-
haired salesman eyed the crowd on either side of the
path, looking for likely customers.

"Lizard on a stick!" he called again.

Caroline Shaw clapped her hands and squealed, as
though she were a girl of half her actual age. She
clung excitedly to her fiancé's arm, pulling him close,
and spoke urgently into his ear.

"Let's get some!" she breathed in a voice too loud
to be truly conspiratorial. "What do you think it
*really* is?"

"Chicken, probably," Karl Lomax replied. "Spicy
fried chicken."

"Untrue, milord," the vendor put in, his bright
white smile belaying the "period" grunge of his
dingy, raglike costume. "'Tis lizard—as the Good
Lord is my witness."

Karl shot him a very skeptical look.

"*Alligator*," the vendor added, whispering. Then,

falling back into character, he threw his arms wide and made a comically frightening face. "This 'gator be a monstrous, dragonlike lizard, hunted in the wild swamps of the southland. Many knights fell riven beneath its claws to bring this delicacy to our fair land."

"I thought hunting alligators was illegal," Karl said.

The vendor frowned at him and spoke out of the corner of his mouth, as though trying not to let the others attending the faire hear. "Okay," he hissed, "it was raised on a gator *farm* down in the bayou."

"Not quite *period* fare, is it?" Karl said. "They didn't have alligator in Renaissance Europe."

The vendor shrugged, and the faux-rags on his skinny frame rustled. "Perhaps 'tis crocodile, from the Nile delta, then," he said. "My sources remain unclear on this point. But 'twas a terrible, great *lizard,* milord. And lizard be a well-known delicacy throughout this fair land." He held out the lumpy fried thing on the thin stick and added, "If you should but try it, your senses would thank you."

Karl remained unconvinced.

"Karl," Caroline said playfully, "they didn't have Renaissance Europe in eastern *Kentucky* either! Get into the mood, would you?" She elbowed him playfully in the ribs. "We're on *vacation*. Seize the day."

"Thy fair maiden's advice be sound, milord," the vendor agreed. Then, laying his hand next to his mouth and speaking in a stage whisper, he added. "'Tis said that the flesh of the dragon has powerful *aphrodisiac* qualities, milord."

Caroline laughed and clapped again. "Let's get some."

"Yeah, okay," Karl said, a begrudging smile tugging at the corners of his lips. "How much?"

"That be four single paper notes per skewer," the vendor said.

"Is this where I should haggle?" Karl asked hopefully.

"Alas, haggling be outlawed by the master of the Vendors' Guild, milord." The lizard seller frowned. "My deepest and most sincere apologies."

Karl nodded at the vendor, then smiled at Caroline as he handed the money over. Keeping his eyes fixed on his fiancée was the only way Karl could avoid wincing at the price—real alligator or no.

The ragged-costumed vendor handed over the food and then bowed, flashing his twenty-first-century smile once more.

"Thank you, milord, milady," he said. "Fare you well." He turned and hobbled theatrically down the muddy street.

Caroline Shaw put her arm around Karl Lomax's waist, and the two walked down the crowded marketway as they chewed on their fried 'gator. Colorful tents of many shapes and sizes lined the sides of the unpaved thoroughfare. Each pavilion shared the common goal of separating the faire-goer from his money. Most were dedicated to selling wares, though a few provided services—massage, body painting, soothsaying.

Karl didn't need a fortune-teller to know his wallet would be a good deal lighter by the time he and Caroline continued on their vacation that evening. The sign outside the town had said, "Knightshead, Kentucky—Sister City to Knightstor, England." Karl thought that if they stayed at the Renaissance Faire long enough, it might have been cheaper just to go to England.

Fog surrounded the tent city, making it seem strange and unreal. The mist added to the period effect that the faire sponsors were trying so desperately to achieve. In the fog, attendees could almost overlook the electrical lines snaking into the backs of most of the tents, or the Velcro fasteners that held so much of the fabric together. The mist made the participants' costumes look better than they were, too. From a distance, Karl could almost believe that he was looking at historical English peasants going about their daily business—historical peasants with great dental work.

This faire midway seemed larger than most of the others he'd been to, though perhaps that was a trick of the light as well. When the fog parted a bit, Karl almost thought he saw a medieval, or early Renaissance, town beyond the woods on the far side of the tents. And was that a *castle* on that distant hill? Probably no more than a painted facade. The AAA guidebook hadn't mentioned castles—or reconstructed historical towns—in Knightshead, Kentucky. Maybe it was something new, though, something tied into the "Sister City" campaign mentioned on the road sign.

Whether a fake or not, the looming castle did add to the atmosphere. Karl almost felt impressed. If he hadn't been to so many Renaissance Faires over the years, he probably would have *been* impressed.

Caroline sighed and snuggled up against him. The neckline of her low-cut top bunched up a bit, giving him a nice view down her blouse. "I just *love* this place," she said. "Don't you?"

Karl smiled and nodded at her. When Caroline wore a scanty top and cutoffs, it was hard *not* to love anyplace they went together.

If the truth were known, though, Karl Lomax *didn't* love the place. Despite the number he'd been to, he didn't much like Renaissance Faires at all. Karl knew the faire circuit well, and there were plenty of things *not* to like about it: too many weirdos, too many aging hippies, too many "arts & crafts" booths (exhibiting neither art nor craft), too damn much strange (and overpriced) food, too many out-of-work actors hoping to be spotted on the off chance of getting their big break, too many dopers hiding out after the dissolution of the Grateful Dead, and *way* too many poseurs speaking with fake accents.

Most of the "history" came from old Hollywood films; Renaissance and medieval cultures were haphazardly blended into a commercially viable whole. The music wafting through the air was often painfully slow and crude (and frequently off key). The colorful tents were fabricated mostly from materials created in a laboratory after World War II. The costumes of the participants were usually about as convincing and historically accurate as the tents.

Not that Karl didn't find some of the costumes the *women* wore attractive—even *alluring*. (Despite his engagement to Caroline, the sight of a chain mail bikini still made his pulse quicken.) Women, in fact, were the whole reason he started coming to Ren Faires in the first place.

Karl had discovered long ago that women were suckers for *chivalry*.

They loved the colorful tents, the sensual costumes, the whole "dress-up" nature of the events. Ren Faires were great places to pick up girls—and they were great places to go on a date.

You could catch a few knights bashing each other and getting all sweaty, listen to some mushy music, dine on exotic foods, knock back a couple of homebrewed drinks, and then finish it all off with a torchlight stroll through a tent city or a fake medieval village. The net effect of all that romance and chivalry practically *guaranteed* a quick score.

Which was why Karl put up with all the other Ren Faire shit he didn't much care for. The faires had been good to his libido—very good indeed.

Of course, Caroline didn't know that. *She* thought Karl was interested in the whole historical re-creation bit; she thought he was just another *rube*, like her.

The two of them had met at a Renaissance Faire very much like this one. Karl had been on his usual babe patrol, and Caroline had come for all the romantic stuff that women like. The two of them had hit it off immediately.

Much to Karl's surprise, the initial attraction blossomed into something deeper. An intense period of courtship had followed, and now they were engaged. Happily engaged. There was only one problem.

Karl hadn't told Caroline the *real* reason they'd met at that Ren Faire eighteen months ago. He didn't have the nerve to tell her that she was just the latest pickup in a long line of conquests. Nor did he dare tell that he was sick to *death* of fake Renaissance events.

He knew she wouldn't understand. She would think it was some reflection on his love for her. (It wasn't.) Or, worse, she would think that their entire relationship was based on a lie. (Maybe in the beginning, but they'd moved far beyond that point now.) In either case, he couldn't tell her. Not now.

The only thing to do was to carry on with the charade; to be as phony as every peasant, knight, and noble in the faires themselves.

Karl didn't much like the corner he'd painted himself into, but Caroline was worth it. One day, after they'd been married for fifteen years and had a couple of kids, he'd tell her. Until then, he'd keep his chin up and try to find things to admire in a series of increasingly repetitive and boring semihistorical attractions.

He *had* tried to steer Caroline away from them. He'd planned out-of-town vacations when he knew the local faires were returning to town. He discarded flyers and sections of the local newspapers before she could see Ren Faire ads. Karl had been pretty successful until today's stroke of bad luck.

He'd never expected to be "ambushed" by a Renaissance Faire while driving through Knightshead, Kentucky, on vacation. The sign for the faire had just appeared out of the fog. Naturally, Caroline *had* to go. Naturally, Karl couldn't refuse—not without revealing his "dark secret."

So, here he was, munching alligator fritter and getting his new Nikes muddy while the chill haze pressed in around them. The fog, Karl decided, was a blessing. Not only did it make the faire look less shabby, but it had the added benefit of making Caroline snuggle close.

"We should have brought our coats," she cooed.

"Yeah," he replied, glad they hadn't. His T-shirt and shorts weren't as brief as hers, but he didn't get cold as quickly as she did. Which always served to bring them closer together, much to his delight. "Do you want to go back to the car?" he asked hopefully.

"Not yet," she said. "We haven't been here that long." She hugged him as they walked. "I sometimes feel like I was born *too late*. That *here* is where I really belong."

"In Kentucky?"

"No, goofball. In the Renaissance. Things were so much simpler then. Life didn't run at you headlong; things were more laid back. Everyone knew their place in society; everybody had a job to do—a niche to fill."

"That's simpler, all right."

"Don't you wish we lived back then?"

"I had a namesake who lived back then," Karl said. "He was burned at the stake."

Her eyes grew wide. "Really? What for?"

"Consorting with witches," Karl said. Consorting was probably a Renaissance euphemism for chasing skirts, he thought.

"Well," Caroline said, putting her arms around him, "*I'm* the only witch you consort with now." She smiled and gave him a quick kiss.

Karl wondered if a man could inherit a tendency for "consorting."

"So, witch burnings aside, don't you think it would have been fun to live during the Renaissance?"

"Forget witch burning, and plague, and famine and all that stuff?"

Caroline frowned playfully. "Yes. All that aside. Wouldn't it be nice to live in a world that . . . *unspoiled*?"

"Sure," Karl lied. "Isn't that why we're here? No sense reliving history if you can't cut out the nasty bits. Of course, living in the Renaissance would be easier if we got the coats out of our car."

"Silly man," Caroline replied. "I'm not *that* cold. Let's look around a bit more. What about that?" She pointed past the tents and small woods to the village looming out of the fog. "We haven't seen that, yet. It looks like a re-creation of a town."

Karl squinted and peered into the mist. Night was fast approaching, and the twilight had taken on a gray, dreamlike quality, so he couldn't be sure what he was seeing. She was pointing where he thought he'd seen a town before, though.

"Is that a castle?" Caroline asked excitedly.

"Maybe. I caught a glimpse of it earlier, through the mist. It's probably just a facade, though."

"It looks real. Let's go see."

"It'll be dark soon," Karl said.

"We've come this far," she replied. "It would be a shame to miss the rest. It's not like we'll be back this way any time soon."

"I guess that's true," Karl answered, thoughts of escape fading from hope. Still, he preferred being "trapped" at a Renaissance Faire with Caroline to being alone most anyplace else. He smiled at her. "Let's check it out before the light goes."

They finished their lizard and dumped the sticks in a trash barrel then walked through the fog toward the dim, angular shapes in the fog. At the edge of the tent city, the couple passed through a small, wild, woody area with an open clearing—probably used for outdoor shows during better weather. The tiny, tree-lined paddock looked like a gloomy wasteland—its surface muddy and rutted with the passage of people and animals. Hoofprints and other animal tracks were clearly visible in the wet earth.

"I wonder where they're keeping the horses?" Caroline asked, glancing around. "I didn't see any in the pavilions." She peered back the way they'd come, but already the faire tents were disappearing into the mist.

"We'll look for them on our way back to the car," Karl said. "The 'village' up ahead doesn't look too promising."

The houses looming out of the fog ahead of them appeared shabby, and ill-kept. There were a *lot* of them, though—far more than usual for a faire this size. In fact, they looked more like part of a historical attraction, or perhaps a theme park (a very run-down theme park).

"Do you think this is some kind of permanent display?" Caroline asked, mirroring his thoughts.

"It could be," Karl replied. "I didn't see anything in the AAA guidebook, though. Maybe we should go back to the car and check."

"After we've walked all this way?" she said. "Honestly, Karl, it's almost like you can't wait to leave."

Karl winced invisibly and reminded himself that now was *not* the time to reveal his Ren Faire history to Caroline. He shrugged sheepishly. "I guess I'm more in the mood for necking than exploring foggy shacks," he said.

She smiled. "Don't worry. We won't stay long. I just want to scope out what's here. It looks pretty deserted, though."

It did. Standing near the first building, they didn't see another soul. The motley village stretched off into the fog, toward the castle on the unseen hill. The exhibit was as big as a real town—but no other fairegoers seemed to be visiting it.

"Maybe this part of the faire is closed for renovation," Karl suggested. The buildings looked as though they needed repairs. Actually, it occurred to Karl that they looked *more* historically accurate than anything else in the faire.

The roofs of the buildings were thatch; the walls largely wattle and daub—a primitive form of plaster. Karl spotted several wood frame and stone buildings in the distance, though those didn't seem in much better shape than the rude shacks nearby.

Many of the houses had small vegetable gardens

next to them, and one or two even had barns. The barnyard fences were rough-hewn rail affairs, certainly good enough to pen livestock, but not much to look at. The barricades surrounding the small gardens were even less appealing. They were cobbled together from sticks, crooked tree limbs, and the trunks of saplings. The vegetables in the tiny patches of protected earth looked stunted and sickly—though this might have been a trick of the failing light and the fog.

The houses seemed deserted and, while this could have been expected in a disused exhibit, it still had a disquieting effect on Karl and Caroline. It seemed as though the couple had walked into a village of ghosts. Caroline leaned closer to Karl, and tried to rub the goose bumps from her arms. Karl put his arm around her and held her close.

"Creepy, isn't it?" she said.

Karl nodded. "No electric lights, no music, no amenities," he said, "just like the *real* Renaissance."

"Ugh." Caroline replied, shivering. "If this is the real Renaissance, I've changed my mind about wanting to live there."

Impending dusk filled the fog with ominous shadows. In the distance, Karl could make out a few flickering orange lights—though he couldn't tell if they came from the ramshackle houses or somewhere else.

Humanlike shapes began to move in the mist. For a moment, the couple felt relieved to see other fairegoers amid this strange and disquieting tableau. Something about the figures seemed odd, though.

They moved slowly, hesitantly, as though they were afraid, or perhaps crippled in some way. As the fog parted slightly, Karl and Caroline saw that the people were dressed in clothes much shabbier than the fried-lizard vendor's faux rags. All of the "villagers" were short and stooped. Greasy, unkempt hair dripped down over their foreheads and shoulders. Their skin looked sallow and spotted. Their feral eyes glinted in the rapidly failing light.

"Maybe this is a re-creation of a leper village," Karl whispered.

"Ewe! Yuck!" Caroline replied, giggling nervously.

The half dozen decrepit figures shambling nearby stopped at the sound. They eyed the couple warily, and made the sign of the cross. Gathering together, the villagers spoke to each other in hushed whispers.

"Okay," Karl said, "I've reached my limit on 'period' charades. This is too much."

"Mmm," Caroline agreed. She kept her eyes focused on the congregating inhabitants of the weird village.

"Let's skip the castle and head back to the car," Karl said.

Caroline nodded. She slipped her trembling hand into his and gave a hard squeeze. The couple turned and walked quickly back the way they'd come. As they did, the voices behind them rose as if arguing, or perhaps angry.

"Maybe the attraction wasn't open for visitors yet," Caroline said. "Maybe they're mad at us."

"They should have posted a sign, then," Karl said, laughing nervously as they walked through the fog. "What are they going to do, arrest us?"

"I hope not."

"We'll be back at the car soon," he replied. "I'd like to see them catch us after that."

"Karl . . ." she said, ". . . why can't we see the tents yet?"

Karl stopped suddenly, his anger fading quickly

into concern. They looked around, peering into the fog, but saw no sign of the faire.

"I'm *sure* we came this way," Karl said, fighting down the worry in his guts. "How could we have gotten lost? The place isn't that *big*."

"Bigger than we thought, I guess."

Trees hung ominously over the path where they stood, and thick scrub lined the trail on either side. Ahead, the trees looked even more dense.

"I'd *swear* this is the way we came."

"Me, too," agreed Caroline. "Maybe we should double back."

"And risk getting even *more* lost? No thanks." He pulled his cell phone out of his breast pocket, turned it on, and punched 9-1-1.

"Karl . . ." she said, her blue eyes peering questioningly at him, "we're just a *bit* lost. It's no big emergency."

"We're strangers here, so being lost *is* an emergency," he replied. "I'm not going to wander around all night, trying to find that damn faire. It's getting colder and damper by the minute. Do you want to be *stuck* out here for the night?"

"I'd rather be somewhere toasty," she agreed. "We could keep following the path, though."

"And what if it just leads deeper into the woods? No. Let's talk to the cops and let them sort this out." He frowned and punched the buttons of the cell phone again. "What the hell . . . ?"

Pulling the phone away from his ear, he tapped the case with his fingertips.

"What's wrong?"

"No signal. How the hell can that be? The signal was fine when we called the hotel from the parking lot."

"Maybe the battery's dead."

"No. It's low, but it's not dead. Not yet."

"I guess we're in one of those cell-phone sink-holes."

"This close to the highway?" he asked angrily.

Caroline shrugged. "Don't get pissed at *me* about it."

Karl sighed and gave her a quick kiss. "Sorry. I guess we'll have to backtrack after all."

"Someone at the village *must* have a cell phone," she said.

"Unless they're taking this Renaissance business *way* too seriously. C'mon."

They retraced their steps down the wooded path, and soon came to the outskirts of the shabby village once more. The fog parted a bit as they left the woods, and they could clearly see the outline of a castle atop the nearby hill. Overhead, stars began to peek out of the indigo sky. Warm yellow lights burned within the castle's windows.

Lights flickered in the village, too—but these were orange, moving lights.

"Torches?" Karl asked incredulously.

Caroline shrugged. "That would be in period."

"Let's find that phone."

They walked to the nearest house, and knocked on the rough-hewn door. Though they heard some movement within the dilapidated walls, no one answered.

"Is anyone home?" Caroline called. "We need to use a phone."

"Or could you just give us directions back to the faire?" Karl added.

Still no one came to the door.

Karl cursed and headed toward the next house. "Talk about lousy customer service . . . !" he fumed.

"Hey, you!" he called to a man hurrying across the street ahead of them. "How do we get back to the faire?"

The man turned frightened eyes toward the couple, then darted between two nearby houses without saying a word.

"Karl, this is giving me the creeps."

"Well, *somebody* here has to know the way back to the faire." Spotting a man nearby carrying a torch, Karl ran up to him. "Hey! You there! Stop!"

The man, a ragged fellow like the ones they'd seen earlier, turned and thrust a burning torch in Karl's direction. "*Back*, spawn of the *Devil!*"

Karl stepped back, barely avoiding the torch's flame. "Hey!"

"The people of Knightstor are God-fearing folk!" the torch-wielder said. "We reject Satan and all his works! Begone!"

"Knightstor?" Caroline said, puzzled. "But this is *Knightshead*, Kentucky. Not Knightstor. Knightstor is in *England*."

"You're taking this period role-playing shit *way* too far!" Karl snapped. "You either take us back to the parking lot, or I'll have your manager stick your head on a pike!"

"Get thee back, minion of evil!" the peasant said, thrusting the torch at Karl once more.

"Shit!" Karl said, barely avoiding the flames again.

"You *asshole!*" Caroline said. "That'll cost you your *job!*"

"Better my job than my immortal soul, vile temptress!" Turning, the ragged man called to his fellows. "They're *here!* I've found them! The witches are here!"

"Right!" Karl said. He lunged forward and smashed

his fist squarely into the man's face. The peasant fell backward into the mud, and the torch skidded out of his hand.

Karl scooped up the firebrand. "Now are you going to *help* us, or do I have to call a cop?"

"Here! The hellspawn are here!" the man shouted, ignoring Karl's threat.

They heard other people coming now. Angry voices filtered through the fading mist; a dozen torches danced toward them through the darkness.

"Shit, Karl!" Caroline said. "Let's get out of here!"

"Yeah."

As the torch-wielding mob closed in on them, the couple turned and ran back the way they'd come. As they went, Karl tossed his torch into a nearby pigpen.

"Why'd you do *that?*" Caroline asked, a note of panic creeping into her voice.

"The light would lead those psychos right to us. I'd rather take my chances in the dark."

They fled down the wooded roadway they'd taken before. As the dark forest closed in around them, Karl spotted a small path branching off to the left. He grabbed Caroline and pulled her from the main track down the narrow game trail.

"Is this the way back to the faire?" she asked.

"The last way we took was wrong. Maybe this is the right one."

She nodded hopefully, but her eyes told him she doubted it.

As they continued running, the voices of their pursuers grew more distant. For a moment they hoped they might be on the right track at last. The woods opened up before them and they paused at the edge to catch their breath.

"Damn," Karl whispered.

"What?" Caroline asked. She had fallen slightly

behind as they ran, and had to peer around him to see what lay beyond the end of the path.

"We're back at the damn village," he said quietly. "Shit. Try the phone again."

The cell phone beeped as Karl pulled it out of his pocket. Caroline looked at him hopefully.

He shook his head. "It's just the low battery warning. Shit!" He punched the numbers into the keypad, with the same disappointing result.

"Nothing. Shit!"

"What are we gonna do?"

"We can't stay out here all night," he said. "Let's try that barn." He pointed to a nearby ramshackle building. "Maybe we can hide out until morning."

Cautiously, they crept from the woods to the barn. No lights or sounds came from inside the structure— a good sign that they might use it for refuge. In the distance, torches moved through both the forest and village. The couple carefully opened the barn door and slipped inside before anyone could spot them.

The building was two stories high, with a hayloft above and animal stalls below. The middle of the room stood open, giving free access to both levels. A wooden ladder leading to the loft leaned against the wall in the back corner of the room. They saw no sign that any animals had been housed in the barn recently. Old, dank straw covered the bare earth floor. Stacks of moldy hay filled the upper level. Several bundles had fallen from the loft and smashed onto the floor below. The shattered bales looked like small haystacks amid the moldering groundcover.

"It could be worse," Caroline said, though her tone made it plain that she didn't think it could be *much* worse.

"It's a good hiding place," Karl replied. "C'mon. Let's get behind some of those hay bales in the loft."

They climbed up the rickety ladder into the second floor and secreted themselves amid the moldy stacks. Outside, the voices of the angry villagers drew nearer.

"This is crazy," Caroline whispered. "Why are they chasing us?"

"Union troubles on the job?" Karl replied, but the jest fell hollow. "Maybe we've stumbled onto a secret government project or something."

"Maybe they're a terrorist cell, hiding out in the castle."

Karl shook his head and shrugged. "It's possible, I guess."

"Maybe they're on drugs."

Karl nodded. Another reason to dislike the faires— though it seemed a very petty reason at the moment. Perhaps all his reasons for disliking the faires were petty. Right now, he wished he'd just told Caroline the *truth* and kept driving this afternoon.

They huddled in the hay for long hours, not daring to move. Their scant clothing ensured that neither of them spent a comfortable night in the chilly loft. Several times, Karl drifted briefly into uneasy sleep. Caroline's shivering woke him, though. Her breathing seemed labored, too. He pulled her closer to him, but it didn't fend off the cold very much.

Near dawn, exhaustion finally took him.

He woke suddenly, and in pain. Caroline was squeezing his arm hard enough to draw blood. "They're right outside!" she whispered frantically. "I think they're coming in!"

"Keep it down," he hissed back. "They won't find us if we're quiet."

They ducked down into the stale hay and, moments later, the rickety barn door rattled open.

". . . thought I heard something," came a gruff voice.

"Maybe it were a trick," replied a more nasal voice. "Witches be good with trickery."

"Aye," said the first. "Be careful while ye search. They may have transformed themselves to deceive us."

The light from the searchers' torches flickered in the dismal barn, casting eerie, dancing shadows on the walls. Karl glanced nervously at Caroline. He said nothing, but even hiding in the semidarkness, he could see his own fear reflected in her eyes. This was madness! They had to find a way out of this insane village.

The sounds of the men searching the barn below drifted up to the frightened couple.

"Did ye see their manner of dress?" the gruff voice asked.

"Not I," the second replied. "But my good wife said it were most un-Godly. She said the woman—if woman she be—were a brazen *succubus*, sent to tempt us and lead us all to damnation."

"Aye, and the man be her warlock keeper."

"Devils from hell."

The men searched without speaking after that, poking into the barn's corners. Suddenly, a sound broke the rustic quiet.

*Beep!*

"What's that?" said the gruff man, a note of fear in his voice.

"A bird?"

"Like no bird *I* ever heard."

*Beep!*

Terror clutched Karl's heart as he realized what the sound was—his cell phone's low power warning!

Frantically, he dug in his pocket for the device. He hit the power button, but the phone *beeped* again before it died. His sudden movement caused one of the hay bales hiding the couple to tumble from the loft.

"Look out!" called the gruff man. He sprang out of the way of the falling straw.

"It's *them!* The devils!" answered the other. He pointed his pitchfork toward the frightened couple in the loft.

"Please! We're *not* devils! Just people like you!" Caroline called.

"Don't listen to her! She's trying to tempt ye!"

"Away, vile succubus!"

"No," Karl said, "you have to *listen!* We're just lost travelers . . ."

"Travelers from the pits of hell!" the gruff man replied. "Back away, William! We'll lock them in the barn!"

Holding their pitchforks and torches in front of them, he and the high-voiced man quickly backed out of the ramshackle building. They slammed the door shut, and Karl and Caroline heard the brace being dropped across the front of the door.

A cry went up outside. *"They're here!"* "We've caught them!" "They're trapped in the barn!" The voices grew louder, as the whole village gathered around the structure.

"What are we going to *do?*" Caroline asked.

Karl shook his head. The building was shabby, but not shabby enough to break down the walls. Trying to leave by the door was futile with the mob outside. He scanned the barn for some other means of egress.

"The hayloft door!" he said, pointing to a square opening on the far side of the loft.

"But it's right over the main door."

"Maybe we can climb to the roof," he said, "then slide down and head for the woods."

"Maybe we should just stay here. Maybe they'll calm down. Listen! Someone's opening the door again!"

The two of them looked hopefully toward the crude portal. "We won't hurt you," Karl called. "We don't mean any harm!"

"Deceivers!" someone shouted from outside.

Beyond the portal stood a huge mob. They brandished torches and rusty farm implements. The shabby people gathered outside looked both frightened and angry. The torchlight made their decrepit faces seem demonic.

"We'll send you back to hell!" a woman called.

At that, three flaming torches sailed through open door. The firebrands bounced across the barn floor. One landed harmlessly on the bare earth near the ladder. The second sputtered on the damp straw covering the floor. The third, though, skidded into the fresh bale that had just fallen from the loft.

The straw went up like dry tinder.

"Shit!" Karl said. He swung down from the loft and ran to a wooden water trough near one of the stalls. It was only half-full, and the water inside smelled like sulfur. He pushed it across the dirt floor and dumped it onto the burgeoning fire.

The fire hissed and sputtered, but didn't go out. The flames spread rapidly to the other hay spilled nearby, then flicked up toward the loft.

"It's no use!" he called to Caroline. "Go to the hay door! Climb out!"

Caroline rushed frantically around the perimeter of the loft toward the hayloft door as he climbed up the ladder to join her.

She threw open the hatch, then shrieked and staggered back, nearly toppling off the walkway. Three flaming arrows arced through the opening where she'd stood a moment earlier. The arrows stuck in the underside of the roof and set it alight.

Karl ran to Caroline's side and seized her in his strong arms. Caroline Shaw alternated between screaming and weeping. "They're going to *kill* us!" she cried hysterically. "Why are they *doing* this?"

A flaming section of the thatch roof fell in. Clearly, the villagers had set the outside ablaze even before shooting arrows through the hayloft door. Beyond the flames, Karl saw the sky, deep blue, the stars fading with the approach of dawn.

The crackle of the fire and the cries of the mob outside built to a deafening roar.

"Burn ye witches!"

"Burn!"

More of the roof fell in, revealing the sleepy countryside beyond the barn.

Holding tight to each other, Karl and Caroline staggered toward the hayloft door again—only to be driven back by another hail of arrows.

"We're going to die here, aren't we?" she said, her voice a hoarse whisper.

Karl didn't reply.

"I'm *so* sorry," she said, looking at him with tearful eyes.

"Me, too," he said. He wished he had the time to tell her all the things he was sorry for; all the lies— the lies that, somehow, had led them to this point.

They embraced and waited for the end. The smoke stung their eyes and burned their lungs.

As the flames licked higher around them, more of the barn fell into ashes—opening gaping holes in the ramshackle walls and roof. The morning sun crested the eastern hills, revealing the landscape beyond the village. A green swath of unspoiled forest and brown farmland greeted the new day. The castle on the hill's summit stood proudly, its walls untouched by the ravages of time.

Karl saw no sign of anything he remembered from the previous day. No faire. No highway. No road signs. No phone lines. No jet trails marring the smog-free sky. No sign of Kentucky—or modern America—at all.

Before him stretched barely-tamed wilderness, farmland, and a proud stone castle—newly completed—standing guard over a shabby Renaissance village.

Despite the fire and smoke, despite the burning in his lungs and the scorching of his flesh, Karl's last thoughts were that everything looked *beautiful*, unspoiled—very much as it must have looked in Knightstor, England, five hundred years before he was born.

Caroline was right. This *would* have been a good place to live.

But it was a terrible place to die.

# THE LAND OF THE
# AWFUL SHADOW

*by*

*Brian A. Hopkins*

Four-time Bram Stoker Award winner Brian A. Hopkins is the author of *Something Haunts Us All* (1995), *Cold at Heart* (1997), *Flesh Wounds* (1999), *The Licking Valley Coon Hunters Club* (2000), *Wrinkles at Twilight* (2000), *These I Know By Heart* (2001), *Salt Water Tears* (2001), and *El Dia de los Muertos* (2002). His short stories have recently appeared in *Weird Tales*, *Historical Hauntings*, *Sol's Children*, *The Darker Side*, *Dreaming of Angels*, *Mystery Scene Magazine*, *Realms of Fantasy*, *Space and Time*, *Bending the Landscape*, *Black Gate*, *Cemetery Dance*, and others. His story, "Diving the Coolidge," was selected by Robert Silverberg and Karen Haber as one of the best fantasy stories of 2001. Darrell Schweitzer (*Weird Tales*) has called him "one of the most intriguing voices to emerge from the small presses since Thomas Ligotti." Brian has been a finalist for both the Nebula Award and the Ted Sturgeon Memorial Award for science fiction. You can learn more about him by visiting his webpage at http://bahwolf.com.

I PARKED OFF THE SIDE OF KLEIN ROAD—the closest I could get to the medieval faire—and walked west up Community Road, which was already crowded with parked cars. The GPS on the dash read N30° 27', W89° 05', but Dalton and I hadn't needed such elaborate technology when we were kids. We'd created our own map for our little corner of the world, a map I remember to this day.

We had named the stretch of pine forest between the neighborhood of Orange Grove and Highway 49 the Land of the Awful Shadow, after a location in Burroughs' fictional world, Pellucidar. That's Burroughs as in Edgar Rice Burroughs, best known for creating Tarzan of the Apes. But Tarzan's jungle was only one of the worlds explored in Burroughs' many fantasy novels. According to Burroughs, Pellucidar exists some 500 miles beneath the Earth's surface. It's lit by a sun that hovers at zenith, creating an eternal noon. The inhabitants of Pellucidar know nothing of night, but there is a moon in the sky—stationary, as is their sun—and that moon casts a permanent shadow on a large section of terrain below: the Land of the Awful Shadow.

Community Road wasn't here when Dalton and I were growing up. There was nothing but the towering Ponderosa pines, sweet magnolias, and a heavy undergrowth of palmetto and scrub brush, a dark hideaway whose close confines had seemed worthy of a Burroughs' tribute. There were pine needle-carpeted trails through the woods and boggy creeks full of water moccasins and copperheads. The sunlight that reached the ground was diffuse and artistic, laying a canvas on which a boy's adventures could be painted with strokes as subtle as his imagination allowed.

The woods were bisected by the Flat Branch

Stream, a tributary to Barnard Bayou. It was the stream that had initially spelled disaster for the forest—the stream and the arrival of dockside gambling in Mississippi.

The casinos irrevocably changed the Gulf Coast. From Highway 90 to marshlands as far north as Shreveport, it wasn't the same South in which I'd grown up. As soon as the gambling laws were passed, real estate became a premium. The Land of the Awful Shadow was bought by a developer who planned to dam the Flat Branch, flood the pine forest clear to Barnard Bayou, and bring in one of those huge, flat-bottomed gambling boats. Orange Grove tried to block the developer, but by the time they were successful, the pine forest had already been plowed to the ground (revealing many a childhood secret—and even one decomposed body). A court battle was waged for years and finally won because of environmental damage to protected wetlands that would result if the Flat Branch were dammed.

Next the land was sold to someone who planned to build a shopping mall, a reasonable proposal since the nearest indoor mall was in Biloxi. However, this developer was soon arrested for tax evasion. Development of the property was stalled again. The grass in the meadow grew tall except where local kids stomped it down to play ball. The few remaining pines were uprooted, defenseless without their neighbors to help break the high winds of tropical storms and hurricanes. A portion of the property was eventually sold to Wal-Mart, and Orange Grove got a Superstore. Another piece went to build a new junior high. But the bulk of the Land of the Awful Shadow's two hundred and twenty acres remained an empty field regularly leased for annual events like the Renaissance Faire.

I paused on the bridge over the Flat Branch, with the tents and pennants and music of the Renaissance Faire beckoning just ahead, and looked down into the tea-colored water. It was deeper than I remembered. A bit wider, perhaps, and with much steeper banks, having had twenty-five years since Dalton and I had played there to carve its way down into the white Mississippi sand. The runoffs and marshes that had once held so many snakes, snapping turtles, and alligator gar were all gone. The meadow's verdant St. Augustine grass kept erosion from bringing them back.

Dalton and I had experienced many an adventure here. In fact, our lives had changed forever in this very stream.

You have to understand first of all that Dalton and I wanted to grow up to be warriors. Yes, I realize that there's not a lot of call for that sort of thing. Knights in shining armor are pretty rare. The Indians are all on reservations running bingo halls and tourist shops. The Hun have retired. Ninjitsu is a lost art. Still . . . we wanted to be warriors. Toward that end, we bought or made every weapon imaginable and practiced with them until we were proficient. The martial arts were our passion 24/7.

We injured each other in so many different ways, with so many different weapons, that there are scores of funny stories from those days—most only funny in retrospect, of course. We each had our strengths and weaknesses: I was better with a bow and a spear; he was better at throwing a knife (coolest thing I ever saw was him nailing a water moccasin's head to the ground when it was about to bite me). I was better at throwing an ax; he was better at sword fighting (but that's only because he *always* hit my hands); and so on. If we sound juvenile, well, we *were* juvenile, but we were boys and growing up together, and we did the blood-brother thing and burned a secret symbol into the backs of our hands and . . . well, you get the picture. We were inseparable. We loved each other as only two young boys can love.

All of that changed here . . . in the Land of the Awful Shadow. Covering my right eye and squinting through my mostly blind left, the stream ran red, as it had on that day long ago. It pulsed with an ancient rhythm, an earthly artery, coagulating corpuscles clotting the reeds and tangled driftwood on its banks. I shuddered. Turned away from the railing. And crossed the bridge to the faire.

\* \* \*

Most of my childhood stories with Dalton involve one of us getting injured. The stories from the Land of the Awful Shadow are no different. The story I want to tell you, the story I *need* to tell you, is one of those. It's not one of our survival stories (those stories always involve us eating something totally gross—like tadpoles, or snakes, or raw catfish—so that we could prove our ability to "live off the land"). It's not one of our fishing stories or canoeing stories or one of our out-all-night-getting-into-trouble stories. It's not the story of how I put ten stitches in Tommy Sproles' head after he stole Dalton's bike and came at me with a butcher knife. It's not the horrifying "Night of the Cockroaches" story wherein we spent the night in a trailer Dalton's father had just hauled home, only to find that the thing was crawling with about a million of the hugest South Texas "cock-a-roaches" known to man—and how we were up all night with machetes battling these beasts, and how, come morning, when the sun finally rose on that grim scene, there stood Dalton and me, splattered with cockroach guts, worn and battered and suffering many a grievous injury, surrounded by thousands of dead, hacked-to-pieces roaches, or how we got in trouble for also chopping the linoleum in the trailer to bits. No, it's not any of those stories. This is the story of how Dalton shot me with an arrow.

In our day, the Flat Branch was what your average redneck would call a "crick." There were times, after a heavy rain, that it might be four-or five-feet deep, but in general I think it wasn't more than twelve-to-eighteen-inches deep in most places—though there were always deeper pockets near sandy bends and fallen trees where a smart boy could fish out a few perch or maybe even a smallmouth bass, if the alligator gar hadn't already eaten them all. Though shallow, it was pretty wide for a stream. Say twenty feet on average. Sandy-bottomed. The color of a good bourbon (like every other stream along the Gulf Coast). Full of water moccasins and crawdads and mudpuppies.

Call it a Saturday—though it could have been any day at all during the summer. We had hiked down through the woods, "stump-shooting" with our bows, mindful of bandits and jabberwockies and scarier things that lurked in the Land of the Awful Shadow, to play in the stream and cool off. I'm guessing I was twelve or thirteen years old at the time. Dalton was a year younger. It was just the two of us that day, though we were often followed by younger boys, disciples who wanted to learn the art of the warrior and saw us as role models. What those younger boys' parents (or anyone else in the neighborhood) thought of us, I can only imagine. Dalton and I typically wore Bowie knives strapped low on our thighs (gunslinger style), carried spears or bows or whatnot, and could generally be seen swinging *nunchakus* (an Okinawan weapon which the next generation would rename/bastardize as "numchucks" and eventually police everywhere would wind up outlawing them).

Casey Colton was following us that day, but we were used to her being around, and to tell the truth, each of us secretly had as big a crush on her as she had on us—though neither of us would ever admit it. Why she followed us and tried to be like us, instead of staying home and playing dolls with the other girls, was something we didn't understand at the time. Tall and gangly for her age, she'd already sprouted breasts (had even shown them to us once, briefly, after an hour of pleading and a bribe of $3.65, which was every cent we had between the two of us). Today we were ignoring her, letting her believe that we didn't know she was back there, a tactic that would surely prove favorable for a later ambush.

I'm not sure who invented the game for that morning, but it went like this. There was this fairly large piece of driftwood floating in the stream. Covered with twisted white branches, rolling and tumbling in the fast-moving water, it looked like some terrible multitentacled sea beast. Because the wood was soft enough to accept an arrow without damaging said arrow (very important!), it was only natural that the beast should become the object of some much needed target practice. It wasn't enough, of course, to shoot this horrible beast one time. No, this was a mighty monster, and only the concerted and repeated efforts of two determined warriors working together might hope to dispatch it. Downriver, there was a peaceful and unsuspecting village waiting. If the beast should pass us, innocent women and children would be slaughtered! (Probably some nubile young female types, too. Females who might want to thank a pair of powerful warriors for all that they had done to thwart evil in the Land of the Awful Shadow.)

So, each of us would shoot his arrow (we probably only had one apiece at the time), then run to collect it from the beast's hide. The beast had all these waving appendages, and it would be certain death to fall within its reach. Thus the trick was to collect your arrow without the beast getting hold of you. This involved a considerable amount of leaping, diving, and generally splashing around in the water. What fun!

At one point in our game, Dalton fired and missed. His arrow thunked into the sandy bank, and he went running after it. I fired and—*kachunk!*—sank my arrow into the beast's broad chest, piercing at least one of its six black hearts. I ran to collect my arrow, leaping over the monster in a grand somersaulting dive, yanking out the arrow in passing. Meanwhile, visualize Dalton retrieving his arrow from the bank, nocking it to his bow string, whirling around and shooting without really taking the time to survey the situation (speed was of the essence, of course, because of all those women and children and nubile young ladies downstream). Picture Dalton's arrow streaking toward the log—uh, the *beast*, I mean—whilst I hang, frozen for an instant in time in the air above the beast. Now picture Dalton's arrow sinking through the top of my foot and out the other side.

In retrospect, I suppose it really isn't funny. That arrow could have just as easily pierced my stomach, chest . . . head. But it didn't. It sank right through my foot. I did my whole splash and roll on the other side of the driftwood monster, came to a sitting position in the water, held up my foot (with about fifteen inches of arrow sticking out of either side of it), and yelled, "You stupid son of a bitch! You shot me!"

Now this is the funny part. Decent arrows cost two or three dollars apiece. That was a lot of money to us back then. We had to steal a lot of Coke bottles from our neighbors and trade them in at the 7-Eleven to get that kind of money, and a fair amount of it had to be rationed for soda, candy, comics, and a million other things necessary to a boy's survival. Like I said, we probably only owned one arrow each at any given time. So I was sitting there in the middle of the river, holding my bleeding foot in the air, with Dalton apologizing like crazy, and wondering how the hell I was going to pull the damn thing all the way out. Fifteen inches is a lot to slide through your foot.

I looked up at Dalton and said, "Do you mind if I break your arrow?" Just as sincere and polite as you please.

Naturally, Dalton said he didn't mind. I snapped it in two an inch or so below my foot. Then I hauled it out of my flesh, feeling the shaft grate against the bones. I can still remember how the jagged, broken end felt slipping back out through my foot as the lips of the wound and then the bones themselves slid back into place. There was more than enough blood to be impressive. Casey looked white as a sheet when she came running down the bank to see how badly I was hurt.

\* \* \*

Bypassing artists' easels, jugglers, belled jesters on stilts, busty women with tables of handmade jewelry, and merchants selling food, baskets, cheap weaponry, and blown glass, I found what I'd come to see in the very center of the Renaissance Faire. There was a ring where combat demonstrations were scheduled to be held by the Society for Creative Anachronism, set off from the rest of the field by a wooden railing. In the center of the ring stood an imposing figure in polished black armor, a long Scottish claymore grasped in his hands with its point resting on the ground in front of his toes.

The sword looked to be at least sixty inches long, with a two-handed grip and leather-wrapped ricasso. The black knight was tall, easily six-four even without the visored helm that hid his face. His breastplate was carefully worked with silver and gold into a large eagle, wings spread and talons extended, as fine a piece of craftsmanship as I'd ever seen at such a faire. His gauntlets were feathered with crimson, as if splashed with blood. His cuisses, greaves, and shynbalds gleamed like black obsidian in the sun.

The knight had a page or squire—or perhaps just an ex-carny who'd found a novel way to make a buck—walking the inside of the crowd-lined circle. "Who would like to try their luck against the Black Knight?" called the page, while the knight stood silent and unmoving. "For just twenty dollars, I'll suit you up and let you show us what you're made of. Defeat the Black Knight and win a thousand dollars! You there, sir—yes, you with the big biceps—would you like to try?"

I squeezed in among the onlookers, working my way to the railing for a better view.

\*    \*    \*

Dalton and Casey helped me to the bank where we briefly debated sending someone for help. I insisted that I could walk, even though it was three miles to my house. I figured I could walk three miles, even with blood squishing around inside my shoe—after all, Casey was there. I couldn't look weak in front of her.

I only made it to the top of the bank, however, before momentarily blacking out.

"Are you okay?" asked Dalton.

"Is it the pain?" asked Casey.

"No," I said, suddenly very frightened, "it's my eye." Inexplicably, I was losing the vision in my left eye. I blinked. I rubbed at it. But my sight in that eye was rapidly fading to black. It didn't make sense; I'd been shot in the foot. Already the initial, shock-induced numbness of the trauma was fading, and my foot was beginning to throb mercilessly. But what did that have to do with my eye?

Then my head began to throb, a resonating dagger of pain that extended from my left temple to a point just behind my ear. This must be what my mother called a migraine, I thought, but then a moment later I realized her migraines couldn't possibly be this bad.

Holding my head in my hands, I began to moan with pain and fear.

Casey sent Dalton for help, then held my head in her lap, stroked my temple, and told me everything would be okay.

There was an arrow embedded in my skull. I could feel it. If I closed my right eye, my left was suffused with blood, pulsating red with every throb. I'd been shot. I don't know how, but it was true. I could remember the sound the arrow had made punching through my skull. I could remember the brilliant flash of white that had accompanied the initial impact, a silent explosion going off somewhere inside my head, like the flash of a camera. I could remember reaching up and feeling the shaft protruding from my head. The cool wash of the stream closing over my face as I'd gone under. Dalton dragging me out and setting me on the bank, where the tip of the arrow had momentarily snagged on a piece of driftwood and *thrummed* in my skull.

As Casey rocked me and whispered over and over that help was on the way, I remembered other things. Things that hadn't happened. Things that couldn't have ever happened.

But I remembered these things as clearly as I remembered getting out of bed that morning.

\* \* \*

The first spectator to pay his twenty and step into the ring against the Black Knight lasted less than a minute. Awkwardly bundled in padded plate and an ill-concealed motorcycle helmet, he marched out bravely enough. The Black Knight had traded his claymore for a foam-wrapped bludgeon of approximately the same size and weight. With it, he proceeded to pummel the would-be warrior. There was very little finesse, but a great deal to laugh about. The crowd loved it.

When it was over, the Black Knight returned to his original spot, completely unwinded, claymore once again in his hands, his only visible victory celebration the dark gleam of eyes behind the narrow slits of the visor.

"Who's next?" the page asked loudly. "Surely there's someone here more capable of testing the mettle of our dark champion!" He paused where I leaned against the railing and smiled. "You," he said. "I can see it in your eyes." And "Yes!" as I slipped under the railing. "At last, a worthy opponent!"

He took my twenty dollars and held out the battered, makeshift plate armor for me to slip my arms into. I shook my head.

"Sir, you have to wear the armor," he whispered. "The swords are padded, but they still deliver quite a whallop. I've seen plenty of bruises even with the armor."

"No thanks."

"But—"

I pushed past him, taking the poorly balanced practice sword with me. The Black Knight saw me coming and swapped out his claymore. I took a few practice swings to limber my arms while the page beseeched me to at least take a shield. I declined, wanting both hands free for swinging the heavy cudgel.

Patient, the Black Knight let me bring the battle to him.

\* \* \*

The pain in my head completely vanished after a few hours, but the blindness persisted. I learned early on not to mention the strange side effect of my accident. At that age, I was incapable of making the adults understand. The only conclusion they could draw was that I was delusional. In spite of the complete lack of bruises or lacerations near my eye, they decided I'd fallen and hit my head.

After weeks of tests, the doctors told my mother that they could find no explanation or cause for the blindness in my left eye. X-rays, CAT scans, PET scans, EEGs, and the most careful examinations all showed that my eye, my optical nerve, and my brain were working normally. They sent me to a shrink to see if I was making it all up or suffering some bizarre, psychologically-induced blindness. Cases were rare, but the doctors said they'd known people who believed they were blind even when they weren't (and, odder still, blind people who were convinced they could see). The mind, they told me, is a strange and complex organ, capable of much more than we know. But the psychological tests were as inconclusive as the medical ones.

Life eventually went back to normal, although relationships were strained between my parents and Dalton's. This latest accident was deemed just a bit too serious. Perhaps we boys were seeing too much of each other. And perhaps it was time to intervene on "this whole weapon fixation thing," as my father put it.

Casey spent a lot of time with me, but much as I loved her, it hurt to be around her. I understood now why she wanted to be like Dalton and me, why she wasn't like the other girls. Looking at her with my blind eye, I saw the things that had been done to her. I saw how she ached and the shame and degradation she hid inside.

Five weeks after the accident, I couldn't take it anymore, so I tucked a note into the collar of Dalton's dog—a standard means of communication between us. I asked him to meet me at midnight in a cane thicket near our homes. For years we'd maintained a narrow path leading into the interior of the thicket. It was one of many secret places we had.

"Your folks lightening up any?" Dalton asked as he joined me that night. He'd dressed all in black and smeared camo paint on his face. There was a wooden sword slung over his left shoulder. He was wearing his Bowie knife. By the light of my failing flashlight, he looked positively commandoish and terrifying.

"Slowly but surely," I answered.

"Mine are talking about moving back to Texas."

"They can't do that!" I knew he'd originally moved to Mississippi from Texas, something to do with his father's business, but I'd never thought about the possibility of them moving back.

"That's what I keep telling them." He drew his Bowie knife and started whittling on a scrap of bamboo. I wished I'd remembered to bring my own knife.

"I need to talk to you about Casey," I told him.

He frowned. "She doesn't come around much since you got hurt."

This surprised me. I had assumed she was seeing just as much of Dalton as she was of me.

"What about her?" he asked when my silence ran too long. He'd stopped whittling and was thrusting the long blade of the Bowie into the soft dirt between his feet.

"Her stepfather . . . does things to her." I didn't know how to put it.

"Things?"

"Like in those magazines we stole that time. Remember?"

"Her stepfather? She told you this?"

"No. I think she's too ashamed to tell anyone. But I know."

"How do you know?"

I didn't answer.

"Oh." He tapped his temple with his index finger, stopping just short of making that twirling motion we used to indicate people who had a few screws loose.

"You don't believe me?"

"When have I ever not believed you," he countered.

"Then we have to do something."

He pulled the knife from the ground and held it up in the flashlight's ghostly beam. "Kill him?"

"I'm serious, Dalton. We have to talk to him. If we tell him we know about it, and we make it clear that it has to stop . . ."

"Then he'll think Casey told us," said Dalton, "and he'll hurt her more."

"We'll tell him that we'll go to the police if he doesn't stop."

Dalton wiped the knife off on his pants leg and slipped it back into the sheath on his hip. "Okay. We'll try it your way." He pulled something form his pocket and tossed it into my lap. "You'll need that." It was his tube of camouflage face paint.

"I didn't bring a weapon."

"I'll cut a bamboo spear for you."

\*      \*      \*

I'd like to say it was romantic and dramatic and so impressive that the onlookers were treated to a once-in-a-lifetime experience, but the truth is I was out of shape and out of practice. I'd forgone the armor for mobility and speed. In the first three minutes that was all that saved me from having my skull split open. After that I was huffing and puffing, unable to raise an offense, struggling merely to parry his blows. By this time the knight was toying with me, as if I'd gained some measure of respect by refusing the armor and rather than beat me down he was content to watch me wear myself out.

The crowd cheered him on as he worked me across the circle. I was beginning to stumble. I couldn't catch my breath. The sword seemed to weigh a thousand pounds, and my arms were as weak as a babe's.

* * *

The Colton house was dark when we arrived. Colton had a toolshed out back, so we hit upon the plan of making some noise that he'd be inclined to come out and investigate.

"What if he calls the cops instead?" I asked.

"Hell, you've been around Casey's old man before," Dalton said. "He calls the police pigs and says they're all crooks. He ain't going to call nobody." He started kicking at the door of the shed, trying to break it down, making an awful racket. When that didn't work, he picked up a rock and tossed it through a window, then used his wooden sword to break all the remaining glass out of the window frame.

A light went on in the house.

"Hide!" I hissed.

We both faded into the shadows. Because Dalton was all dressed in black, he was instantly invisible. I had turned my jacket inside out because the lining was navy blue. My jeans were new enough to be dark. My sneakers were white, but I had planned to squat in the shadows with my shoes hidden behind me.

Colton came out of his back door with a baseball bat in hand. Wary, he checked around both corners of his house, probably figuring whoever had been trying to break in had fled in that direction. Then he started slowly across the yard, crouched down as if he expected an opponent to materialize out of thin air and leap on his back. He wasn't wearing anything but white boxers. His bare feet left long dark streaks in the dew-glistening grass.

Though it had been my idea to come here, I was ready to chicken out now.

"Dalton," I whispered. "Let's get the hell out of here."

"Too late!" he rasped. "We'll jump out and scare the shit out of him, then run like hell."

"What if he's not scared?"

"Quiet!"

Colton spotted the broken window and started cursing. He came forward fast then, crossing the yard in a dozen quick strides. He smacked the side of the building with the baseball bat. "You better be long gone, you chickenshit son of a bitch!" he yelled.

This was our chance to speak up, to threaten him into leaving Casey alone, but neither of us said a word. I was shaking like a leaf. He was a big man. An adult. And I was suddenly just a very small boy. A real warrior would have stepped out of the shadows. A real warrior would have stood up for Casey.

I prayed that he wouldn't see me.

"You ever come around here again, I'll cave your goddamn skull in!" he bellowed into the night.

He turned to go back to the house then, but something caught his attention, something seen from the corner of his eye. Whirling back around, he brandished the bat and leaped at Dalton's hiding place. "Come here!" he growled viciously, swinging the bat.

Dalton scrambled back out of the way, sword drawn. Moonlight off the pale wooden blade must have alerted Colton. The bat just barely missed my friend, shattering branches from the dead bush behind which Dalton had been hiding. Colton's second swing shattered Dalton's sword. His third would have done serious injury, but I had leaped from the shadows with my bamboo spear by then.

I jabbed Colton in the back, hard enough to draw blood. He yelped, spinning to confront me and swinging the bat. I raised the bamboo and the bat dashed it out of my hands and sent it tumbling across the yard. As Dalton distracted Colton by hurling what was left of his sword at the man's broad back, I scampered after my spear, the only weapon I had.

Colton must have thought I was running for his house, because he pursued me rather than attack Dalton, who was much closer. Colton had to know who we were by this time. Two neighborhood kids with wooden swords and spears—even with our faces blackened, it couldn't be much of a mystery. Maybe he thought I was going to wake up Casey, and he'd have her to deal with as well since he knew we were all friends. He couldn't very well teach us a lesson—at least not a *physical* lesson—in front of his step-daughter. Regardless, he came after me, wheezing a bit now from the exertion of swinging the bat.

Things happened fast. I snatched up the bamboo and turned as he leaped at me. I saw the sharpened tip line up with his abdomen, saw his eyes go wide as he saw it, too. It might have only grazed him or penetrated mere inches, but he was a big man and he was moving fast. I fell back and the butt of the spear came up solid against the ground. The tip sank into Colton's belly as if it had no more consistency that butter. Colton screamed, trying to twist away, but the bamboo held him. When he twisted to the side, I saw the tip of the spear straining to come through his lower back. His skin was stretched in a taut little Bedouin tent, six inches high.

"I'll kill you," he gasped, spraying spittle. He shoved himself forward, reaching for me. The tip of the spear erupted from his back, and he slid down its length, reaching for me with one hand and drawing back the baseball bat with the other.

That's when I heard the unmistakable sound of Dalton's Bowie knife spinning end over end in the night air. The knife caught Colton in the thick cord of muscle where his neck met his shoulder, sinking deep. Colton seemed not to notice. He just kept coming down that length of bamboo, reaching for me. His hand found the collar of my jacket, and he closed it in a fist so tight and large that I felt as if I was strangling. I saw the bat arch for the blow that would blind me forever, but then Dalton was there, grappling the bat away from him.

I reached up to try and push him away. My hands found the Bowie knife. Before I realized what I was doing, I'd torn the blade from his shoulder and stabbed at him. Once, twice, and his cheek gaped bloodily. A third time and I caught him in the side of the neck. A great gout of blood sprayed out, and we both stared at it in disbelief and horror. He stumbled back from me, one hand attempting to stem the flood from his neck, the other clutching at the bamboo shaft protruding from his belly.

Dalton struck Colton a haymaker with the bat, and he went down. The bamboo snapped somewhere inside him. Weakly, Colton tossed one half aside, but seemed unable to locate the end protruding from his lower back. He lay there on his side on the ground, reaching for it, while blood continued to jettison from the side of his neck.

Dalton and I stood trembling as Colton's struggles grew weaker. He reached out to me once and gurgled something that might have been a plea for help, blood bubbling from his mouth, legs twitching in a vain attempt to inch him closer. I watched his eyes glaze over with moonlight, knowing I would never be the same again. Nothing would ever be the same again.

It seemed to take him forever to die.

When Colton was finally still, Dalton wanted to collect our things and run, but I convinced him that we had to hide the body. We loaded Colton into a wheelbarrow we found behind the shed. We rolled him through the darkened neighborhood streets of Orange Grove and into the Land of the Awful Shadow, where we buried him in one of our secret places.

The eastern horizon was turning gray by the time we were done. We parted out in front of my house, just minutes before I knew my dad would be waking to get ready for work. Neither of us seemed able to look at the other.

\*      \*      \*

There should have been the great clash and clangor of steel on steel. Sparks and metallic shrieks as edges grated on one another. A familiar face from the crowd, cheering us on, knowing we both loved her.

I was spent and the Black Knight knew it. It had reached the point where it was a mercy just to finish it. He forced me back against the railing, scattering the nearest spectators as his sword swept past my head and clattered down on the top rail. I reached over his arm, pinning his blade there momentarily, just long enough to plant a boot against chest. Using the railing behind me for leverage, I shoved him back with my leg, hoping the heavy armor would take him off balance and spill him to the ground. He recovered well enough, but I had time to strike at his sword hand with my blade. Despite the gauntlet, his weapon was knocked from his hand. My next blow struck him lightly over the head, just enough to make my point.

He bowed his head in acknowledged defeat. "Well done, Sir."

Smiling, I cast my weapon aside. "I just took a page from your early training."

He removed his helm and smiled. "When did you know it was me?"

"Months ago, when I started looking for you," I joked. I opened my arms and reached out for him. "It took two private investigators and more money than I care to think about. Who'd have thought to look here first?"

We embraced while the Renaissance Faire spectators cheered.

\*          \*          \*

There was a police investigation. Blood and the signs of a struggle were found in Colton's backyard, where it was believed he had caught two thieves breaking into his toolshed. A tire track showed where his body had been removed from the yard in a wheelbarrow, but what became of the body and the wheelbarrow was a mystery. No one realized that two old rusty shovels were also missing from behind the shed. Nor were the shovels ever found where they'd been thrown into a deep bend of the Flat Branch.

It would be nearly twenty years before the pine forest was leveled and bulldozers uncovered his remains. The investigation was reopened, but there was nothing found to give the police any more than they'd had.

I saw Casey three days later. She cried on my shoulder and told me how much she had loved her stepfather. To hear her speak, he'd never been anything but a kind and loving man. A few weeks later, her mother moved them somewhere up north . . . and I never saw her again.

Six months later, Dalton's family moved back to Texas. We met in the bamboo the night before he left and swore we'd keep in touch. Things had been strained between us since that night. Despite the clarity of my visions and newfound memories, neither of us could be certain there'd been any reason to kill Colton. Dalton blamed me for getting us into the situation. I blamed him for escalating it.

We would lose touch almost immediately, the promises and blood-oaths of childhood failing to hold before an adulthood all too soon thrust upon us. My own family would leave Mississippi a few years later, taking me that much father from a map of my own making. Society would impose its own maps, and the worlds of Edgar Rice Burroughs would give way for the bitter pill of reality and responsibility.

They say on a quantum level that there's a constant division of possibilities, instances when particles can go left or right, up or down, spin clockwise or counterclockwise, and there are those who believe that each of these outcomes exist somewhere in some independent universe. Our every action, conscious and not, creates a parallel dimension whose inhabitants are completely unaware of the myriad others living and dying, each in their own time and space, an infinite cascade of realities.

But what if there's a part of the brain the purpose of which is to suppress this knowledge, a failsafe to keep us from going mad? And what if that part of the brain was damaged? It wouldn't have to be my brain. Damage to any quantum twin of mine might ripple across the dimensions like wildfire, might leave us all conscious of each other's individual experiences, leave us all blind in one eye but with a gift of sight reaching beyond our own dimension.

I'm convinced that a door was opened in my brain, opened on a cerebral Land of the Awful Shadow in which I can see as many possibilities as I'm insane enough to look for. In my life, I've seen the myriad of possible consequences resulting from my best and worst actions. I've seen how the tiniest degree in course correction can affect our lives, how every choice we make yields new dimensions in the grand dance that is life. I've seen my own death a hundred times. And I saw Casey's stepfather abuse her—here, in some other dimension, a year or two after that night Dalton and I murdered him, a year before we ever met her. It had happened, was happening, would happen some place, some time, some when.

I've spent my life hiding from most of the things I've seen in my blind eye. But then one day I saw Dalton alone and bitter and ultimately dead by his own hands. Whether in this world or an infinite number of others, I couldn't live with that.

But I've found him now. Here, in this universe— the only universe over which I have any real influence. And he shall never enter the Land of the Awful Shadow alone, not so long as I am here to hold his hand.

*For Dalton Smith*

# FAIRE LIKENESS

## by

## *Andre Norton*

Andre Norton's writing career spans more than seven decades. Beginning in 1932 with Graustarkian adventures and historical novels, and progressing to science fiction in the early fifties, she opened the Gate to the Witch World—and to her work as an author of fantasy—in 1962. Her books have garnered nearly every award in the field of imaginative literature and have been translated into numerous languages, and they command a loyal following of several generations of readers. Miss Norton currently lives in Murfreesboro, Tennessee.

THE RENAISSANCE FAIRE AT RIDGEWOOD HAD, within the past few years, become a national tourist attraction. The center of the festival was the castle that Margaret and Douglas Magin had made the focus of their retirement; and, though the fortress was somewhat modest in mass, it was, nonetheless, a castle. Leading to the pile was a lane, lightly graveled, that was lined on either hand by the "town": a collection of three-room cottages, each with a display area for handicrafts on the side facing the "street." Beyond the booths to left and right lay

wild land, where a growth of brush quickly gave
way to woods. On the far side of the fortress was
the famous Rose Garden—often put to service these
days for weddings—and the tourney field.

Deb Wilson, my friend and sponsor at the Ridgewood Faire, was well used to these romantic surroundings. She not only displayed and sold articles
made by herself and her classes in fine needlework,
but also held seminars here. I had felt truly honored
this year when she had asked for my help at her
shop-booth during such times as she had to be
elsewhere.

At that moment, though, I was beginning to regret
my enthusiastic assent to be part of this year's faire,
of which I was not a member. The heat clung to me
like yet another layer of the archaic clothing in which
I was already wrapped. Irritably, I pulled at the tight
bodice-lacings of my "authentic" period dress,
pushed at the heavy folds of the skirt. Deb was wearing a twin to my garment, save that she was allowed
a touch of embroidery to enliven it, since her persona
was that of a leading guildswoman. In addition, she
was also a judge of correctly-chosen and constructed
clothing, as Margaret Magin was a stickler for historical accuracy.

"Good day, me bonny wench! 'Tis a fine sight for
the eyes that ye are."

Attempting to respond to this strange salute, I
turned too fast and cracked an elbow painfully
against a screen. Then I realized that the greeting had
been meant for my booth mate.

The man standing by the supports for the counter
we had not yet set into place was short—no taller
than Deb, at least. He was also certainly no paladin
come riding. His faire garb was the drab stuff of a
very common commoner and looked as though it

needed a good washing. Beside him stood two train cases lashed together so that one handle served both.

"Sterling! I thought you were banished!" My friend's jaw tightened in a set that suggested she wished her statement were truth.

The shabby newcomer grinned. "Well, now, Deb m'dear—let's just say that fickle Fortune beamed upon me again. And she continues to smile, for behold! She has given me a roost beside the beauteous needle wielder herself." He nodded to the right, where indeed another booth-cabin stood unclaimed. "And," he continued conspiratorially, indicating his double bundle, "*you're* lucky, too. I've a little something here that'll pull visitors aplenty in this direction."

Deb was flushing; this encounter was obviously no meeting of friends, as far as she was concerned. From a woman of usually even temper, such an attitude was puzzling. The needleworker turned a little toward me.

"This is Sterling Winterhue," she sated, as one person might call an unpleasant mistake to the attention of another. Then she gave a single curt nod at me. "Miss Gleason." The cold voice and bare-bones introduction were extremely unlike my friend.

"Yes sirree, ol' Winterhue hisself." The man pulled off his peaked cap, bowed awkwardly, and patted the top case. "Come with a real treasure. Gimme 'bout an hour to get set up; and then, Deb m'girl, you bring Miss Gleason over and get a preview."

"*Lemme alone*, Mark! Hey, mister—got any monsters this year?" The interrupting voice, shrill and willful, was that of a boy. Winterhue scowled, but only for an instant.

"So you like to see monsters, do you? Well . . ."

"Sir, I beg your pardon. Roddy—"

" 'Rod-dy, Rod-dy Rod-dy!' " the boy singsonged mockingly. "I don't hafta listen to you, you—cop! You been *no*-ing me all morning, and I'm gonna tell Nana!"

I had managed to push aside the embroidered screen that would shield one corner of the sales area and was now able to see the speaker. Very few Ridgewood residents would have failed to recognize that ten year old in spite of his page's dress: Roddy Magin, the pride of, and heir to, the castle.

The youth's companion was an archer, bearing an unstrung bow and a quiver of arrows across his back, but wearing on the breast of his jerkin a pendant in the form of a massive shield embossed with the royal arms of the court. A member of the security force, then. Just as I caught sight of the man's charge, Roddy threw a piece of pastry at him. The boy edged backward; however, he did not escape the hand that closed on his velvet-clad shoulder. He yelled and tried to twist free, but his guardian's hold failed to loosen.

As if the pair did not exist, Winterhue repeated to my partner, "Give it an hour, Deb, an' come along." With no further word he headed toward his booth, twin cases in tow.

Deb scowled openly after him. "I thought that man had been—" she began, then set her lips in a locking line.

The Magin boy now swung a kick at the archer. "*Lemme go, lemme—*" His protest cut off with a squawk as he was picked up and held fast by his much-tried chaperone, who growled: "Be quiet, you brat!"

For a wonder, the child obeyed, giving Deb the chance to finish what she had begun to say a moment before. "Doesn't court banishment still hold?"

"Not if it doesn't please the Magins." Mark's tone was dry.

Roddy turned his head sharply and snapped at the hand still restraining him. The security officer looked to Deb, shaking his head as the boy mouthed an obscenity and spat: "Nana'll get rid of you! Wait'll I tell her—"

"Wait till WE tell her," the archer corrected, controlling his temper heroically. "And we're going to do it right now. Sorry, ladies—" Giving a last nod, Mark set off down the lane, steering the pugnacious page before him.

Deb dropped onto a box, pushed a wandering strand of hair back under the edge of her frilled cap, and pulled her wristwatch out of the pouch at her belt. "Look at that—it's already eleven. I have to meet with Cathy and get the seminar leaflets. Don't wait lunch on me, 'Manda—I'll grab a burger or something on the way back."

I did not wish to make Deb late for her appointment, but I felt I *must* have some answers. "What was all that 'monster' business?"

Deb shook her head and picked up a tote that stood propped against the cabin door. "I'll tell you when I come back," she promised, adding grimly, "I do hope Mark can get Margaret to put a tight rein on that little pest."

She was out of the shop before I had a chance to protest. I knew there was no use in simply sitting and thinking up more questions, but I was determined to see that my booth mate answered those that had already occurred to me when I could get her alone again.

I fetched a Coke from the cooler. My head ached, and I wanted noting more than to lie down on one of the cots. But rest, I knew, would not be sufficient to banish the disturbing thoughts that crowded into my mind; if I tried to relax, those would torment me even more. It was best to keep busy.

Regiments of thread packets had to be mustered out according to color, needles and other tools placed in plain sight. Books of tempting patterns required arranging, and some needed to be opened to a particularly intriguing design. As the display grew, I began to feel pride in my artistic ability.

When I broke off at last for a sandwich and another Coke, I glanced over to Winterhue's hut, but no sign of life was to be seen. Scents aplenty filled the air, however, chief among them the smell of barbecue from a cookshop down the street. The savory odor made me take an extra-large bite of my chicken salad.

"And where's the lovesome Deb, m'lady?"

I jumped. The packed earth and springy grass between the huts had deadened the sound of his approach, but Sterling Winterhue was back.

"She had to meet with one of the committee," I answered after a hasty swallow.

"And to see what brought me here." With this comment—and without invitation—the artist stepped into the outer section of the shop. He had removed the peasant's cap with its towering peak and, as he bent briefly over my display, the top of his head showed a few grudging strands of gray-brown hair that looked as though they had been painted across his scalp.

Suddenly he looked up, and even in the dim light I could see his eyes glint. "So—Guildswoman Wilson is willing to miss her tryst with Sir Sterling, is she? Well, now, mistress, *you* won't."

Before I realized what he intended, Winterhue strode up and put a hand on my arm. Nodding and grinning, he drew me out into the road, then laughed as he set me free.

"Think me a lusty rogue, do ye? Nay, I am not such. Also—" Winterhue gestured toward his hut, "—what I have to show is displayed in sight of all."

I shall never understand why, but, without a murmur of protest, I went with him.

We came up to the outer "shop" section of the artist's cabin. Its front now stood fully open and was further extended by a wide table that doubled the show space. However, what was displayed there seemed scarcely able to be contained even in so generous a frame. If a giant whose hobby was miniatures had taken the entire faire for his collection, Winterhue's Renaissance panorama would be that scene. Here, wrought to impossible fairy-scale, were the castle, the lane with its shops, the tourney field, the famous rose garden. But these settings, impressive as they were, were eclipsed by the inhabitants. Those were plentiful, and every person, from high to low, was an individual portrait, rendered with almost disquieting accuracy. In spite of the afternoon heat, I shivered, for I now knew who Sterling Winterhue was.

"You did the Lansdowne goblins!" I exclaimed. Late in the spring, a craft fair had been held at the castle, and at that festival, two disturbing life-sized goblin figures had been the main draw. They had been assigned a price that had astounded most viewers, but they had been purchased for that astronomical amount for—rumor had it—no less a personage than a screen director.

The sculptor nodded again. "Yessirree, that was me." He made a sudden predator's swoop upon the tabletop world and, scooping up one of the of the figures clad as one of the nobility, he lifted it to my eye level.

"Our hostess—and a fine lady she is."

The resemblance was unmistakable—this was indeed Mrs. Magin, clothed in the richest of court dress. Winterhue smoothed her full skirt of green satin; then, after patting her on the back with a forefinger, he leaned forward to insert her once more into the rose garden. There a stout, gray-haired doll in red velvet waited, using a silver-headed cane for support.

"Yeah, Court and Faire," the miniaturist stated as she positioned the figures. "This is going to be good PR for them both. And there are only a few more people to be added—"

My host reached under the edge of the table and pulled out a drawer. In that receptacle lay more images, each dressed in the garb of a different social rank of the past. Here was a country woman, there a glittering courtier.

"Are you going to sell these?" I asked. I did not have to give any of the small sculptures further scrutiny to be assured that they were works of art.

"Sell them? Yes, but kind of—backward." Winterhue's tone had lost the jovial well-met quality it had earlier held. "You want to appear here, you pay for it."

From the drawer, the artist selected another figure and held it up. This one was, as yet, bald of head and blank of features, but something was familiar—I drew in a breath as recognition struck. "It's *Deb!*"

"Just so," Winterhue agreed. "Our good needle mistress."

"But why—" I began, then stopped. I could not believe that my partner had paid to have herself represented among the works of a man she so obviously disliked. I held out my hand, wanting to look at the poppet more closely, but its creator was already fitting it back into the case.

"Her doll's got to be done by tomorrow," Winterhue declared. "You might remind her of that, Miss Gleason." His hand still on the drawer he had just closed, the sculptor was now staring at me. "Gleason," he repeated. "Amanda Gleason, maybe? Wouldn't have thought you'd be interested in all this." He made a gesture that took in not only the table but our general surroundings. His stare grew more penetrating as he queried, "What do you think of it?"

In spite of the heat that had glued much of my clothing to my body, I felt a chill. "Do you intend it as a permanent exhibit at the castle?" I asked in a tone I hoped was calm.

"Right you are," Winterhue assented. "This display'll go into the main hall of the castle, and tomorrow CNN will be here to tape it for the news." Abruptly he changed the subject. "Ever hear from Jessie these days?"

If the image-maker meant to disturb me by that inquiry, he did not succeed.

"I believe she left town some time back," I answered.

"Hmph," he muttered. "Hope she'll have better luck wherever she lights."

Here was another question. How had Winterhue come to know the would-be mystic who had caused so much trouble for several of the Ridgewood citizens?

" 'Manda—" Deb's voice called. She had passed our cabin and arrived at that of the artist, carrying a covered basket whose lid heaved as though something within fought for freedom. Though she did not offer Winterhue the animated container, she spoke to him. "Margaret Magin wants you to include this. . . ."

" 'Zat so?" The sculptor asked casually. In another of those snake-quick strikes, he shot out a hand. His fingers did not encircle Deb's wrists; rather, they touched the lid of the basket for an instant, and that top settled quietly into place. Then he did reach for the handle, but Deb swept the container out of his reach.

Her movement bumped the lid askew so that we could see the basket's contents: a black kitten who, at the sight of us, opened its mouth in a silent mew.

Sterling Winterhue . . . Jessie Aldrich . . . I thought back to some nasty gossip from the past concerning the sculptor and the supposed mystic—rumors of so-called black magic and the discovery of a suspiciously dead cat. I was only guessing, but there was no question about the throbbing that had begun in my head, and which was growing worse with every breath I drew.

" 'Manda, you brought a camera—get it!" Deb had suddenly become a drill sergeant barking an order to a slow-moving soldier.

I hastened back to our shop, remembering where I had set the Instamatic on one of the shelves. As I reached for it, I could hear my friend's voice; she was speaking more loudly than usual, as if increased volume would make her words more forceful, so I was able to catch most of what she said.

"We'll take some pictures for you, Sterling," she was telling the artist when I emerged from the cabin. "Hallie's birthday is tomorrow, and this kitten is one of her gifts from Margaret; she says she wants it placed on Hallie's lap."

Winterhue did not answer immediately; Deb's

take-charge tone and behavior might have put him into a state of slight shock. Not until I came up to his booth did he take a step toward the display table.

"Over there," he said, "under the pine tree."

By now I was close enough to follow that pointing finger. Hanging from the miniature evergreen was a swing, and the doll seated in it depicted a small girl who wore a puff-sleeved dress and had her hair caught up in a net of fine gold thread. This was Hallie Magin, Roddy's younger sister.

"So—" Deb nearly hissed the syllable; I could tell that her anger was barely suppressed. "You dared to use her—"

"And why not?" The sculptor's reply held something of his usual flippancy. "Our patroness wished it. All that witchcraft nonsense is over—and remember that the faire-in-small was Douglas Magin's idea to begin with."

Suddenly the basket tipped in my partner's hold, and a handful of black fur half jumped, half tumbled out. No sooner had it landed on the ground than it streaked into the brush behind Winterhue's booth and was gone.

Just as quickly, an expression that had probably been around since long before the Renaissance shot through my mind. Ramming the camera into a pocket of my skirt, I started after the runaway, but it had the advantages of youth, speed, and a good head start.

To my surprise, Deb laughed.

"Foiled!" She grinned, chuckling again. "Lucky for us the little thing's house trained; if we get some food, we can coax it back."

"That would be better for you." With this cryptic and somewhat sinister remark, the artist turned his back on my partner and placed both hands on the world-table. Under his careful urging, it gave way before him, sliding into the space at the shop front. Deb beckoned to me as she stooped to pick up the lid of the basket.

Back in our own private quarters, I settled myself on the edge of my cot. By now I felt thoroughly confused. Our neighbor's mysterious behavior was strange enough, and Deb's lack of effort to locate the kitten was another piece of the puzzle.

"You have got to tell me what this is all about," I declared.

Deb had bent over the cooler of food we had brought with us and was probing among its contents. When she stood up, she was holding an oversized shaker that I knew contained her sea salt.

"Okay," she replied. However, her tone suggested that her focus for the moment lay elsewhere.

I had already had a good many surprises that day, but I was about to have another: Deb stepped to the nearest window and began to shake salt along the sill. Another sharp thrust of pain began above my left eye and headed inward, and I bit my lip to stifle a gasp, lest I interrupt the ritual. For ritual it was; I knew what she was doing, and I could guess why. She was now closing—according to Pagan belief— every opening in our temporary home that could be used as a means of entry by the Dark.

I have always believed that the needleworker's unique art flowered during her New Age research, which had, in itself, branched from her delvings into the past. As far as I knew, Deb was not a Wiccan, but she did accept a great many beliefs held by walkers of the Old Way. When, in the past, a group of us had been roused to action by the unethical conduct of Jessie Aldrich, my friend had been emphatically on our side.

My own interest in the early religion had been piqued at that time, but my convictions were too strong to allow surrender of the faith I had observed through my life. However, what I could accept, I did, and in no way would I question that which others felt to be true.

Deb's silence lasted so long I feared she did not intend to answer. At last, though, she set the shaker down on top of a box and seated herself on the opposite cot.

"Most of what I know about started at Hentytown over in Kentucky a couple of years ago. That was the first time the local Renaissance group held a faire, and they asked our people to give them tips."

Deb looked grim. "You know, after what we went through with Jessie, that fantasy has a dark side, and that, used for the wrong reasons, it can become truly evil. Well, Sterling likes to portray those unsavory aspects in his work. That kind of sculpture was never shown to the public, only to select customers; we always thought he made the shadow-ones to order. Anyway, he was still discreet about them.

"Then he brought a couple of boxed panoramas to Hentytown." Deb's mouth pursed as though she tasted something bitter. "It got around that he had a live monster in one of them. Our adorable Roddy, who'd been taken to that faire with his sister, broke into Winterhue's booth when the banquet was on; apparently another boy had dared him to. The kids took the box, but Hallie had followed them and they caught her. They were making her look at it when Mark Bancock found them."

Deb paused.

"What was in it?" I demanded.

"Hallie was screaming like a banshee, but she never would tell what she saw. Roddy and his friend claimed it was nothing really scary—just a scene of a girl in the woods at night with something looking at her from behind a bush. But the boys kicked it apart, so no one ever knew what it really showed."

My friend shook her head. "There was a lot of trouble; Sterling had done that box to order and had already taken a down payment. Nobody outside the inner Court knows what settlement was made to his customer, but it was said to have been a huge sum. Shortly after that came the nasty business with Jessie that I'm sure you don't care to remember—" (I raised a hand in a defensive gesture, wanting indeed to ward off those memories.) "—and witnesses said Winterhue was seen at two of her so-called Black Masses. The Court banished him; but apparently, after the craft fair here in the spring and that big sale he made with the goblins, Margaret Magin took him back into the fold.

"Now he's managed to interest CNN—they want to do a story and get pictures once his miniature faire is set up in the castle. That may sound like good publicity, but I keep thinking we're in for more trouble."

*Perhaps more than you suspect,* I thought. Then, hesitatingly, I told her, "Sterling showed me an unfinished doll he says is you."

Deb actually snarled. "Just let him try to use it! Margaret said he has to get written permission to do anyone's likeness in one of those things."

"Miss Wilson?" Deb was being hailed from the front of the store and rose to see what was wanted. I followed a few minutes later, after invoking the magic of two aspirin to banish the pain-demon who had taken up residence above my left eye.

The newcomers were a large woman and a boy who were wearing the coarse clothing of medieval villagers. "How do we look?" the matron was demanding of Deb as I came out.

"We're entering the contest as a family," she continued. "I'm Helen Quick, and my husband is Robert—he's playing the cloth merchant. Will we pass for a merchant's family?"

The boy, who plainly wanted to be elsewhere, shook free from the hold his mother had on his shoulder. "That guy with the little clay people," he said, pointing to Winterhue's display. "*He* liked what we had on—he said he might even put us in his table thing!"

Mrs. Quick's face flushed an even deeper red than the heat had already colored it. "Shut up, Mike!" she snapped, shooting a hostile look toward the sculptor's booth. "I've heard about him, and we sure don't want to get mixed up in *his* stuff! Well, Miss Wilson?"

Deb inspected the pair for a moment before she nodded and delivered judgment.

"Very good. Except—" she pointed to the child's footgear, "—those should come off, Mike. We're supposed to be in a small village. You might wear clogs in winter or bad weather, but you'd go barefoot on a day like this."

The boy's mother caught up her wide skirt to reveal simple black shoes. "Do I go bare, too?"

Deb smiled. "No, Mrs. Quick. For the wife of a merchant, you've chosen exactly right."

"Okay, then." With no more in the way of thanks, the matron stepped back into the street, pushing her reluctant son ahead of her.

I shook my head in disbelief as I watched them disappear into the crowd. "Are they all like that?" I wanted to know. It might be the needleworker's duty to pass on the authenticity of costumes, but it appeared she had a thankless task.

My friend laughed. "Well, there are enough like them to keep us in our places! Now that this faire has gotten important enough to draw the big media, we're getting twice the usual number of people signing up to do characters."

"Is Mrs. Quick in the SCA?" I inquired. "I don't remember her from last year." I knew some members of the Court, but I had never witnessed such rudeness from any of them.

"Not that I know," Deb answered, adding dryly, "If she's a newcomer, she may be an equally quick goer."

At that moment, the call of a horn rang out, making both of us jump.

"The parade is staring through town," Deb explained. "The Court will be making their entrance now; this is their first appearance all together." She gave a silent whistle of relief. "Glad I didn't have to be involved with *that*."

Afternoon slid into evening, bringing a welcome breeze as we finished our preparations. Several of our fellow "merchants" hung out lanterns. No such lighting beckoned passersby to the front of Winterhue's booth, but a dim glow in the back of the shop suggested that the artist might be busy there. Was he, I wondered, engaged in finishing the poppet that would link my friend to his miniature world, whether she wished to be so connected or not?

Deb's attention was also fixed on our neighbor's quarters. "Trouble!" she said tersely. "Not my affair, though—I refuse to get involved again." She made that statement as though repeating a solemn oath.

Turning away, she lit three lanterns, two of which

were to be suspended outside, and a camp lamp of contemporary design (and greater power) whose use must be confined to the hut's interior. Next, she delved into a suitcase and brought out her second costume—that of the guildmistress—which she would be wearing to the banquet.

While Deb was dressing, I went down the street in search of the barbeque that had been teasing my nose all day. It was when I left the "tavern," supper in a bucket in my hand, that I saw the sculptor again. Unlike other merchants in the village, he had not changed his drab work clothes for more colorful and festive ones in preparation for the evening's activities, nor did he seem to notice me.

As I returned, I saw that my friend had two escorts waiting for her at the front of our shop. One was Mark Bancock, who was saying crisply to his companion, "If that kid tries to break into Winterhue's booth again, they'll have to lock him up. I've got no time to babysit the brat."

The other man was the first person I had seen in mundane clothing the whole day. Sighting me, he lifted a hand in salute, and I returned the gesture, recognizing an old acquaintance. Jim Barnes was the closest thing to a feature writer the modest Ridgewood newspaper possessed.

"Press on duty, Jim?" I asked teasingly. "Shouldn't you be wearing a town crier's outfit?"

He nodded toward the archer and returned my banter. "Nay, mistress—merely making the rounds of the crime scene with yon constable."

In the context of what I had seen and heard about our neighbor, the reporter's joke did not seem amusing. I certainly hoped that the already much-put-upon security man would not be forced to perform actual police duties.

" 'Manda . . ." Deb beckoned me inside to where she stood, well away from the shop door and the waiting men. When she spoke, her voice was hardly above a whisper. "Be careful, please. I don't like you being alone."

Such a warning was very unlike my friend, and I found it unsettling; I waited for her to tell me the reason for her concern, but she said no more. In fact, she seemed so eager to be gone that, as she stepped out and greeted her escort, I had only a moment to wish them an enjoyable evening before all three left.

After fixing the shop bell so that it would announce any visitors, I brought my supper out into the front portion of the booth. I ate slowly, watching the street.

Winterhue's hut was totally dark now; and indeed, all the world had grown gray, since the light of the period lanterns did not carry far beyond the fronts of the shops.

However, though the faire was shadowed, it was by no means silent. From the direction of the castle came a cry of trumpets, probably to announce the seating of the Court; then, more faintly, a burst of music followed, of the kind I had heard being rehearsed for several months. Light (albeit dim), and sound, and scent, too, had messages for the senses in the evening air. I was aware of incense burning, though not near; the night breeze brought no more than a hint. The unreal world that was the faire seemed to be waiting for something.

Having finished my supper—most of which, due to my nervousness, had ended up in the trash—I returned to the inner room and took a paperback from my tote. Almost immediately I put it back again. Perhaps if I rested . . .

After a moment's struggle, I freed myself from the

heavy skirt and the laced bodice that held me in the grip of an Iron Maiden and put on my Chinese cotton robe. On impulse, I pulled out several boxes and pushed aside a limp curtain to look out of one of our two windows at Winterhue's shop. Nothing moved there.

In the suspense stories I read for relaxation, a cold wind, or some equally disquieting phenomenon, always announces the arrival of danger. I, however, was simply unable to settle down. This was a strange feeling and one I had never had before; time might have ceased to exist.

The moon was favoring the faire tonight, and a bright beam carved a path between our booth and that of our neighbor. Without warning, something dropped from the air into that ray-path. Leaves and bushes rustled.

"Darn you, cat!"

The intruder from the woods could now be clearly seen: it was Mike Quick from the merchant family. The boy dropped to his knees to grab at a small black blot, but with a bound, the blot eluded him. Overbalancing, he fell forward, and his prey vanished into the dark.

"Sneaking around, eh?" A second, much larger shadow moved into the moonlight and pulled Mike halfway off the path in the direction of the artist's hut. "Well, I have a cure for *that*—"

By this time I was up, thrusting my feet into my shoes, sure I was hearing choking sounds from the merchant youth. When I looked out again, his captor was dragging the wildly-kicking boy toward the Winterhue booth, but the man halted abruptly when he sighted more movement at the trees' edge.

"Mike!" cried a second young voice. "You got that kitten yet?"

"You, is it?" the man roared. "You miserable little vandal, I'll have you now!"

His captor gave a forceful shove, and the Quick boy fell back again into the moonlit path. He did not get to his feet but scuttled for the safety of the wood on hands and knees.

Quietly as I could, I left my vantage point and moved to the front of the shop. Unlatching the outer door and loosening the alarm cord, I took up the flashlight we had set on one of the shelves. As I stepped outside, I almost echoed the leap of Mike's prey as a small furred body fastened onto the hem of my robe.

A rise and fall of words began, none of which I could understand. Tugging my robe free from the kitten's grip, I ran toward the speaker, who I did not think was addressing anyone in this world.

The chant cut off abruptly, and Winterhue (I could not see his face, but I knew it was he) spoke the merchant boy's name, making of its single syllable a drawn-out siren call: "*M–i–i–i–ke . . .*"

Hardly had he completed the word when the youth cried out. The artist moved onto the path to meet Mike, who was returning as summoned. The boy crawled back into the moonlight, body close to the ground, fingers crooked like the claws of an animal. Roddy simply stood to one side of the way, his mouth open as though he were screaming but making no sound at all.

I stepped up behind Winterhue, so that I, too, stood facing the boys. As I moved, the sculptor was lifting one arm; then he leaped toward them, and the moon caught the glitter of a knife blade as he raised the weapon. His other hand closed on a loose dark curl that lay over Roddy's forehead. Still the boy remained silent, his face a mask of mindless fear.

"No!" I cried. Snapping on the flashlight, I caught the three figures full in its powerful beam.

Startled, the sculptor loosed the lock of hair, twisting round so he faced partly into that light, and I clung to the hope that he could not see me behind it. Even his goblin figures had not worn such terrifying expressions as his own features now formed.

Stepping back from Roddy, Winterhue wheeled in a crouch, a soldier facing a charging enemy. The Magin boy made no attempt to run as Mike Quick wormed his way up beside him; the older youth's mouth was working as though he were shouting, but he, too, was held by the spell of silence that gripped his friend.

"Drop that light, bitch!" the artist spat in my direction.

To my horror, my grip on the barrel of the flash was loosening. At the same instant, I felt a renewed pull at the hem of my robe: the kitten was climbing, but I dared not try to remove it, lest I lose control of the light, which I was now holding in both hands. I fully expected Winterhue to attack me and tried to edge backward, only to discover I was rooted there. I had no more power over my own body than the sculptor's small dolls—or the two large, living manikins who stood before me—had over theirs.

"I said, *drop it*—!"

A force that might have been an extension of the artist's will seized me, shaking me painfully, and only with great effort did I manage to keep hold of the light. The small cat had reached my shoulder in its ascent. Against the arm up which it was now making its way, its frail body weighed very little; however, it could interfere with any defensive move I might have to make.

Vicious laughter burst from the sculptor as he saw my predicament. I was sure he would reach out and take the flashlight easily from my helpless hands to complete his triumph; but he did not. What he did do was far more frightening.

For the second time he raised the hand holding the knife, but he did not strike at me; instead, he placed the blade between his teeth in the manner of a storybook pirate. From the breast of his jerkin, he brought out a poppet on which the moonlight seemed to center with added intensity. It was smaller than those he had shown to Deb and me, but it was unmistakably another portrait-figure. The head was still bald, but the features were those of Roddy Magin.

Returning the knife to his hand, Winterhue turned and twisted the weapon over the doll, as though seeking the most vulnerable spot to stab. Again he laughed.

"Needs a little trimming up—I was going to give him some hair, until you showed up, damn you! You've done enough already to spoil my plans with your bleeding-heart blabber in that letter to the paper about Jessie's animal sacrifice. Now, Miss Lady-in-Shining-Armor, you just watch old Winterhue, because he's going to show you a real artist's secret."

I could do nothing but obey in a body that had become an imprisoning shell. The kitten had settled on my shoulder, and its soft fur brushed my cheek as it shifted position. It was purring with surprising volume for its size, yet the vibration told not of contentment but of mingled fear and anger. And from that so-small source, power was expanding. Downward into my body it flowed, warming my arms until I once more felt the prickling return of life to my hands.

The sculptor moved the knife point closer to the head of the doll, aiming at one of the unblinking eyes.

"Easy—so very easy—to handle folk who come a-spying . . ."

That threat I head, but it was the last understandable thing the artist said. Yet again he spewed forth a series of meaningless sounds which, though discordant, had a rhythm to their flow. Winterhue took a quick stride to the edge of the light, revealing Roddy to my view. The boy was on his knees, swaying back and forth, his hands pressed over his eyes.

I tried to scream, but nothing came from my mouth. Then the rough tip of a tiny tongue flicked across my lips, and suddenly sound broke forth—no words I knew, but strange noises I had made no effort to form. The artist answered with cries that were loud enough to muffle my own, but still I continued. His fingers clenched as he tried to keep hold of the knife; even as I had fought to keep the flashlight steady earlier, so now he was struggling to retain his weapon.

It was the doll that fell though, thankfully, the knife did also a moment later. At the same time, the flow of Jabberwocky from my lips ended and I was free to move. Winterhue had gone to hands and knees to retrieve the blade, but only inches before his fingers, the thing was sliding itself away over the ground like a stray moonbeam.

" 'Manda!" a familiar voice cried.

"What's going on?" someone else called, followed by a chorus of other shouts to which I paid no attention; I had just achieved my goal of recovering the doll. Now, with Roddy's image in my hands, I started toward the boy himself. In that instant, the youth charged the still-kneeling sculptor—an attack

I could see by the light that blazed from the poppet in my trembling hands.

Mark and two other members of faire security separated the youth from the object of his wrath, while Deb pulled the flashlight gently from my hands and held it steady. I became aware that the small weight on my shoulder was gone.

I felt completely bewildered by the events of the night—to such a degree that I could actually sympathize (a little) with Roddy Magin, who was crying with the force of a two year old and still struggling, in Mark's grip, to reengage his enemy. Winterhue, however, was no longer a threat.

That being so, there was something I had to do. I edged away from the light, though my friend tried to hold me, repeating my name in alarm. A few moments later, hardly knowing how I had come there, I found myself kneeling at the edge of the woods. With one hand, I felt the ground until my fingers sank into a soft patch, then set about digging as a squirrel might open an earth pocket to hide a nut. Tearing off one of the ruffles of my chemise, I wound it about the doll, fitted the manikin into the hole, scooped back the soil, and flattened it.

Deb knelt down beside me. My friend no longer held the flashlight, so only the moon witnessed the "burial service" we gave the poppet, she pronouncing more of that unintelligible language over its "grave." I, meanwhile, sat rubbing my eyes, behind which had erupted a headache of migraine proportions.

Questions . . . so many questions. Who—or what—was Sterling Winterhue? The dolls he shaped—were they dangerously bound in some manner to the persons they represented, or was this fear only a dark fancy born of the torture in my skull?

I do not remember the ride to the hospital; once there, however, I know I was visited by dreams that left me weak and sick. When I finally began to rise from the utter debility and the pain that—I discovered later—had actually lasted for days, I made a decision about my experience. I had been drawn into the uncharted territory of the psychic realm, and I would not, in future, knowingly venture so, away from my earthly home. Never again—not I.

Before I was discharged from the hospital, my friend left town, having taken a position as a lecturer with a traveling exhibit of Renaissance needlework. She had visited me daily, but neither of us was comfortable with the other any longer. In the encounter with the sculptor, I had learned that the Deb Wilson I thought I knew was but a costume, like one of her period dresses, for the woman of power who had come forth that night. I found I did not even want to ask questions, though I had a daunting number of them to answer myself when the sheriff and a state trooper visited me. The most crucial query had yet to be posed, and not to me but to the organizers of the festival: Would there be another Ridgewood Renaissance Faire?

On the day I came home to a safe and sane life again, someone was waiting at the door. This was one friendship I would not avoid, and my new acquaintance would ask no questions. Moonshadow, the kitten, was the only piece of miniature magic I cared to own—or be owned by.

# TAD WILLIAMS

*Memory, Sorrow & Thorn*

**THE DRAGONBONE CHAIR**
0-88677-384-9

**STONE OF FAREWELL**
0-88677-480-2

**TO GREEN ANGEL TOWER** (Part One)
0-88677-598-1

**TO GREEN ANGEL TOWER** (Part Two)
0-88677-606-6

To Order Call: 1-800-788-6262

DAW 42

# Tad Williams

## THE **WAR** OF THE **FLOWERS**

"A masterpiece of fairytale worldbuilding."
—*Locus*

"Williams's imagination is boundless."
—*Publishers Weekly*
(Starred Review)

"A great introduction to an accomplished
and ambitious fantasist."
—*San Francisco Chronicle*

"An addictive world ... masterfully plays
with the tropes and traditions of
generations of fantasy writers."
—*Salon*

"A very elaborate and fully realized setting
for adventure, intrigue, and more
than an occasional chill."
—*Science Fiction Chronicle*

0-7564-0181-X

To Order Call: 1-800-788-6262

# Kristen Britain

## GREEN RIDER

As Karigan G'ladheon, on the run from school, makes her way through the deep forest, a galloping horse plunges out of the brush, its rider impaled by two black arrows. With his dying breath, he tells her he is a Green Rider, one of the king's special messengers. Giving her his green coat with its symbolic brooch of office, he makes Karigan swear to deliver the message he was carrying. Pursued by unknown assassins, following a path only the horse seems to know, Karigan finds herself thrust into in a world of danger and complex magic....　　　　　0-88677-858-1

## FIRST RIDER'S CALL

With evil forces once again at large in the kingdom and with the messenger service depleted and weakened, can Karigan reach through the walls of time to get help from the First Rider, a woman dead for a millennium?　　0-7564-0209-3

To Order Call: 1-800-788-6262

DAW 7

# KATE ELLIOTT

## *Crown of Stars*

"An entirely captivating affair"—*Publishers Weekly*

In a world where bloody conflicts rage and
sorcery holds sway both human and other-
than-human forces vie for supremacy. In this
land, Alain, a young man seeking the destiny
promised him by the Lady of Battles, and
Liath, a young woman gifted with a power
that can alter history, are swept up in a
world-shaking conflict for the survival of
humanity.

| | |
|---|---|
| KING'S DRAGON | 0-88677-771-2 |
| PRINCE OF DOGS | 0-88677-816-6 |
| THE BURNING STONE | 0-88677-815-8 |
| CHILD OF FLAME | 0-88677-892-1 |
| THE GATHERING STORM | 0-7564-0132-1 |

To Order Call: 1-800-788-6262

# Irene Radford

"A mesmerizing storyteller." —*Romantic Times*

## THE DRAGON NIMBUS

## THE DRAGON NIMBUS HISTORY

## THE STAR GODS

To Order Call: 1-800-788-6262

DAW 31